Jerusha

Prejudice, Passing, and Personal Growth in the United States of America

A Novel

Dolores McCullough

Levellers Press
AMHERST, MASSACHUSETTS

Copyright © 2016 Dolores McCullough

All rights reserved including the right of reproduction in whole or in part in any form.

Published by *Levellers Press*, Amherst, Massachusetts
Cover design and illustrations by Aline Hoffman

Printed in the United States of America

ISBN 978-1-945473-20-3

In Dedication to

*My Parents,
Bernice and William H. McCullough
who had the courage to encourage their children
to follow their dreams.*

Prologue

The United States in 1955

Emmet Till, a fourteen-year-old Negro* boy from Chicago, Illinois, on vacation in Jackson, Mississippi, was accused of winking, some said whistling, at a white woman. Because of this, he was beaten beyond recognition and killed by white men. The children of the country knew nothing of this for years.

In a northern town that same year, the parents of a particularly vulnerable daughter and son committed themselves even more strongly to the silence of the their chosen path.

---

*Although the term, Negro, is not used today, it was a common word in 1955. Its use wasn't challenged until the '60s, when Black became Beautiful.

New Crossing, Connecticut

"Who do I look like?" fourteen-year-old Danielle McKinnon whispered to her full-length reflection in her new pink wallpapered bedroom. The mirror reflected a slim girl with a dark olive complexion. She wore plastic-framed glasses and a long-waist dress of polished blue cotton with matching flat shoes and purse. Her dark brown hair, in a poodle cut, framed her face. It wouldn't frizz on this cool June day, and she relaxed a bit. She wanted to look pretty for high school orientation. Like the movie stars. She picked up the latest issue of *Photoplay*, a movie magazine, from her old wooden desk, flipped through the pages for the tenth time, returned to the mirror and wondered again, *Who do I look l like?*

"Whom," she said aloud, correcting her reflected image which looked unhappy that her family moved away from her Bayfield Junior High friends in Massachusetts. She dreaded meeting a bunch of rich high school freshmen in New Crossing, Connecticut.

Her father, Mac, who now owned a Chevrolet dealership, had moved his family from their small Cape Cod house in Bayfield into a large brick colonial. He and her mother, Lynn, planned the move so Danielle and nine-year old Phil could make a smooth transition into their new schools.

She was applying Tangee lipstick and rubbing her lips together when she heard the quick click of her mother's high heels. The combined aromas of Chesterfield cigarettes and Heartbeat perfume floated into the room with her mom, who everybody said looked like Bette Davis. When she saw her mom in the mirror behind her, Danielle instantly absorbed the hint of tension she saw in her mother's long-lashed hazel eyes. She watched those eyes as her mom slowly exhaled her cigarette smoke and assessed her daughter's reflection. Lynn looked stunning in a green silk dress and glowing gold earrings that highlighted her wavy light brown hair. She smiled, and Danielle experienced that precious moment of self-esteem when a mother expresses her unqualified approval of her daughter. "Let's go find your father," she said.

Mac, too, had splurged on clothes. He was sitting, one leg crossed over the other, on an overstuffed parlor chair, sporting a light brown summer suit. He smiled, stood and tilted a brown derby hat onto his head. Tall, dark and handsome, with a pleasant hint of cigarettes, he would remind people of the movie star, George Raft, on that day.

Together, the three walked out the front door of their new home. Blacky, their shaggy-haired mongrel, barked a hello from the back yard next door where he and Phil were being looked after by their new neighbors, Pat and Jean Richardson. Danielle had called out, "Here, Blacky," a few days earlier, before realizing their first hired help, a Negro, was washing the windows. The woman, her back to them, just kept working, as Danielle and her mother stifled embarrassed giggles and pulled the dog into the house.

A few days later, she overheard her father tell her mother that the woman was offended and wouldn't be back. He sounded upset.

Phil and the two Richardson boys, in freshly ironed cotton pants and shirts, sat around the picnic table. Phil was throwing dice onto a Monopoly gameboard, when Mac called out to his son, "Wish your sister good luck!"

"Good Luck," said Phil, glancing up from the gameboard and smiling.

"Thanks," said Danielle in a trembling voice.

"Look at my two girls," Mac said, taking Danielle on one arm and Lynn on the other. "People will wonder what a guy like me did to deserve the love of two such women." And with that, they stepped into their new Chevrolet Bel Air and drove through New Crossing to officially enter what her Bayfield friends called the upper class.

New Crossing, Connecticut in 1955

When Principal Wallace told the assembled students and their parents that academically, Tarkington High was rated eighth among the top public schools in the country, Mac gave his daughter an approving nod. "Nearly one hundred percent of the graduates will go to college, many of them to the Ivy Leagues," Mr. Wallace said.

The elegant yellow brick school smelling of clean, freshly polished wooden floors, enticed Danielle, and she longed to linger in the library's literature section. In a classroom, she sat at a wooden desk, whose top was on hinges. She opened it, inhaled the ghostly scent of pencils and erasers that had once been there and imagined studying the classics.

At the buffet table, she bit into a white sandwich with cucumbers, mayonnaise and no crust. "They forgot the meat," she said to her mother and laughed.

"That's a cucumber sandwich," whispered her mom. Danielle looked around, as she chewed, to see if anyone had overheard her blunder. "Everyone looks so rich and so…" She didn't know if 'snooty' or 'confident' was the right word. "I miss my friends," she said.

"You'll feel better when you get acquainted," said her mother. "Invite a few of the girls over for a picnic."

"I can't invite girls I don't know!" she whispered. *They won't come,* she thought.

"Are you the new family with the Chevrolet dealership?" asked a woman with precise diction. Her blond hair, drawn into a chignon, was elegantly set off with pearl teardrop earrings. In her gray linen suit with a fitted jacket and straight skirt, she looked like a model in *Vogue* magazine. A pink and gray silk scarf was gracefully draped at the round neck of her white blouse.

Danielle felt her mother's tension mount and wondered if her mom's silk dress was stylish enough for New Crossing. She stifled an urge to see if the seams of her own nylons were straight.

"Yes, I'm Lynn McKinnon," she heard her mother say.

"Marilyn Osborne," the woman said, assessing them.

"Mac McKinnon," said her father, arriving with glasses of ginger ale he handed to Lynn and Danielle. His smile was genuine and his diction, just as good as hers, was unaffected. He extended his hand to Marilyn Osborne, whose smile finally reached her eyes. Danielle felt safe in the relaxed atmosphere he inspired so effortlessly. "And this is our daughter, Danielle."

"Nice to meet you, Mrs. Osborne," said Danielle, extending her hand.

"Lovely dress," said Mrs. Osborne, and she called out, "Mark, Kimberly, come and meet the McKinnon family."

So, on a July morning, right after a family vacation on Cape Cod, preparations for the picnic were in progress. Spatula in hand, Danielle nervously shoveled freshly baked Toll House chocolate chip cookies, just out of the oven, onto a glass platter while her mother filled small powdered rolls with tuna fish salad. Kimberly Osborne, Joy Bentley, Sue Harris and Laurie Smith were coming to lunch!

"Why can't we have hotdogs and hamburgers like we used to?" Danielle said.

"Put the ham and cheese sandwiches on the platter," said her mom, ignoring her as she poured a bag of State Line potato chips into a bowl.

"Can't we leave them in the bag?" she asked, raising her voice. Her informal Bayfield life was over. Her mother took a glass pitcher of lemonade from the refrigerator. "What happened to the Coca Cola cooler? We had it at the beach!"

"Take out the cookies and lemonade. They'll be here any minute," said her mother, picking up the platter of little sandwiches, pushing open the screen door with her shoulder and walking quickly across the professionally tended lawn to the tree-shaded picnic table. In Bayfield, she and her mother, on their hands and knees, had weeded crabgrass and dandelions with their immigrant neighbors to plant a vegetable garden.

Danielle kicked open the screen door, and the dog dashed out. She wished she could run with him into the woods behind Bayfield Junior High and up a hill where, like the tomboy she was, she'd gallop to the top and whinny like the Arabian stallion in the Walter Farley series, *The Black Stallion*.

"Tie Blacky to the dog house," said her mother, arranging trays, luncheon plates and utensils on a flowered tablecloth with matching napkins.

"You're acting like we're better than Bayfield people!" Danielle said, setting the pitcher onto the table hard.

Her mother stopped rushing and just stood there in her pretty mint green dress.

Danielle saw hurt in her eyes before she regained her composure and said, "So you're not going to give these girls a chance? Is that what you want?"

"No. I'm sorry," Danielle said, barely audible. She felt wretched. She knew her mother was feeling her way in this new neighborhood and that she wanted them both to fit in. Danielle wanted it too. She had spent the morning under a hot hair drier, her curls stretched onto rollers to create waves, then stood before the full-length mirror in her bedroom to see how she looked in her white sleeveless cotton shirt, pale blue shorts, white sneakers and socks. Her slim athletic body had tanned as she'd ridden waves onto the Cape Cod shore. She was still nice and dark like her father. Her mother and brother tended to burn.

When she was a little girl, she'd asked her parents, "Why do people say I look like Daddy and Phil looks like Mommy?"

"Because you and I have dark olive complexions, and your mother and Phil have light olive ones," said her father.

"But we're all olive," said her mother.

An hour later, sipping lemonade and munching on little sandwiches with girls from New Crossing in their shorts, sleeveless shirts, white socks and sneakers, Danielle was beginning to feel she belonged. "Autumn Leaves," played by pianist, Roger Williams, rippled through the air from her portable record player, as they studied the back-to-school issue of *Seventeen* magazine.

"I just *have* to have five sets of dyed-to-match sweaters and skirts in different colors for each day of the week," said Kimberly Osborne, delicately picking up a chip.

"I just *have* to have matching pocketbooks and loafers in black, brown, beige and navy," said Sue Harris.

"What about maroon?" asked Joy Bentley. The next forty-five record dropped from its holder onto the turntable, and they heard Bill Haley and the Comets sing "Shake, Rattle and Roll." Nibbling on a chocolate chip cookie, Laurie Smith stood and demonstrated a basic rock and roll step. They all got up and danced. Danielle bopped awkwardly up and down, hoping they wouldn't notice. Mac had once ridiculed Lynn, when he came home to find her teaching seven-year-old Danielle the Swing, and her mother had cried. Her parents rarely danced, except for a fox trot and waltz they walked through.

They'd given Danielle ballet and tap dancing lessons during her grammar and junior high school years. Recently, her mother suggested she take ballroom dancing lessons.

Danielle hoped she'd forget about it, but knew she wouldn't.

Joy danced easily, flipping through the pages of *Photoplay* at the same time. Danielle tried to copy her footwork. When Joy turned to the centerfold, featuring head shots of perky blond Doris Day, exotic violet-eyed Elizabeth Taylor, curvaceous brunette, Esther Williams and glamorous blond, Betty Grable among others, she said, "Laurie looks like Doris Day!"

The girls danced over to the movie star magazine to find themselves mirrored there.

"You look like Kim Novak, Kimberly," Laurie said. The girls nodded, acknowledging Kimberly's voluptuous figure and her sculpted blond hairstyle that was an exact copy of the star.

"You have her name, too," said Sue. "You'll probably win Most Beautiful in junior year." Kimberly smiled like a beauty queen receiving her fans.

"But you look like Debbie Reynolds, and you sing and dance like she does," said Danielle. Sue perked up.

"Joy looks like the mother in 'Father Knows Best,'" said Kim. "I can see her as the wife of a successful man, pretty and down to earth."

Joy, who currently couldn't decide on a shoe color, lit up. "Really?"

"Well, maybe not down to earth," Kim amended, and they all laughed. Then there was silence, while Danielle waited for her turn. Kim was on a roll. She looked at Danielle. "Sapphire," she said.

Danielle saw the girls' eyes widen in surprise. She heard stifled laughter. They studied her face, and she wanted to hide.

"You don't look like Sapphire," Joy said. "You look like…"

"You should have stayed out of the sun at the beach," said Laurie.

"What's wrong with a tan," asked Danielle. "My Bayfield friends get darker ones."

"Well, that's Bayfield," said Kim, disparagingly. "And with your curly hair, well it's just not your best feature. Danielle turned away to hide her tears. "Oh, I was just joking."

"You look a little like Ruth Roman," said Joy. "She's dark."

"I have to use the bathroom," Danielle said and escaped into the house. Splashing cold water on her face relieved her reddened eyes, but not Kim's stinging ridicule. She stared into the mirror at her tanned face. Sapphire was Amos' wife on the Negro television comedy, "Amos and Andy." Comedienne Ernestine Wade played his strident complaining spouse. "I don't look like her," Danielle told her reflection.

When she returned, the girls were eating strawberry ice cream, and Laurie was holding forth on another article from *Photoplay*, "Is Eddie Leaving Debbie for Liz?" The girls crowded around the article, blithely forgetting Danielle's distress.

When they finally left, Danielle grasped the magazine, raced to her room and looked again for a movie star she resembled. She found no one.

That evening, she tiptoed into the large family room, where her parents and brother were watching "Father Knows Best" on television. Standing behind an overstuffed chair at the far end of the room where her father and brother couldn't see her, Danielle caught her mother's attention by waving the incriminating issue of *Photoplay*. Her mother looked up at her daughter and sped across the room.

"I don't look like any of the movie stars. The girls said I look like..." Tears rolled down her cheeks. "Sapphire."

She heard her mother's voice, suddenly tight and angry, as she called out, "Mac, the girls said she looks like Sapphire."

Her father turned down the volume on the television set and walked quickly to them.

Phil turned around to look. "Remember you're part Indian," Mac said easily, as if he'd been anticipating this moment for years. "If anyone says you look like a Negro, just tell them it's your Aztec ancestry. They were a highly civilized people." This *non sequitur* did nothing to restore her self-esteem.

"Don't worry, Dan. You'd look like an Aztec movie star, if they had one," her brother called from across the room, and he tapped out a rhythm with his new drumsticks for emphasis. He'd just started drumming lessons, to his father's distress, and was rarely seen without them. She saw honesty in Phil's hazel eyes, and she trusted him. He always told her the truth.

Guilt set in. "It's not because Sapphire's a Negro," Danielle said. "There's nothing wrong with that. I'm not prejudiced!"

"We know that, and we're proud of you both on that score," said Mac. The sincerity in his voice calmed her. He turned up the sound on the television just in time to catch the end of "Father Knows Best." She liked the show because it celebrated her Dad. Like the father played by Jim Anderson, he too, knew best.

After the program, her mother said, "I've got raspberry sherbet from Howard Johnson's. Who wants some?" Everyone did. The restaurant line was famous for its twenty-eight flavors of ice cream. "Help me, Phil," she said, and they moved on to the kitchen.

Danielle looked at her father. "Aztec?" He nodded. She gestured to an old drawing, hanging on the wall by the fireplace. "Is that why you have that picture?" She walked to it, and he joined her. Together, they looked at an ink drawing, framed in wood, of the receding figure of an Indian, who had one long feather at the back of his head. He sat tall on his horse, as he guided it down a path, away from the viewer. Beneath the picture was a quotation. Danielle knew it by heart. "Great Spirit, Help me never to judge another until I have walked a mile in his moccasins." Her father had quoted it to steer his children away from prejudice.

Once he'd walked in on eight-year-old Danielle and her friends who were watching one of the many popular cowboy and Indian shows on television. They were shouting and rooting for the cowboys to kill the Indians, when her father's voice broke into the clamor. "Don't think of them as the enemy!" The children froze and looked up at him. "Think of them as the other side." And he'd smiled.

The ink drawing of the Indian had always intrigued Danielle, and she wanted to see his face. "I'm going to write a story about him," she said. "What could he have done?"

"Do you like to write?" asked her father.

"I love it," she answered, and her voice broke.

It was in the pause that followed, as they continued to look at the picture, that Mac said, "Maybe, one day, you'll write, and if you do, perhaps you'll write a story about an honest, straight-forward sort of fellow who means no one any harm, but who is beset by others."

"Beset?" she asked, and thought, *Dad does have a way with words.* When he didn't answer, she looked away from the drawing and saw her father walking from the room.

They never spoke of it again, but Danielle knew he was talking about himself.

PART ONE

*"People, people who need people,
Are the luckiest people in the world."*

From "People," lyrics by Bob Merrill, popularized by Barbara Streisand in the 1964 Broadway musical, *Funny Girl*.

Chapter One
December 1981, New York City

There's a new age notion that we choose our parents.

It woke her again. At least thirty-nine year old Danielle thought it did. Not just the morning sickness, "the cleansing," she called it. Not just that. Just before "the cleansing" sent her running, jaw clenched and bent over, for the bathroom, she lay in the bed of her Gramercy Park apartment, just for a moment, awakening in the multi-colored glow of a recurring dream. This morning, it was jangled by a rhyme: *Don't need a disclaimer-*

She reached the toilet bowl just in time! *Don't need a disclaimer,* came the ditty again, as the first wave of vomit gushed from her mouth. And then, the rest of the rhyme: *Abortion's a no-brainer!*

Where did that come from? It struck her half-awake brain as funny, and she giggled, causing the second wave of vomit to get stuck in her throat. She couldn't breathe! Fully awake now, she straightened up, slammed her hands into her abdomen and executed her first Heimlich maneuver. The nauseating mess shot from her mouth onto the upended toilet seat and ricocheted into her face.

Blindly she reached up for a towel, slid down the wall into a sitting position beside the toilet bowl and wiped the sweat and vomit from her face. With glazed eyes, she stared at her panting stomach. *Don't need a disclaimer; abortion's a no-brainer,* sang over and over through her mind.

It was at this moment that Danielle McKinnon was moved to speak her first words to the unborn child. "Is anybody there?... If you are, did you just choke me? If you did, you've got every right. That thought... I don't know where it came from... was obscene." Still shaky, she flushed the toilet, took a clean rag from under the sink and cleaned the seat. "But I've got to give you a heads up. I made a mistake. I can't have you." She rinsed the rag and dropped it right into the wastebasket, washed her hands, face and mouth and dropped her pajamas into the hamper. She set the shower's faucet to Warm, stepped in, opened a bottle of sweet almond olive oil shampoo and squeezed the golden liquid into her curly, dark brown hair. "Look, it may sound strange, but if it's true we pick our parents, shop around! You can do better than me. I'm almost forty, for God's sake." She remembered she had to buy doughnuts, and that gustatory memory called up a mini-wave of liquid which belched out of her mouth, dribbled down her chin, rolled between her breasts, down over her belly and nestled in her pubic hair. She shot the shampoo in its wake and washed her whole body.

Carefully, she focused on her day. She had to buy orange juice. Her students were expecting a Christmas breakfast before the vacation break. The principal had sent out a circular: No Parties at Central West High School! Central West, recently dubbed Wild West High by a New York newspaper, did have its problems. Danielle and many of the other teachers thought the biggest problem was the administration. So, this day, she'd break the rules for her Literary Arts class of seniors and for her precocious ninth graders, too.

A little after six that morning, she was drying off, when the phone rang. *Who would call so early? Unless!* Fear for her father's heart condition propelled her down the hall to the living room, tying her robe as she ran. Twenty years earlier, her mother told her that her father had a heart condition to scare her so she'd stop dating a Negro student at college.

At first, she refused and continued to date him. After all, her father had praised her for being an ambassador for the United States when she brought home a male student from Columbia, two young men from India, an Israeli whom she dated, and a very dark-skinned African. Mac enjoyed them all. So why did he object to a Negro from his own country?

Then, one day, when she visited her folks for a weekend, her father was in bed and had been there for three days, seeing no one. Her mother was very stressed. She told Danielle that her father was really ten years older than they'd told her, which was true, and that he had a heart condition. Terrified, Danielle traded in her self-respect for her father's health and told the young man she could no longer go out with him. Something within her died that day. Not that she was in love. She wasn't, but she'd violated her principles, and resurrecting her spirit wasn't easy. Dad, by the way, had been hale and hearty ever since. She grabbed the phone. "Mom?"

"No. It's me."

"Phil!" How could she have forgotten? Her brother had been on prime time TV the night before, playing drums at the Chicago Coliseum with The Dreamers, a famous black singing and dancing group. He was the sole white musician that night, and she'd proudly watched television while her thirty-five year old brother's staccato rhythms supported the sharp, precise movements of the dancers.

When the emcee announced, "Phil McKinnon on drums!" she'd jumped up and cheered wildly until the tenant above her banged on the ceiling.

"You were great!" she said into the phone.

"Thanks! I wanted to catch you early. I just accepted a gig at The Greenwich Village Jazz Club."

"Wow! Congratulations."

"Thanks. Can I stay with you until I find a place to live?"

She looked up to see her embarrassed reflection staring at her from the living room mirror. *I'm pregnant and puking all over the place.* "Sure," she said.

"Great! I'm flying in this afternoon." Danielle stifled a groan. She wanted to hide this pregnancy from her family, from her significant other, Josh Freedman, who was the father, and from the world. "Let's have dinner with Josh at the club tonight. I want to look it over before I start work. Seven o'clock? My treat."

She consulted her reflection again and smiled. "Dinner at seven is great. I'll be there and I hope Josh can make it." She hung up the phone and rushed back to the bathroom to apply light lavender eye shadow and mauve lipstick to complement her dark brown eyes and dark olive complexion. Then she combed her frizzy hair into an Afro, popularized among white people by singer Barbara Streisand. It was a godsend for Danielle.

The late-bloomer had long since grown into a pretty woman, though a feeling of insecurity she couldn't identify surfaced when she received an unfriendly look from an occasional stranger or felt her mother's tension. When she was nine, she'd asked her parents if she was adopted. The question threw them into such confusion, she knew she'd guessed wrong. *I'll wear red today.* She put those memories down, but others arose in their place.

Four-year-old Danielle was climbing a blue slippery-slide in her pink cotton pants and shirt. Her brown and white saddle shoes had been tied firmly by Mommy.

The wall that separated the kitchen from her large playroom had an opening. Across the room, she saw a robin perch on the branch of a maple tree in the yard. She waved. "Hold on to the railing!" said her mother, leaning through the opening. Her body tensed, as she looked up into her mother's worried eyes.

The scene could have been a Norman Rockwell painting for the cover of the *Saturday Evening Post* that July of 1945. "I am holding on," could have been the caption, and that was what Danielle said. Her tight dark curls bounced as she climbed up the last three steps, both hands back on the railing. "See?" she said proudly, but Mommy was casting a net of worry over her. They heard the hiss of liquid boiling out of a pot onto the old stove, and they smelled the pungent aroma of corned beef and cabbage drifting into the playroom.

"Be careful," said Mommy, rushing farther back into the kitchen.

Knowing Mommy would return to worry again, Danielle decided to hide. She climbed down the slippery slide, opened one of its side panels and took out a slim hard cover book. Cartoon figures of a fawn, colorful birds and forest creatures played on the cover.

"Bambi" was written in gold script across the top.

She picked up Fido, her favorite stuffed toy, pressed her nose into his tight white curls and inhaled. Fido smelled like salt. "I'm going to read you a story," she said, looking at the black button-like eye on the side of his head, the only one he had left. She walked past a wooden cradle where her doll Pam slept, past a rocking horse and left her playroom to walk down the hall of the elegant eighteenth-century wood-framed house. It was divided now, into three rentals.

"Such a serious little girl," friends and neighbors would say, smiling down at her.

Danielle knew life was serious. She just didn't know why.

She stopped at the coat closet, opened the door and walked in, leaving just enough light behind so she could read to Fido. The closet smelled of woolen coats and fragrant wood. She walked past the boots to her favorite corner, where she sat on the floor and relaxed. She stood Fido beside her and opened the book.

She knew the story by heart, knew when to turn the pages and recognized many of the words. "Bambi's mother worries about his safety, just like Mommy does," she told Fido. "Man is their enemy." She pointed to one of the forest creatures on the cover. "That's Thumper the Rabbit." She giggled. "Thumper's mother told him, 'If you can't say something nice, don't say anything at all.'"

The front door opened and closed. Footsteps creaked on the wooden floor and stopped outside the closet door. "Shh," she told Fido, as the door opened further, exposing their enchanted corner.

"Danielle! What are you doing in there? Come on out." She heard the smile in Daddy's voice and looked up to see him peeking at her through the woolen coats, and she was happy in spite of herself. He removed his brown derby hat and placed it carefully on a shelf beside his gray one. "You'll hurt your eyes reading in there."

"I can see."

Daddy set down his sample case, which Danielle knew held a volume of the *Encyclopedia Americana*, gently wrapped his fingers around her and trotted her out of the closet. She looked up at him in his brown and beige pinstriped suit, starched white shirt and brown tie and laughed as he picked her up, way up into the air.

"How much do you love Daddy?" he asked her.

"One hundred and fifty-nine," she said laughing.

"Why a hundred and fifty-nine?"

"Because that's how many pancakes Little Black Sambo ate."

"That's a lot!" he said. They enjoyed this routine. He set her gently down and asked, "Will you stop reading in the closet?"

"But I can see!" she said.

"It's too dark in there."

"The hall light illuminates the pages."

"*What* did you say?" Daddy was smiling but Danielle tensed. "Lynn, come here. Quickly!" he called out, and Danielle heard the banging of a pot cover and Mommy's running steps.

"What happened?" said Mommy, looking at her.

"Tell Mommy what you just said!"

Danielle looked up at the two people she loved most in the whole world. "I can read in the closet."

"Because?" said Daddy.

"The hall light illuminates my book."

Mommy sighed, and Danielle saw her smile.

"Il-lu-min-ates! Four syllables!" said Daddy.

"What a big word! Say it again," said Mommy. "Illuminates." In the combined glare of her beaming parents and the overhead light, the little girl may have left her body and hovered over the scene for an instant because she saw herself, all alone and vulnerable, looking up at them. She vowed never to say another big word again.

The hiss of water boiling over again sent Mommy running back to the kitchen. Daddy followed her. Danielle walked back into the closet and closed the door.

Chapter One

Recalling that time, Danielle told herself, "I was autonomous reading in that closet!" She had long since retracted her vow never to say another big word again. She walked into the old-fashioned Gramercy Park living room and admired one complete wall, lined from floor to ceiling with books. *I'm autonomous here, too.* She thought of Josh and dropped down onto the overstuffed maroon couch, where she'd lain in his arms when they first made love, where she first considered giving up that autonomy.

Danielle had lived independently for a long time. She'd had two lovers over the years, a Puerto Rican actor/dancer, and a Jamaican professor/writer. She joked that she was prejudiced towards her own race, but didn't admit, even to herself, that she didn't feel accepted by them. A simple detail like whether her hair frizzed made the difference in how many of them reacted to her. On the days her curly hair frizzed, some people would turn away from her or just ignore her. So she remained married to theatre and acting; she valued her freedom to close her door on the world to rehearse, to read and to write. But, as her enthusiasm for acting diminished, she began to teach full-time. Eight years later, she was yearning for something more once the day was over. Two years later, she met Joshua Freedman. A couple of months later, she threw open the door to her sanctuary and invited him in! Danielle picked up the phone and dialed his number. "Hi," she said.

"Hi." She heard surprised pleasure in his deep voice and pictured his dark olive Sephardic features, piercing brown eyes, full eyebrows, aquiline nose and dark curly hair.

"Phil just invited us to dinner at the Greenwich Jazz Club tonight at seven."

"Count me in. I saw his show on TV last night. He's great!"

"He is, but we may be the only two people beside my parents who'd call it his show." Josh's companionable laughter warmed her through and through. "He'll be working at the jazz club for a while and living with me until he finds a place to live.

"I'm impressed!"

She hurried on before he could ask her to move in with him. "I'm running late. Let's meet at the club."

"Fine. Danielle?"

"Yes?"

"Move in with me."

Her stomach rumbled. "That's a great idea," she said quickly. "I'll need a bit of time, but let's plan it tonight!"

She hung up the phone and made a cup of tea. Food was out of the question. *I'll tell him about my pregnancy and – my plans.* She realized she'd just used the word, plans, as a euphemism for abortion, in case the fetus read her thoughts… *This is ridiculous!*

She took the steaming tea into her bedroom.

She pulled a red velvet pants suit with blue tones from the closet and held it under her chin before the mirror. *Stay away from greens and oranges. They give our complexions a sallow look.* Her father had given her that advice when she was sixteen. She'd never forgotten it because his voice had deepened and his comment seemed to come out of nowhere. He'd never counseled her on her appearance before. Her mother did that. She'd even counseled her on her nose, and with that thought, up cropped more memories of life as a four-year-old.

In the late afternoon of a warm summer day, Danielle was sitting between Mommy and her doll Pam on the back porch steps, where the white paint peeled. All three wore identical red and white checked seersucker dresses Mommy had made for them on her Singer sewing machine. They were waiting for Daddy to come home from work and take them to the Canton for fried rice and shrimp.

She and Mommy were stroking their noses downward with their thumbs and forefingers and repeating, "I think I can, I think I can, I think I can." In Danielle's favorite new story, "The Little Engine That Could," the train made it all the way to the top of the hill, chugging out those words. Danielle was trying to reshape her nose with them.

"Keep stroking your nose down, and it'll grow longer like Mommy's.

"When?"

"In a few years." *A few years?* She gripped her nose and jerked it down.

"Not so hard! Like this," said Mommy, gently stroking her daughter's nose. A man, his face black as coal, rounded the corner of the house. Mommy gasped, "Mac!"

He spied Danielle, grinned and broke into a silly dance, twirling and two-stepping.

"Daddy, you look funny!" She bumped down the stairs in a sitting position and, with arms outstretched, ran laughing through the crabgrass and dandelions.

"Mac! Wipe your face!" Mommy said. Daddy gave Mommy a confused look and swooped Danielle up into the air and continued to dance. "There's soot on your face," she said, wiping it off with a white handkerchief. "You look like a Negro," she whispered, glancing over her shoulder.

"What's a Negro?" whispered Danielle, looking wildly around the yard.

"Oh!" Daddy said. "The car's engine died, and I was turning the crank to get it started, when smoke blew into my face."

"Change your shirt and clean up before anyone sees you!" Danielle saw tears and, worse, fear in her mother's eyes.

"Don't cry Mommy," she said and started to cry, too.

"Mommy and Daddy are just fine," said Daddy, setting her gently upon the lawn.

"Mommy's going to get you a baby brother or sister soon, that's all. I'll be right back, and we'll go to the Canton." He leaned over to kiss her forehead, stopped, wiped his sooty mouth with the back of his hand and rushed up the porch stairs into the house.

"Mommy and Daddy are fine," her mother repeated, dabbing tears from Danielle's eyes with the checked skirt of her dress. She lifted her daughter onto the porch and sat the doll beside her. "Stay right here with Pam, while Mommy gets a clean hankie."

Danielle watched her mother open the screen door and run up the back stairs.

"Mommy? Can we go to Bradley's Bookstore before dinner?" All Danielle's favorite books and toys came from Bradley's. "Mommy?" She looked for her mother in the first- and second-floor windows. Then, she remembered there might be a Negro around, so she picked up Pam and ran around to the front of the house to wait safely by the family car.

"It's a beat up old Ford," her father would say, "but it's all ours!" She sat Pam on the running board, the rubber-lined step along the side of the car, and scrambled up to sit beside her. A man and woman walked along the sidewalk toward her. She put Pam on her lap so she could see them too.

Mommy said not to talk to strangers. The woman stopped and squinted at her. The man frowned. They looked at each other and looked back at her, as if she had been bad, very bad. Danielle gripped Pam. Suddenly, the couple looked up and quickly walked away. Danielle looked up and saw Mommy staring at them with a wild look in her eyes like a cat about to attack. Then she looked Danielle over and asked, "Did they do anything to you?"

"They *looked* at me." Mommy sat on the runner beside her daughter and pulled her close. Danielle thought about what Bambi's mother said. "Is Man our enemy, too?" she asked. Blinking back tears, Mommy gently stroked her daughter's nose down, then just stopped and dropped her hands onto her lap. "I think I can, I think I can, I think I can," said Danielle, looking into her mother's eyes and stroking her own nose down and down and down.

Soon after, Mommy told Danielle she had a pug nose like many people do, and that her nose was cute.

* * * *

Danielle looked into the mirror and smiled. She liked her nose. It was just broader than the rest of the family's. "I've got to get a move on," she said aloud. She still had to buy juice and doughnuts. Her stomach rumbled again. She buttoned her insulated, lavender coat and slung an oversized black leather book bag, stuffed with students' papers, over her shoulder. Then she slipped in a dog-eared paperback of *Pride and Prejudice*. Danielle never travelled without a novel. She loved great literature; she also needed a place to hide.

She was at the door when she remembered the unfinished conversation with her unborn child, and paused for closure. "Shop around, if you're there. Find yourself a real mother. Like mine." To Danielle, motherhood was an overwhelming responsibility. *Give me a hundred and fifty students. I have a chance with them.* She dashed out of the apartment and down the stairs.

Chapter Two

*"Trust thyself: Every heart vibrates to that
iron string." – Ralph Waldo Emerson*

Covering their bent heads against stinging snowflakes, the well-dressed folks of Gramercy Park scurried to work. Gazing up into the cold December morning, Danielle invited the snow to pelt her cheeks and spit into her eyes. A born New Englander, maple syrup flowed in her veins. She inhaled a deep dose of winter's tonic and felt better.

On the bus, she chose a window seat and was reaching for her paperback when the recurrent dream she'd awakened with resurfaced. It was crystal clear, with scenes in two different centuries. She pulled out a pad and pencil, and like an old-fashioned sepia-toned photograph springing to life, the first scene played out on a mercantile street.

I was in my twentieth-century blouse and jumper, observing ladies in fashionable, long nineteenth-century dresses and large graceful hats, some with feathers, walking along cobblestone sidewalks. Gentlemen in top hats and pinstriped suits were tending to banking, haberdashery shops and clothing stores. The buildings were one and two stories high. I knew my grandfather was on that street! A horse-drawn carriage pulled up. I climbed on, and it turned into an omnibus that transported me into the twentieth century. It stopped in front of my grandparents' Tudor house in Brooklyn, New York.

This second scene was in Technicolor. Note: I was seven the last time Dad drove us there to spend Thanksgiving with his family.

Stepping off the omnibus, I walked across the flagstones and climbed the brick steps to the front door, opened it and walked into the high-ceilinged living room. It was empty, except for a space to my right where a section of the parquet floor, sunk about a foot deep, held a black-and-white television set, circa 1950s. A man on the screen made an announcement that amazed me, but I don't remember what he said.

I crossed the living room, climbed the mahogany staircase to the second floor, walked directly into a large bedroom with a sliding closet door and slid it open. It was lined with shelves. One shelf had a piece of black fabric, folded over. I lifted the top fold and saw small jewels – rubies, emeralds, diamonds and blue sapphires, sparkling on black velvet. Or maybe it was colored glass. Either way, I knew they were precious! Note: Are there jewels in the house? Or do they symbolize something to be treasured?

I should tell Mom and Dad about the dream. She'd been raised to keep an open, but not a foolish mind about dream interpretation and psychic phenomena.

She put her notebook away and watched for her stop. *It's a beautiful old house, but Dad doesn't want us to visit our aunts… What did that man on TV say? He sure surprised me.* She saw her stop coming up and pulled the cord. Stepping onto the sidewalk, she felt like she was standing between two worlds. *Was that a past life dream? Or a pre-cognitive one?*

Donuts and juice! The past melted away, and she was back in 1981, hurrying along Eighth Avenue to the delicatessen. Ten minutes later, laden with two full grocery bags and her book bag, she rushed toward Forty-Seventh Street. In spite of the cold, she was sweating under her coat. The late bell rang!

She thought of her student Kamara Briggs and hoped he'd memorized his lines from one of the original stories of Uncle Remus. Her father had entertained her with the Walt Disney version when she was a child. But she'd chosen the original version in Black English to teach to her Literary Arts class. She'd studied it in a graduate course and had fallen in love with its gentle sounds and strong message. In her imagination, she heard the compassionate voice of an old slave quietly instilling self-esteem into the hearts and minds of slave children who gathered around him to hear his stories. Kamara, an ex-convict, was not so sanguine.

She rounded the corner and saw security guard Felix Mendez with him on the top of the ramp by the teachers' entrance. It looked like the guard was trying to keep the gesturing six-foot-two-African-American student from going through the teachers' door. She broke into a run. Getting closer, she realized, *Felix is holding the script and coaching Kamara with his lines!* She heard the young man alternate between mumbling, "Didn't the fox never catch Brer Rabbit? the little boy asked Uncle Remus the next evening," and bellowing, "Where's McKin?"

"Don't worry! She'll be here," said Felix. "You need to get to class son."

"I gotta pass!" said Kamara and muttered, "He come mighty nigh it, honey, sure as you're born, Brer Fox did."

Danielle was tickled. Both she and Felix remembered when this twenty-year-old entered the school two years earlier, after being released from a short prison stint, too angry to care about passing a class. She heard him say, "I gotta graduate, man. I gotta graduate!" and she saw Felix smile and point to her, as she rushed up the ramp.

"C'mon, Teach," Kamara yelled, bolting toward Danielle, taking the grocery bags from her arms and leading her up through the teachers' ramp into school.

Panting, Danielle followed him. "Happy Holidays, Felix."

"Happy Holidays, no parties, sorry, the rules," Felix answered.

"Want a doughnut?" she asked, pulling a box from one of Kamara's bags. He smiled, shook his head and took one.

She checked in late, unlocked the elevator and pushed the button. In the elevator, Kamara shot Danielle his fiercest look. "I've got my oral interpretation. You better pass me this time!"

Danielle shot Kamara her fiercest look. "You know the rules!" It was how they related. They'd really disagreed, two years before, when the young ex-con rose up from his seat in Danielle's tenth-grade English class, crumpled his homework paper in his fist and yelled: "You just

Chapter Two

don't like me! I'm not doing your stupid homework!"

Danielle had shot back: "I don't have to like you, although I do, but I have to teach you! You don't have to like me, but wouldn't you like to graduate?" Kamara glared at her, and his anger morphed to cynicism. He dropped his crumpled paper onto his desk and growled: "You better pass me."

She held his glare with a stern look. "I don't pass anyone! You pass yourself!" But, before he could change his mind, she picked up the crumpled homework, turned from him and proceeded with the class. Her students suspected Kamara was Teachers' Pet. Danielle denied it.

In those days, anything could set him off. On his first day in class, mischievous ninth-grader Luis Rodriguez said he had a girl's name. Suddenly, Kamara was on his feet and towering over him. "Do I look like a girl to you?" Luis jumped up from his desk.

"Take your seats and let's begin," Danielle said quickly. But Kamara was moving toward Luis, who was backing away. Danielle put her hand on the doorknob, ready to open it and call a security guard. *He could end up in jail again!*

Kamara took another step toward him. Luis bumped into his desk and couldn't move. Still looking up, he made a fist. No one moved.

"Kamara's right," said Danielle. "The romance languages influence English. So Carlo, ending in 'o' is a male name, but Carla, ending in 'a' is a female name. Other countries have different rules."

Kamara looked at her. "Like in Roots?" The students were riveted. They all knew the story of the African boy who was abducted from his tribe, taken to America and enslaved there. They'd either seen the 1977 TV mini-series "Roots," or read Alex Haley's novel. "Kunta Kinte's name ends in a," said Kamara.

"That's a perfect example," she said.

"And they called him Toby," he muttered. Danielle's hand slid from the doorknob.

"I forgot," said Luis. Kamara nodded, and with the slow dignity of boys, they took their seats.

Now two years later, in the warm airless elevator, Kamara handed her his assigned reading from Joel Chandler Harris' *Tales of Uncle Remus* and said, "I'm doing it *now!*"

"You can rehearse it *now*," she said, and unbuttoned her coat to let her sweating body breathe.

Kamara's eyes moved up left to retrieve his memorized lines, and he recited in fast, agitated tones, "Didn't the fox never catch the rabbit, Uncle Remus?" asked the little boy the next evening. "He come mighty nigh it honey, sure as you're born."

"Sho's you bawn," Danielle said, wiping sweat from her forehead.

"Bawn?" He looked at her. "Man, they talked funny."

Danielle's stomach turned, and she felt dizzy. "It's a beautiful language."

"Bawn, bawn, bawn!" said Kamara. "Sho's you..." Danielle, leaning against the elevator wall, began to slide down it. Hazily, she saw him bend toward her. He was holding the two bulging grocery bags. "Grab my arm, Teach!"

She grasped the sleeve of his woolen pea coat, and he pulled her up. "I'm fine. There's just no air in here," she gasped. The elevator door opened. As she staggered out of the elevator and down the hall, clinging to Kamara's coat sleeve and too dizzy to trust her balance, a strange thought entered her mind for the second time that morning. "Some say you enter the gates of heaven on the arm of someone you've helped," she said, and saw Kamara look warily down on her wet face and unfocused eyes.

"Don't die on me now, Teach. I've gotta graduate!" Her knees buckled even more, and laughter shook her weakened body, as she clung to Kamara and stumbled along the corridor. Across the hall from her room, she saw history teacher, Mr. Spatz, look up from correcting papers, witness the scene and apparently decide Danielle was in good hands.

"Why can't I do a modern version in Ebonics? Make it real," said Kamara.

"Because Black English is a grammatical and poetic language."

Chapter Two

"How would you know?"

"I studied it," she said, ignoring his real question, which was about her racial identity.

It was a question her black students thought they kept a secret from her, but she knew they'd shortened McKinnon to Mc'Kin, meaning My Kin.

Kamara pushed open the door to reveal her Literary Arts students sitting expectantly in a two-tiered semi-circle. They'd covered a table with a red paper tablecloth, paper plates and napkins. "Ms. McKinnon!" Sixteen-year-old Tamika, prettily adorned in a corn-rowed and beaded hair style that was just catching on, jumped up and motioned to her own chair. "Sit here."

"You all right?" asked Louis Rodriguez, taking one of Kamara's grocery bags and quickly unpacking it onto the table.

"I am now," said Danielle, already healing from the energy of the class. Putting down his sketching pencil, Jamal Jackson, a quiet black student, took the other bag and helped Louis.

"We thought you booked," Louis said, pouring juice into paper cups.

"We did not!" said Marisa Encarnacion, handing a glass of orange juice to Danielle, who took a sip. Her stomach began to settle.

She saw Kamara, under a poster of Frederick Douglass, pacing and muttering his lines. "Okay, everyone. Help yourselves to juice and doughnuts and settle down for Kamara's oral interpretation."

At that moment, Richard Spatz opened the door and looked into the room. "Is everything all right?" he asked.

"Hey, Mr. Spatz," said Louis. "Come on in!" Danielle's students often did readings from American literature for Mr. Spatz's American History class. Since this was his free period, he'd occasionally drop by to listen.

"Join us for a juice and doughnuts," Danielle said. "Kamara's doing a reading."

Mr. Spatz caught Kamara's distracted eyes with his own. "Okay with you?"

"Come on in. It can't get any worse." He took center stage, sat down and started to rattle off the lines from rote memory.

Danielle interrupted. "A couple of questions first."

Kamara exhaled loudly. "Hurry up before I forget this shi'"... He stopped and looked at her. "Sho's you bawn stuff." Danielle sensed he liked the story, but wasn't about to give her an inch.

Nor she him. "Remember the assignment. As Uncle Remus, get the message across to the little boy."

"How am I gonna do that?"

"What does Uncle Remus want to do?"

"Tell a beat up slave kid a story about a smart-assed rabbit."

"Why?"

"To show him how to get over in this lousy world."

Tamika piped up. "Remember *Roots*. He probably wants to tell that little boy a secret, in code, so he can respect himself."

"That boy," Jim Chang added, "probably worked day after day in the fields, has been beaten like an animal and is so messed up, he's not even sure he's human."

Kamara groaned and looked at the Chinese student. "Okay Man, since you know so much about being a little nigra slave, come up here and *be* him!"

Chang got up, walked to Kamara, sat down at his feet and looked up into his eyes.

"Convince me." Danielle appreciated that the class was stifling giggles for Kamara's nerves.

"Take your damn glasses off. Only Massa has those." Chang removed his glasses and squinted at him. The two boys grinned at each other, and Danielle saw Kamara begin to relax.

Softly, she said, "Look into the boy's eyes, Kamara, and convince him that he is just as good as any man that God has created. If you forget a line, Tamika will cue you." She handed Tamika the script and sat back down.

Kamara had to pass, so he told the tale of how Brer Fox tricked Brer Rabbit into hitting a human-like form made out of tar and getting himself so stuck together, he could barely move. While Brer Fox considered what to do to Brer Rabbit – barbeque him, hang him, drown him or skin him alive, Brer Rabbit kept pleading for Brer Fox not to throw him in the briar patch. So, of course, Brer Fox threw him in the briar patch.

With each phrase, Kamara sought to show the little nigra boy, played by Chang, his worth, and, as he did, something within him slipped, and his deep rich voice became a healing balm in the gentle sounds of the old language. Suddenly, he *had* to make the boy decode the precious message in the story of how Briar Rabbit, symbolic of the so-called inferior black race, outwitted Briar Fox and Briar Bear, symbolic of the so-called superior white race, and escaped, laughing into freedom.

"Bimeby, Brer Fox hear somebody call 'im, en way up in de hill he see Brer Rabbit koamin' de pitch out'n his ha'r wid a chip. Den Brer Fox know dat he bin swop off mighty bad. 'Bred en bawn in a briar-patch, Brer Fox – bred and bawn in a briar patch!' en wid dat he skip out des ez lively ez a cricket in de embers…"

Danielle watched Kamara emerge from a light trance to hear stillness in the room.

She knew he felt the fear of failure in the pit of his stomach. She'd been there herself. When the applause began and his classmates were telling him how great he was, she saw a reaction rise up within her student and brace him like the cold winter air had braced her that morning. He sneaked her a gleeful look, and she sensed he'd be a handful for the rest of the morning.

Tamika brought him a doughnut, and Marisa brought him orange juice. He patted the head of the little slave boy and said, "Thanks, man." Chang jumped to his feet and got his own juice and doughnut.

"Color makes no difference," Marisa said softly.

"Ms. McKinnon?" said Jamal, the quiet one. "Can people have doubles?"

Here it comes again, Danielle thought. "Could be."

"I…I saw a woman in my neighborhood who looks just like you."

"Oh?"

"Do…do you have any relatives?" he stuttered.

"No. I'd love to meet her, though. Do you know her?"

"N…no, I just saw her in the neighborhood."

Danielle saw through their questions and hated what she saw. Apology. Fear of offending her. Jamal never stutters. *They've got to think – to feel their way through this… brainwashing!* To make that happen was her undercover mission as a teacher.

Kamara stood. "Jamal is just too polite to ax you."

Now it's coming. Danielle was thinking of the handful she figured he'd be after his success and so chose to ignore the implied question and to correct his grammar instead. "Asss-k," she said, emphasizing the k-sound. "We're going back to Standard American English after vacation."

Kamara would not be deterred. He stood up and looked to enlist Tamika. "Right, Tamika? Right?"

"No, Kamara, no!" Tamika said, as though she were commanding a frisky dog to sit.

Danielle glanced at Mr. Spatz, but his expression was unreadable.

Kamara picked up his chair and carried it to where she was sitting and sat down, face to face with her. "Can I asss-k you something?" he said emphasizing the k-sound right back at her.

Quickly, Tamika joined them. "Ms. McKinnon, he doesn't mean to insult you."

"Don't ever apologize for being who you are, Tamika." She turned to Kamara. "It's, "May I." A loud silence sounded throughout the room.

"May I asss-k you a question?" he said.

"Yes."

"Is you black?"

"*Are* you black."

I'm black. Is *you?*"

She knew he was intentionally holding on to Black English, and she almost laughed, but, "No," stuck in her throat because the class was… so still… and she saw in Kamara's eyes, in Tamika's eyes and even in Chang's eyes how important her answer was. "I'm not, but I've been asked that before." She saw Kamara's cynical disbelief and Tamika's disappointment. Chang was inscrutable, and Marisa looked kind.

Louis whispered loudly, "She doesn't even know what she is."

"Yes, I do! I'm Scotch, Irish, English, Welsh and Aztec."

The changing bell rang. Danielle stood. "You were superb, Kamara! Happy Holidays, everyone." Greetings, like snowdrops, pelted the air and cleared it. She intercepted Tamika. "Kamara may be pushy, but he was right to ask. And, if I felt insulted, whose problem would that be?"

"Yours," said Tamika and hugged her. Danielle hugged her back.

"Ms. McKinnon!" said Assistant Principal James, bursting into the classroom. Teacher and student switched roles. Tamika raised an eyebrow and studied Mr. James, while Danielle put her tail between her legs and walked over to him. "A party, Ms. McKinnon," he said, writing in his notebook.

Tamika joined them and said, "It was a great class, Ms. McKinnon." She smiled at Mr. James, added, "As usual," and walked out.

"Just doughnuts and juice," Danielle said. "They deserve a reward for all."

"Against the rules." He peered at her over his bifocals. "You checked in nine minutes late, and you just engaged in physical contact with a student."

"But I...Yes, well, I'm sorry." Assistant Principal James frowned, turned to leave and bumped into Mr. Spatz, who chose that very moment to bite into his doughnut.

"Mr. Spatz?" Dr. James said pointedly.

"Mr. James," Aaron Spatz returned in kind and turned to Danielle. "I'd like Kamara to perform the Remus piece for my American History class."

"I think he'd love to. He can rehearse here first. Ask him." The late bell rang and the two men left, though not together.

Standing alone in the empty classroom, Danielle suddenly felt empowered. She thought about her unusual morning: awakening from a strange dream, racing to the bathroom with morning sickness and talking to the fetus. *Fetus. That's so impersonal.* Aloud, she said, "Maybe I can do it. Maybe we can... Little One. Want to?" She waited for a tiny congregation of cells deep within her to answer, and though no little voice piped up, "We can do it, Mommy! Let's go," happiness overtook her. She pulled a book order form from her desk and danced across the room and out the door.

The holiday spirit had already transformed the corridor, but her radiance turned heads. A girl from one of her ninth grade classes, called out, "Are you in love, Ms. McKinnon?" Danielle laughed and a renegade silliness bubbled up.

She tried to keep her euphoria in check as she escaped into the English Department. As teacher of the Literary Arts elective teaching creative writing *and* oral interpretation, she was one of the most right-brain English teachers in a department used to right-brained teachers. She hoped her behavior might just slip by.

* * * *

"We're wanted!" said Nicole Johnson, looking up from correcting papers at the long worktable. Compared to Danielle, Nicole seemed more left-brained than she actually was. Her close-cropped Afro framed her flawless cinnamon complexion and thick lashed oval eyes. She slid her pinkish gold wire reading glasses down her nose and gave Danielle a conspiratorial look. "Dr. Norton's waiting."

"What did we do now?" grinned Danielle. The two women had been hired at the same time. Danielle, upon graduating from Ivy League Smith College in New England, studied acting in Manhattan and performed in out-of-town theaters before teaching. Nicole, upon graduating from New York University, taught English in Liberia with the Peace Corps. From the start, Danielle and Nicole formed a professional alliance rooted in their determination to place the students' education above the political needs of the teachers and administrators. Two years earlier, they alerted a New York newspaper to investigate why a thousand ex-cons were enrolled in their school in its first fall term, Kamara among them, without telling the teachers.

"I don't know what *I* did, but *you* didn't order your books for February," said Nicole. She stood.

"I'm ready now." Danielle waved her order form and followed her colleague, who looked svelte in her tailored pinstriped pants suit and low-heel pumps, to the Assistant Principal's door. Nicole knocked.

"Come in," murmured a bored male voice. The two women exchanged a "this should be fun" look and walked into the office. Their relationship reminded Danielle of Bill Cosby and Robert Culp in *I Spy*, a secret-agent adventure series, the first of its kind which aired on NBC for three years in the late sixties. The detectives, one black and one white, worked together to solve crimes. Their conversation was really banter and, even though they were both the good guys, they didn't hang out together, share a beer, talk about race and their feelings the way friends do. Danielle felt they were self-consciously acting like equals instead of being equals, and that made her uneasy. In spite of that, she and Nicole hadn't crossed the line to friendship either.

Dr. Jonathan Norton, beginning to bulge in his Brooks Brothers' suit, kept them waiting without so much as a greeting while he finished writing. His relationship with them was a perfect foil for their limited relationship with each other. By comparison, theirs seemed normal. Like two students called to the principal's office, they stood before his desk, gazed upon his balding pate and tried not to giggle.

Jonathan Norton was a generic white bureaucrat in a school top heavy with white male bureaucrats, so top heavy that a faculty member dubbed it Dolly Parton High after the bosomy country and western singer. Thanks to the Equal Opportunities Act, there was one black bureaucrat. Someone on the staff named him The Cork because, as the last one hired, his position corked up this bulging bottle of white bureaucrats and kept their jobs secure. If cuts in the bureaucracy were ordered, The Cork would be the first to go and, of course, all would cry Racism! While many other public schools had voluntarily begun to make their appointments democratically and according to ability, Dolly Parton High's often inept bureaucrats held onto the easy life with the tenacity of the last of the plantation owners. Danielle, Nicole and others found this unacceptable.

Finally, Dr. Norton looked up and smiled. "Good Morning, Ladies." The "ladies" smiled and replied in kind.

"Here's my order for twenty copies of "Self-Reliance," said Danielle.

"If I'm too late, I'll purchase them from a bookstore over the holidays."

"Ms. McKinnon." Dr Norton savored her name in such a way that, if Danielle were the student and he the teacher, everyone would call her the Teacher's Pet. "I'll order the books, but do you really think they'll understand it?"

"Oh, they'll understand it. The question is: Can I *teach* it?"

Dr. Norton indulged her with a look that said, "How charming you look in your rose-colored glasses." He took her order form and sat back in his chair. "As to why I summoned the two of you,"... He drew out each phrase, as if savoring a favorite pudding... "As head of the English Department, my position... will become available this autumn." He appeared to puff up. "I've been promoted to the Board of Education."

"Congratulations!" Danielle and Nicole chorused. Not only were they glad to see him go, they both had applications on file for his position.

"You've both applied for my position, and we *should* have a female Assistant Principal on staff," he said magnanimously. He looked at Danielle, and her breath caught. "I've recommended Ms. McKinnon for the position."

Dad will be so proud of me, she thought, floating into a bubble of success.

She heard but didn't listen to him say, "And you, Miss Johnson, as next in line, will be given a reduced teaching schedule to assist her."

Danielle turned to Nicole and heard her ask, "Upon what did you base your decision, Dr. Norton?" Only then, did the words, 'And you, Miss Johnson, as next in line, will be given a reduced teaching schedule to assist her,' arrive, as if by a late messenger to Danielle's bubble.

"Ms. McKinnon's literary expertise, of course," he said. "She has her Master's in the classics from *Smith College*! A rare find for this school."

"Nicole's thesis was on the Transcendentalists." Danielle said this without fear she would change his mind.

Dr. Norton smiled at Danielle. "Can you cut your vacation short two days to begin your internship?"

"Yes."

"Very good." He turned his back on them to lock his file cabinet and said, "Miss Johnson, your attendance, for those two days are optional, but I'm sure Ms. McKinnon would appreciate your help. There will be compensation, of course."

Danielle watched Nicole nod to his back. Her teeth must have been clenched hard to cause so tense a jaw.

He turned back. "Happy Holidays, Ladies." Nicole nodded again and walked out. He smiled at Danielle. "Call me John."

She caught up with her colleague, who was walking quickly down the empty corridor. "You can contest this," she said, speaking lightly and smiling into Nicole's eyes, vaguely aware of how phony she sounded.

"On what grounds?" Nicole exhaled a shaky breath and appeared to compose herself with anger. "You got the job, you're qualified, and you'll be wonderful at it! I'll assist you," she said, looking directly at her.

Danielle was searching for words, when unbidden, the remembered feeling of being a white person talking to a Negro, *someone not as good as me*, emerged. It shocked and horrified her, and she hoped Nicole couldn't sense it.

"Merry Christmas," Nicole said and rushed away down the hall.

"Merry Christmas!" Danielle called after Nicole's receding back. The euphoria was gone. She watched her disappear around the corner. A sickness crept into her stomach that had nothing to do with her pregnancy. *That's not me! I don't believe that! Then a question arose. Who's more qualified for the position?* She couldn't move. *It's a draw.* The sick feeling retreated into her subconscious and passed an old memory arising from the same place, as she walked to her classroom.

It was January of 1958 in New Crossing, Connecticut, and Danielle was President of the Senior Youth Fellowship in a protestant church. The hierarchy had mandated that the second Sunday in January be set aside yearly to invite a minority group to visit. Since laws called covenants had prevented Jews and Negroes from moving into their town until 1948 and was still in effect, the Reverend Peterson arranged for a

Negro Youth Fellowship, three towns away in Waterfalls, Connecticut, to visit.

But the Youth Fellowship wrote back a refusal. Reverend Peterson, a fatherly figure who looked remarkably like the nation's president, Dwight D. Eisenhower, told the New Crossing fellowship, "They declined our invitation because they felt that setting aside the same day each year to be friendly to them was demeaning."

"*Good for them,*" thought Danielle.

"Be Kind to Animals Day," whispered the boy next to her. Sporadic giggling erupted, but abruptly stopped, when the laughers saw their minister waiting. Some assumed appropriate expressions, while others smiled at their laps.

He continued. "I spoke to Reverend Johnson who said his fellowship would be willing to visit on any other Sunday. He suggested the second Sunday in February and I told him we'd be available." The smiles disappeared.

So, on that winter night, Danielle opened the doors of their cozy New England Church and welcomed the Waterfalls Youth Fellowship in out of the cold. Twelve negro teenagers, the boys in suits and the girls in skirts with blazers, walked in, looked around and, except for one girl in a red plaid skirt, who caught her eye and smiled, did not return Danielle's greeting. One handsome unsmiling teen looked over her head and across the room. Feeling affronted that a *Negro* ignored her, she turned to see what he found so interesting, and saw her fellowship had gone!

"Excuse me," she said and found them crowded into the adjoining kitchen, slouching in their cashmeres and jeans and having their own party. "Our guests are here! Take out the food and greet them," she whispered. The little Christians ignored her. Danielle had been elected president by a fluke, when two popular contestants, Kimberly Osborne and Michael Adams, had weakened each other's votes. "Michael, they'll follow you. Get them out there. We have guests!" So, Michael, who was a Junior Minister, led his people out of the Kitchen and into the Promised Meeting Hall, where they immediately regrouped as the Chosen,

Chapter Two | 39

across the room from the Negroes. They put one platter of sandwiches, cookies and sodas on a near-by table.

Danielle took their tray, whispered, "Get the rest!" and walked back across the hall to where their *guests* were still standing by the door. "Would you like a sandwich?" she asked. The smiling girl in the red plaid skirt had straight black hair tied back with a red velvet bow. She took a tuna fish sandwich. A brown skin girl with dyed blond hair picked a ham and cheese and two boys chose peanut butter and jelly.

Encouraged, Danielle said, "Let's go over there for soda and cookies." *Over there* was where the sweater and jeans set leaned into each other and sneaked looks across the room. Still holding the sandwich tray, she walked all the way back and whispered, "Bring the sodas and food to the center table." So the white fellowship carried trays of food and drink to a large center table, placed there earlier for that purpose, and the Negro fellowship walked to it, drank sodas and ate sandwiches and homemade cookies. Silently.

"I like your red plaid," Danielle said to the girl with the ribbon in her hair.

"Thank you," she smiled.

"My favorite is black watch."

"Mine too. I have a black watch skirt."

"Me too!" Danielle turned to the girl with the blond hair. "Do you like plaids?"

The conversation was getting pretty thin, but the girl nodded anyway. The white teens were exchanging eye-rolling looks with each other. The Negro teens occasionally locked and unlocked eyes with one another. When the evening was finally over, Danielle walked their guests to the front door.

As soon as the door closed, everyone began talking at once. Danielle was incensed. "Why were you all so rude?" Nobody answered her. "You could have talked to them." They ignored her. "They were our guests!" she said loudly.

"They're not like us," said Joy.

"Yes, they are!"

"Well, I wouldn't marry one," said Kimberly, an elegant hand on her hip, the other on her sweatered endowments.

"I would!" said Danielle. At sixteen, she was the shy one, the quiet one with glasses and limp curly hair. She wouldn't bloom until college.

The Chosen looked at her. "You wouldn't really marry one," said Sue Harris.

"Yes, I would!" Suddenly the room exploded with everyone telling everyone else why they wouldn't marry one, as if the evening had been a matchmaking event.

"I'm free, white and will be twenty-one in five years," said Kimberly, as if that popular saying encapsulated all the wisdom one needed on the subject.

"Everyone knows that they're, well, you know," said a boy too smitten with the voluptuous Kimberly to speak coherently. The fellowship filled in the blanks.

"Lazy!"

"Stupid."

"Inferior."

"They smell."

"Did you smell any of them?" asked Danielle.

"I didn't get close enough." Laughter.

"Me neither."

"They don't smell!" Danielle said and remembered how she'd found out, when Reverend Peterson's voice brought quiet. They thought he was in his office.

"It's twenty to eight, and your parents expect you home by eight-thirty."

"Oh, I'm sorry. I forgot to assign a clean-up crew," Danielle said and turned to her fellowship. "Who'll help out?" No one answered.

"Everyone pitch in," said Reverend Peterson. Quietly, they swept floors, emptied trash, washed and dried dishes and put them onto shelves.

Buttoning up her woolen coat, Danielle thought, *I'm glad he heard them. The bigots!* She remembered the attendance list and walked down the dimly lit hall to the office and filed it in the fellowship's drawer. When she got back, everyone was gone. Except Reverend Peterson.

"I'll drive you home," he said, locking the door to the church. They walked together onto the dark empty streets. She usually caught a bus, but the Reverend drove her home that night… to talk her out of marrying one.

"But they're just people," she said timidly, as he drove.

"You'd be socially ostracized, Danielle."

"But the Negroes are equal." He didn't answer. "They're Americans."

"Your father's business would close down. People wouldn't buy from him."

"But that's not fair." Danielle's voice caught in her throat on 'not,' and she choked on 'fair.' She felt awkward, explaining right and wrong to a minister.

"People would become violent if you dated a Negro," he said, parking in front of her house.

"What would Christ have done?" In one night she'd gone from being a wallflower to a theological contender. Her voice was disappearing.

"You don't want to be crucified, do you?"

"Isn't that the challenge?" she whispered.

He didn't answer, and they looked at each other for a long moment. When she opened the car door, they said good night, and he drove away.

Her shaggy-haired dog, Blacky, whined expectantly at the front door. She opened it and whispered, "Come on." The dog raced out into the snow, raced back, circled her and raced ahead again. Danielle walked into the crunching snow and slid over patches of ice. "Reverend Peterson is prejudiced," she said to Blacky as he rushed by. And she kept walking and sliding, until her mother called her to come in.

Her parents listened quietly, as she told them what happened that night. "I'm withdrawing my membership," she said. No reply. Three days later, she called the church office and told them she was quitting. They said they'd keep her membership on file in case she changed her mind. She expected the minister would call her parents, but, if he did, they didn't say.

"What a bigoted time I grew up in," Danielle said to the Little One, as she prepared for her next class. "It's much better now, but…" She remembered what her father had said when he explained to her and Phil why they had to go to Sunday School.

"*You'll attend the closest Protestant church to the house. For the experience. Your mother will attend service on Sundays. I'll be there for Christmas and Easter. Jesus was a great prophet, but over the centuries, the churches have persecuted people in his name. We chose a Protestant church so that, if you or Phil fall in love with a Jew or a Catholic, you won't feel guilty marrying one.*"

After the holiday party for her fifth class, Danielle outlined future lesson plans. The room was glowing in the late afternoon sun, when she checked her watch. *Time to meet Josh at the jazz club.*

Chapter Three

The Salvation Army bell trilled in the chill air, reminding Danielle to slip a dollar into the donation box. "Thank you," smiled the volunteer.

"Happy Holidays," she called back and rushed down the stairs into the subway. She dashed through a closing car door, slid into a seat as the train lurched away and pulled her dog-eared copy of Pride and Prejudice from her book bag and joined the rest of the readers. *Darcy*, she thought. *Josh isn't a Darcy. Oh no. He's more like Jane Eyre's Mr. Rochester!* She was reading Jane Austen's novel for the third time since she was fifteen and still didn't see what Elizabeth saw in that stuffed shirt.

Josh was Danielle's Mr. Rochester, sophisticated and cynical, but with a surprisingly sensitive and playful core. When she'd read the novel in her twenties, she actually inhaled a breathless, "Oh," when Mr. Rochester's surprise embrace caused plain Jane Eyre to swoon. Danielle had become a pretty woman, but the plain Jane of her teenage years was deep within her psyche.

Josh, like Mr. Rochester, disenchanted by the shallow beauties of his day, opted for a woman of substance. So, one month, two weeks and three days earlier, at a Victorian style inn one autumn night in the Berkshires, Danielle swooned in Josh's embrace and abandoned, just once, birth control. She looked up from her book and remembered how they met.

It had been at a spring conference in Queens given by APEX, The Association for Paranormal Experimentation. The program featured lectures and workshops on reincarnation, a topic she'd had intuitions about since elementary school.

Just before she saw Josh at the conference, she saw what she could only describe later as a bearded English shepherd of centuries past, in loose woolen clothing, carrying a walking stick. As the ancient shepherd faded away, the modern day Joshua Freedman stood in his place. She was drawn, not only to his rugged good looks, but to a strength of character she sensed he possessed and a smile she warmed to that cool April night in 1980.

After the conference, she heard Josh's deep resonant voice, "Does anyone need a lift?" A wave of women shored up around him. Danielle politely waited behind everyone. When her turn came, she smiled hopefully. "Are you going to midtown?"

"The car's filled up. Sorry," he said. The hopeful smile dropped from her lips so quickly, he couldn't help noticing, and it embarrassed her. She was walking to the exit, when she heard running steps and his voice. "There's room after all." She turned. He looked too confident in his fitted jeans, open leather jacket and maroon sweater over a gently muscled chest into which she had a powerful urge to snuggle. But she felt too vulnerable. And too proud. "I've got a ride, thanks," she said, walked alone into the cold night and took a subway without even getting his name. A New England child of the fifties, Danielle learned never to run after a man. Regret set in.

For two months, she attended APEX'S weekly meditation sessions throughout the city, Manhattan of course, hoping to find him there. A new Manhattan resident, she took The City's tongue in cheek prejudice seriously and never thought to look for him in its boroughs of Brooklyn, the Bronx, Staten Island and Queens. She called those "the Boondocks." When APEX reconvened in June for a weekend Dream Interpretation Workshop on a Staten Island campus, she arrived on Friday evening in time to attend the opening event, a wine and cheese party, held under the stars on the roof-top of the conference center.

She saw him! Across the crowded roof! Talking with three other women conferees. A changed person, Danielle grabbed a glass of red wine, a small plate of cheese and crackers and flew straight across that roof. He looked at her and smiled. Does he recognize me? And she joined the conversation that turned into a "Can You Top This?" competition on personal psychic experiences. She led with, "We lived in a very old house when I was about five, and one night, the ghost of a tow-headed boy about my age walked into my bedroom. He wore a blue and white striped shirt over white pants. He was smiling and playing with a yellow yo-yo…" and she kept talking until the last woman drifted away.

Danielle and Josh talked on into that enchanted evening, sipping wine by the rooftop's fence, facing into the soft night air. When he told her where he lived, she blurted out, "You live in *Brooklyn?*" and tried to cover her shock with a show of interest. "For long?"

"Raised there. Graduated from Brooklyn College."

"Nice! What was your major?"

"Psychology."

"So you're a psychotherapist?"

"Not yet. I worked my way through college at Careers Central, an executive search firm in Manhattan. After graduation, the boss offered me a partnership."

Good grief. He's a headhunter! "A friend of mine got a job through your agency. Do you enjoy it?"

"I did for a while. It's good money, but I'm ready to move on. I have my PhD. in Clinical Psychology, and I'm building a practice, while still running the agency."

"Congratulations on your new career!" she said with the same enthusiasm she'd use to congratulate a truant student who started to attend classes regularly.

"Thanks. It's not easy leaving a sure thing to start over."

"But you light up, just talking about it."

"I love working one on one with people, helping them find solutions to their problems… and perhaps making a difference in the world."

"That's just how I feel teaching at Central West High School."

"Wild West High School? The one in the news?" he blurted out. She nodded and saw him try to cover his shock with a show of interest. "Isn't it dangerous?"

"It's a challenge. The students are just cynical, sophisticated New Yorkers, who don't want to be conned. Particularly by the white man." Josh raised his own sophisticated, cynical eyebrow. Danielle didn't like phonies. *I need to know how he thinks.* "Last year, one of my students, Kamara Briggs, fresh out of Rikers Island and older than my sophomores, was put in my class to make up the work he failed before going to jail." She told Josh his story.

"It *is* a chance to make a difference," he said. "What was he in for?"

"Selling marijuana."

Josh paused. "I sold grass in college. Many of us bought or sold it."

"Anybody go to jail?"

"One guy got caught, but his father paid someone to drop the charges."

I think I like him. She knew she was attracted.

The following day, when it came time to practice interpreting dreams, Danielle and Josh paired up and pulled their chairs to a private corner of the auditorium. "I had a silly dream last night," he said.

She sat facing him. "Do you want to go first?" He opened his notebook. "Sure. I dreamt I was following an orphaned kitten running down a back alley toward the scent of a meal." He laughed. "Large hungry rats were running after her, but they scattered when I ran by. I knew that kitten was in real danger, but each time I got close, she'd round another corner and disappear again. I woke up in a cold sweat, wanting to…tell her something."

"So you're being eluded by something you call 'she' who you're trying to protect. Does that make any sense?"

"I don't know."

"It's your dream."

"I've never had a cat, much less an orphaned one." He was about to laugh again, when his jaw dropped. "My daughter… I need to protect her more than ever since the divorce. She's having a hard time with it."

"Does she live with you?" Danielle asked, derailed from her task.

He shook his head. "Sharon lives with her mother. I have her on weekends and, after school on Wednesdays, I take her to therapy. This weekend she's with my parents. But usually, we do things together like roller-skating in Central Park, going to movies, museums…."

"But it's working out?"

"In a way, but… I just don't think I'm cut out to be a father."

Chapter Three

"Sounds to me like you're under-estimating yourself. How old is she?"

"Fourteen."

"Just a kitten?" she smiled. Back on track.

He smiled back. "Yeah, just a kitten, but she can be a handful. After four years of divorce, she still wants Kathy and me back together again."

"Is that a possibility?" She was trying really hard to stay on track.

His eyes caught hers and held them. "No. It's over. For both of us." Danielle wanted to dance.

During the weekend, they participated in the same groups, as much as the rules would allow, and lingered over the breaks, while interpreting their dreams and sharing their lives. At the end of the conference, they made a date to meet for drinks at an outdoor café in Greenwich Village… to talk some more. He didn't seem to be a phony, but she still wanted to know more about him.

By late July, settling onto the couch in her living room, she thought he'd never stop talking about his new psychology practice. *Doesn't he know I know he'll succeed?* Her fingers took on a life of their own and traced the curves of his chest she'd been eyeing long enough. He stopped talking, slipped his arm around her waist, pulled her across the couch, and they began with snuggling. No bottled cologne ruined his fragrant mix of maleness and sweat. She tasted it along his neck and let him move her onto her back. He opened a button on her blouse, and her exposed skin tingled under his breath, as he said, "Let's take this slow." He kissed her there, and she felt she'd come home.

In early August, Josh introduced her to the "kitten." With straight dark brown hair, long-lashed almond eyes and a slim body already developing, Sharon Freedman was a beautiful child. The three began to spend weekends together. At first, the girl was moody and quiet. Then she'd become animated, talking to her father. *This must be awfully hard for her.* Danielle tried a couple of unsuccessful conversation starters, then gave in and became a supportive audience.

In late August, Josh drove them to Marty's Lobster House on Long Island to celebrate Sharon's fifteenth birthday. Danielle gave her the front seat so she'd feel included. Then she leaned into the back seat behind Josh, closed her eyes and let the warm salt sea air caress her face and hair. *One teenager will be easier to handle than my five classes*, she thought. Then Sharon said, "Dad, I've got to tell you something."

"What?"

"I can't tell you."

"Okay." Danielle gazed at waves breaking onto the rocky shore.

"But I've got to tell you."

"What is it?"

"I can't tell you."

Through the rear view mirror, Josh looked at Danielle. She smiled at him, and his eyes smiled back at her. "Tell me another time," he said to Sharon.

"But I have to tell you now!"

Exhaling exasperation, Josh made a sharp turn into the parking lot of the restaurant. A bag with Sharon's birthday presents banged against Danielle legs from its hiding place on the floor. It hid a blue sapphire ring from Josh and a mint green sweater set from her. She'd wrapped them in colorful birthday paper with a balloon motif and used the edge of an open pair of scissors to curl the green ribbon, just as her mother had done for her.

They sat in reserved seats by a window, overlooking the harbor. "Look how pretty," Danielle said to Sharon, who barely glanced at it.

"Dad, I've got to talk to you."

"Spit it out," Josh said.

Danielle stood. "I have to use the women's room. I'll be back in ten minutes."

Twelve minutes later, as she sat down at their table, Sharon stopped talking and pointed to a bar with a room of its own. "Can we talk in there?" Josh looked apologetically at Danielle. She smiled at the two of them and nodded.

Chapter Three

"Okay. Let's get this over with." Josh stood, as a waiter arrived with two glasses of red wine and a Shirley Temple. "I ordered you a Merlot."

"Perfect." She watched them both walk out of sight into a room with cushioned chairs around small tables. *I should be in there with him.* She felt guilty. She gazed down upon white boats tinged orange by the sunset, sipped wine and savored her new relationship with Josh. Today, she witnessed how understanding he was of his daughter, and she admired that, but... *Would he be sterner if it wasn't her birthday? She's qualifying for brat...but it's so complicated with the divorce and his guilt.* She glanced at the cocktail lounge, sipped more wine and looked back upon the harbor.

Twenty minutes later, after staving off starvation with cream of crab soup, she welcomed them back with a smile. They were quiet as they sat down. The waiter returned, and they ordered the house special, boiled lobster with butter, french fries and a salad. After the waiter left, Josh said, "Sharon thinks you're after my money."

"When she could speak, Danielle said, "I earn a living teaching."

Calmly pouring blue cheese dressing over her salad, Sharon said, "Teachers don't make good money."

"It's good enough for me! I'm glad you brought it up, though. Do you want to talk about it?" Sharon continued to eat her salad, as if Danielle hadn't spoken. She felt Josh give her hand a gentle squeeze under the table. The lobster dinners arrived, and they filled the silence cracking hot, red shells with pliers, extracting lobster meat with metal picks and dipping it into melted butter. Danielle noted that the French fries were made from freshly cut potatoes, Josh said how delicious the food was, and they let the real issue drop.

For dessert, they ordered ice cream, and Danielle brought out the birthday gifts.

Sharon immediately slipped the sapphire ring onto her finger and held up her hand to display it. "Thanks Dad," she said.

"Glad you like it," he said, smiling.

"It's beautiful," Danielle said, and offered her gift.

Sharon unwrapped it, looked, mumbled, "Thanks," and closed the box.

"It's a good color for you," Josh said.

"Feel free to return it for something else. There's an exchange certificate in the box," said Danielle, putting the gift back into the bag. Sharon nodded without looking at her.

The ice cream arrived, and cake, Sharon's piece with a burning candle. Danielle smiled encouragingly at Josh, and they joined the waiters in singing, "Happy Birthday."

After that day, about every three weeks, like a recurrent pre-menstrual cycle, a Sharon-related incident would arise to challenge their relationship. Josh asked Danielle if she would join him at Sharon's weekly session with her psychologist, Alison Altman. She'd never been in therapy, and she jumped at the opportunity to solve their problems together. For months she worked doggedly at understanding Sharon, but then, one night, alone in the privacy of her Gramercy Park apartment, like a spontaneous combustion, she exploded, "Kitten, my ass! She's a baby cougar."

Danielle floated up the subway steps into the old-fashioned Charm of Christmas in Greenwich Village and walked toward the jazz club. Colored lights glittered through the paned square windows of small shops. Spruce and balsam trees scented the cold night air, as the villagers purchased them from sidewalk vendors and pulled them along the streets to their apartments.

Tonight you're going to meet Josh, Little One. Remember him? He's the one who knocked us up. Laughing, she opened the door to a round dimly lit lobby. The murmur of early diners and the soft strains of a piano issued from the adjoining room. She looked for Josh. He wasn't there, but framed black and white photographs of legendary jazz musicians surrounded her. She looked for and found a picture of one of her favorite singers, Louis Armstrong.

She moved on to another room where an oval bar was filling up and looked around. *No Josh.* Quickly, she moved to save them seats by the wall. For privacy, she hoped. She squeezed past an animated circle of people and was putting her book bag on one swivel chair and her coat on another, when an aging but stylish woman on the seat beside her got her attention. She had a glamorous worn look that suited her in that milieu. Relaxed in a slimming black silk dress that draped just below the knee, she swung her shapely legs and spiked black heels. Her silver-streaked red hair was drawn back from her lined patrician face into a ponytail. A well-worn woman, that's how Danielle thought of her, cradled an oversized martini glass in tapering fingers with maroon and silver claw-like nails. She turned to Danielle and looked at her from under thickly mascaraed eyelashes. Her earrings of marcasite swung and glittered. "Don't miss Lena Horne's Broadway show," she said.

"I saw it. Wasn't she great?"

"And disturbing," said the woman. "In 1947, she married the white pianist and composer, Lennie Hayton, in Paris. They kept it a secret in this country for three years because of racial threats!"

Her circle of four companions, well into cocktails and conversation, joined in. "What did you think of her Stormy Weather reprise?" asked a woman in a navy business suit.

"That alone made the evening worthwhile," said Danielle.

"Who would have thought The Surrey with the Fringe on Top could be so damn sexy," said one of the men. They all laughed and agreed.

"Join us," said the woman, sipping her martini.

"Thanks, but I'm meeting someone for a… private talk."

"Here?" asked the woman in the navy suit.

"I was going to swivel the chairs toward the wall… Not good planning," she admitted to their amused faces.

"What will you have," asked a waiter with the modulated speech of an actor.

"Gin and tonic and a Pellegrino." She felt Josh's arms encircle her.

"Merlot McKinnon? Pellegrino?" he asked. The group laughed politely, and Josh smiled at them.

"We were talking about Lena Horne's show," said Danielle.

"She's a great performer," Josh said, hanging his leather jacket on the chair. He looked relaxed in his business suit. "We saw the show. Her family was successful and in the middle class as far back as the 1880s."

"And still faced prejudice," said the well-worn woman. The waiter set down the drinks before them. Josh looked at Danielle.

"That's our cue," the woman said. "Have a good talk and enjoy the show."

"Thanks. Nice talking to all of you," said Danielle, and the friendly group swiveled back into their circle, as Danielle and Josh turned their chairs to face the wall. "I thought we'd have more privacy." Josh handed her the bubbling mineral water. They toasted silently and watched their silhouettes toast with them. She thought of the Little One and whispered, "To you."

"What?" Josh asked. When she didn't answer, he looked at her and smiled. "What?" He looked so open, so happy.

"I'm pregnant," she said softly. She almost said, "I have someone I'd like you to meet!" Fortunately she didn't because, as it was, Josh was looking at her as if he didn't understand what she meant. He seemed frozen in the happy moment that just passed. The fantasy Danielle created with the Little One left her unprepared for his silence and for the shock that was crossing his face as it unfroze.

"Pregnant. When?" he asked in a monotone.

"November 15th at the Berkshire Inn." Such left-brain accuracy was way out of character for her, but those prosaic words were magical, calling up a memory of his mouth tracing a line from her breasts to her belly, of her body melting into his.

"Didn't you use birth control?… I guess you didn't." He stared down into his gin and tonic.

Somewhere behind them, a glass slammed onto the counter and, for an unnerving moment, she wondered if the group had heard.

Josh looked up at her with eyes that, just seconds before, were alight with joy and trust.

Now they were blind-sided by betrayal. She blinked back tears. "I didn't use birth control because… oh, it seems so foolish now, but…" She swallowed hard. If she explained, the whole experience would seem pathetic.

"But?"

Chapter Three

To protect her private Victorian fantasy from expiring under the rational light of twentieth century sophisticates, she lowered her voice. "That inn was right out of *Jane Eyre*. "I love…" The words caught in her throat. Music played, conversations buzzed and Josh waited. If she was going to lose him, it might as well be on her own terms. "I love you the way Jane loved Rochester. The moment was too… classic for birth control." Their eyes were locked, his in confusion.

"How romantic!" whispered the well-worn woman.

"Don't fall for it, guy," one of the men said gently.

Josh turned to him in confusion. Danielle touched his hand, and he turned back. "I was planning to have an abortion until this morning, but…" Shock crossed Josh's face a second time.

"An abortion?" he said hoarsely. "Why didn't you tell me?"

He's hurt. It was warm in the crowded bar, and sweat broke out under her sweater. "It was my choice not to use birth control, so it's my responsibility to…" Unable to say the word again, she turned to the wall and saw a silhouette of claw-like fingers holding up a large martini in a toast.

"Let's have the baby," Josh said.

She turned back to him. "It's my responsibility to – dispose – of the baby. Or give birth to her." She waited for his reaction, but he didn't say anything. He seemed to be waiting for hers. She felt light-headed.

"Let's have the baby," he said again. *Did I hear him correctly?* "Her?" he asked.

"Did you say *her*?" She nodded. He smiled, reached for her, and she swooned into his arms.

"He fell for it."

"Can it, Jack."

"To romance!"

"To Charlotte Bronte!"

On the last toast, Danielle turned to the well-worn woman and smiled. She and Josh received the listeners' good wishes, both enthusiastic and cautious. The band was playing "Take Five," as they walked hand in hand to the dining room.

She saw her brother stand and wave them over to the table. He looked handsome in his green crew-neck sweater and blue jeans. A black couple, also at the table, smiled at them. Phil introduced them as Darren Walker, his colleague and friend from music school and Darren's fiancé, Cheryl Green. Danielle could barely wait until the introductions were over to announce the advent of the Little One.

"Uncle Phil, I like the sound of that," said her brother, hugging her and the still stunned Josh.

"Did you choose a name yet?" asked Darren, a slim young man in a denim suit.

"Not yet," said Danielle. She wasn't about to admit she'd just decided to have the baby in school that morning. She looked at Josh. "We could name her after our mothers, Lynn Bess… or Bess Lynn."

"Or Danielle," he said, caressing her fingers.

"Or the right name may just come along," said Cheryl, a full figured black woman, who looked striking in her midnight blue sheath, full Afro and wood-carved earrings.

"That's what I think too," said Danielle, catching fire with her.

"Wait until Mom and Dad hear!" said Phil.

Mom and Dad… A subtle disharmony hummed through Danielle's euphoria. "Let's eat," she said, to divert the feeling. She picked up the menu and concentrated on the fish selections. But her father's voice broke through: *We're family enough. We don't need anyone else. You and Phil have your education and your independence.* Mac had said that, in passing, when Danielle, at thirty, mentioned, in passing, that she wasn't married yet. *Was Dad suggesting we don't marry?*

Now that the memory popped up again, she told herself, *Dad knows Josh and likes him*, put it out of her mind and selected prawns with black bean sauce.

"Something wrong?" Josh asked her. She smiled and shook her head.

"What are you doing for Christmas?" Cheryl asked.

"Spending it in Connecticut for a few days," she said brightening.

Chapter Three

"We have a neighborhood tradition of caroling, followed by a Wassail party at our house.

"Sounds like fun," Darren said.

"It is," she said, then thought how uncomfortable it would be for the black couple.

Her joy dropped a few notches.

"How about leaving at three from my place?" Josh said. Phil nodded and Danielle pulled an extra set of keys to her apartment from her bag and handed them to her brother. "Would you bring the gifts for tomorrow? They're in a pile on the living room floor. I just want to stop by the apartment tonight long enough to pack a suitcase and then go to Brooklyn with Josh."

"Good! I could use a little privacy," said Phil, grinning.

"Oh. Are you back with Alma?" Darren asked him.

"No." Danielle watched happiness fade from her brother's eyes. How joyful he'd been with the young black woman. She had no idea why they had stopped dating, and Phil was too private a person to ask. She watched him squirm from Darren's inquiry by asking Josh, "Is Sharon coming with us?"

"I won't know until the last minute," said Josh, his happiness dimming too.

She watched Phil hide his feelings behind a menu, then saw Darren pick up his menu, lean into Phil and heard him say quietly, "Don't wait too long, man."

Touched by the warmth of their little group, she raised her glass. "I know it's a bit early, but let's toast to 1982. It's just around the corner, and I feel it's going to be a wonderful year." "With new careers!" Darren raised his glass.

"New friendships!" Cheryl raised hers and smiled at Danielle and Josh.

"Weddings!" Phil raised his glass to the two couples.

"And a child." Josh raised his glass and took Danielle's hand in his. The little party clinked to affirm their toasts, and ordered their meals.

The band was on break, and a vintage recording of Louis Armstrong singing, "What a Wonderful World," filled the room. Danielle had the odd sensation that he was alive and singing in that very moment, just as a medieval painting or an ancient Egyptian statue, at times to her, felt sentient. *I wonder if the aura of our little group will live on and add to the vibes of this club.*

Chapter Four

It was two a.m., when Danielle and Josh, happily leaning into each other, entered his Brooklyn penthouse. Josh had celebrated his fatherhood with two more gin and tonics, and Danielle had driven them home. In the dark foyer, she brushed her lips against his, and he responded with a deep, slow kiss. Then, he yawned, his breath warming her cold ears.

Danielle understood. Tomorrow was the packing, the driving to Connecticut and the Wassail party with the carolers, a yearly tradition at the McKinnon's, but a street light which romantically lit the living room couch by the bay window, beckoned to her. She waited until he locked the two locks and hung their coats in the closet, before she unknotted his tie. Then Josh remembered his new identity. "Mr. Rochester, huh?"

She laughed and unbuttoned his shirt collar. "Yeah, rough-edged, sensitive and sexy." She felt his cool hands move under her sweater and up her back. She raised her arms, as he lifted the garment over her head and dropped it. She led him across the room until he turned her back into his arms. They slid to the floor somewhere between the couch and the coffee table under the bay window. "Definitely not a Darcy."

"I don't know what you are." He stifled another yawn. "But it turns me on." She too felt that sleepy mixture of love and desire, which enfolded them in a trance so deep that, at first, when she heard the door's lock click open, it seemed as though it was far away in someone else's apartment. Then the second lock clicked open!

Josh jumped to his feet and grabbed a metal object in the dim glow of the streetlight. Danielle reached blindly for a weapon and picked up a bowl of sloshing liquid on the coffee table. She saw the outline of a telephone, grabbed the receiver and tried to dial emergency, as a shadowed form slipped into the foyer and quietly lowered a large bag onto the floor. Lights clicked on!

It was Josh's daughter, Sharon, sixteen, looking eighteen, in a black leather jacket and jeans. The girl's incredulous dark brown eyes stared at them from a beautiful face framed by long brown hair that touched down onto her shoulders.

Danielle's relief turned to humor, and it seemed to be all around her. Josh was standing beside her with his fly unzipped, brandishing a menorah. She giggled then realized she was down to her black lace bra and red velvet slacks. Her forefinger, which had been trying to dial 911, was knuckle-deep in a milky cereal bowl, which he must have left out that morning, and the receiver was drowning in milk and Cheerios.

She looked up and grinned at Sharon, who just stared at her. Laughter bubbled out of her, and she looked at Josh. He finally came to life, quickly put down the menorah, turned his back to his daughter and zipped up his fly, saying, "Sharon, why are you out so late?"

"What's she doing here?" said the girl. Danielle stopped smiling.

"She belongs here," said Josh.

"And I don't?"

"Of course you do, but it's two o'clock in the morning!" Sharon threw her bag and jacket onto a coat hook. "Does your mother know you're here?" No answer.

Danielle put her hand over her belly to include the Little One. Not that they noticed. Sharon walked past her into the kitchen. Danielle retrieved her sweater from the floor, pulled it down over her head and followed. "Are you coming with us for Christmas? My parents are looking forward to meeting you." No answer. "We'll sleep over tomorrow night and Christmas Eve, then leave on Christmas Day."

Josh walked into the kitchen, and Sharon turned to him. "I'm not going."

"Does your mother know where you are?"

"Can we talk alone?" she asked her father, as she opened the cupboard, pulled out a box of crackers and slammed the door shut.

Chapter Four

"Want some eggs and toast?" asked Danielle.

Sharon swung around to face her. "You are not my mother," she said spelling out each word. Then she walked back to the living room. Josh ran his fingers through his curls, looked into Danielle's eyes and put an arm around her waist. She felt his helplessness, as they followed her.

Sharon stood with her back to them, eating crackers. "Come, sit down," said Josh. He and Danielle sat apart on the couch. Sharon slumped into the Queen Anne chair opposite them, forming a crooked circle. "The timing could be better, but we need to talk." Sharon leaned down to put the cracker box on the table, and a golden crucifix on a chain fell from her shirt.

"What's that for?" asked Josh. Both Sharon's parents were Jewish.

"Just keeping a low profile, Dad. Not everyone likes Jews."

"Won't you lose track of who you are?" Danielle asked.

"Sharon picked up the cracker box and looked at her father. "Can we talk alone?" By now, Danielle wished they would.

"Yes, but first, the news," said Josh and put his arm around Danielle. "We want you to be the first to know."

Sharon stopped chewing and looked at them. "You're getting married?"

"Yes," they said together.

"Da-ad?" said Sharon, which translated to Danielle as, "Are you nuts?"

Determined to set her straight, Danielle said, "In August, you'll have a sister. I feel it will be a girl." A flash of jealousy in Sharon's eyes told Danielle that she'd just become the girl's worst nightmare, and in spite of herself, she savored the moment.

Slowly, Sharon stood. Then Josh stood and asked, "You want to talk in the kitchen?" It felt like a showdown to Danielle, so she stood too, just as Sharon threw the cracker box. It bounced hard off her forehead.

"Sharon!" said Josh. Danielle's hand flew to the side of her brow.

"I didn't mean it. What did you have to stand up for? I was aiming at the wall."

"Sharon," Josh said again.

"She threw me out!" his daughter yelled. She ran into the bedroom she used when visiting and slammed the door behind her.

Josh removed Danielle's hand from her head and gently touched it. "I'm all right," she said. They heard the lock to Sharon's room click shut. Then muffled sobs. He caressed Danielle's cheek, then walked to his daughter's door and knocked. She saw Sharon looking down as the door opened.

When they disappeared inside, Danielle scooped up the cracker box from the rug, threw it onto the coffee table, dropped down onto the couch and stared. She was angry!

At herself! At all of them! Not only at what just happened but at nearly a year and a half of this screwball behavior! Of these father-daughter chats! Of trying to please!

Hot tears ran down her face.

She looked at the door to Sharon's room. *This is one conversation I'm not going to wait out. I'm going to bed.* She crossed the living room to the front door and reached for her suitcase. A large black garbage bag, the one Sharon brought in, slouched beside it. No twisty held it closed. She looked in and saw cassette tapes mixed with sweaters, jeans and underwear. Her hand flew to her belly. *She's moving in! Oh my God, Little One. She's moving in.*

It was four a.m., when Josh slipped into bed beside her. She woke right up. *Maybe she's gone back to her mother!* But when she looked at Josh's desolate expression, she said, "The poor kid." She imagined her mother saying that.

Josh just lay there staring at the ceiling. "I feel so guilty. The divorce..."

"We'll become a family, she said. "It'll just take time." *I hope.* Josh rolled over to face her. Tears were in his eyes. She stroked his brow. "Sharon's had a few shocks today, getting thrown out of her home, then hearing about our plans to marry and to have a baby. She needs to know she's wanted here." *And I need to want her.*

She heard Josh's cry, a high sound he tried to control. She pulled him to her and gently massaged the back of his head and shoulders. His tears were wet on her bosom. As she held him, their breathing fell into sync, and they slept.

Near noon, she awoke with a rumbling stomach and heard Josh showering in the master bathroom. She hurried to the hall bathroom next to Sharon's room. Quietly, she closed the door, dropped to her knees and retched loudly into the toilet bowl. She envisioned Sharon shooting up from her sleep into a wide-eyed sitting position. She giggled, but didn't gag.

She cleaned the toilet, then sat back on the rug and gazed at the cracked white tiles for a few moments to insure the crisis was over. She was thinking how clean Josh kept the place when the cracks appeared to merge into the figure of a woman in a long old-fashioned dress, and a fragment of a dream resurfaced.... She was standing alone on an outdoor train platform... Danielle could feel her grief.

I've dreamt this before. She got up and was washing her hands and face, when a knock startled her. "Just a minute." She dried off, opened the door and looked into Sharon's guarded eyes. "Morning. I'm just leaving." Eyes averted, Sharon squeezed past her. "Did I wake you?"

"Uhn." Danielle translated that into, "Yeah, but whatever."

"Sorry. Morning sickness." Sharon pulled her toothbrush from its holder, and Danielle walked down the hall.

"How..." It was Sharon's voice. Danielle turned. "How far along are you?"

"A little over five weeks. This phase is usually over in the first three months."

"Yuck!" said Sharon, and shut the door.

Forty minutes later, Danielle, refreshed from a shower and shampoo, was dressed for the day in a claret cashmere sweater and indigo jeans. She was ready for the dinner and Wassail party only five hours away. Lured by the aroma of freshly brewed coffee, she walked quickly across the wooden hallway floor and onto the kitchen's linoleum with a red brick design. Josh wasn't there, but the coffee pot was warm on the ancient stove. She poured a mug, took a soothing sip, then opened the old

General Electric refrigerator and brought cream cheese, butter, jam and milk to the table.

She took another sip of coffee and dialed her parents' number in Connecticut.

"Hello?" said her mother. How good to hear a friendly voice.

"Mom, hold on." She opened the door to the hallway, heard noises that told her Sharon was showering, so she got right to the point, which finished with, "Sharon's angry and hurt. Just so you know in case she decides to come."

"The poor kid," said her mother, which discouraged Danielle from telling her about the baby and her plans to marry right then.

Josh walked into the kitchen, carrying a brown bag smelling of warm bread. His brown eyes looked serious under his full dark eyebrows, as he unzipped his jacket.

"See you around five," she told her mother, hung up, and snuggled into the cool leather corner of his free arm. "Mmm. Warm bagels, onion, cinnamon and raisin," she said as aromas escaped from the bag. "I wanted to make a hearty breakfast this morning, but I just couldn't."

"I know. I heard you in the hall bathroom." He smiled.

She poured fresh mugs of coffee, as Josh unpacked the bag. She felt a part of things this morning. "Is Sharon coming?"

"Maybe. If she doesn't, I'll probably stay, too."

"I understand." She was surprised that she meant it.

"Kathy called this morning in a panic." Danielle handed him a mug. "She said she didn't throw her out of the house. Sharon snuck out after she went to bed." He sat down at the table, lost in his thoughts.

"What happened?" she asked, pushing the plate of bagels toward him.

"Did I tell you Kathy has a degree and experience as a chef?" Danielle nodded. "Well, she just invested in a classy tavern here in Brooklyn with a guy who already runs one successful restaurant and wants to open another. It sounds like a great opportunity." He paused to spread cream cheese onto an onion bagel. "I told her I'd help out financially or – otherwise."

"And?" Danielle asked, holding her buttered bagel in mid-air.

"She needs to devote at least a year to help this guy renovate, get the business on its feet and train the cooking staff. It could be a gold mine for her. She wants Sharon to stay with her parents or mine in the meantime, but Sharon's having none of it."

Danielle examined her bagel. "Sharon may be too much for them."

"I know. Anyway, they got into an argument last night, and, in a fit of anger, Kathy said, 'Maybe you should go live with your father for a while. I've had it with you.'"

"Not a nice thing to say to your child." *But I'd sure know how to play that role on stage*, the actress within Danielle thought. She bit into the bagel and asked, "Do you think Kathy can make a go of it?"

"Absolutely. In any case, I want to be there for Sharon."

"Of course."

They were on their second cup of coffee when Sharon, dressed in a green sweater and jeans, sat down at the table.

"Good Morning," said Josh.

"Uhn."

Danielle interpreted her response as a positive one and said, "That hunter green is fabulous on you."

"Thanks." Sharon selected a warm cinnamon raisin bagel from the plate and buttered it. Danielle waited for her to enjoy a few bites before asking, "Are you coming with us?"

"Unh."

Chapter Five

Gentle sounds of an ancient mystery issued through the open window of Josh's car radio, as a choir sang, "Do You See What I See?" Danielle stood on the tree belt between the car and the mailbox in her purple coat and gazed up into the graying sky. She waved a green envelope in a large arc and said, "It will snow on the drive there."

"Another miraculous vision," teased Josh, carefully placing bags of colorfully wrapped Christmas and Chanukah gifts into the trunk.

"Just New England forecasting," chuckled Phil, setting suitcases beside the bags. "We'd open the windows each day to double check on the weather report."

Danielle smiled to see how relaxed and ready for a holiday break the two men were in their leather jackets and jeans. Then she reread the address on the green envelope and frowned... *Tessie and Charlotte McKinnon, 1077 E. 38th St., Brooklyn, New York...* Phil, our aunts live ten blocks from here." *I'll send it from Mom and Dad's.*

"Really? Let's visit them."

"Dad said not to! You know that." She paused at the mailbox and explained to Josh, "I was seven, Phil was almost three, and our grandparents and Uncle Robert were still alive, when Dad and Mom stopped taking us there."

"But you send cards," said Josh eyeing the green envelope.

"Yes, and we'll phone them from Connecticut on Christmas," said Phil. Dad visits, but never talks much about it."

Danielle was still standing by the mailbox, thinking, *How odd to have that dream about finding precious gems in their house and then to move so near.* Musing on the synchronicity, she didn't feel Josh slip the Christmas card from her gloved hand or see him drop it into the mailbox beside her. But, when the box clanged shut, she swung around. "No!" I have to send it from Connecticut!" She yanked open the mailbox door and peered into the darkness.

Josh closed the mailbox and looked at her. "Let me get this straight. Your aunts live ten blocks from here, and you want to mail it from Connecticut?"

"Our aunts are a little weird. I don't want them to know where I live."

"Dad could be wrong about them, you know," Phil said.

A tote bag whizzed past their heads and landed in the trunk. Sharon strode by, climbed into the front seat on the passenger side and shut the door. Josh rushed to reopen the door, but Danielle slipped her hand into his wide gloved one and said, "At least she's coming." He looked at her to argue the point, but they got lost in each other's gaze and just stood there, because it felt so good.

"Come On Baby, Light My Fire!" sung by The Doors, blasted from the car radio.

"Turn it down!" yelled Josh. Five minutes later and a few decibels lower, they were on their way, with Josh and Sharon in the front, Danielle and Phil in the back.

"Let's drive by our aunts' house," Phil said.

"Phi-il! Dad told us to keep away from them!"

"Would you explain why again?" asked Josh.

She repeated the reason that had satisfied her when she was twelve. "He said they're old maid busy-bodies who'll run my life and turn me into an old maid like them."

"You made it to old maid without *their* help," said her brother.

She laughed and swatted him with her glove. "Maybe he had reasons he couldn't tell a child." Danielle saw Sharon roll her eyes at her father, as she moved to the music, and she stopped talking.

Snow began to fall as Josh drove along East 38th Street. Phil peered through the rhythmic windshield wipers to find the address. Heat fogged the side windows, and Danielle welcomed the cover, until Sharon glanced back at her and said, "Hiding from the old maids?"

"No," she lied. *Should have put her in the back seat.* She wiped the moisture from her side window with a glove, revealing a block of Tudor houses. Her breath caught. "Oh!" She loved her parents' red brick colonial because it was home, but she'd always dreamed of living in a Tudor house with gables, stone turrets, stained glass windows, dark wood around cream stucco…and window seats! She pictured herself, sitting on a bluish-green velvet window seat, reading a novel.

"Snow's covering all the addresses," said Phil.

"Let's go!" said Sharon, punctuating "go" by punching the leather armrest with her fist. No one objected, and Josh speeded up.

In the tenth block, a rather modest Tudor appeared, and Danielle yelled, "Stop, that's the house!" Josh hit the brakes and the car slid into the curb. "Turn off the radio," she said, and Sharon actually did. Danielle rolled down her window…

Snow was falling in soft whispers onto the flagstone pathway to the three-story Tudor. A black wrought iron railing wound up the brick steps to a heavy wooden door. It rounded at the top over a stained glass window. A black iron knocker was centered below it. A holly bush and an ivy bush covered the darkened house on one side of the staircase, and a soft golden light glowed through the sheer curtains of windows on the other side.

"How do you know this is the house?" asked Josh.

"A dream jolted my memory. There's a window seat in bluish-green velvet right behind those curtains."

As if on cue, a hand moved the curtain aside. Amber lampshades and Christmas tree lights glowed blurrily through the fogged and icing window. Danielle saw an elderly woman, silvery hair tied back with a blue ribbon, holding a blue cardigan sweater to her neck. Behind her, fading into the shadows, was another old woman in an apron over a maroon dress through which Christmas tree lights glittered.

"I see someone," Josh said.

"Me, too," said Sharon.

"One?" asked Danielle.

"It must be Aunt Tessie, the older sister," said Phil. The silvery haired woman in blue dropped the curtain back.

"Let's go!" said Sharon. They departed in a veil of snow.

"When did you dream about the house?" asked Josh.

"Night before last." She'd wanted to discuss it with her fellow dream enthusiast, but that might get Sharon started. And she'd been pretty good so far. Danielle settled back into her seat, slipped her hand under her coat and laid it gently on her still flat stomach. *Do you dream, Little One?*

When Josh turned off East 38th Street, Danielle turned for one last look through the rear window. And that triggered a memory.

She was six years old, looking out the back window of her father's 1947 blue Buick. Hard rain beat against it. She smelled the savory lunch New York Nana had packed in a brown grocery bag. It lay on the seat beside her. "Mommy, may I have a sandwich?"

Danielle's mouth watered with the remembered taste of that sandwich. "Phil, remember New York Nana's sandwiches on the drive home from Brooklyn?"

"I didn't have my teeth yet."

"Oh. They were delicious!"

"How did she make them?"

"With Dreikorn's Bread," Danielle said, picturing the orange and white wrapped loaf beside her grandmother's wooden cutting board. She heard snickers trickle into her reverie, but she continued anyway. "Left-over roast beef or baked chicken, mayonnaise, salt and pepper."

Josh sang a take-off on the MacDonald's commercial: "At McKinnon's, they do it all for you."

Everyone laughed, except Danielle, who was compelled to say, no matter how out of sync she seemed, "They were the best sandwiches I've ever tasted."

"No sesame seeds?" giggled Sharon.

Danielle touched Josh's shoulder. "Remember that wonderful meal at Lutece?" He'd taken her to one of the finest restaurants in Manhattan for her birthday. They had Pate Beau Sejour, Chicken Bordeaux and Crepes Suzette.

"Mmmm!"

"Mmmm!" she agreed. "Those sandwiches were better," she said quietly.

There was a pause, quite a long one, after which Sharon gleefully said to her father, "We have a nut-case here." Phil frowned at Sharon and looked out at the falling snow.

Danielle leaned back and wondered just what she had seen through her aunts' window. *It was probably Aunt Tessie who drew the curtain back. But the other woman? An illusion created by ice, fog and lights? New York Nana always wore an apron...* Voices in the car faded, as a long ago memory of a visit in that house emerged.

Six-year old Danielle was crawling around on her knees, pushing all her pick-up sticks into the parlor rug by the dining room in her grandparents' home in Brooklyn. Her parents, grandfather, aunts and uncle were deep in a boring grown-up conversation on the other side of the living room. She paused to look through the mahogany legs of the dining room table and chairs and saw a hand darker than Daddy's on a white apron. *New York Nana sees me!*

Clutching the last three sticks, she stood up in her pink cotton dress, white socks and Mary Jane shoes, peeked over the table and saw the top of New York Nana's apron. It covered her maroon dress-up dress. Guiltily, she looked up into her face.

Graying black curls escaped from a hair net onto a high forehead over her eyes…It was New York Nana's eyes that drew her because they kept changing. Danielle saw them begin to fill with laughter, and she opened her pink-sleeved arms and reached out to be picked up, but New York Nana stayed on the other side of the dining room table and didn't move. The little girl almost cried, but her grandmother's eyes changed again and turned so tender it felt like a caress. She continued to see more in those eyes. She saw pride – and felt worthy, amusement – and felt forgiven for pushing the sticks into the rug. Suddenly, she saw alarm followed by loneliness in her grandmother's eyes, and it reminded Danielle of the day a dog snatched up her Raggedy-Ann doll from the grass and ran away with it. How she'd screamed as the dog disappeared across the meadow. She wondered if New York Nana was remembering losing her doll too…

Earlier, she'd walked into the kitchen and found New York Nana cutting cooked chicken on a wooden board. When she thought her grandmother wasn't looking, she put flour from a canister on her nose and was rewarded with a smile. New York Nana was making chicken sandwiches when Mommy came in, took her daughter's hand and led her back into the living room. "Stay out here with us. New York Nana is cooking. Play with the pick-up sticks."

But now, for a few precious moments, Danielle and her grandmother, separated only by the dining room table, were sharing time together. She saw longing in New York Nana's eyes. Then she saw a tear roll down her cheek. They both stood very still, and somehow Danielle knew it had to be this way. They shared a secret, though she didn't know just what it was, as she stood, arms raised, looking up at her….

In the back seat of the car, Danielle drew a circle on the foggy window. She couldn't remember how their time together ended. She tried but couldn't remember New York Nana eating dinner at the dining room table or sitting with them in the living room. But she remembered looking into her eyes that day and knowing she was loved.

Chapter Six

"Maybe one day you'll write, and if you do, perhaps you'll write a story about an honest straight-forward sort of fellow, who means no one any harm, but who is beset by others."

—Mac McKinnon

Josh lowered the volume on Michael Jackson's "Rock With You" to drive into the quiet community of New Crossing. "No! Make it louder," whined Sharon, stamping her foot.

Danielle didn't hear them. She was so immersed in remembering a suggestion her father had once made to her that she barely saw the wooded park-like neighborhood where each turn-of-the-century style house rested on a couple acres of land. Josh pulled into the rounded driveway in front of the McKinnon's brick colonial home.

"Lynn, they're here!" Mac called from the open front door, and the joy in his voice ignited joy in his daughter's heart. Vibrant and trim at seventy-seven in brown slacks and a muted plaid shirt under a beige Perry Como sweater, he quickly descended the front steps. People often took him for Mediterranean, so he'd explain he was Scotch and Aztec. Behind him, a decorated balsam wreath hung from the dark oak door and to his left, a blue spruce tree with blue lights glowed in the early dusk.

Danielle ran to greet him, saw silver in a renegade black lock of hair that curled onto his high forehead and the realization that he was getting older tugged at her heart. She flew into his arms. "Dad, we've got to talk! I need material for a story I'm going to write about you."

"Where did you get that idea?" he laughed.

"From you."

"From me?"

"Don't you remember?" He shook his head. "We were in the family room. I was fifteen, and we were looking at the framed drawing of the Native American hanging by the fireplace. And you said that maybe one day I'd write…" She saw memory flicker in his eyes and stopped talking.

"Oh. You'd be writing up the wrong tree. Write about your students. That's where the real drama is."

"I still want to talk. May I visit next week?"

"Of course. This is your home." He disengaged one arm and reached out. "Josh! Good to see you. How's business?"

"Good to see you, too. I could use your advice on growing my practice."

"Anytime, for what it's worth. Come next week with Danielle."

"Hi, Dad," Phil called, dashing by with two overnight bags. "We're on the third floor, Josh."

"Phil!" Mac broke away from Danielle and Josh to embrace his son. The bags were in the way, so he patted Phil's shoulder. "How's the celebrity?"

"Good." Danielle saw an uncomfortable moment pass between them, before Phil smiled and said, "I'd better finish unpacking while the weather holds." He started up the steps, as Lynn was running down. He set the overnight bags right down and embraced his mother. Her light brown hair blended with her son's and framed her gently lined face in soft waves. A kelly green sweater and slacks outfit flattered her still trim figure and highlighted her hazel eyes. She hugged everyone and looked around.

"Where's Sharon?" she asked.

"In the car," said Josh.

Lynn raced to the passenger side of the car. Josh started to follow. "Let her go," Danielle said. "Mom and Dad are good with kids."

"Okay, if you say so," he said, taking their overnight bags from the trunk.

Phil picked up the other ones. "I'll take one," Mac said to his son.

"I've got it. Mom could use your help with Sharon, though," Phil said and sprinted up the steps, past Danielle and Josh.

"Is Phil always so distant with him?" murmured Josh.

"Pretty much. I don't know why."

They climbed the stairs to her second floor bedroom. Josh set down the bags and looked around. "Your room's on the third floor, as usual," she said and laughed as he rolled her onto the bed and kissed her.

They heard a breathless Mac say, "Slow down, Sharon. You're too fast for me."

"Where's my father?"

"Delivering suitcases." Danielle and Josh drew apart and listened.

"Let's wait for them in the family room." It was her mother's voice.

They started down the stairs, but halted on the landing, when they heard Mac say, "Sharon, do you celebrate Christmas?"

"No!" Danielle and Josh exchanged a confused look.

"Well, I saw that crucifix around your neck and wondered," said Mac. "You *do* celebrate Chanukah?"

"Yess!" she hissed.

"He's skating on thin ice," Josh whispered.

"Good!" Mac said cheerily. "Because some guy who called himself Sam Goldberg left this for you." By now, Danielle and Josh were leaning over the railing and craning their necks to see what *that* could be.

Mac, Lynn and Sharon were standing before the glowing fireplace inside the family room in what could have been the scene of an old Hollywood Christmas in Connecticut movie. Hanging from the mantle was a blue and white knitted stocking, bulging with gifts. Three other stockings in red, in green and in gold, hung along side it.

"I know it's still two days before Christmas, but why don't you open your stocking now?" said Mac. Beamed upon by what looked like two indulgent grandparents, Sharon just stared at them and said nothing. Danielle's heart ached for her folks, as Mac persevered. "Young Lady, you're never too old to get a little pampering, while we adults entertain ourselves with a cocktail." Sharon still said nothing. "Lynn! Bring out

Chapter Six

the hors d'oerves. Let's open these stockings and get the party started."

"You're supposed to open them on Christmas," Sharon said stubbornly.

"What do you care? You're Jewish," said Mac. Lynn gave Sharon a quick pat on the shoulder and hurried to the adjoining kitchen. Danielle and Josh walked all the way into the family room, as Phil approached from the far side, where he'd apparently been putting gifts under the tree. Mac gestured wildly. "Phil! Josh! Danielle! Open your stockings! I'll make the drinks." He dashed out of the room.

For a moment, the three adults didn't look at the disgruntled girl. Then Josh gestured toward the four stockings hanging from the mantle, made a heroic attempt at levity by throwing out his arms in feigned surprise and saying, "Santa came!"

"No!" said Sharon, and turned from her deflated father. "Sam Goldberg." She unhooked her Chanukah stocking from the mantle. Careful not to look at her, Danielle, Josh and Phil reached for their stockings.

"Oh! Quotable New England Writers," said Danielle, pulling a miniature book from her red stocking and adding it to a small pile of gifts on the rug beside her. "Santa's been to Bradley's Bookstore."

"Where else?" smiled Mac, sitting beside Lynn on the couch, while the "kids" sat on the rug in front of them, opening gifts. His Irish crystal tumbler sparkled in the light of the fireplace as he sipped a Chivas Regal on the rocks. "Pass the chips." Danielle handed it up to Lynn who handed down a bowl of salted cashews.

From a green stocking, Josh opened a box with a matching Cross pen and pencil set, nesting in brown velvet.

"To celebrate your new business," said Mac.

"Thanks," Josh smiled, toasting Lynn and Mac with his gin and tonic.

"Doesn't this family ever get out of Bradley's?" said Sharon hastily pulling pencils, pens, erasers, ring enforcers, a miniature dictionary and other students' needs from her stocking and dropping them into a pile on the rug. She reached for the cashews.

"Don't stop now. The best is always in the toe," said Phil, pulling a brand new set of drumsticks from his gold stocking and tapping out a complex rhythm on his sister's back, her quotable poet's book and the side of the couch.

Sharon sped through the stocking, pulled out a small gift in blue tissue paper from the toe and opened it. She lifted up a silver chain with twin female figures, finely crafted in silver and crystal, symbolizing her astrological sign, Gemini. She let it swing in the firelight, and her eyes sparkled. She smiled at Lynn and Mac. "Thanks, Sam." They laughed. "Who is he, anyhow?"

Mac sipped his scotch. "Years ago in Brooklyn, I sold the *Encyclopedia Americana* by passing myself off as Sam Goldberg in the Jewish neighborhoods, Sean O'Reilly in the Irish section,-

"You passed yourself off as a Jew?" Sharon asked wide-eyed.

He nodded. "I did."

"Cool. I do some passing off myself."

"We noticed."

Red candles in old brass holders flickered over shrimp creole, a holiday favorite at the McKinnon's. Under the dining room table, Josh's shoes tapped Danielle's to ask, "Do you believe how Sharon and your father are getting along?" They'd been locked in friendly conversation, since the cocktail hour.

"Crabs in a barrel?" Sharon asked.

"Watch out or they'll drag you right down to the bottom of that barrel!" said Mac, refilling his wine glass.

"You been dragged down in that barrel?"

"Yep." His answer startled Danielle.

Sharon put a fork layered with a green pepper and shrimp into her mouth and talked as she chewed. "Who was the crab?"

"Well..." Mac balanced a shrimp, a green pepper and an onion with creole sauce onto his fork, shoveled it into his mouth and chewed, while he considered his answer.

Danielle put down her fork and listened. Her father had used that very metaphor to encourage her as a child to follow her sense of truth instead of someone else's. Never had she thought to ask him if *he'd* been a crab in a barrel.

"The real crab," he said, "is Fear." With the same respect he would give to an adult, he added, "Do you really think you need a crucifix, Sharon? There's nothing to fear any longer. Your people are organized and strong"-

"My civics teacher said some towns in Connecticut still have laws to keep Jews and blacks out," Sharon shot at him. "Is New Crossing one of those?"

Mac's surprised eyes looked at Josh and back to Sharon. "You're talking about laws called "covenants," of all things. They were racist housing laws that are illegal now.

"But aren't they still… followed?" asked Josh.

"They are," Mac said, his voice hardening, and on a sudden impulse, he raised his wine glass high and toasted, "To Hell with New Crossing's laws!"

As one, the delighted adults lifted their glasses and toasted, "To hell with New Crossing's Laws."

Sharon lifted her coke and, with a cynical but intrigued half-smile, said, "Okay."

"Another toast," Lynn said, and Danielle's body, like a Geiger counter, registered her mother's tension. "To Phil's new job at the Greenwich Village Jazz Club." Congratulations and toasts ensued, leaving her no time to ponder the source of the tension.

Josh raised his glass. "To Danielle becoming head of the English Department!"

"It's not definite yet," she said, waving away the congratulations. "But here's to Josh's full-time psychology practice!"

"That hasn't happened yet, either," Josh said quickly. Everyone laughed. Danielle noticed Sharon sitting back, not in her usual closed down manner, but rather as an observer at a peculiar gathering. She wagged a finger in the direction of her father and Danielle. "No one's toasting their engagement?"

"I was waiting for the right moment to"— Danielle's parents jumped to their feet and rushed around the table.

"We saw that coming months ago," said Mac. More hugs and congratulations. Lynn reached out to Sharon and said, "I've always wanted a grand-daughter." Sharon took her hand.

"You're going to have two grand-daughters," Danielle said softly, putting one hand on Sharon's shoulder and one in Josh's hand. Sharon didn't pull away. "We're going to have a baby."

The Geiger counter was very active in Danielle now, as Lynn said, "Congratulations, honey." It sounded more like "Good Luck." She gave her daughter a full-bodied hug and Danielle's heart beat with a nervous happiness. She saw her father's smile had frozen on his lips.

Carolers in the distance were singing, "What Child Is This?" Danielle and Josh laughed. Sharon stood and looked through the windows for singers.

"Over there," Phil said, gesturing to a window across the room.

"C'mon, Dad," she said, taking her father's hand and pulling him across the dining room to catch glimpses of carolers with flickering candles walk among darkening trees and houses in the falling snow.

Danielle turned to her father. "You'll make the best grandfather in the world." She opened her arms to embrace him.

"Aren't you over the hill for this?" he asked without moving.

She mustn't have heard correctly. *Over the hill?* She stood there, arms extended. Once when she was ten, she'd been hit on the back of the head by a soft ball during a game. Her stunned body knew it was hit before her mind registered it, before she'd found the bump and felt the pain. She stared into her father's steady gaze, unable to locate the source of the hit.

"There's too much on your plate already, isn't there?" His eyes narrowed with incisive reasoning. Her stunned mind tried to remember what was on her plate.

As if from afar, she heard her mother say, "Phil! Mac! Take Josh and Sharon out front to hear the carolers!" She felt her mom's hand grip hers and heard her say, "We'll set up the buffet."

Chapter Six

She looked around for Josh. He smiled at her from across the room, and she realized he hadn't seen or heard what had passed. She smiled back.

She didn't register the pain until she and her mother entered the large rectangular ballroom. Through the glass doors, she glimpsed carolers with candles a few houses away. "We have about twenty minutes before they get here," said her mother.

Two buffet tables were already set with glass cups and a large punch bowl on one and silver coffee and tea urns, cups, plates and napkins on the other. She followed her mother to the kitchenette, a long narrow room behind the bar. They took pitchers of wine spiced with roasted apples and sugar from the refrigerator, returned to the buffet and poured the Wassail into the punch bowl. She followed her back to the kitchenette and carried trays of crackers, cheeses, dips and chips back to the first table before she could say, "Josh wants the baby, too! It's not really Dad's business if I take on too much." Her words unleashed tears. "How could he say that?"

"I've got to talk to you and Phil. You both deserve to know," her mother said, disappearing into the kitchen again.

"What's *Phil* got to do with this?" she said, hurrying after her. Lynn was tense and quiet, as they put trays of Christmas tree cookies and gingerbread men on the table.

"Need help?" Danielle froze at the sound of her father's voice. Neither woman answered. "I'll check the bar," he said. He filled an ice bucket and poured himself a scotch on the rocks. "I'm sorry I was so abrupt." Danielle wiped away her tears. "The last thing I want to do is hurt you. You're my heart."

"But why" – Her voice broke.

Mac placed the ice bucket on the bar and said, "It's just that you have so much happening right now. Marriage, Sharon and your promotion! I'm so proud of you. I just don't want to see you take on more than you can handle. Even if it's not my business. And it's not."

"The promotion isn't a sure thing." Her voice shook.

"When is the baby due?" he asked in a neutral voice.

"August 15th."

"And your new career? When does it begin?"

"After Labor Day. If I get it."

"You will," he said, his voice tinged with pride. "It's a lot, that's all. I know you'll make the decision that's right for you." He picked up a chip and chewed thoughtfully. "But consider this. While you're deciding, why not let your mother make an appointment at the clinic here for the end of the first trimester? In case you change your mind?" He glanced briefly at Lynn, then back to her. "That would be?"

"The winter break, around Valentine…" Her voice petered out. "Josh wants the baby too," she said instead.

"I like Josh. I couldn't have picked a better man for you myself. He's a fine person and a good provider." Danielle relaxed a bit, and Mac took a swallow of scotch. "Now, please take this in the way it's intended." He paused. "Divorce is common among those in your generation, and, sometimes, that may be for the best." Danielle's stomach tightened. "Years ago your mother and I scrimped and saved to put you through Smith College to insure you'd never have to be dependent on anyone, if it came to that."

"It won't."

"I hope so. But perhaps your Alma Mater gave you an edge on that promotion?"

The memory of Nicole's face, when Dr. Norton chose Danielle for the position, citing her Ivy League education as the reason, angered her, and she didn't answer.

Phil walked into the room. "Dad, Mr. Preston and Mr. Page want to talk to you. They said it's important." Mac frowned.

"I love you, Dad, but…" She couldn't finish.

"You're my heart," he said, turned to go, then paused. "And your writing! Don't let your dreams get away from you!" He smiled. And was gone.

What her father said was reasonable. Very reasonable. "Have I been cavorting around in my own little bubble?" she asked her mother and brother.

Chapter Six

"It's your body; it's your decision," said Phil, his voice shocking her with quick anger. His young "Leave it to Beaver" all-American boy look had faded with his freckles. The principled man, who was her friend, shone hard in his hazel eyes.

"I want to do the responsible thing, especially for the baby," she said to her mother who was looking as if she were about to deliver her a death notice.

"Your father…" Her mother stopped, her lips pressed together, her hands in fists.

Danielle's old fear returned. "Dad's… sick?" Lynn was frozen in place. "Mom?" No answer. She looked at her brother.

"Is it his heart?" Phil asked.

Their mother looked from one of her children to the other. "When I tell you… you'll leave home and never return." Danielle felt the grip of her mother's tension within the center of her whole being.

"Tell us what?" she asked. "What?" They waited. And waited.

"I hate this," Phil said quietly to Danielle.

Why does he want me to have an abortion? The thought invited a question that took all her courage to ask. "Are we—Do I have a disease? Am I going to die?"

Their mother reached for the buffet table to support herself. Phil rushed over, but before he could touch her, she said, "You have black blood!"

Silence.

Danielle was still processing the death fear. "How long do we have?" she asked in a diminishing voice. Her mother didn't answer.

"She means we're part black," said her brother.

"I never should have married him," said their mother.

Terror slowly released first Danielle's stomach and then her voice. "We're… part black? That's it?" Her mother nodded. "That's all?"

"The baby could be born black," her mom said. "Josh is as dark as you are. We never thought you'd have a child at forty."

"*That's* why Dad wants the abortion?" Danielle asked. Their mother was looking at them, as if she would never see them again. Phil took her arm and guided her to the couch.

"Mom," Danielle said, "I'm glad you married Dad. He's a wonderful father." She remembered she was going to live and smiled. "Do you want a drink?" No answer. As she walked to the bar, Danielle searched for words to soothe her. "Our culture… spawned this fear of being black, long before we were born. It's past now."

"It's not," said their mother.

"So, why did you and Dad have us?" Phil cautiously asked, sitting beside her.

"We almost didn't," she said. The story came out in broken phrases. "I was terrified Danielle would look Negro. I rented a horse in a park …in Brooklyn… and kicked it into a trot… to bring on a miscarriage." Tears rolled down her face. "Your father and your Aunt Charlotte caught the horse and stopped it. They said we wouldn't have a Negro baby… because I'm white."

Danielle pictured her mother, young, thin and frightened, bouncing on the trotting horse. She gently slid a tumbler of scotch into her hand and sat on the arm of the couch to be near her. "You didn't get rid of me. I'm here," she joked, but her mom was too deep in her memories to hear.

"I was so in love with your father." She took a sip of the scotch and put the glass down. She looked at them again. "You and Phil were the best thing that ever happened to us." A cry rose up out of her with a sound so desolate that Danielle reached around and cradled her mother.

"We'd never leave you," she said. "Why would we?" Phil, who had found tissues, pushed them gently into his mother's hand, put his arm around her shoulder and they sat there… A family.

"I can't believe we got through this," said their mother.

"I can't believe you thought we'd leave," said Danielle. "You and Dad are usually so rational. It's 1981, for God's sake. Martin Luther King has come and gone. It's not a big deal… anymore."

In between the words, big deal and anymore, the first piece of a puzzle arose as a fleeting feeling of inferiority at knowing she was black moved in on her. Her shamed mind denied and forgot it. The cynical look on Kamara's face and the disappointed one on Tamika's, when she told her Literary Arts class she wasn't black, took its place. "My students know," she said quickly, crossed to the mirrored wall and peered into it. "What do they see?"

Phil joined her at the mirror where they examined their features. "Darren and Cheryl saw it, too. In you. I told them we're Aztec," he said with an ironic smile.

"I've told hundreds of students that," Danielle said, and a second piece fell into place. "I think they see it in my nose and eyes."

"And your eyebrows," Phil said. "Mine too."

Danielle imagined their reflections turning a dark brown. "Phil?"

"What?"

"When you played drums with the Dreamers….."

"Yes?"

"You weren't a token." They laughed, and a silliness born of relief began to infect them. She saw her mother reflected in the mirror, just behind them. "Mom, you look like you just picked a Get Out of Jail Free Card and don't know how to use it," she giggled.

"Doesn't this upset you?" asked her mother.

"No!" Danielle said too loudly. And a third piece fell into place. In repertory, she once played the part of a Negro field worker in a production of *Cat on a Hot Tin Roof*. When she darkened her face and wrapped a white cloth into a turban around her head, she was immediately transformed into a Negro and felt very proud of her make-up and costuming skills. Then she heard giggling and whispers. She looked around and saw that no one else playing a field worker had been so transformed. She pretended she hadn't heard, but she no longer felt part of them.

To shake off the memory, she asked her mother, "Why did you think we'd leave?"

"Your grandfather's sister, Thelma Mae, left and never returned because she could pass."

"Grandpa McKinnon had a sister? I didn't know that."

"There's a lot you two don't know."

Caroler's voices, just outside, broke into the Wassail Song. "They're here," said Phil. "I'd better get my black ass upstairs to greet them." Danielle doubled over with laughter to hear him claim his heritage with such dry humor.

"I'm going to fix my make-up," she said. "I cried it off."

Their mother snapped to! "Don't tell your father you know! I'll tell him."

"Okay. Don't worry, Mom. Meet you downstairs."

In the privacy of the dimly lit stairs, she said softly, 'What child is this, Little One? Irish, English, Welsh, Scottish, Aztec, Jewish, African American… who came to rest?" She bounded up the rest of the stairs. "Ho! Ho! Ho! Do I have a story!"

Flipping on her bedroom light, she thought of Josh and felt a surge of love for him. *He doesn't even know, yet. Will it make a difference?* She decided it wouldn't. Probably. At the bathroom mirror, fluffing her frizzy hair, a fourth piece of the puzzle… *That's why I didn't get that job in Beldome!*

It was in 1963 on that rainy morning she applied for a high school teaching position at the prestigious Beldome High School in Connecticut. The day she arrived for the interview, the smiling principal hurried along the driveway, holding up a large umbrella to shield her from the rain. But when he got closer, his smile faded. He asked her just three questions: "You're Ms. McKinnon?"

"Yes, Mr. Grant." She held out her hand to give him the firm handshake she'd been practicing, but he was busy with his umbrella.

"When did you graduate from Smith College?"

"This June." That was on her resume. She smiled and waited to be invited in. He looked directly at her. "Why is your hair frizzing?"

"Oh! The rain and humidity must have frizzed it a bit." She'd sat in rollers under a drier and sprayed her hair in place, just two hours before. She was never invited in. He took his umbrella and left her standing in the rain. Her mother, waiting in the car, observed it all and said nothing. Danielle wrote him off as a snob, one of those blue bloods like Kimberly Osborne's mother.

Chapter Six

The snub was just the push she needed. She got work substitute teaching in Manhattan, studied acting and was happier than she'd ever been in her life. She was applying a mauve lipstick when the fifth piece fell. *That's why the casting directors asked me if I was black.*

It was 1973, and Danielle was making the rounds trying without much success to get acting work. She was drinking coffee in a Howard Johnson's in the theatre district and searching the trade papers, Backstage and Show Business, to find auditions for her type, which was an ongoing mystery, when a man and a woman in business suits approached her, introduced themselves as casting directors from a Madison Avenue agency, Kenton and Kools, well known for casting commercials and soap operas. They invited her to come to their office to be interviewed for a role in a soap opera. Now, she knew she was not the Proctor and Gamble type, the all-American type like her mother was, but she was unprepared for what they were about to offer.

"We're looking for a light-skin black actress for the role. Frankly, we're in violation of the Equal Opportunity Law, and the only light skin actress we know is busy with another network." It wasn't the first time agents thought she was black. She'd been sent out on auditions to sing spirituals or to dance, and she couldn't do either.

"I'm not black," she told the agents and thought, *"It's the only chance I've ever had to audition for a nationwide television role that could bring the prestige and fame that would make my parents proud I chose acting."* She was tempted to lie. After all, Paul Muni and Louise Rainer played Chinese roles in "The Good Earth," and Anthony Quinn played Zorba the Greek! But it wasn't the same thing and she knew it.

"Perhaps there's – something in your background you don't know about?" The woman agent smiled. "We were certain we discovered you! – Like Lana Turner in that coffee shop years ago." She remembered Cat on a Hot Tin Roof and knew she could pass for a light skin black, particularly the Proctor and Gamble version. She was the type! Finally! She just wasn't black.

"I'd love to play the role. But, after Martin Luther King's assassination and all that the black people have been through in this country, I can't say I'm black and take a job away from them. I couldn't live with that." How righteous she'd felt.

The casting agents smiled. "Ask your parents. Just in case."

That night, she phoned her parents. "There are no Negroes in our family tree," said her father. Her mother said nothing.....

Danielle stared into that memory for one long moment before she raised her arm and threw her lipstick across the bathroom with such force that it smashed into the expensive ivory wallpaper, staining it a greasy mauve.

"Good King Wenceslaus looked down / On the feast of Stephen" was being sung in the ballroom. She descended the stairs to the feast of McKinnon. *Maybe Sharon would like to join the singers around the piano.*

But the first person she saw, as she entered the ballroom, drove that thought from her mind. A tall black man with a close cut Afro in a smart-looking jeans suit and white crew neck sweater stood there. *How did he get in?* His eyes were hard and dark, and one of his strong-looking hands was opening and closing into a fist! *What's he doing here? It was a knee-jerk reaction, and the prejudice governing it shook her. I only thought that because he's acting strange,* she told herself. She looked across the room and saw an attractive black woman in a purple turtleneck sweater and matching slacks, standing at the buffet, pouring glasses of ginger ale for two black boys of grammar school age, who were putting Christmas cookies onto their plates. The woman smoothed back her wavy black hair, looked up and gave the man an inscrutable look. He took a deep breath and rubbed his fist-making hand down his hip and thigh.

It was when Danielle looked back that she saw her neighbor, Mr. Hendrix, on the opposite side of the table, staring at the woman, eyes glittering with hate. Unexpectedly, her body went rigid with fear. Jean Richardson, their next door neighbor, appeared and guided the woman and her sons across the room to the group singing at the piano. But Danielle couldn't take her eyes off Mr. Hendrix... the man who owned the hardware store in town, who'd always smiled and asked young Danielle how she was doing in school, who'd congratulated her on becoming a teacher, whom Danielle had thought of as a nice man. She watched his malicious eyes follow the two children and their mother. *The hate stare!* Slowly, she remembered the times it had been directed at her. *When I dated that black student in college… When I was on tour with a show in Nashville, Tennesee…* Details rushed in. *The first one demeaned me. But I was safe. Not the second. It sent me running for my life… And oh! Sitting on the car runner with my doll, just before Mom drove that couple off. I was only four…*

"That's Leo and Viola Stokes and their sons," said Phil. Startled, she looked at her brother and realized she was trembling. Relaxed in his blue crew neck sweater and jeans, he'd obviously missed the scene with Mr. Hendrix. "The Richardsons are selling their house. When the Stokes family came to see it tonight, Pat and Jean invited them to meet the other neighbors."

"What real estate agent around here would show them the house?"

"I think it all happened through the Richardson's." Danielle watched the various neighbors look at the black family and thought Norman Rockwell might well have painted that collage of facial expressions… distrust, tension, cautious good will, open-mouthed surprise, amusement, disdain and shock. Leo Stokes was still on their side of the room.

"Let's say hello," she said. They walked over to him. Danielle held out her hand and said, "Welcome to the neighborhood, Mr. Stokes." She sounded so serious, she embarrassed herself, but he smiled and shook her hand.

Phil offered his hand. "Phil and Danielle McKinnon."

"Our hosts," he said. His handshake was firm, his voice deep.

"Brother and sister," said Danielle.

"Not much resemblance," he said, and Danielle saw the familiar questioning of her racial identity in his eyes. She looked for her father. He was watching them from across the room. Her mother was watching *him*.

"Dad's over there." She gestured to the far end of the bar by a maroon love seat.

Leo nodded at Mac, who nodded back. "I'll go say hello," he said.

His steps seemed measured, as he approached Mac. "Let's join them," she said.

"Not me," said Phil, watching his father. Danielle was about to follow when she felt Josh's broad hand on her back. Reluctantly, she turned to him and saw Sharon cautiously smile at her. She smiled back.

"It looks like some walls are crumbling around here," Josh said.

"I hope so," said Phil.

"You have no idea," said Danielle. She glanced across the room and saw her father's hand, the one holding a tumbler of scotch, trembling. *I've got to get over there!* Want to join the carolers?" she asked them.

"Okay," said Sharon. Quickly she took three song booklets from a pile and handed them to Phil as the group began to sing, "I Heard the Bells on Christmas Day."

"Page seven. I'll be right back," she whispered.

Mac and Leo Stokes were shaking hands, as she rushed across the ballroom and entered the kitchenette behind the bar. She found her mother at the far entrance, standing in the perfect place to overhear the two men without being seen. She was filling platters with hors d'oeuvres brought by their neighbors. Danielle joined her.

"Go back!" whispered her mother.

"I want to hear this," Danielle whispered back.

She heard Mac's voice. "I see my daughter and son have already introduced themselves." He sounded so reserved, like Kimberly Osborne and her "blue blood" parents, who so casually elevated themselves over everyone else. She'd never heard her father speak to someone that way. She tried to look out, but her mother pulled her back and put a platter lined with a paper doily into her hand. As Danielle placed hot appetizers on the platter, she wondered if Mr. Stokes was clenching and unclenching his fist.

"Nice-looking boys you have there," said her father. She breathed easier and smiled at her mother whose hands paused in mid-motion.

"Thanks," said Leo Stokes and then added, as if in a tit for tat, "Nice looking son and daughter you have there."

As the singers heralded in "Peace on earth, good will to men," Mac and Leo Stokes moved their conversational comments like pieces on a chessboard.

Chapter Six

"You're making a courageous move," said Mac.

"I suppose," said Leo.

"But will it work?"

"I don't know."

"The children here will snub your boys. Your wife will be shunned. You're not wanted here. You saw the look." Danielle's hands flew to her face. *He means Mr. Hendrix.* She felt sick to her stomach.

"You won't be happy here," said her father.

"You are," said Leo Stokes.

Silence.

"How does he know?" whispered her mother.

"He saw it in my face," she whispered back. "My students see it, too. And the black musicians at the jazz club and…" Pain and guilt in her mother's eyes stopped her.

Her Mom handed her a tray of hors d'oeuvres and repeated, "Don't tell your father what I told you and Phil. Give me time to talk to him." Danielle nodded, and looked to where her father and Leo Stokes were standing. But Mac was halfway across the ballroom, beckoning to Roger and Tom, who'd met with him earlier.

A piano chord sounded and Danielle saw Leo Stokes, his wife and sons in the group singing, "Here Comes Santa Claus." She saw her father leave the ballroom with the two men. One was Roger, a banker in town, but she couldn't place Tom. *They must be going to his den.* She started to follow.

"Danielle!" her mother said. "Circulate!" She watched her mother move on. *Why did Dad tell Leo he wasn't wanted here?*

"Are you all right?" Josh picked a mini-hotdog from her tray and dipped it in mustard.

His deep voice was gentle and his dark eyes searched hers. She put the tray on the bar, took his hand and led him out of the ballroom, down the hall and into the family room. A few people were having quiet conversations by the fireplace, so she took him to a secluded spot on a leather bench between the back of the Christmas tree and a window.

It was snowing out. Christmas tree lights of red, blue, green and white twinkled in the cold black palette of the window. Danielle looked through it all and began to talk. When she got to the part where she found out she was black, she saw Josh's eyes widen in surprise. He enclosed her hand in his two large ones and listened. Relieved and gratified by her choice of this man, she talked on. She pleaded with him not to prejudge her father.

"I've always known him as a fair and decent man," said Josh. *Was Josh thinking,* Until now? The thought tore at her heart.

"Dad! Where are you?" It was Sharon's voice, but it could have been Danielle's.

"Over here by the window," called Josh.

The singing had stopped. Danielle checked her watch. "We've been here an hour! I promised Mom not to talk about this yet," she whispered, just before Sharon rounded the tree with an excited look.

"Sorry we ran out on you," Danielle said. "It was my fault."

Sharon seemed too excited to notice. "Everyone's gone home. We've been looking for you!" She smiled like someone in the know. "C'mon," she said and disappeared back around the tree. They stood, and Josh took Danielle's hand.

"Sharon's happy here," he said.

Chapter Seven

"Here they are!" said Mac in a voice a bit too loud and with a smile a bit too wide, as Danielle and Josh walked into the empty ballroom. *Has he been drinking all this time? He can usually hold his liquor.* She began stacking dirty dishes. "We'll clean up tomorrow. But, before hitting the hay, let's have a nightcap to toast you and Josh!"

She looked around. A smiling Sharon was pushing chairs into a circle, apparently for the toast. Josh shook his head in amazement, and she laughed. Her parents did have a way with kids. Phil was at the bar with their mother. She was pouring scotch into two crystal tumblers. Mac joined them. "Gin and tonic, Josh?" he asked.

"Why not," he said.

"I'll have the usual," giggled Sharon. Mac filled a champagne flute with Coca Cola. Danielle saw them share a conspiratorial look.

"I'll have a beer," said Phil.

"Not tonight," Mac said, selecting a Sam Adams from the refrigerator. "A frothy libation." Her father and brother laughed together, and it warmed Danielle's heart.

"I'll have Merlot in a fancy goblet," Danielle said and thought of the Little One. "Cut it with Pellegrino." She slid a table with hors d'oeuvres and a bowl of potato chips into the center of the circle.

Mac put an arm around Lynn and tapped his tumbler of scotch with hers. They all gathered into a circle and stood before their chairs. Sharon took a chip and scooted between Josh and Lynn. Danielle felt Josh's arm slip around her waist, and joy re-entered her heart. Mac raised his glass and said, "To a lifetime of fulfillment." His voice broke on the last word, and he stopped to gain control. Phil repeated his father's toast. Danielle and her mother, near tears, smiled at each other. Sharon seemed about to burst, as they all clinked glasses, sat down and looked at Mac.

He looked up from studying the ice in his drink and smiled. "Tonight, Lynn and I found out that our friends, Mike and Pat Richardson, are selling their house next door." He smiled. "We also found out that Danielle and Josh are engaged to be married. So we told Pat and Mike we'd like to put a bid on their house as a wedding gift, providing…" He paused when Sharon squealed in delight and looked expectantly at her father whose mouth had dropped open. Danielle, in much the same condition, looked around and saw Phil send a questioning look to their mother who was smiling, or seemed to be. Mac continued, "Providing, of course, you want to live in the neighborhood. If not, we'll find another place."

"What about the Stokes family?" Danielle asked.

"They and four other families have shown some interest, so nothing's settled," said Mac. "Needless to say, Pat and Mike are thrilled by the idea of you and Josh moving in." Cold air seeped through the window frames, clearing Danielle's thoughts. Hail tapped what sounded like an urgent Morse code message on the dark panes. "We're in for some weather," he said, rising and refreshing his drink. "Tomorrow morning, Danielle, you can take Josh and Sharon on a tour of the house. They are expecting you anytime after breakfast."

Danielle looked at Josh. He was looking at her. "What do you think?" she asked.

"Jews in New Crossing?" he said, and she knew he'd love to make that happen.

Sharon raised her flute of coke. "To Hell with New Crossing's laws!" She toasted everyone in the circle, then ran to toast Mac at the bar.

"To Hell with New Crossing's laws," he said quietly and drank. A strong wind blew the hail in one hard slam against the windows.

Danielle's thoughts seemed to race in many directions at once: *I was miserable here as a teenager, but things can change. I love Manhattan, but Josh wants us to be the first Jewish family in New Crossing. Can't blame him for that. And Sharon's so upbeat here. If it doesn't work, we can move back before the Little One starts school. The commute's short. I can still work in the City.*

Chapter Seven

Her father returned to the circle. She hugged him. "It's a very generous gift."

"We're a very fortunate couple," he smiled.

She hugged her mother, who looked around and said to everyone, "I'd always find her reading on the Richardson's porch or in the gazebo."

Danielle nodded. "I used to imagine living there. Even though I loved our house," she said with a guilty smile.

Mac returned her smile. "I understand. It captured your imagination… a house built in the eighteen hundreds."

"Seventeen ninety-five," she said. "We'd won the American Revolution and George Washington was President!"

"He probably slept there!" said Sharon. They all laughed.

"You can feel the history in that house," Danielle said.

"Take it, Dad," said Sharon, pulling her father's sleeve.

Josh turned to Lynn and Mac. "It's a beautiful gift, but Danielle and I will have to talk. If we decide to move in, a down payment would be more than gift enough." Danielle's love for him deepened.

With a nod, Mac toasted Josh. "You don't have to decide tonight. Think about it. If you want it, it's yours. In the meantime, let's get some shut-eye." He smiled at Sharon. "Tomorrow's a big day." He downed his scotch and swayed slightly, walking to the door.

"I'll bet Mr. Hendrix discouraged the Stokes," said Danielle, standing. "He gave Viola a hate stare that was awful."

"I saw that," Mac said, his voice dropping in pitch. "It was obscene. Dangerous."

"Too bad about the Haley family though," said Phil.

"They're still better off with their own kind," Mac mumbled, reaching for the door to the hallway. The hailstorm slowed to a steady tap, tap, tap. Danielle and Phil looked at each other. Lynn squeezed Danielle's arm and stared hard at Phil.

But Danielle was compelled to ask, "What do you mean, 'their own kind?'" Her father turned in apparent surprise at having been overheard.

As Mac paused to collect his thoughts, Phil asked, "Do you want to buy the house to keep the Stokes out?"

"Danielle! Phil!" their mother said in a voice as staccato as the hail. She turned off lights, putting them into semi-darkness. "That's it. Go to bed."

"Your mother's right. We'll talk about this in the morning," said Mac.

But Danielle knew her father as a just man, and she needed to clarify his intentions for Josh and Sharon. "Dad wouldn't do that. They have a right to live here."

"They're moving too fast," he said.

"That's not like you, Dad. Let's talk."

"There's no talking about this!"

"But what about the Stokes?"

"Danielle, there's so much you don't understand."

"You mean that we're part black?" she asked. And smiled.

If the hail was raging again, and it was, nobody heard. She saw fear flash into Mac's eyes, just before they narrowed. "What did you say?"

"I told them," said Lynn.

Mac looked at his wife. "You *told* them?"

"Because of the baby," Danielle said.

"Damn you to hell!" Those words to his wife, the woman he loved, were a growl.

"Dad, we've always talked things out. Let's—"

"There's no talking about this, Danielle," he said walking back into the room. "Either you go along with the way your mother and I are living, or you don't. And, if you don't, I'm sorry to have to say this, but… You're out."

"Mac!" Lynn said. Danielle heard her mother's voice, as if from a distance, as she looked into the deadly serious eyes of her father.

"Then I'm out." It was Phil's voice from the same distance.

"Phil…" Her mother's voice was a plea.

Danielle, aware that Phil was leaving the room and Lynn was following, that Josh and Sharon were staring, cried out, "Dad!"

Her father gestured in a wide arc. "Danielle, do you see all of this? This house, these grounds, this neighborhood?"

"Yes, Dad, I do."

"Were you not raised here? Fed? Clothed? Sheltered?"
"Yes but…"
"No worries? A happy child?"
"A very happy child." She heard her voice weaken.
"And did you not go to the finest schools, and receive the best education that money can buy?"

She heard the plea in his anger, and her heart answered. "The best, Dad, yes."

"And now that you and your brother are launched, strong, able to survive, not worrying about life and liberty, but pursuing your own happiness, don't your mother and I deserve our time to enjoy our lives without worrying anymore about surviving?"

"Yes, Dad."
"Then talk to your brother… Make him understand."
"But what about the Stokes?"

Suitcase in hand, Phil walked back into the ballroom. His mother gripped the arm of his coat. A warning of danger like fire alarms screamed through Danielle's whole being, but she pushed it away. Mac swayed to the bar and poured himself another scotch. It sloshed into his glass and onto the bar. "Tonight, this man, Leo Stokes, whom you say has rights, has threatened *my* rights."

"How? How could he?" asked Danielle and rushed on, "Besides, Phil and I are happy about this. Why, I want to write about it!"

Mac swung around. "You pampered fool!" He grabbed her arm and pulled her across the room to the mirrored wall where she had once practiced ballet exercises. Reflected there, Danielle saw an elderly man with a runaway silver curl on his forehead, his face distorted with rage. He held the arm of a confused woman she barely recognized as herself. Sharon stood by the circle of chairs, as if frozen, a flute of Coca Cola in her hand.

"Do you see a black woman there?" her father said loudly.
"Yes, I do. *And* a white woman." Her voice was strong again.

Josh and Phil moved in the reflection and flanked Mac. Her mother was beside her.

"The point is – it's there, Dad," said Phil. "That's all. Why deny it?"

"Why deny it? Because it can drag you down!" said Mac, his voice spiked with liquor and rage. "Like crabs in a barrel, it drags you down!" He looked from Danielle to Phil and back again, his voice rising to a crescendo. "Is that what you want? To take everything I've built and reduce it to *rubble?*" On the word, rubble, he hurled his crystal tumbler at the mirror. There was a loud crack, and like one caught in a nightmare, Danielle watched their reflections splinter and crumble. She turned to her father.

"Dad…Dad, I love you. Phil does, too." She reached out to embrace him. Her mom rushed between them, and Mac pushed her away with a quick, rough movement. Phil caught her in mid-fall. "I love you!" Danielle said again.

"Then honor me!" He gestured broadly, lost his balance, stumbled backward into a buffet table and slid quickly to a sitting position on the floor. His hand landed on a shard of glass from the broken mirror. He pulled it out and blood trickled down his wrist, staining his muted plaid shirt bright red. Danielle moved to help him, felt Josh's hands restrain her, and she tried to pull away. Mac looked up at her and waited.

"I do honor you," she said, and thought of her students. "But I can't hide!" She thought of the Little One. "And I won't have the abortion. That would be committing genocide!"

Suddenly, Mac's face changed, as if he saw something so horrible, it obliterated rage… After a long moment and without taking his eyes from her, he said in a quiet voice… "Then, leave. Leave the house." He turned and crawled to the buffet table, shakily grasped its sturdy wooden leg and pulled himself up.

Sharon ran to him and tried to staunch the bleeding with paper napkins. His eyes remained on Danielle. "Get out, now" he said, almost tenderly.

Danielle cried out, "You understand, Dad. I know you do."

She heard her mother say, "Phil, get the suitcases. Danielle, go. Go! We'll be fine."

Chapter Seven

Danielle's eyes were locked into her father's eyes. His rage was gone. Unwavering determination had taken its place. Her mother quickly wrapped her coat around her shoulders.

"Mom?" she cried, still looking at her father.

"We'll be fine. Just go!"

Somehow, she found herself sitting in the front seat of the car. She heard the dull thud of the trunk closing, the back door of the car opening, and she felt Phil's hand on her shoulder. The engine turned over, and she saw Josh beside her with a gentle look in his eyes, one hand over hers and the other on the steering wheel. She turned around to see if her father had changed his mind and come out—to talk. She saw Sharon instead, backpack slung over her shoulder, walking toward the car. The girl glanced back at the house before getting into the back seat beside Phil and shutting the door.

Josh's hand left Danielle's to take the wheel. The car moved around and down the circular driveway. She looked through the windshield and saw the storm had ceased. Moonlight was glimmering on hail-encrusted snow.

She was leaving the place that had been home since the summer just before her high school years were about to begin. Her father and mother had taken her to orientation day at the public high school in New Crossing. Together, they'd entered the upper class of society, so she could be sure of an education in one of the finest schools in the country. As the car turned onto the country road, a high wail left her body, and sobbing shook her.

PART TWO

Chapter Eight

Danielle dropped two crispy potato pancakes and then a side of applesauce from the serving spoon onto her plate. It was her favorite Chanukkah food, but she had no appetite for it that night. Across the room, Josh's mother was cuddling Sharon to her ample bosom, while wagging a finger at the girl's nose. The gangly teenager was snuggling happily with Grandma Bess and glancing at Danielle, while talking behind her hand. Danielle hoped Bess, in her firm but gentle New York accent, was telling her granddaughter not to spread stories about what happened in Connecticut.

Josh, his parents – his whole family all know what they are…Russian Jews. All around her, loquacious family members of all ages chewing, talking, touching and joking sat in straight-backed chairs around the formal dining room table or sank casually dressed bodies into overstuffed furniture in the comfy living room. It was her third Chanukah party, but for once, she didn't want to be there. Normally, she loved the playful sparring and just plain fun of being part of a big family. But, that night, she stood aloof, held hostage by a new paranoia and the pain of being ordered to leave her father's house.

Only four nights before, she, with Josh and Sharon, dropped off Phil at her Gramercy Park apartment and drove back to Josh's penthouse. On Christmas Eve day, Danielle and Sharon unpacked their bags. Sharon refused Danielle's offer of help and told her father, "She's poking her nose into my things." On Christmas Day, Danielle phoned her father, but he wouldn't come to the phone. Her mother said he needed time.

Sharon phoned *her* mom and was invited to Chanukah dinner with Kathy and her business partner. Now it was Monday with a Chanukah party at Bess and Jacob Freedman's home.

On the short drive there, Danielle said, "I'm not telling anyone what happened with Dad, yet."

"You'll talk when you're ready," Josh said. Sharon said nothing.

At the Freedman's front door, Bess, in a blue jersey dress, lifted her arms to enfold Danielle in a hug. Her graying black hair curled softly around her face. "How's my little girl?" asked Bess.

"Fine," Danielle lied, smiled and hugged her back.

Jake Freedman, broad-shouldered like his son, confronted Josh in his deep sonorous Brooklynese. "What kept you so long?" Confronting was the loving way this father and son related. "You're ten minutes away, and the last one to arrive?"

"We're still moving Danielle and Sharon into the apartment," said Josh, matching his father in tone and physique.

Danielle put her plate of potato pancakes on a tray. She knew she was welcome that day, but wished she could take a book to a private corner. Instead, she poured a glass of ginger ale and took her food to a love seat in a corner by a darkened TV. She saw Sharon still talking behind her hand. A golden mezuzah glowed on the girl's pink sweater. *Passing for Jewish today?* She looked away and smiled to see children peeking under a sheet covering blue and white wrapped Chanukah gifts. Josh's hand caressed the back of her neck and slid down her back and around her waist, as he sat beside her.

"Look at Sharon. I bet she's telling your mother I'm black."

"You're not black."

"I'm part black."

"Don't advertise it though. We have a couple of racists in the family."

"We have a couple of anti-Semites in ours! And, besides, who advertises themselves more than the Jews!" she snapped.

"Touché. But don't make more of it than it is."

"I need to claim this! How can I do that if I'm busy hiding it?"

Chapter Eight

At that moment, Bess called from across the living room, "So! You were keeping it a secret!"

"She told her!" whispered Danielle and called back, "It's not a secret."

But Bess, standing hand in hand with Sharon, was advancing on them. "Quiet, everyone!"

The room went silent, and Danielle saw all eyes turn on her like a spotlight in a police interrogation. "It's not a secret! It's not a secret!" she called out to them.

Bess stopped next to her, paused, turned to the family and announced: "Josh and Danielle are engaged to be married."

The room exploded.

"Congratulations!"

"It's about time."

"Welcome to the family."

Twenty plus people jumped up, hugged and congratulated Danielle and Josh, who tried to look as though they knew what was happening all the time. Out of the corner of her eye, Danielle saw Sharon walk away.

On the drive back to the apartment, Josh said, "Don't forget, we have an appointment with the psychologist tomorrow. I'll pick you up at six." Sharon groaned. Danielle held up a plastic bag. "Bess gave me food from the buffet. We can have corned beef sandwiches before the session."

"Perfect," said Josh. Sharon said nothing.

Danielle and Josh took seats on a comfortable light green couch and looked across at Sharon and her psychologist, Alison Altman, sitting in equal comfort on matching chairs. Sharon liked Alison and listened, as she encouraged her to explain her real feelings to Danielle.

The girl looked down at her hands. "It's aggravating when you try to take my mother's place because I want *my mother* to do things for me." Danielle was moved by the hurt Sharon's chip-on-the shoulder manner couldn't conceal.

"I understand what you're saying. It hurt me to be around your family at Chanukah because I lost… my family." Her voice broke.

Josh gestured to Danielle and Sharon. "The two of you should –

"Hold on, Josh! This is between Sharon and Danielle. You're triangulating," warned the therapist. As Danielle understood it, to triangulate meant to butt into the business of two other people. Alison had been coaching them all in this discipline for a while.

"Danielle and I should give each other space. Lots of space," said Sharon.

"You have to live with her though," said Alison. "And after what you've both been through, you may be able to understand each other better, when one of you acts out."

"It's not a secret! It's not a secret!" Sharon yelled in perfect imitation of Danielle's acting out at the Chanukah party. The triangle laughed, and Alison looked intrigued.

Danielle took a deep breath. She glanced at Josh, who was still smiling, relieved, she supposed, because his daughter had made a funny, and said, "Four days ago, I found out I'm part black." She saw Sharon quickly take in Alison's surprised and Josh's neutral reactions and then match her father's expression. "Last night, at the Chanukah party, Josh and I were discussing whether or not to keep my color a secret from his family."

"My stupid idea," said Josh, and Danielle took heart.

"I saw Sharon whispering to her grandmother and thought she was telling her all about it." Alison glanced at Sharon, who still looked neutral, and Danielle continued. "But she was really telling her grandmother about our engagement. Then, when Josh's mother crossed the room and said, 'So, you were keeping a secret!' referring to the engagement, I started yelling, 'It's not a secret! It's not a secret!'"

Alison laughed and asked, "How do you feel about their engagement, Sharon?"

"Whatever," said Sharon, without blinking an eye.

"Did you tell your grandmother that Danielle's black?" asked the psychologist.

Sharon looked like a card shark who accidentally showed her trump card. But only for a second. "Yeah. Why not?" she asked, her beautiful eyes opened wide. Danielle's face fell.

"How does that make you feel, Danielle," asked Alison.

"I feel hurt by you," Danielle said to Sharon, "and angry with myself for not telling them."

"Why didn't you tell them?" Alison asked.

Danielle fought back tears. "Family problems… I wasn't ready."

Admitting that, she became ready.

Sharon spent the next few days of the vacation fixing up her room and socializing with her friends.

Danielle spent hers packing boxes in her Gramercy Park apartment. Her neighbor across the hall, Jill Martin, poked her expensively coiffed head through the open door of Danielle's apartment, saw her packing books into a box, and looked around. Recently retired from her career as an executive secretary on Wall Street, she appeared to have time on her hands. "Would you like some help?"

Danielle, who was just thinking how easy it had been to tell Alison she was part black, turned to her. Until recently, this woman had been too busy to do more than half-smile when Danielle said hello. Now, here she was at her doorstep. "How are you at taping boxes?"

"I can do that, but don't ask me to lift them." So, Danielle filled, moved and stacked boxes while Jill taped them, asked her what her rent was and if her apartment was rent controlled. At noon, Danielle offered to take her to lunch as a thank you.

They settled into seats facing each other at Szechuan East around the corner from the apartment. Jill ordered egg drop soup and beef with orange. Danielle ordered hot and sour soup and sesame shrimp. When the soups arrived, Danielle told Jill she was pregnant and getting married.

"Congratulations! When are you due?"

"The last week in August."

"August? Oh dear! I had Michael in August. Too hot! Stay cool and raise your feet." This was the most conversation they'd ever had. Danielle decided to take a chance. "Over Christmas, I discovered a family secret." Jill looked up from her meal. "My father's passing for white." She saw Jill's expression go on hold, but she continued. "So, the baby may be some shade of brown or even black." She heard herself babbling, but couldn't stop. "You'll see the baby when I visit my brother here, so I thought I should warn – tell you."

Jill examined a piece of beef on her fork. "It must have been quite a shock for you."

"Yes!" exploded from Danielle, and she said quickly, "I want this baby very much." She said it as much for the Little One's benefit as for Jill's. She stuffed a whole sesame shrimp into her mouth, chewed too fast and swallowed with difficulty. The food hit her stomach in a lump. "This is only the second time that I've told anyone, and…" Jill forked a small mouthful of beef into her mouth and kept chewing, as if she were eating popcorn and watching a film… "I thought I might meet with – well you know, prejudice." She laughed to show how foolish that was.

"Of course, dear. But you do have choices, you know…adoption, abortion," she said as if reading choices from the Columns A and B on the menu. Danielle nodded and pushed a sesame shrimp around her plate with the chopsticks. Jill went on to tell Danielle about a Christmas Eve robbery in the neighborhood. "He ripped the chain right off Mrs. O'Brien's neck! They go after gold chains, you know."

They? Danielle picked up the check, as soon as the waiter put it on their table. "Thanks for the taping. I'm going to leave the rest of the packing for another day."

"And I've got to get going." Jill stood. "By the way, let me know if you decide to give up your apartment." Danielle smiled and beckoned to the waiter.

On Thursday, she tried again. She went to an exhibit at the Metropolitan Museum of Art with Laurie Smith. They'd studied at both Tarkington High and Smith College in the late fifties and early sixties and had performed at the college playhouse. Laurie, who resembled Doris Day, was the leading lady. Danielle had the character roles. Other than that, they rarely socialized. Danielle's friends were in the literary club and Laurie's were in the sororities. Now that they both lived in Manhattan, they occasionally met for a cultural event.

Chapter Eight

During lunch in the museum's café, Danielle listened to gossip about some intrigue at Gucci's where Laurie was a buyer, followed by a dramatic monologue on the breakup with her boyfriend. She listened throughout the long lunch. Then, she suggested a walk in Central Park to tell her news. It was a safe choice. If Laurie's reaction demeaned her, Danielle would never have to see her again.

The snow crunched under their feet, and the ice-coated trees glistened above their heads. They paused beside the statue of Alice standing on a mushroom, talking to the other characters in Wonderland. They reminisced about their high school trip to see this sculpture in their senior year of 1959, the year the statue made its debut in the Park.

She told Laurie her news. When she got to the part about her father passing for white, Laurie responded with a downward sounding, "Oh."

"So the baby will be part black."

Laurie looked at her as if for the first time, then said quickly, "How much? What per cent?"

"I don't know. I never thought about it." She changed the subject. "By the way, I've been recommended to become the head of the English Department this fall."

"Do they know you're an ethnic?"

"I'm not an *ethnic!*" She blurted it out before she realized how prejudiced it sounded. "I'm white, Aztec and black!" Danielle held Laurie in her gaze until she acknowledged this. She watched Laurie break from her steady stare by pulling up the arm of her winter coat and checking her watch. "I'm late! I forgot! I'm late!"

"For a very important date?"

"No, no, I told you we've broken up! My manicurist! Nice seeing you again."

Danielle watched her scurry away and called out, "Brava Rabbit! Brava!" The comment was lost on Laurie, but an unnoticed bystander laughed, applauded and walked on. Danielle circled the statue until she and Alice were facing each other. "So what's it like in the rabbit hole?" She lingered a moment, then checked her watch. It was after four. She decided to drop in on Josh at work. She needed a friend.

A brisk thirty-block walk brought her to his search firm on the second floor of an office building on Madison Avenue in the fifties. She pushed open the glass doors of Careers for You and immediately felt better. She could open her heart to Josh.

His door was closed, so she sat on a dark blue vinyl chair and slipped out of her coat. His eyes lit up, when he came out and saw her. He was escorting a young black man in a business suit to the door. "It's slow after the holidays," she heard Josh say. "I'll call you if anything opens up, but thanks for dropping by." The two men exchanged firm handshakes.

"Shall I call *you*?" he asked in a clear, well modulated voice. *My students should hear this guy take control of the English language.*

"Give it about a month," Josh said and closed the door behind him.

No one else was in the waiting room. He pulled her up from the chair into his arms and kissed her slowly and deeply. Then he looked into her eyes. "I don't have any more appointments. Let's go home. I'd suggest dinner in town, but I told Sharon to be home for dinner."

"Sounds good to me." They walked into his office, and she sat opposite him at his desk and gazed up at two framed Monet city prints, while he finished up. From down the hall, she could hear the murmur of someone still making calls. "That black guy looked very professional," she said. She read the name on the resume. "Andrew Davis. Is that the one?" Josh nodded, ripped off the top page of his day calendar, threw it into the wastebasket and jotted notes down on the page of the next and last workday of 1981. Danielle read Andrew Davis' resume aloud. "Graduate of Baruch College with a major in business."

Josh laid down his pencil and smiled at her. "He's been looking since June."

"Will something open up soon?"

"I hope so. He's well qualified." He sighed. "I actually have two openings now, but the companies won't accept black trainees." He took the resume from her, turned it over, wrote a six and circled it in the upper right hand corner and filed it, while she stared at him. He saw her distress, as he was closing the cabinet. "That's the reality, Danielle."

"What if you just sent him to their offices anyway? He might sell himself."

"They'd find themselves another search firm. I get a lot of business from them."

At a loss for a comeback, she asked, "What's the circled six for?"

"It's a code we use in the office to let the other agents know a client's black."

"How do you live with this?"

"With colitis." He smiled. "Soon I'll be out and into a new career."

"Where you can do some good."

He frowned. "Let's go." He rose to get his coat.

She slipped back into hers. "Let's pool our money, live more simply, and get you out of here sooner."

"Come," he said. "There's no need to sink the ship."

The car crawled slowly along the Belt Parkway. In the silence, she felt Josh glancing at her. "Are you all right?"

"Fine." But she couldn't open her heart to him, as she'd planned.

"Let's get take-out," he said.

"Sharon likes eggplant Parmesan from Antonucci's."

"Sounds delicious." His voice was warm and deep. They rode on in silence.

It was dark by the time Danielle put the dinners to warm in the oven and shook a vinaigrette dressing she made for a tomato and lettuce salad. Her mind pelted her with questions. *How can Josh do that? Why did I feel so insulted when Laurie called me an ethnic? Why won't Dad talk to me?*

She phoned her parents. Her mother answered. "Why won't he talk to me?"

"I told you. He needs time."

"Can we meet?"

"Of course."

The front door slammed. "Sharon's back. I'll talk to you later," she said and hung up. Sharon burst into the kitchen and looked around.

"Where's my father?"

"In the shower. Hungry?" No answer. "We have eggplant Parmesan!" Still no answer. To compensate for the girl's silence and her own inner turmoil, Danielle talked with exaggerated enthusiasm and gestures, as she checked the garlic bread in the oven, poured dressing onto the salad and tossed it. "Let's have some dinner and talk about our new life!" In her exuberance, she missed an individual salad bowl and tossed the oily lettuce onto the counter. "Our feelings, our goals…" She was facing the window with her back to Sharon. She picked up the salad bowls, looked up into the dark mirror of the window and saw Sharon mimicking her behind her back. Quietly, she said, "Let's try," turned around and put salad bowls at each place setting.

"We're supposed to be giving each other space," Sharon said.

"*And* trying to live together," said Danielle. She took the eggplant Parmesan from the oven and set it on the table with warmed garlic bread and a bowl of shredded Parmesan cheese.

Josh walked in. "Sharon, we need to talk," he said serving steaming portions of eggplant to each of them. "Just before the holidays, the Dean called." Danielle saw Sharon tense and begin to pick at her salad. "I waited until after Christmas, Chanukah and our moving in together to talk about this." No answer. "He said you're cutting English." Sharon kept her eyes on her plate and began to eat. Danielle marveled at her nonchalance. Her own stomach was doing flip-flops. "You're failing class!" Josh's voice began to rise. "With a bunch of losers! Why?"

Danielle leaned toward her. "Want help catching up?"

"No."

"Sharon!" said Josh, slamming his fork onto the table.

Sharon shoved her dish aside and stood. "If I want help, I'll get a good teacher from a good school." She walked quickly to her room and slammed the door. Seconds later, Josh followed her. Danielle, too stung by Sharon's words to triangulate, just stared at the door. She heard him knock on his daughter's door and call her, and she heard the door open and close. As she tried to eat the eggplant, their voices escalated. She put down her fork and listened.

"Whadya want? I don't have a mother! I don't have a father!"
"I'm your father!"
"Until that baby comes!"
Danielle put a protective hand over her womb.
Josh's voice softened. "That's nonsense. Come to dinner."
"I've got a date."
"Sharon. Sharon. Come back here."
Danielle walked into the hallway in time to see Sharon slam the front door behind her, leaving her father standing alone.

She went to him and touched his arm. "It's good it came out. Now we can talk to her about it." He didn't answer. "With Alison. She'll help us."

"The divorce has damaged my relationship with her." He looked lost.

"Would staying with Kathy have improved it?"

He turned to her. "No, it wouldn't have. We were wrong for each other." He gathered her into his arms and put his face into the crook of her neck, then stood back and looked at her. "Let's eat."

She took his hand, as they walked back into the kitchen. He sat down and stared at his plate. "How about a glass of Chianti?" Josh began to relax even before she set down the wine glasses and poured the dark red liquid into his glass and the Pellegrino into hers.

"No wine for you?"

"Not while I'm pregnant." He looked disturbed by her answer, and that confused her, until she thought, *He's still thinking about Sharon.* They toasted and ate in companionable silence. Then he pushed the plate aside and stood.

"Delicious. I have to pay some bills," he said and went to his office. Danielle did the dishes. Then she settled into her favorite Queen Anne chair in the cozy living room alcove that faced onto the street. It had been a wearing day. Her eyes closed and she slept.

"Did Sharon come back?" The urgency in Josh's voice startled Danielle awake.

"Oh! Maybe. I might not have heard her."

Josh rushed to her door, knocked and called out her name. No answer. He opened the door and shut it. "She's not back. I'm going to look around the neighborhood. Want to join me?" The grandfather clock said eight-thirty. She nodded.

The night air was invigorating. Hand in hand, they covered a four-block area of quiet streets. "Did you call Kathy?" she asked, eventually.

"Not yet. Let's go back." His steps quickened. As they walked into the living room, Josh called out, "Sharon?" Danielle checked the kitchen and made tea while Josh checked the other rooms. He was sitting on the couch, just staring at his hands, when Danielle brought in a tray with a piping hot pot of chamomile, two mugs and a plate of oatmeal cookies. She set it on the coffee table between them, sat down and poured. "No answer at Kathy's." Danielle dipped a cookie into her tea and searched for encouraging words.

"She said she had a date. She'll be home soon."

"You were probably right," Josh said.

"About?" He didn't answer right away, so she second-guessed him. "About Andrew Davis? You're going to send him out?"

"To an all-white company? That would be stupid."

"Are you calling me stupid?"

"I'm calling the idea of sending a black man to apply for a job with a bigoted firm, stupid."

"It's just not fair," she muttered, still stung. "My students will have to face this shit."

"I didn't say it was fair." He glanced at the grandfather clock and checked his watch. "I meant right about the baby."

"The baby?" She began to lighten up.

He nodded. "Maybe we should wait."

"For?" She was smiling, now.

"Until Sharon's feeling more secure," he said carefully.

She stared at him. "Are you saying end this pregnancy because Sharon's feeling insecure?"

"I'm worried about my *daughter!*" he said in an explosion of angst.

She put down her cup. "Then maybe it's *we* who should wait."

Chapter Nine

The taxi sped onto the highway toward Manhattan, away from Josh, but not from the remembered touch of his hand on her arm or the confusion in his voice, when he said, "Why are you so angry? You were planning an abortion yourself less than a week ago."

He has a point. What if something happens on the street to Sharon! Teens do foolish things…

She tried to assuage her guilt by concentrating on the soothing glow of the tall apartment buildings across the river. Instead she remembered how Josh's eyes lit up when he saw her, and she felt again how right he was for her. *If he hadn't suggested the abortion, would I have done it myself? Would the Little One have responded with a miscarriage?* She had heard of such things happening.

The cab turned into Gramercy Park, and she pushed the thoughts away. *I need time, and I'm taking it.* Her resolve seemed to strengthen on the elevator ride up, but when she stepped out onto the second floor, she heard a beautiful but lonely-sounding melody coming from her apartment. Her unexpected arrival startled Phil at the piano. He looked at her and immediately asked, "What's wrong?"

The words, "I left Josh," got muddled in crying sounds, and tears blinded her. She felt her brother take the suitcase from her, lead her into the living room, sit her in the overstuffed chair and slip tissues into her hand. When she could, she looked up and saw him sitting on the couch across from her. She looked into his steady hazel eyes. "Josh wants me to have an abortion so Sharon will feel secure." Phil's sigh told her he was sympathizing with Danielle and Josh as a couple, not as her advocate. "It's my choice," she said. "He has no right pushing me into a decision like this!"

"Did he push you?"

She was annoyed. "What do you mean?"

"What if you just said, 'No.'"

"It's not just that," she said evasively. "He refused to send a perfectly qualified black applicant out for a job with a firm because they don't hire black people. When Phil didn't respond, she said, "That makes him a bigot. Right?"

Phil leaned forward. "Josh isn't a bigot, Dan. He's overwhelmed by Sharon and the business right now."

"I don't have to put up with it!"

"I understand, but give him time." She slumped back into the overstuffed chair. "Give yourself time, too."

"Sharon can be such a brat."

"Give her time, too." When she didn't respond, he returned to the piano, as if to an unfinished conversation. He played a few lines of the melody she'd heard in the hall. "That's lovely. What's it from?"

"Me. But I can't seem to tease out the rest of it."

"It's…haunting." She settled into the cushions and closed her eyes, and Phil explored his melody. Her thoughts wandered to their father. She said it quietly. "Dad is a bigot." Phil stopped playing and looked at her. "Remember when I dated a black student in college. He nodded. "I told Dad, and I thought he was going to be sick."

Phil was quiet for a moment. Then he said, "Once Dad visited when Alma and I were studying at the apartment. After she left, he told me not to have black people visit. I accused him of bigotry, but he didn't get angry. He just looked sad. He said that it was dangerous, more than I knew, that it wasn't their fault and that they'd never had it easy in this country… My anger just melted away. He was paying for the apartment, and so I complied. Dad and Mom thought inter-racial dating was particularly dangerous…Do you think they were right?"

"I don't know. Once I got a hate look from a very respectable-looking man when I dated that black student in the early sixties. I never told anyone, but it terrified me."

"Write about it."

"Yeah? Just this week, I told Jill Martin, who lives across the hall here and Laurie Smith from New Crossing, that I'm part black. Jill hinted at an abortion, and Laurie demanded to know the percentage of black before she ran off."

"I told a black musician today that I found out I'm part black, and he told me he found out he's part white."

She laughed in spite of herself. "You're living in a civilized world of musicians. In my world, I'm losing my membership in white society."

"Not all our friends are bigots."

"Most of them aren't. I hope."

Phil returned to his melody, and Danielle was easing back into the cushions, when another memory took hold of her. "In my junior year at Smith, police were beating negroes on the streets down South for trying to vote. We saw it on television."

"I was just starting high school," said Phil.

"Students from my college were marching on Washington, and I wanted to join them. Dad said I would have to support myself before making such a dangerous decision. He was paying the bills, and, like you, I obeyed him… I didn't go. I missed being there when Martin Luther King gave his 'I Have a Dream' speech… missed participating in the greatest movement of our time. Because Dad said it was too dangerous!" Her voice broke, and she fought not to cry.

"There's so much we don't know about him. We still don't."

"Did you ever get back with Alma?"

"Right after graduation, I got my first gig on the road and have been on the road pretty much ever since. Alma went to graduate school and began to teach. We drifted apart."

"Dad broke you two up."

"I've blamed him for years, but now, I'm not so sure."

"I'm going to call Mom and get some answers from her."

The next day, Danielle looked into the full-length mirror at her still slim figure. She wished herself good luck and slipped into her purple coat and boots. She was meeting her mother.

Twenty minutes later, she was driving north on Route 91 to Fair Hills, a village near New Crossing. For the first time since the wassail party, Danielle spoke to her unborn child. "A train whistle woke me this morning, but the whistle was in my dream. A Negro woman, middle-aged, standing on a country railroad platform, got smaller and smaller, as the train traveled north. I saw people she knew, perhaps her family, get on that train. She just stood there in a long dark dress and watched as the train chugged away. And, Little One, I cried I missed them so."

She turned off the highway at the exit for Fairfield. A familiar country road led to the Fair Hills Fish House, circa 1850, and she parked beside her mother's mauve Chevy. The heavy wooden door opened into a cozy country lobby, smelling of fresh fish cooking in butter and spices. A waitress hurried by with a tray. "Hi Melinda."

"Hi Danielle. Your mother's on the water side."

Danielle saw her sitting along the windowed wall with a view of a frozen pond lined with leafless trees, its branches stark against a white and yellow sky. For years, the Fair Hills Fish House was their favorite spot for lunch and conversation. Cautiously, she approached her mom, so trim and smart in an avocado pants suit. Her brown, flat-heeled leather boots, however, were made for walking over ice and snow. "Hi Mom," she said softly. Her mother glanced up from her reverie and looked at Danielle without changing expression. Just looked at her. Danielle felt afraid and didn't know why. Her mother stood, they hugged without speaking and sat opposite one another along the windowed wall. Melinda arrived with menus.

Her mother smiled. "I'll start with a glass of Chardonnay." She looked at Danielle.

"A bottle of Pellegrino and a glass with ice." She thirsted for a Merlot to recapture old times.

"Shall we share an appetizer of clams casino?" her Mom asked.

"Let's," smiled Danielle and waited for Melinda to leave before asking, "How's Dad?"

"Coming along." Danielle knew that meant he wasn't ready to talk to her.

Chapter Nine

A basket of bread arrived with their drinks. She also knew they would have to make do with that and the appetizer until each had said the things they had come to say. As they toasted, the clinking glasses reminded her of the bell that rings to announce Round One in a boxing match. They looked at one another, sipped their drinks, and Danielle led with a hard right. "You and Dad brought us up not to be prejudiced. Dad didn't even join the country club because it was restricted. Was he just afraid of being found out?" Her mother exhaled and was about to reply, but Danielle kept on punching. "Why is it such a big deal to say I'm black?" Her mother looked quickly around, and Danielle pressed on. "If we're all so liberal, so unprejudiced, why can't I say I'm Celtic and African American?" Her Mom looked down and touched her forefinger to the cool, moist base of the glass, and Danielle steam-rolled on. "If I said I'm Celtic and German or Celtic and Swedish or Celtic and Italian-

"You have no idea, do you?" she said, looking up from her glass, and Danielle fell silent to see tears in her mother's eyes.

More quietly, she asked, "Why should I have any idea?" You've both been so secretive. What is our history?"

Her mother paused, said, "Our history." And she exhaled deeply... "Your grandfather's mother on your father's side was Jerusha, a kept negro woman, who lived in a cottage on your white great Grandfather's plantation. Master McKinnon was your great grandfather."

Danielle's dream jolted into focus. To her left, opposite the window, she imagined she felt a Presence – was it from this history? – sit down on the free seat between them in the aisle. She didn't look because she was afraid. Instead, she remembered sitting around the dining room table in Brooklyn with her father's family when she was five. New York Nana and Grandpa McKinnon were there. Reach back one more generation and Great Grandpa McKinnon would be.... "A slave owner?" she asked.

"A former slave owner."

"Jerusha was a former slave?"

"Yes. She had your grandfather by him."

"Plantation?" A word she thought she understood, but could only define. She looked at the empty chair. In her imagination, a wealthy southern gentleman, leaned in to put his arm around her shoulder. Danielle sat back and struggled to get a perspective.

"I thought Dad grew up in California."

"South Carolina."

"How many lies-

"Do you want to hear this or not?"

She fell silent, and waited for her mother to speak.

"When your grandfather came of age, Master McKinnon sent him to tailoring school and then provided him with clientele, his own rich and influential friends."

"Grandpa was very lucky," she said testily.

"That's right," her mother said just as testily. "But he knew his children wouldn't be lucky if he stayed in the South. So he moved his family north to…

"To pass for white?" Danielle shot at her.

"To live the American dream!" she shot right back.

"Okay, but why pass for white up North? The North fought for emancipation!"

Her mother fell back in the chair and passed a hand over her eyes. She took a sip of wine and looked straight at Danielle for what could only be Round Two. A broken Negro man now sat between them. She swallowed her Pellegrino, avoided his eyes and barely noticed that the Clams Casino had arrived.

Her Mom began. "When I was twelve…"

"You were raised in Massachusetts? That's true, isn't it?"

"Yess!" Lynn hissed, and Danielle's back flattened against her chair. "And your white grandfather, my father, owned a lumber business and was the richest man around."

"Way out in the wilds of Tewksberry, Massachusetts? I've heard all this. Your parents beat you, your father shot your kittens for meanness when you were a child and kept you from graduating high school to stay home and clean the house. So you ran away. Is that true?"

"Yess!"

"You weren't that different from a runaway slave down South yourself."

"Wrong. I was running for my freedom, but only from my family. Twenty miles from your Alma Mater." Lynn took a sip of wine and looked into her daughter's eyes. "There's more." Danielle's hand trembled as she drank. Round Three. "When I was twelve, your grandfather took me to a business meeting, in the middle of the night, way out in the Tewksbury woods."

Danielle fought for her footing. "That was in?"

"Nineteen twenty-nine. We came to a clearing in the woods. It was pitch-dark except for a burning cross. Figures I thought were ghosts floated towards us. My father got out of the truck; I scrambled into the back and peeked out. I saw my father pull a white hood over his head, and I…I knew they weren't ghosts. I don't remember all that happened next except there was a Negro man… his arms were tied to his side, and he was being dragged. I heard a crying sound and…"

Danielle was trembling. "You heard a crying sound…and?"

"I heard a scream…" Danielle looked at her mother's contorted face, twisted in horror, and she leaned in to her. "And I hid… in the bottom of the truck. I don't remember anymore. I don't want to remember. Your father once suggested I try hypnotism to remember. I refused, but little by little, the memories come up."

She reached for her mother's hand. "I didn't know," she whispered and realized that's how her mother had begun their conversation. "I didn't know," she repeated, and waited for her to speak.

"That was the North, Danielle. Your father lived in the South. When I fell in love with him, it was illegal to marry a Negro in Massachusetts if he came from a state in which it was illegal. And it was illegal in South Carolina."

"But that was in the forties."

"And the fifties." She sounded so weary. "Maybe I shouldn't have married him, but he was the best thing that ever happened to me."

"I'm glad you married him, Mom. He's a wonderful father, a wonderful…" She remembered the wassail party. She turned and looked into the imagined eyes of the broken Negro. She looked for herself and for her mother at eyes that had known the unspeakable… When she could speak again, she asked humbly, "Why did Dad become prejudiced?"

Her mother looked surprised. "Prejudiced? I don't know if prejudiced is the right word, but… he had no safe place to speak his truth. He'd cut himself off from his family. Maybe the prejudice of others – infected him." She held her daughter's gaze. "It's infected me." Tears welled up in her eyes.

"Jerusha," Danielle said, unable to absorb her mother's last statement. The vowel sounds sang. "I love that name." Her mother looked surprised. "Did she ever come up North?"

"No. She was too dark to pass."

"So everyone moved north and left her?"

"Your grandfather lived in the South with her most of the time to manage his tailoring business. The clients were there. And your aunts and uncle would visit."

In the pause she realized she was hungry. The Clams Casino had long since gotten cold, so they ordered clam chowder and fried clams with salad.

"I dreamt about her last night," Danielle said.

"Jerusha?"

"I know I did, and I know how she felt, when they left her." She told her mother about the dream. The synchronicity of it at that particular time wasn't lost on them. "You know, you and Dad were the only adults I knew who were open to dream interpretation, reincarnation… mystical things. How come?"

"Your father and I were always interested in it. We wanted to understand our lives. And we learned a lot from your Aunt Tessie. She was constantly reading about mysticism in the East and the West."

"Really?" It was unusual for either of her parents to mention her aunts, but this was an unusual day. "It's too late now, but can we talk about this sometime?"

"Yes. Now's not the time." The fried clams arrived and they ate in silence, until her mother said, "I begged your father to tell you you're black, so you could audition for that soap opera…even if it meant losing you."

Danielle put her fork down and took her mother's hand. "You wouldn't have."

"I know that now."

"Mother and daughter embraced before parting. She didn't tell her mother she'd left Josh. And she didn't mention the Little One.

Phil was about to leave for work, when Danielle returned. "I just had lunch with Mom!"

He checked the time. "I've got about twenty minutes. Shoot." He almost forgot his hurry, when Danielle told him what happened.

"Are you saying Dad wouldn't talk about it out of fear?"

"I didn't talk to him, but I think so. Remember how his voice would get deep and serious, as if he wanted to say something more than he *could* say? Phil nodded. She lifted one of a pair of bronze Lincoln bookends from a bookshelf, held it carefully in both hands and imitated her father. "These bookends were given to me by a man whose last name also happened to be McKinnon, and who thought there might be some distant relationship between us. They were in his family since the Civil War, and he gave them to me as a gift."

"Maybe he was our great grandfather, the plantation owner," said Phil. She traced the familiar lines of Lincoln's face with her finger. The green felt backing on the bottom of the piece was smooth with age. "These bookends are heirlooms." They looked at their mysterious treasure.

"Dan, you know that baby picture of yours Mom and Dad had framed with your first shoes bronzed at the base?" Danielle nodded. "When I was about seven, I was upstairs with Mom while she was making your bed. We were talking about something, I don't remember what, when I looked at that picture and said, 'Danielle looks like a little Negro girl.'"

"What did she say?"

"Nothing. She kept making the bed and said nothing. But the silence was loud."

"They never took the picture away."

"No."

That afternoon, Danielle had seen fear at something only partially remembered on the face of the little girl who was now her mother. Over Christmas, she'd witnessed the terror of a small boy on her father's face, just before he ordered her out of the house.

"They were both terrified," she said.

"They still are." Phil stood. "I've got to go." He looked at his sister. "Want to come by later and welcome in the New Year with us at our table?"

Without Josh? She shook her head. Phil turned to go. "Call Alma," she said.

He turned back. "Write your story."

"I don't know my story."

"You got part of it today. Our aunts probably know more."

She watched her brother wrap a cashmere scarf with brown, beige and maroon stripes around the neck of his brown leather jacket. She was there when her mother bought it to keep her son warm in the cold countries behind the Iron Curtain, where he played drums for the black singing and dancing group, The Dreamers.

"Does it bother you being black," she asked quickly, as he was shutting the door.

He looked directly into her eyes. "No. It makes me feel more American. You?"

"No," she said in a tiny voice.

He rushed back in, gave her a brotherly hug and a kiss on the forehead. "Happy New Year!" he said. Then he was gone.

She stood alone and lonely in her cozy apartment. "Get a hold of yourself," she said and turned on the television. It bombarded her with holiday cheer. She turned it off, paced the living room, stopped to pick

Chapter Nine

up her notebook and put it down again. She picked up the phone to dial Josh, and put it down. How she wanted to celebrate New Year's with him, to laugh, to talk, to make love.

She pulled a bottle of Merlot from the wine rack, uncorked it, filled a wine glass and toasted,

"Happy New Year, Little One. Don't worry. I won't make a habit of this." She sipped the wine, picked up her old copy of *Pride and Prejudice*, snuggled into the overstuffed chair and put the glass on the table beside her. *I'm proud, and Josh is prejudiced. Or I'm prejudiced and…*" She took another sip of wine and quietly said aloud, "Should we consider a miscarriage, Little One, you and I? The timing now is so complicated with Sharon, my new job, my relationship with Josh and you happening all at once… Maybe postpone your coming into the family for just a little while, a year perhaps, until I can do right by you. You could come back, when Sharon is ready for a sister. If you still want to, that is… Let's keep it in mind."

She reached for the wine glass again and paused. Desperation inspired her next move. Quickly, she called information and dialed her aunts' telephone number. They always call us in Connecticut. *They don't know I live in Manhattan. I won't tell them.*

"Hello?" said the melodious voice of her Aunt Charlotte. *Hang up. They'll think it's the wrong number.* "Hello?" Aunt Charlotte sounded irritated now.

"Happy New Year. It's Danielle."

"Danielle?"

"Yes." She heard a smile in her aunt's surprised voice.

"Happy New Year! Tessie! Danielle is on the line!" Danielle felt a glow. Charlotte had always been her favorite aunt, had always noticed her and played with her. "I'm glad you called. We couldn't get through to you on Christmas Eve or Christmas Day. Tessie and I were beginning to worry. Is your father well? Danielle?"

"That's right. You didn't hear from us." And Danielle told her why. Before going to bed, she wrote a note and taped it to the bathroom mirror.

Phil, I called our aunts, and we're invited to New Year's dinner at four o'clock. I accepted for us both, but they'll understand if you can't make it, since you don't know about it until right now! I hope you can make it. They sound nice! We'll see. Happy New Year!

Chapter Ten

New Year's Day, nineteen eighty-two, dawned crisp and cold. The streets of Manhattan and the Belt Parkway gave no warning of how icy Brooklyn's streets would be. Danielle took the Flatbush exit and pulled up to an open variety store. "Let's get Barricinni chocolates. Dad always brought us a box when he came back from visiting them," said Phil.

"Good idea. They're delicious," said Danielle. She watched her brother walk into the store. He'd dressed for the occasion in a brown tweed sports jacket, tan crew neck sweater and slacks. She refreshed her lipstick. *This could be a mistake.* Her father's old warning nagged at her still, so she'd worn a purple jersey dress that complimented her figure with high-heel designer boots to make it clear she was *not an old maid!*

"I got the two-pound variety box," said Phil, getting in and shutting the door. "Dark chocolate, milk chocolate and white chocolate," he said grinning.

"That's our family," she said, laughing. She drove out of her way to avoid passing Josh's apartment. It was only ten blocks from her aunts' home.

"I'd ask if you called Josh, but you'd ask if I called Alma, and I don't want you to do that," said her brother.

"Good thinking." She turned onto East Thirty-eighth Street. "I was six last time I saw them."

"I was three."

She found the address easily this time and parked. Sheer ice lined the walkway and covered the three steps to the front door. Danielle slipped on the first stair, lost her balance, grabbed the wrought iron railing and slid in a half circle to a sitting position on the second icy step. "Damn boots!"

"Take my arm," said Phil.

"I can do it," she said, waving him away. Stubbornly, she gripped the railing with both hands and climbed sideways up the steps. "They may still be weird, you know," she said, inching up.

"At least we'll know where you get it from."

Just then, the curtains parted and closed quickly.

"Weird!" she said. Triumphantly, she stood on the icy landing, just as the front door swung open, startling her into a jump and a high-heeled skid into the open arms of a short, sturdy woman who appeared to be in her sixties. "Aunt Charlotte!"

"Happy New Year!" laughed her aunt, embracing her. "You look like a McKinnon." She reached for Phil, hugged him and her eyes filled with tears. She gave his arm a playful shake to get control of her feelings. "I'm glad you phoned, Danielle. It's been almost thirty-five years." Oblivious to the cold, the three stood there, looking at each other. Charlotte, in her dark brown slacks and matching turtleneck sweater, looked quite normal, Danielle noticed. "You both resemble Mac... How is he? Her guarded expression was not lost on Danielle.

"Well, he's healthy, and the business is going well."

"Good," she growled, then paused as if to regain self-control and led them into a small foyer.

"Where's Aunt Tessie?" asked Danielle, looking around.

"Oh, my God! I left her basting the turkey all by herself!"

"I'll help," said Danielle.

"No, no. Take off your coats and make yourselves at home. We'll be right out." She hurried through the living room, dining room and into the kitchen from which the savory aroma of roast turkey drifted.

Danielle and Phil watched from the darkened foyer. "Did you see her change when she mentioned Dad?" she asked Phil. He nodded. "Weird," she said.

"Give her a chance," said Phil. He opened the coat closet and she reached for a hanger.

"Hang your coats outside the closet," Charlotte called out from the kitchen. Danielle froze in mid-reach, and Phil looked in the direction of his aunt's voice. "Mama's and Robert's ashes are in there." Danielle and

Chapter Ten | 123

Phil looked down and saw two cardboard boxes, side by side, on a table.

Neatly printed on one was – Remains of Ruth Williams McKinnon, June 15, 1963 and on the other – Robert Henry McKinnon, December 8, 1975. Danielle looked up at Phil, whispered, "Last one in shut the door," and threw herself into a giggling fit.

"Shhh!"

She hung her coat on a hook and was trying to stifle her hilarity, when she looked across the dimly lit room and sharply inhaled. The shadow of a man's face was smiling at her.

"What is it?" asked Phil.

"I… I saw a ghost on the mantle," she whispered. She looked back. Red candlesticks in brass holders stood on each side of a mahogany clock. "It's gone now."

"You might have imagined it."

"Maybe, but I don't think so." Carefully, she looked around. A maroon oriental rug covered the large living room floor. Across the room next to the dining room stood a baby grand piano. Moving along the living room wall to the right was a fireplace with a mantle under a stained glass window. Beside it, an unlit Christmas tree filled the corner, and a long window seat ran along the wall overlooking the street. *Bluish-green.* Chills played along her neck and arms.

At the next corner, she saw the foyer and the off-limits coat closet. Along the wall, leading back to the dining room was a couch, a bookcase and a dark blue wing chair in front of a staircase to the second floor. "I remember this wing chair," she said, walking to it. "Aunt Tessie gave me a book of Grimm Fairy Tales and told me to sit there and read because I'd woven all my pick-up sticks into the rug. She was so stern, and that book was so frightening… I remember looking around the chair and seeing Uncle Robert sitting on a stair behind me… with a gentle smile on his face."

"Maybe he was stationed there to watch you," said Phil.

"Probably." A chill shot through her. *The same smile as the one on the mantle.* To get distance from him, she walked quickly across the room to the window seat and sat down. Guilt set in. *Uncle Robert was so kind.*

She looked up at the mantle and smiled at the place where she had seen him.

Phil sat down at the baby grand. "A Knabe," he said respectfully.

"What's a Knabe?"

"An excellent piano." He raised the lid and played chords softly.

He's falling under the spell of the house's charm too. She ran her hand over the dark velvet window seat. "I used to crawl along here, peek through the curtains and bark."

"Why?"

"To protect the house from strangers."

"Ever think you were a brat?"

"Never."

Phil laughed, opened a 1940's songbook and played "Sentimental Journey."

"Haven't heard that one for years!" piped a voice from the kitchen.

Danielle jumped up and called out, "Do you need any help?"

"No, no! Stay right where you are."

She remembered Tessie as a stern middle-aged brunette whom she didn't dare approach, so she sat right back down on the window seat and looked across the living room to the dining room and kitchen door. Just as she remembered, turn of the century mahogany furniture lent the room a quiet elegance. A long dinner table with cushioned Queen Anne chairs stood beneath a brass chandelier. A china cabinet with glass doors, showcasing fine china in a rose and leaf design, lined the far wall, and a small cabinet, holding crystal glasses stood on the opposite wall by the staircase.

Her eyes roamed to the kitchen door and her recent memory of New York Nana, standing at the threshold of the kitchen, seemed to return in the flesh! "You're McKinnons, all right," piped the same voice. Phil stopped playing. Danielle blinked and saw the same silver-haired old woman she'd seen through the icy window over a week ago. Now she stood at the kitchen door in a long white apron over a pink sweater set and gray skirt that stopped at mid-calf. Her long silver hair was tied back with a gray ribbon.

"Aunt Tessie," said Phil standing. Tessie opened her arms and hugged him, as Danielle crossed the living room. Then she gave Danielle a frail but energetic embrace.

Charlotte joined them to hear Tessie say, "It's about time you two came. Your Grandmother and Uncle have been waiting for you." Danielle smiled at Tessie's casual reference to those whose ashes were in the closet.

Charlotte rolled her eyes and said, "Tessie is entering a time in her life when the past appears to join the present."

"Check the rice, Charlotte," Tessie said sternly. The sisters stared at each other.

"Shall I set the table?" Danielle asked, trying not to laugh.

"Yes, and I'll help you," said Tessie.

"Here you are at last," said Charlotte, her soft southern tones warming northern ones, "braving the ice to slide back into our lives."

"Do you have an ice chopper?" Phil asked.

"Oh, don't bother. The handyman will be here tomorrow."

"It's on the back porch through the kitchen," said Tessie. Phil left for the kitchen and Charlotte followed him. "The wood for the fireplace is in the garage."

"Tessie!" They heard Charlotte's embarrassment followed by Phil's laughter and then, Charlotte's chuckle.

In the dining room, Tessie muttered, "Charlotte's so independent!" She switched on the Christmas tree lights. Danielle inhaled balsam, looked at her reflection in a large colored bulb, touched the tinsel and wondered what occasions had brought the variety of ornaments to their tree.

"Your tree is so much like ours at home," she said. Home… To dispel her heartbreak, she crossed to the china closet. "The rose and leaf design?"

"Yes, said Tessie. "Our best for tonight."

"It's still slippery out there," said Phil, entering the living room with an armful of wood and kindling. He set it into the dark fireplace and went back outside to chop ice from the front steps.

Danielle took a long wooden match from the mantle, struck it and ignited the kindling. She wondered what Christmas Past in the McKinnon homestead had been like. Then she lit two tapering bayberry candles on the dining room table and glanced curiously in the direction of the mantle and the closet.

"Your Uncle Robert has been gone seven years, and your grandmother eighteen," said Tessie, startling Danielle, who hadn't realized how closely her aunt was observing her. "We need to get those ashes down to South Carolina."

"Perhaps, we can all drive down together in the spring," said Danielle, surprising herself with a burst of family feeling. The sound of ice crackled outside the curtained window, as Phil's shadow bent over his work.

"It's more complicated than just delivering the ashes," said Tessie. "Years back, the government took over a few miles of land outside of our home in Edmundton for nuclear testing. The Negro cemetery was on that land."

"What?" asked a shocked Danielle.

"Oh, they didn't blow up the grave site, but the whole area is radioactive and off limits to the public. We have to make application to arrange for the proper authorities to place grave markers on our plot and to bury the ashes. We went through the whole procedure once before, in the late fifties, to bury Papa." Tessie sounded very tired.

"So let's do it when you and Charlotte are ready," Danielle said softly, wondering how long Tessie herself had.

"We'll talk more about it. Let's help Charlotte now," she said, perking up.

Half an hour later, Danielle and Phillip sat down to dinner with their aunts for the first time in over thirty years. Tessie's fork pointed at Danielle. "I remember you walking around with flour on your nose to get attention."

Danielle squirmed. "There wasn't a lot to do around here. Phil was still in his cradle, and the rest of you were all so serious."

Chapter Ten

She looked at Phil whose fork was pointed at Charlotte. "I remember you playing the piano." The conversation picked up with each one carefully selecting memories to get them through dinner without inadvertently giving each other indigestion.

After the dishes were cleared, Phil asked Charlotte to play melodies from the old songbooks. They hummed along with "That Old Black Magic," sang a phrase or two from "Carolina in the Morning," then leaned in around Charlotte to sing all the lyrics to "Satin Doll." Charlotte finished with a flourish, and they took their places around the crackling fire for dessert and coffee.

"Your grandmother was an English and Speech teacher just like you are, Danielle," Tessie said, pouring cups of coffee. "Self-educated, of course. A schoolmarm."

"You graduated from Smith College, didn't you, Danielle?" asked Charlotte.

"Yes."

"June 1963?"

"Charlotte." Tessie's stern voice held a warning.

"Mama died that month, a few days after you graduated."

"Charlotte!"

Did she wait for me to graduate? Danielle wondered. Then she felt foolish. She'd pretty much forgotten about her grandmother, since she was six years old. *Why would New York Nana remember me?* A Kodak photo of her graduation picture came to mind. Phil was in the picture with Mac, her mother, Holyoke Nana and Uncle Albert on her Mom's side of the family, the white side. "Did Dad know she was dying?" she asked her aunts.

"He knew she was failing," said Tessie. "When she passed, he came in for the funeral."

"Did she know Danielle was the first in the family to graduate college?" asked Phil.

"Robert was the first," Charlotte said sharply. "He graduated from New York University in 1925, and I graduated in 1939."

"I wish I'd known," said Danielle. "I wish I'd known a lot of things."

"Mama was well enough to enjoy the note you wrote to us with your graduation picture," Tessie said gently.

Charlotte leveled Danielle with a steady gaze. "Were you aware that she'd passed on a few days later?"

"I…I don't remember." She turned to Phil. "Did Dad tell us?"

"I don't remember."

"In either case, you two have no memory of it," said Charlotte, with a chilling bitterness. Danielle looked at Phil, who looked down into his coffee cup.

"Well, the two of you need to know about your family," said Tessie.

"Yes," said Danielle. *That's why I'm here.* But now she felt like a spy.

A plate of cookies appeared under her nose. She looked into Tessie's inscrutable eyes. "Try a gingerbread man. I made them myself."

She tried one, but barely tasted it. "I was so self-involved back then," she said apologetically.

"Your parents weren't much help," said Charlotte.

"How about a glass of Scuppernong?" asked Tessie.

"What's Scuppernong?" Phil asked.

"Wine from the scuppernong grape in South Carolina. It was your grandmother's favorite. With an energy Danielle was surprised to see, Tessie walked with a perky step to the breakfront and set out four small wine glasses. Charlotte uncorked the bottle and poured the golden liquid into stemmed glasses. They glowed in the firelight.

Danielle sipped the wine. "It's not sweet, but it's not tart either. How unique. The grapes must be delicious." She was about to sip again, when she remembered the Little One, looked down at her flat stomach and gently touched it. When she looked up, two very savvy women were sizing her up with a knowing look. "I'm pregnant," she said. As one, Charlotte and Tessie leaned in to her. She felt a strong warm hand on her left arm and a cool fragile one on her right.

At first, she faltered and spoke haltingly. "Three days ago, I walked out on the baby's father…his name's Josh, Joshua Freedman, because…" And she explained what happened with Josh and Sharon the night she left. There was a long silence, and to fill it, she said, "I was shocked by the racism out there."

Tessie leaned forward. "Tell no one about your color! Except for family."

Danielle's back straightened. "Why not? It's the truth."

Charlotte sat back. "Even if people aren't prejudiced, your own fears may cause you to think they are. Just as they did with you and Josh."

"It may also affect how you feel on the inside," said Tessie.

"I feel angry on the inside, and…" She looked at her brother and saw he was trying to give her space by studying his drink.

"Inferior? Nauseated?" Charlotte prompted. Danielle hesitated and Phil went to the piano and quietly played his melody.

"No, no! Well, sometimes inferior." She remembered Josh calling a remark she made stupid. *And he didn't mean anything by it.* She looked at her aunts. "I love Josh, but I don't know what to do."

"While you're deciding, why don't you… Oh dear, I should speak to Charlotte first," said Tessie.

"No need," said Charlotte. "Would you like to stay here for the time being? You can sleep in Mama's room."

"Yes," Danielle said. "Yes, I'd like that." It felt right, and she was amazed that it did. "What do you think, Phil? You'll have the apartment to yourself." He stopped playing.

"I think it calls for a drum roll," he said, executing it with his fingers on the top of the piano. They laughed, and the tension broke.

Charlotte opened the box of Barriccini chocolates and set it beside the plate of cookies. "Our favorite, and you two *did* remember that," she said with a smile and added, "This is your home too, Phil. Robert's room is available whenever you want to visit."

Tessie raised her glass of Scuppernong. "To new beginnings in 1982."

"To new beginnings," they toasted. The clinking crystal made a happy sound and Danielle realized she and Phil made the same toast with Darren and Cheryl at the Village Jazz Club two weeks earlier. She sipped the wine and settled back into her chair.

"We need to think about getting some things for the baby," said Tessie.

"I already have two family heirlooms from you and Charlotte," said Danielle.

"What heirlooms?" Tessie asked.

"The amethyst ring and the Aztec bracelets."

"Not Aztec. Catawba. We're American Indian, not South American," said Tessie, and her face turned serious, as anger fired up in Charlotte's eyes. "That was the last time we saw you and Phil. We wanted to give you something to remember us by. Papa put together a bag of items, silver cufflinks, a finely crafted jackknife among them and told Mac to give them to you, Phil, when you were older."

"I have them," he said, "but I had no idea why."

"I remember now," said Danielle, looking at Charlotte. "You took me to your room, took that beautiful amethyst ring from your jewelry box and gave it to me. You were smiling and serious at the same time. She turned to Tessie. "And you took me to your room and gave me one brown leather Catawba bracelet decorated with red beads and leather fringes and a white leather one decorated with green and clear beads and leather fringes. I love them."

"Why was it the last time?" Phil asked.

"Your father decided to separate you two from the rest of us," said Charlotte.

Danielle pictured her gentle young father. "Why would he do that?"

"We all tried to get him to change his mind," Tessie said.

"Except for your mother, of course," said Charlotte. "She couldn't wait to get out of here." Danielle envisioned the frightened young woman her mother must have been, but couldn't call upon words to defend her.

"Papa said Phillip, referring to your father, was acting too hastily," said Tessie. "But Phillip said…" She looked as if she didn't want to continue.

Charlotte steam-rolled on. "You broke away from our people down home for the good of *your* family. Now, I need to break away from you, for the good of *my* family."

Silence.

Gently, Tessie said, "Mama begged him not to take her grand-children away, but all he would promise was that he'd visit her. And he did."

"He tore the family apart," said Danielle.

"But why? Why would it be for the good of our family?" asked Phil.

"To keep your race a secret. Your grandmother and uncle couldn't pass for white. Their features and complexions gave them away," said Charlotte.

So do mine. Danielle felt like she was drifting out to sea, all by herself. "That's wrong," she called out, as if from afar.

"You don't know the half of it!" said Charlotte. "He-"

Tessie interrupted. "Danielle. Phil. You did not know your father in the old days!"

"This is no time to return to the *old* days," said Charlotte.

"Right," said Phil. "It's getting late."

"The half of what, Charlotte?" Danielle asked, grasping her aunt's arm.

"Let's go, Danielle," said Phil.

"The half of what?" She held on to her aunt's arm as if it were a buoy in deep waters.

Tessie stood. "We need another dinner."

"I can move Danielle in on Thursday. How about then?" asked Phil.

"That will be fine. You both need to understand!"

Back in her Gramercy Park apartment, Danielle showered, wrapped up in her flannel nightgown and robe and curled up in her overstuffed chair with a pad of lined paper. Warm, yellow lamplight flowed over her hands, one holding a pencil with a sharpened point. But, instead of writing, she doodled. Phil sat down at the console piano, turned on its light and searched for his elusive melody. Danielle's doodling turned to scribbling and the scribbling got wilder and wilder, until she threw her note pad across the living room to where it smacked against the wall. Phil banged a chord of the piano in agreement and stopped playing.

"Let's get some sleep," he said.

"How could Dad do that?" she yelled. A neighbor knocked on the ceiling and yelled, "Quiet!"

"Shh, I don't know. Let's go to bed. Aren't you meeting Nicole at school tomorrow?"

She nodded and retrieved her notebook. "How can I write about him?"

"Write about yourself. You're getting your story."

I'm getting my story. My aunts are telling me their story and mine. I'm moving into their home in a few days. What else will they tell me?

Chapter Eleven

The next morning, Danielle awoke with her Aunt Charlotte's words still in her mind. *Their features and complexions gave them away.* She rushed to the bathroom and looked at herself in the mirror. *Do I pass?* She splashed cold water onto her face and brushed her teeth. Painful as it was, that story, as if with a firm hold on her shirt collar, was pulling her to the task.

But she had committed to joining Dr. Norton and Nicole on that vacation day. Moodily, she pulled on an old sweater and jeans, buttoned up her quilted lavender coat, stomped across the room and slammed out of the front door.

Walking toward the bus stop, she muttered to the unborn child, "Grandpa? What a travesty."

A car pulled up by the curb. "Taxi service to Wild West High School!"

She swung around at the sound of Josh's voice, her face betraying any idea she had about playing it cool, when they next met. "Josh! What are you doing here?"

"Danielle, who are you talking to?"

"The baby," she said defiantly. Josh jumped out of the car and opened the door for her. *He just wants to make sure I get in.* She did and drank in the look of him as he walked to the driver's side and got in. "How did you know I'd be going to school today?"

"I have my sources."

"Phil?"

"My sources are confidential." His poker face slipped into a smile.

"Phil," she said and suddenly felt happy. "So much has happened."

"With me, too. We have to talk."

"What's happened with you?" she asked, watching his large gloved hand turn the key in the ignition and steer the car out of the parking space. She wanted to pull that hand from the wheel, just to hold him. He drove on.

"Let's have the baby. I want it," he said.

"Her." He looked at her, almost missed a light, braked quickly and put out his arm to keep her from jolting into the windshield.

She stopped talking, so he could concentrate on his driving. Besides, she couldn't think of a light conversational topic. She wanted to ask, *Will it work with Sharon? Do you really want the baby? Do I?* But her painful independence was making her feel alive, and she didn't want to lose that. So she didn't say anything. After a while, he said, "Let's have dinner tonight."

"This week's full."

"You're angry."

"No. How about next Wednesday? Want to try Jezebel's? It's a soul food restaurant I've heard a lot about."

"I can't. The psychologist said I have to stay home nights."

She stared at him in alarm. He stared back at her and swerved onto Tenth Avenue just in time to avoid a collision. Horns honked, and road rage had its moment. Danielle forced herself to look ahead again. "You're seeing a psychologist?"

"Alison. With Sharon."

"Of course. I forgot."

"I wish I could. She's cutting classes, coming home late." He braked to a stop in front of the school. She put her hand on the car door handle. He put his hand on her arm. "We have to talk. I'll send car service for you."

"Forget car service. I'm moving back to Brooklyn."

"Welcome home!" Josh said and slid his arm around her.

"No, no! With my aunts! I'm moving in with my aunts."

"Your aunts?" The surprise on his face was comical. She couldn't have confused him more if she'd tried.

"We have to talk," she said, stepping out of the car.

Chapter Eleven | 135

"So what are you angry at?"

"Bigots!"

"I'm not a bigot!"

"I know." She waved and walked into the building.

When she arrived, Nicole was already working in the book room. Danielle flicked dust from a stray book to read a title and sneezed. "Damn dirty book room."

"Not when we finish with it," said her colleague, drawing a diagram of the place.

She doesn't seem upset. Danielle relaxed. "What are you doing?"

"Reorganizing the room according to grades." Nicole always looked stylish, even in her old blue jeans and peach sweater. A matching scarf, folded into a triangle over her Afro was knotted at the nape of her neck. Gold wire glasses perched on her nose. She smiled at Danielle. "Do we have a list of book titles and prices?"

"We should have an old list. I'll ask Dr. Norton when he comes in and update it."

"Great…How was your Christmas?" Nicole asked, as she sketched.

"I've got news," said Danielle and instantly regretted her words. All enthusiasm about the baby, about being black, and about her engagement to Josh had lost its luster. Plus, she was feeling like her old, white liberal self again, and for the first time in days, she was relaxing.

"News?" Nicole looked up expectantly.

Just then, Dr. Norton briskly entered the book room. "Good Morning, Ladies," he said, placing a possessive hand on Danielle's shoulder. In quiet protest, she dropped the volume she held. It landed on the pile of books, causing a dusty cloud to rise up around them. Dr. Norton got a sneezing fit, pulled out a handkerchief to cover his face with one hand while he tried to dust off his suit with the other. He backed out of the room. "Give Miss Johnson instructions on how to clean and reorganize this room and meet me in my office to order books," he said, escaping down the hall.

"You sure got rid of him," Nicole said, and they shook with silent laughter. "Any instructions on reorganizing the book room?"

"Of course not. I'll send a custodian or two to help with this mess. See you later." She was almost out the door when Nicole said,

"Mc'Kin?" Danielle whirled around. "Your students think you're black."

"I know." Her stomach tightened.

"They call you Mc'Kin for My Kin. It's their secret nickname for you."

"I know." Danielle risked a smile and turned back to the door.

"What's your news?"

She turned back. "Oh. Josh and I were talking about getting married, but we're not sure yet. I'll be back," she said and escaped. She rushed into the English Department and called down for the custodians. She felt disoriented and uncomfortable with her dishonesty. As she typed a revised book list, she heard the laughter of her colleague and the two custodians, Gary and Bridgett, in the book room. Two lonely hours later, she handed the list to Dr. Norton.

"This could be the start of a new career for you," he said. You can move from Assistant Principal to Principal and then to an appointment at the Board of Education and be out of the classroom entirely."

For the first time in her career, she thought, *Maybe I will*.

At noon, she checked on Nicole and the custodians. "Hey, Ms. McKinnon," said Gary, a large, easy-going black man in his fifties.

"Happy Holidays," said Bridgett, a wiry, wrinkle-faced woman with an Irish accent.

"We're getting there," said Nicole, wiping books with a damp cloth.

"This is beginning to look like a book room again," said Danielle. Let's break for lunch."

"I'm working through lunch and not stopping until the books are cleaned, counted and stacked," Nicole said.

"I'll join you," said Danielle.

"Great. By tomorrow, we should have this room organized."

Chapter Eleven

Danielle took sandwich and coffee orders for their little crew and called the delicatessen. Everyone wanted the deli's special, hot corned beef sandwiches and coffee. "Be back in fifteen minutes."

"I'll join you," said Nicole. The two women got their jackets from their classrooms and met at the front door. They walked silently through the cool, crisp air to the store. Danielle bought four sandwiches. "Isn't Dr. Norton eating?" Nicole asked.

"He's having lunch out with some of the other department heads."

"He should have invited you."

"He did, but I told him we had too much work to do."

On the walk back, Nicole said, "Tamika was so disappointed. She was sure you were black."

Danielle shrugged. "Can't be what I'm not."

"They need black role models."

She nearly told Nicole the truth, but her heart was closing like the door, behind which she could only hide and peek, like her aunt hid and peeked behind the living room curtains of her protective Tudor home. She smiled at Nicole. "They've got you for a role model, and it doesn't come any better than that."

"I thought you were black, too."

"Most black people do," Danielle said and thought, *We can never be friends now. Real friends.* Her heart hadn't hardened enough not to feel the pain of that.

"You know, you could submit date and place of birth on yourself, your parents and your grandparents to the Schomburg Library. Just in case. They have a computerized ancestry search dating back to Africa." Nicole's gaze seemed to burn into her.

Looking ahead, she said, "That would be a great project for my students!"

"It would."

For the rest of the afternoon, while Danielle and Nicole wiped dust off books with damp cloths, stacked and counted them, Bridgett and Gary washed and polished floors, swept away cobwebs and wiped down bookracks and walls.

At three o'clock, Bridgett dropped her mop and said in her strident brogue, "Tamarra, we'll need to get some help to take down the glass globes from the chandelier, change the bulbs and polish the brass chains." Danielle nodded. "You two slaves can work y'rselves t'death here, but I'm leavin'. C'mon, Gary. Y'r wife wants you home for Qwanza."

"You've done more than your share," Danielle told Bridgett and Gary, as she left the building with them to buy another round of coffee for Nicole and herself. The "slaves" worked until the last book was wiped clean, stacked and counted. "Tomorrow, I'll submit the book order," said Danielle.

"I'll estimate shelf space and label the areas," said Nicole. "Then we can put the books back on the shelves."

"And leave by noon, at the latest."

"Good work, ladies!" The two women turned to see Dr. Norton, happily inebriated from lunch with his colleagues. "Ms. McKinnon, meet me in my office tomorrow morning, and I'll show you how to issue directions for the end-term exams and the Regents." Danielle pictured him handing her the same old sheets with the same old directions to prepare the students for the exams, and she heard him making the same aggravating comment about how "nothing ever seems to improve our students' scores."

She turned to Nicole. "Perhaps Ms. Johnson will join us?"

"Sure she can. I'll see you tomorrow," said Dr. Norton, not noticing that Danielle had asked Nicole, not him.

It was after dark, when the two colleagues finally left the school, pulling their coats protectively around themselves. Danielle muttered, "How do you *really* prepare the students for those exams?"

"Beside giving them a good education from the first day they enter school?" asked Nicole. The teachers exchanged a wry smile. "Do you want to have dinner and brainstorm *now*, before we meet Nort?"

Danielle's hands flew up, and she feigned shock. "Nort? Where's your respect?"

"Wherever his respect is when he calls me Miss and you Ms."

"Touché," Danielle laughed.

Chapter Eleven

The aroma of charcoal-broiled hamburgers greeted them as they crossed the street to a dimly lit nineteenth century restaurant the faculty nicknamed the Teachers' Tavern. They stepped over the threshold into a dark wooden interior and passed through a long bar with shining brass cash registers ringing up purchases. As they entered the dining room, they glimpsed an opening in the wall to the kitchen, where steak and hamburger juices dripped from racks and sizzled in the fire.

Nicole found a table in a secluded, well-lit corner. They hung their coats on hooks, settled in and ordered glasses of wine. "We'll need to work on the students' self-esteem as well as their skills," she said.

"We may need after school hours. How do we get Nort to agree to that?" asked Danielle.

"I don't think he'll be a problem. The willing members of the English Department will do the work. When the students' scores improve, he'll look good."

"And for the students whose grades don't improve?"

"We'll debrief them on an individual basis, have another dinner here and keep on planning."

The wine arrived and Danielle toasted Nicole's plan. They ordered charcoal burgers with sautéed onions, salads and hand-cut potato fries, then brainstormed ideas for revamping the four-year English curriculum to prepare their students, not only for those final tests, but to inspire a passion for literature within them. "We'll challenge the students with the great questions – Who am I? Why am I here? – and begin the great quest for self, while honing their reading, writing and speech arts skills," said Danielle. The women were deep into their plans when the burgers arrived. They bit through warm crusty rolls into juicy burgers, and all talking stopped for a time. Then it started again, at a slower pace, and thinking shared delicious space with eating. Suspended in time, Danielle and Nicole enjoyed each other as professionals. They finished with mugs of dark roast coffee and headed home.

The next morning's work flew by. In high spirits, Danielle, Nicole, Bridgett and Gary took leave of one another at eleven o'clock and hurried from Tenth Avenue and Forty-seventh street in different directions.

Danielle walked toward Rockefeller Center because she had no place to go. She wasn't welcome in her parents' home, Phil was working, and she hadn't yet moved in with her aunts. *Why didn't I make time to see Josh? To talk.*

She paused at the corner of Fiftieth Street and Fifth Avenue and glanced uptown at Saint Patrick's Cathedral a couple of blocks away. She stood there in her quilted lavender coat, jeans and boots and remembered a cool autumn evening in the sixties, when she'd worn an elegant, long old-fashioned-style coat which covered her mini-skirt. She had congregated with a hundred other New Yorkers on the cathedral's steps to protest the Vietnam War. Each held a candle flickering in the darkness. For a moment, she felt what it was like to be twenty-five again, gathering with strangers in passionate protest. *What had changed?*

She heard the melody of "Have Yourself a Merry Little Christmas" coming from the skating rink in Rockefeller Center and turned to see the giant Christmas tree rising up from the ice-skating rink below street level. *What are my chances of getting a seat at a restaurant with a view of the rink? Not good.* She walked the angel-flanked corridor anyway to where lines of people, four and five deep, looked down upon the skaters and took a small elevator to a restaurant below.

Call it a Christmas miracle, but Danielle entered the crowded restaurant just as a single person was leaving a small table with a view of the skaters. She ordered roast turkey with all the trimmings. Slipping out of her coat, she looked up at the scores of people freezing and looking down at the skaters and diners, and suddenly she remembered a day in 1950, when her parents, too poor to eat at the restaurant where she now sat, were part of that crowd up there. Eight-year old Danielle, her mittened hand secure in her father's big gloved one, looked down through a barred fence at the skaters. She and her pretty young mother held Phil's hands. Later they would have soup and sandwiches at the automat. *We were so happy.*

Chapter Eleven

The waiter placed the meal before her. Fragrant gravy covered sliced turkey and dribbled into crevices of mashed potatoes and stuffing. She combined cranberry sauce with gravy and mashed potatoes onto her fork. The taste momentarily distracted her from the pain of remembering that happy time. Strains of "I Heard the Bells on Christmas Day" accompanied the skaters, and she watched the facile and the occasionally clumsy in colorful jackets, scarves and leggings. One girl went into a spin, lost her balance and fell. Two other skaters pulled her to her feet and guided her to the railing.

Danielle herself, just three years before, had lost her balance in that rink; she'd gone into an impromptu dance trying to get her balance and was caught in the strong arms of her interesting new date, Joshua Freedman. Danielle and Josh, with a married couple, laughed a lot that day. The couple was divorced now. She looked away, pulled a copy of Jane Austen's *Sense and Sensibility* from her bag, stared at blurred print through tear-stained eyes, and barely tasted her meal.

When the little elevator returned to the street level, she decided she'd seen enough happy people shopping, lunching and meeting friends. Near the silver-white windows of Saks department store, she hailed a cab for Gramercy Park. It continued downtown to Forty-Second Street, past the magnificent statues of lions guarding each side of the marble staircase leading up to the Mid-town Library, to lines of people filing past Lord and Taylor's window displays with Christmas scenes of old-fashioned stores and moving mannequins in old-fashioned dress. Soon, the cab turned east into the twenties and dropped her off in Gramercy Park.

She entered her apartment. Phil had left. She threw off her coat and kicked off her boots. Emotionally depleted, she lay on her bed and slept.

She dreamed the doorbell rang, and she cowered behind the front door, staring at the drawing of the Native American on horseback that now hung on the inside of the door, and she wondered how it had gotten out of her father's house. Her fear grew. The doorbell rang again. Her eyes flew open. The clock said 3:20. *I've been asleep only fifteen minutes!*

On the third ring, she realized it was the phone, and she reached for it. "Hello?" She could barely speak.

"What's wrong?"

"Josh! Oh, nothing." She sat up. "I was sleeping. I've just spent two days cleaning a filthy book room." Her mind raced. *I'm not meeting him at his place for dinner. I haven't decided about the Little One.* "It's good to hear your voice."

"I have a New Year's gift for you. Will you accept it?"

"What is it?" She smiled.

"Tonight and Saturday night at a lodge in Vermont."

"Oh!"

"Sharon is staying with my parents."

"Oh!" Her exhaustion was rising like heat in a cold room. "Josh, what we really need to do is talk."

"Right! We need to talk without anyone or anything interrupting us, and the Vermont Inn is the perfect place!"

"That's true." Somehow it seemed logical.

"Is an hour enough time for you to get ready?"

"I think so," she said, checking her hair in the mirror.

"I'll be at your place at four-twenty," he said and hung up.

As she replaced the receiver, she saw the answering machine's red light blink five times. *Has he been calling all day?* She tore into the bathroom, shampooed and showered. Quickly she applied light eye shadow and lipstick. *It's not logical to go to a lodge to talk.* Too late. She was already grinning at herself in the mirror.

Dressed and packed, she was writing a quick note to her brother to let him know she'd be out of town with Josh for the week-end, when the buzzer sounded. *Why doesn't he just let himself in? He's got a key.* But she knew why and loved him for honoring her decision to separate. She buzzed him up.

She was rushing into her jacket, scarf and boots, when the doorbell rang. She reached for the doorknob, checked the peephole in the door and saw a tiny Josh standing in the hallway looking distorted and far-away in the little round lens, but when she opened the door, he loomed larger than life and she could feel him even before he drew her to his chest and kissed her. When she reluctantly slid her hands back down from his neck, he picked up her overnight bag. "Come," he said in a hoarse voice. He pushed the elevator button, while Danielle double-locked and alarmed the door. The elevator arrived, and they were on their way.

Chapter Twelve

They were silent, at first, leaving the city, occasionally glancing at one another, content with the novelty of just being alone together. As the white landscape became a darkening wintery retreat from the world and fir trees mingled with bare black maples, she had to resist the urge to entwine her fingers with his. He was driving. Instead, she said, "We have the whole week-end... What a gift."

He took a hand from the steering wheel for a second to run his forefinger down her cheek. "How did your internship go?"

She chuckled and told him about her two days of stepping into Dr. Norton's shoes, of conspiring with Nicole at the tavern to improve the curriculum, and of Nicole's giving him the nickname, Nort.

He laughed. "You'll be a big improvement over Nort because you'll put the students' needs first."

"I hope so, but I think my biggest talent will be as delegator. Nicole is organized, has great ideas and knows how to motivate the students."

"So do you! – Have great ideas and know how to motivate the students, that is."

She laughed, and the car purred along the quiet country road. The trees were slipping into the darkness now, and she pulled her jacket collar and scarf closer around her neck. "Nicole tried to find out if I'm black."

"Tried?"

"I wasn't sure I wanted to tell her, so I lied."

Josh glanced at her. "You lied?"

"Why are *you* so surprised? *You* lied to Andrew Davis."

"True, but I need to make a living. Why did you?"

She looked at the black windshield and saw the dusty book room there and heard Nicole say, "*Mc'Kin?*"

"Why? I guess because I feel so vulnerable. Maybe you were right. I don't have to tell the whole world."

"Can you live that way?"

"I don't know." *Why is he so uncooperative?* "Can you?"

"I don't know," he said quietly. "I don't want to fight, Danielle."

"Me either. But I'm glad you brought it up. Really."

He squeezed her hand and they drove on in silence for a while. Then Danielle said quietly, "How's it going with Sharon?"

Josh sighed. "Not good. I'm worried about the trouble she might get into." He looked quickly at her and back to the road. Danielle's stomach clenched so hard she thought she'd cut off the Little One's blood supply before realizing it probably didn't have one yet. She leaned back anyway, stretched out her legs, took long deep breaths and waited for Josh to continue. "In therapy, she told Alison I blame *her* for your moving out. She said I don't want her around, that she only feels wanted when she's with her friends."

Danielle concentrated on deep, even breathing. "What did you tell her?"

"That I want her! That my relationship with you is my responsibility, not hers!" On the dark screen of the windshield, Danielle now saw the green and beige chairs in Alison's office, heard Sharon's accusing voice and Josh's controlled anger. "Alison suggested I stay home every night until she starts coming home on time and improves in school."

"How long would that be?"

"Could be months. More."

"Did she say your folks could stand in for you this week-end?"

"Yes."

"Your parents are a God-send, but you'll need breaks." He said nothing, and she clamped her teeth down on all of her usual knee-jerk rescue suggestions like, *Maybe I could join another one of your sessions with Alison – or – Should I try my relationship with her again? Invite her on an outing? Just the two of us?*

Josh glanced at her. "I want my relationship with you!"

She concentrated on snowflakes beginning to fall through the car's headlights. "And I want mine with you." *But I won't offer myself as a sacrificial lamb again. They have to help themselves.*

Josh took her hand in his and held it. The country road was nearly empty. She saw a wooden arch over a sign, and read it aloud, "The Vermont Country Inn." He took back his hand, slowed down and turned left across the road. Ice crunched beneath the tires, as they drove under the arch onto a narrow clearing flanked by high snow banks. The headlights lit up the deep dark road. Danielle sat forward and looked up through the windshield. "Stars! You can see stars."

He looked up and braked. "Amazing." He looked at her. "I made dinner reservations for six o'clock at a restaurant just outside the inn. This whole place is set up like a Winter Wonderland with little shops, restaurants, sleigh rides and snow sports…" His eyes met hers. "Danielle, let's leave all talk about Sharon and the Little One here in the clearing. We can pick it up on the way out. Unless, of course, one of us has an epiphany."

"Let's," she said and relaxed.

He too appeared to breathe more easily. "We have just enough time to check in and get to the restaurant."

The inn itself was a wood frame colonial. They checked in and carried their overnight bags up one flight of creaking wooden stairs to their room and put down their bags. It was pitch dark except for a yellow glow from an old-fashioned street lamp outside their window. Danielle looked into Josh's eyes, vulnerable under dark eyebrows and eyelashes, wet with the melting snow, and she was caught there. As their clothes fell away, the soft blue and green colors of the colonial wallpaper seemed to wrap around them. Urgently, he lifted her onto the bed, bumping her head against the headboard of the four-poster. "Sorry," he murmured, and the skin on her neck tingled from his warm breath. He kissed her cold breasts and erect nipples, and she felt grateful. So grateful.

"Are my hands still cold?" she asked, hoping not to break the spell by stroking icy fingers down his back over his tender parts.

"A little." Gently, he pulled the soft comforter over their heads, and Danielle inhaled the sweet, masculine smell of him. Shivering bodies heated as they kissed and caressed in new and remembered ways and melted into each other. If sex is a portal, then she traveled through its tingling, fragrant space with him to a place under those covers where her body and mind broke free and found peace. Wondering if he felt the same way, she pulled the comforter under their chins to see his face. They gazed into each other's eyes and slipped into a short, deep sleep.

They awoke refreshed and lay there for a few minutes. "Hungry?" Josh asked.

"Yes," she said, surprised it was true. Josh called the restaurant and made a new reservation for eight-thirty. They freshened up, dressed quickly in their discarded jeans and sweaters, pulled on boots, buttoned up their jackets, wrapped scarves around their necks and raced down one flight of stairs to the lobby. In the hurry, Danielle slipped on the icy threshold.

"Careful. Rushing in. Rushing out. Must be from New York," drawled a Vermonter, shoveling snow from the steps. "You'll calm down pretty soon."

"A week-end may not be enough time," said Josh.

"Ayup. You may have to come back." He brushed snow from a red sleigh, drawn by a muscular brown horse with half-closed eyes.

"Want to ride over there?" Josh asked Danielle.

She looked down a snowy incline the length of a short city block to a wood frame building with a sign that said Farm House Restaurant. Along the path, lights twinkled in windows of old-fashioned stores. "Let's walk. I feel invigorated, and that horse looks bushed." They walked and slid along the pine-scented lane toward the restaurant. "Oh! Look at that!" she said. Like children, they stopped and stared into a store window showcasing an array of cheese and crackers. Gourmet delights beckoned from within.

"We'll catch it later. If we miss this reservation, we miss dinner," said Josh, pulling her along and then slowing his pace to peer into a leather goods store. The shops, selling jewelry, unique household gifts, clothing, toys, artwork and sports equipment were interspersed with decorated trees and moving mannequins in nineteenth century garb.

"It's like we've just entered a Lord & Taylor window display!" she said. A mannequin with pearl earrings and long-lashed brown eyes blinked, turned to the tune of Winter Wonderland and gestured to a window displaying earrings and necklaces in old jewelry boxes. A pair of dangling garnet earrings on gold chains caught Danielle's eye. "Oh, look! That would look great on – Oops!" Fortunately she slipped on the ice before slipping up on her promise to leave talk of Sharon and the Little One in the clearing. "Good thing I didn't wear my designer boots."

"I've never seen you in your designer boots."

"And you never will. I bought them on impulse, and never wore them – until I visited my aunts this week."

They reached the restaurant, stamped snow off their boots and entered the lobby of what looked like someone's country home. Danielle admired a balsam tree decorated with strings of cranberry, popcorn and tiny white lights, while Josh apologized to their host for missing their earlier reservation.

They sat at a table for two near a window in a lively dining room, and opened menus.

"Spiced pumpkin soup," Danielle said reverently. They ordered two bowls and complete prime rib dinners, one with a well-done end cut for Josh.

"So, tell me about your aunts," he said.

"Well, they're nice, not really weird. Aunt Tessie is in communication with the family ghosts, namely New York Nana and Uncle Robert. Aunt Charlotte thinks Tessie's getting senile. I'm not sure Charlotte's right, though."

"Why?"

"I thought I saw Uncle Robert or some smiling male ghost, and–

"Wait a minute. Why do you call your grandmother New York Nana and what did you see?

"Phil and I were taught to call Dad's parents New York Nana and Grandpa and Mom's parents Holyoke Nana and Grandpa. They were named for where they lived. I don't know why. It's less personal than Grandma Bess and Grandpa Aaron, isn't it?"

"Maybe that's the idea," said Josh.

"I never thought of that. It makes sense. Now." The pumpkin soup arrived. "Mmm. Miso's in it," she said.

"Tell me about the ghost you saw."

"Well, it was just for a second, but, as I walked from the coat room, where New York Nana's and Uncle Robert's ashes are boxed and stored… That sounds weird too, doesn't it?" Josh shrugged his eyebrows and she continued. "I thought I saw the face of a man, by the mantle clock, smile at me."

"Just the face?"

"I think so. I wasn't expecting him. It was only for a moment, and then he was gone. I was too shocked to look him over."

"Did Phil see him, too?"

"No." She saw Josh trying to maintain a neutral face.

"Are you having second thoughts about me?" she asked.

"You mean, do I think you're weird?" She nodded. "No. Unique."

She grinned. "Unique. I can live with that."

"What's Charlotte like?"

"Well, she's very angry at Dad, discredits Mom and advises me to pass for white so I won't get paranoid like I did with you, saying you were prejudiced because you called me stupid and because you didn't….."

"Hire that black guy?"

Danielle nodded and watched Josh stare down into his soup. "Your business is too new and fragile for you to take risks. Right?"

He nodded without looking up.

"Well, you're not going to have it much longer anyway. Listen, I'm not as cocksure about how to handle these things, as I was last week. That's also why I want to live with my aunts. I want to understand this family. My parents too. I'd want that even if I weren't writing about them."

Josh looked up at her. "Can't you do all that, living a few blocks away from them with me? Then, at least, you can take breaks."

Breaks! Living with you and Sharon! They looked at one another, through the elephant in the room that was sitting between their soup bowls. She banished it to the clearing. The waiter replaced their empty soup bowls with crispy green salads dressed in vinaigrette and quietly moved on.

Danielle and Josh played throughout the weekend. They started with a late brunch in the breakfast room of the inn. Josh ordered a cheese omelet, Danielle ordered pumpkin pancakes with bacon, and they shared. Then, they rushed outside to go cross-country skiing and came back snow-caked and wet, but enthusiastic about skiing. Drying and warming by the inn's fireplace, they drank hot chocolate from huge saucers and talked and laughed with other week-enders in the comfortably crowded room.

In the late afternoon, they returned to their room and snuggled under the covers. Later, Danielle showered and dressed for dinner in the purple knit dress, the same one she wore to meet her aunts, because Josh liked it on her. They joined some of the cross-country skiers for dinner in the large, lively dining room of the Farmhouse Restaurant, and returned early to the inn for one more night of love.

After Sunday brunch, dressed in fresh jeans and sweaters, they poked through the stores, looking to take something of the weekend back with them. Danielle bought balsam-scented sachets for the bureau drawers she would enjoy now in her grandmother's bedroom, a magenta silk scarf for Charlotte and a lavender one for Tessie. She bought Phil a large brick of Vermont cheese and English biscuits. For Josh, she selected a pair of soft, dark brown leather gloves. She found the dangling garnet earrings and bought them for Sharon, while Josh was busy selecting a winter white and lavender ski suit for her to try on. When she emerged from the dressing room to show off a stunning fit, he presented her with a pair of Amethyst drop earrings to wear with her purple knit dress or her jeans. Finally, with no other excuse to stay, they packed their bags and ate an early dinner.

It was dusk, when Danielle stroked the nose of the sturdy brown sleigh horse whose name she learned was Daisy, and Josh told the old Vermonter who worked there, "This is a great place. We'll be back."

Chapter Twelve | 151

Then, having run out of reasons to tarry, Danielle and Josh got into his car and departed. They left talk about Sharon and the Little One in the clearing for a while longer, as they drove through. Conversation bubbled, as they reviewed their weekend, and it didn't fizzle out until they could think of absolutely nothing else to say.

When they stopped for gas, Danielle took a pair of sparkling garnet earrings dangling on golden chains from a little box in her bag and held them up for Josh to see. "These are for Sharon. Will you give them to her from me tonight?"

"Why don't you give them to her yourself?"

"I don't know when I'll see her again, and I want this to feel like a gift, not a bribe. When we do meet, it's myself I'll be offering."

"They're beautiful. I'll give them to her tonight."

She put the glittering earrings back into their little box and carefully placed it in the glove compartment. Josh paid the attendant, and they followed the signs to New York. "Any ideas for what to do about... our challenge?" she asked.

"You could move in with me and that would be that."

Her stomach tightened. "Shouldn't you and Sharon work on your relationship first, as Alison suggested? At least get a start?"

"Probably."

"And I'll decide what I'm going to do about the pregnancy."

"Have the baby, if you want it." What Danielle heard was, *I don't want this inconvenience, but I'll go along with it as a favor to you.*

From a place of deep hurt, she asked, "Do you want it?"

"If things were different...." His voice petered out.

"But they're not." *Unless you get rid of that fetus.*

The drive back seemed interminable, until Josh said, "Tell me about Holyoke Nana."

"Why bring her up? To pass the time?"

"Yep."

"Well, you hit upon a real diversion!"

"Divert me."

"Okay. Once upon a time in the early nineteen hundreds, Holyoke

Nana and Grandpa lived way out in the mean wild woods of Massachusetts, not many miles from all the Ivy League Colleges in the Amherst area. They beat my mother and her brother regularly. Mom ran away when she was seventeen, waited on tables, met Dad and married him."

"Good move."

"It didn't seem that way at the time. Marrying a Negro, as they were called in 1939, was dangerous, even if it was legal. But, in Dad's case it wasn't legal because his home state was in South Carolina, and there was a law there, preventing him from intermarrying.

"I didn't know that. I just thought it would get you socially ostracized."

"Well, you could go to jail for it… Remember that old saying, "I'm free, white and twenty-one?"

"I'd forgotten that one. Did Holyoke Nana have any redeeming qualities?"

"Yes! She was white." Josh shook his head at the irony, and she continued. "New York Nana and Grandpa were honest — except for lying about their color — kind, hard-working and educated. But Holyoke Nana was white!"

"And legal… Free, white and twenty-one," he mused.

"By the way, I had lunch with my mother this week." She told him about the Ku Klux Klan meeting to which her grandfather had taken her Mom, when she was twelve, in the backwoods of that hometown.

"The Ku Klux Klan operating up north? You're real good at diverting. It's amazing your mother turned out so well."

"That apple fell nowhere near *that* tree. My mother never abused us or taught us bigotry. She and Dad brought us up to have values and the character to act on them." *Am I doing that now?* She ignored the question and said, "Sharon's not a bad apple either."

"I know. She's felt hurt and angry since the divorce," said Josh.

"I've been hurt and angry since my father kicked me out of the house." They drove on in silence. When Josh pulled up in front of her apartment building, he left the motor running to carry her suitcase and to walk her into the lobby. "I hope I didn't freak you out with my sto-

Chapter Twelve

ries," she said, and would have said more, but he was kissing her. They held each other closely.

"I'll call you," he said and pulled away.

"Remember the earrings," she said quickly.

"I will," he said.

And it was over. The elevator lifted her up to her apartment away from Josh and the life she wanted with him. Alone there, she remembered Sharon's and Josh's words before his daughter ran from the apartment into the night, the night Danielle left him.

Whadya want? I don't have a mother! I don't have a father!

I'm your father!

Until that baby comes!

"I'm still Sharon's victim," she said into the empty elevator and hit the wall with her fist. "I want to be living with Josh, not moving in with my aunts. She's wrecking my life and I can't do a thing about it."

In her dream that night, Danielle floated in pitch-black outer space between a half-moon and a star trying to get a hold of one or the other. She lunged at the half moon, missed and toppled screaming into the darkness. Out in the void, she heard banging. Her flailing arms hit what felt like a tree branch. She grabbed it, and it bit into her hands. She looked up to see she was dangling from a garnet studded moonbeam. All alone. In the distance, a dark pregnant woman and a very, very ugly old white lady with stringy, silver hair were smiling and sitting on moonbeams. They waved. She tried to call to them for help, but could only moan. The banging began again!

"Danielle! Are you okay?"

She opened her eyes. "Phil?" she croaked. He was knocking on the door.

"Are you okay, Danielle?" The mattress felt solid beneath her.

"I had a nightmare. I'm fine."

"Are you sure?"

"I'm sure. Sorry I woke you."

"That's okay."

Her nails were digging into her palms. Her hands shook as she switched on the light, grasped her pencil and picked up her dream journal. She suspected the exaggerated images of Charlotte and Tessie sitting on moonbeams represented parts of herself. *Just like the old maids in that card game I played when I was ten.*

"Old maid," she said out loud, ran to the bathroom, switched on the light and stared into the mirror. "You don't look like an old maid, but you are one," she told her reflection. The alarm clock sounded. *School!* She thought of her students with an uncharacteristic anger. *They won't want to work after vacation, and I don't want to deal with their attitudes!* Her stomach heaved. She dropped to her knees over the toilet bowl and vomited.

Chapter Thirteen

An angry old maid stomped into the high school an hour early with two containers of black coffee and a croissant. She checked in, picked up her mail, hung her coat in her classroom closet and slammed the door, before she remembered the book room. Grabbing a coffee, she sped down the hall, unlocked the door and entered into its darkness. The smell of newly waxed floors transported her back to her own school days in New England with clean rooms and an excellent public education. Blindly she reached up into the air, felt a dangling chain, grabbed it and pulled. Light sparkled from clean glass globes hanging from gleaming brass chains, and shone upon racks of clean books organized by grades and titles. She sipped the fragrant coffee and, for a moment, forgot her anger.

"What a difference we made." The old maid turned at the sound of Nicole's voice. Her colleague stood at the threshold, her rose-colored wire glasses perched prettily on her nose. But the first thing Danielle saw was the cinnamon color of her skin.

Together, the two women walked the aisles of the small book room, admiring their work. "It seems like we've been gone a lot longer than two days," said Danielle. They lingered for a moment in the doorway. The sparkling chandelier reflected in Nicole's fashionable glasses. For a fleeting moment, Danielle felt an urge to say, *I just found out I'm part black*, then thought, *Why expose myself this way? Charlotte and Tessie may be right.*

Nicole tilted her head and raised her eyebrows slightly, as if to ask, "You have something to say?"

"See you at lunch?" asked Danielle. Nicole smiled, nodded and walked toward the English Office.

Danielle returned to her room. Suddenly, the world seemed flat and gray. All the desk-chairs had been pushed to the sides of the empty room to let the wax dry on the floor. The angry old maid threw her empty coffee container into a wastebasket and pushed the desk-chairs roughly into a double semi-circle. She sat at her desk, bit into an almond croissant, her favorite pastry. It tasted too sweet and the second coffee tasted like the paper cup. She scanned the weekly calendar and saw that Dr. Norton would announce her upcoming appointment as head of the English Department at the Wednesday meeting. *I'll be Queen of the Old Maids.* The nightmare was still with her. *My whole life is suspended in space because of Sharon.* She grabbed a piece of chalk and assaulted the blackboard:

Date: January 5, 1982

Aim: To introduce a quotation from one of the transcendentalists.

Do Now: Review your one-minute speeches. We'll begin in three minutes.

She'd been enthused about easing her students into the language and philosophy of the nineteenth century transcendentalists. Now it seemed like a chore.

"Morning!" Mr. Spatz stepped into her room and read the Do Now. He was casually but appropriately dressed in a brown suit, open jacket and red tie, and she began to relax. There was something reassuring about Aaron Spatz's presence. The students seemed to feel it too. "Looks like we have another opportunity to combine the literature and history of the Civil War. Will your students be willing to perform again?"

"I'm sure they will."

"Great. See you later." He returned to his classroom across the hall. The school bell blasted. She threw the croissant in the wastebasket and put the unfinished coffee in a desk drawer. The memory of hanging in space by herself from a gift she offered Sharon made all young people suspect this morning. *Selfish, self-absorbed teenagers!*

"Morning, Ms. McKinnon," said Tamika.

Danielle noticed the girl's new book bag was a copy of her own. *Why is she always role modeling me?* She was more aware of the blue highlights in the girl's black complexion than in Tamika herself this morning. *Why not role model Nicole?* She returned the girl's open smile with a forced one.

Kamara danced in singing his version of Black English. "We be fam-i-ly! Hi Teach!"

Where does he get off always acting so familiar? "Good Morning. We're speaking Standard American English this term," said the old maid with a thin smile.

"Quotin' ole white folk who have nothin' to do wid us?" asked Kamara.

"Nothing to do with you? That's bigotry!" she said coldly and saw surprise and confusion transform his face. *Well, he'd better grow up!* "Ralph Waldo Emerson spoke out against slavery," she said. "Henry David Thoreau and Louisa May Alcott were part of the underground railroad."

"That was brave," said Tamika.

"My bad," said Kamara.

Danielle heard her voice hardening, as if it belonged to someone else. "They rose above the common prejudice of the day for justice!"

"Okay, okay." Kamara opened his notebook and copied the Do Now.

The rest of the class arrived. *Self-involved teenagers!* She saw them size her up and quietly take their seats while she ranted on without even greeting them. She softened her voice, but the split between her words and her heart was still there. "Thoreau wrote an essay on non-violent protesting which inspired Gandhi to lead a non-violent protest which, in turn, inspired Martin Luther King."

"I didn't know. I like them. I do," said Kamara.

Danielle ignored him. She knew he didn't know, and she'd wanted to share this great history with her students, not to use these facts to whip them for their ignorance. In high school, she hadn't known either, until someone taught her. But Danielle wasn't a teacher that day. She picked up a piece of chalk. "They were Transcendentalists. Take this down." The only sounds in the room were of fluttering papers, of book bags snapping and unsnapping and of Danielle's angry chalk hitting the blackboard. "Trans means across or beyond. To transcend means to go beyond the range or grasp of human experience, reason or belief."

"Like a religious experience?" asked Tamika.

"Sometimes. Or like some other true knowing that comes from deep within when, for instance, you're out in nature."

"What if it's a false knowing, like prejudice," asked Marisa.

"That's Decendentalism," said Kamara. The students laughed, and the old maid let Danielle speak.

"I think you've coined a new word."

"Give me credit!" He pointed to her marking book, and that grated on her nerves.

"Let's hear from the transcendentalists," she said, ignoring him. "Take three minutes to practice your speeches with one another. When I call time, choose your own order, and we'll begin." She took a seat in the back row and concentrated on the minute hand of her watch, while her students paired up and rehearsed their speeches. "Time!"

The old maid looked up to see Tamika take stage, exhale deeply and shake out her hands to relax. Her cornrows, laced with little blue beads, complemented her denim dress and her blue and white sneakers. *She's copied my dress too!* But as she watched the girl compose her nerves, she thought, Tamika's so authentic. Danielle gave her an encouraging smile and waited for her to begin.

"A foolish consistency is the hobgoblin of little minds, adored by little statesmen and philosophers and divines. Ralph Waldo Emerson," said Tamika. "Whenever a teacher pigeonholes a student, that teacher blocks a student's growth."

"You can say that again," said Louis.

Tamika continued, "For instance, the school rules say you need two years of English to improve your grammar before taking a creative writing elective. But a tenth grader I once knew was just as good at grammar as most seniors. She wanted to take creative writing and Ms. McKinnon broke the foolish consistency of the school rules and let her take the course."

"Who was that?" asked Louis.

"Me," said Tamika. The students applauded as she took her seat.

They smiled at Danielle. The old maid, remembering all the trouble she'd had bucking the authorities on that one, ignored them, as she penned a ninety-five by Tamika's name.

She looked up to see Chang standing studiously in his horn-rimmed glasses, patiently waiting for his classmates to settle down. "Quiet! Let my man speak!" said Kamara. And there was quiet.

"Make your living by loving. Henry David Thoreau. If you make your money by doing something you love to do, and you love law and become a lawyer, you could make a lot of money. If you love to teach, you will earn a good living, but you'll never be rich. And if you love to play the bass like I do, you may not always have a gig, and you may have to get a job to survive while you do what you love. H.D. Thoreau loved to write, but he had to get a job as a surveyor to pay his bills. Playing bass makes me happy. Like Thoreau, I will earn money where I can and continue to march to the beat of a different drummer. My own."

Applause. Kamara raised his arm and they high-fived. "Two quotes! You aced it, man." Danielle forgot why she was angry.

Erika Schmidt stood and walked quickly to the front of the room, as if to get the assignment over with as quickly as possible. Danielle was ready with an encouraging smile, but Erika didn't look at her. A short utilitarian hair cut framed her unhealthy-looking light brown complexion. Unlike other students of Puerto-Rican descent in the class, she seemed tense and guarded in her white starched blouse and straight brown skirt. The diamond star, or whatever it was at her neck, looked too rich for her outfit.

Doesn't that girl ever relax? "Take a deep breath or two, if you want, and begin when you're ready." Danielle smiled, but a veil had dropped over Erika's eyes, and Danielle's eyes moved back to the doo-dad around her neck that now looked more like a letter. She leaned forward and squinted … and couldn't believe her eyes.

"Trust thyself. Every heart vibrates to that iron string. Ralph Waldo Emerson," said Erika. "What a stupid statement. How can I trust myself? I'm only sixteen and my father tells me what to do."

"Erika, what's that around your neck?"

"A necklace," she said in a tone that said it's none of your business.

Danielle stood and walked to the first row. The students looked too. She approached Erika and stood a few feet from her, just to be certain. "It's a swastika!"

"It's a fashion statement," Erika said.

"A fashion statement? You can't wear that in a free country!" Danielle was yelling.

"If this is a free country, I can wear it." Erika was not yelling.

Danielle had meant to reason with her, but her righteous anger caught fire with her old maid's ire, and she grabbed the girl's arm. Erika swatted her hand away. "Let go of me!" Behind Danielle, large, gentle hands, she knew belonged to Kamara, took hold of her arms and backed her away from the girl. She saw Louis move between herself and Erika.

"I'm reporting you!" said Erika.

"I'm writing you up!" Danielle said, pulled away from Kamara, marched to her desk, grabbed a referral from the drawer and wrote, with a shaking hand, words that incriminated her more than it did her student. She was aware of stillness in the room. She looked up and saw that Erika had returned to her seat. *I could lose my job.* She tore up the referral and started again, as if a rewrite could change what just happened.

As she wrote, she heard Tamika gently ask, "Why are you wearing a swastika?"

"My father gave it to me."

She said her father gave her the swastika, Danielle wrote.

"Is your father Puerto Rican?" asked Marisa

"My mother... It doesn't mean anything," said Erika, referring to the swastika.

"But won't you offend the Jews?" asked Tamika.

Danielle looked up. Erika's face was still expressionless, but she was opening up to Tamika. Danielle waited like a spider for Erika's words to get caught in the web Tamika was unwittingly weaving. "They don't care. They come up to me on the street and ask me about it."

"They want to know how you think," said Kamara.

Chapter Thirteen | 161

"It's just a fashion statement, repeated Erika. "They weren't upset."

Danielle pictured a couple of elderly Jewish women, whose coat sleeves covered arms once branded in a Nazi concentration camp, now standing on a street in Manhattan, asking Erika why she wears a swastika. She was about to verbally whip the girl with that image, when Kamara took stage, struck a tone somewhere between a serious lecturer and a comedian and said, "If someone walked into my neighborhood wearing a KKK tee shirt and said it was a fashion statement, we wouldn't ask him what he thought. We'd show him how we felt!" Danielle put down her pen.

Louis Rodriguez faced Erika. "You better believe it."

Erica looked tense. "You know it says hate. Right?" Jamal asked quietly, looking up from a sketch he was drawing of her.

Danielle remembered she was a teacher. She pocketed the referral and joined them. "Erika, I apologize for grabbing your arm. You're right about this being a free country." The girl looked away from her and said nothing. She continued, "I'm pregnant with a child who'll be half Jewish and part b—" She saw surprised smiles and heard muted exclamations. "Will my child be safe with you?" No answer. "Will she?"

Erika headed for the door and opened it. Danielle rushed in front of her and barred the way. "Move!" said Erika.

"The class isn't over, and you didn't answer my question, Danielle said, her voice rising again.

The door across the hall opened and Mr. Spatz walked quickly to them. "Is everything all right, Ms. McKinnon?" Danielle pulled the referral from her pocket and handed it to him. The class held its collective breath, while Mr. Aaron Spatz read the referral. He looked at Danielle. "May I?"

Take one giant step and clobber her? Danielle nodded.

He looked at the girl and spoke evenly. "You have a choice, Erika. Come to my room for a series of discussions on this topic for the next week, or I'll get a security guard, right now, to accompany you to Counselor Cohen." Erica stood tensely and didn't answer.

Caught between the devil and the deep blue sea, Bitch? thought Danielle.

"While you decide, why don't you spend the rest of the period in my classroom?" he said. Erika brushed by Danielle and walked across the hall to the history class.

Mr. Spatz nodded to Danielle, followed Erika to his classroom and closed the door.

Danielle closed her door and just stood there. "Are you having a girl or a boy?" asked Marisa. She turned at the sound of her voice and said absently, "I don't know."

"Ms. McKinnon?" said Tamika, gleefully drawing out the vowels of her name, to call her back to the present. "Congratulations!" Danielle looked around at a classroom of smiling faces. Their affection, mixed with a new gentleness upon finding out about her pregnancy, reopened her heart. The old maid was gone. She'd started losing power when Tamika got up to speak.

"When are you due?" asked Marisa.

"In August." They all seemed to realize at once that their class would have graduated by then, as they looked around at one another.

"Don't worry, Teach. If Erika reports you, we'll all give you good character references," said Kamara. Danielle smiled.

"You lost your temper. That's all. I do it all the time," said Louis.

In the pause, Kamara said, "Did you almost tell Erika your baby is black?"

"Native American," she said quickly.

Kamara shook his head. "Your lips were pressed together to form a bee or pee, like you taught us." She could see no way out. "I wanted you to know, but some people are so narrow-minded…" A few nods. They waited. "My father and grandfather passed for white so we could have more opportunity than…"

"we have," said Tamika.

That sounds terrible. Danielle couldn't think of an answer that wouldn't offend them.

"Times have changed," said Jamal.

"I know, but…" *Is he sketching…this?*

"Don't you want to be black?" asked Marisa.

"It's just that when people find out, they don't see me as white anymore, and that's my heritage… Most of it!" A quiet like thunder preceded darts of lightning.

"So, you want to pass and you don't want a baby that can't. Is that what's going down?" asked Kamara.

Danielle's arms rose in a helpless gesture. "Well, I…It's just easier if…"

Into the silence, Marisa asked, "Are you going to have the baby?"

"Ye-es. I don't know."

"Maybe you shouldn't," said Kamara.

His words landed like a punch to her solar plexus. "I'm still deciding what to do about her," Danielle said.

"Her? You just said you don't know if it's a girl or a boy," said Louis. Danielle's heart pounded, and her face was hot. "I don't really know. I just have a feeling it's a girl." *Even the truth sounds like a lie, now.*

"You can always put her up for adoption," said Marisa.

Does the Little One know what's happening? "For three generations, the whole family has been passing for white… I'm not explaining this correctly."

"You're explaining it." The breaking voice was Tamika's, and the hurt in her dark eyes was unmistakable. The blue highlights in her black complexion were a luminous aura that transfixed Danielle, as the girl said, "You're saying you don't want to be like us and you would even have an abortion to prevent it."

"No," said Danielle. They waited, but she had no follow-up. It was as if she had stepped into an out-of-control dream and was hanging in space. She saw Jamal put down his pen without looking up, disillusion dawn on Marisa's face, cynicism return to Kamara's and disappointment everywhere. The bell blasted. She still couldn't find the right words.

She never met Nicole for lunch. Instead, she moved through a haze of misery as what she had said and implied became clear. As the speeches were given in her Creative Arts Class the next day, the words of the great philosophers mocked her. This was not lost on the students, who covertly looked her way. She looked around for Tamika. She was absent.

Back at her apartment, she found a note from Phil, saying he'd meet her at four o'clock the next day to move her into their aunts' house. She hadn't told him what happened at school. She'd told no one.

On Wednesday, Tamika looked straight ahead as she walked to her desk and opened her notebook. Danielle assigned an in-class essay entitled, Marching to the Beat of a Different Drummer, to avoid questions she didn't know how to answer. She worked at her desk and didn't think about her own march. She wondered, instead, if anyone in school knew what had happened in her class.

At the English Department meeting, Dr. Norton announced she would replace him in the fall. Applause and congratulations erupted. For a fleeting second, she saw pity in Nicole's eyes, as she smiled and applauded.

On the way home, she remembered Tamika's speech… "She wanted to take creative writing and Ms. McKinnon broke the foolish consistency of the school's rules and let her…" Suddenly, Danielle knew why the girl role-modeled her. *She was role-playing me as a writer… and I was blinded by color.*

Chapter Fourteen

"I'll miss you," she whispered to her Gramercy Park apartment. Boxes of books and other precious belongings she'd packed for her new life with Josh were stacked in closets to wait, like the boxed ashes of New York Nana and Uncle Robert that waited in her aunts' hall closet… for a home. Phil walked in, told her that the car was packed, and they headed for Brooklyn.

She dropped into the passenger seat, dropped her book bag onto the floor, shut her eyes and pretended to sleep, while her brother drove out of Manhattan. Her mind raced ahead to her new home with the other old maids, back to Josh's apartment dominated by Sharon, to her classroom where she wanted to be invisible, and finally to her Gramercy Park sanctuary. When she opened her eyes, they were already on the Belt Parkway to Brooklyn.

"Go back! I'm not moving in!"

Phil gave her a blank look. "What?"

"I've changed my mind. I don't want to live with those crazy aunts. Turn around!" It was rush hour, they were in it and speeding along.

"Why?"

"I don't want to write that damned book. I don't want to teach!"

Phil pulled out of the fast lane into the middle one. "What's wrong?"

"I'm a bigot. That's what's wrong." The confession burst out almost as a surprise. Self-hate streamed from her eyes, but when she saw Phil's concern, it became a plea for help. "I lied about not being black to my students and got caught."

"Why did you lie?"

"To pass. When I explained that, I offended them. Hurt one of them." She would not let herself cry. She didn't deserve it. "And all because I don't want to separate myself from my white background, don't want to be called a black, an ethnic… Did it always have such a demeaning connotation? Sometimes I've even felt revulsion."

"Toward your students?"

"No! Not them! Toward the idea of being black. But not toward them! Oh God, I hope they don't think that!" She broke down and cried hard, very hard. Pulling tissues from her bag, she blew her nose and wiped tears from her face. When she finally looked up, she saw that Phil had parked on a side street off the highway. She searched for more tissue to avoid facing him.

"That's not you, Danielle. Too much has happened too fast," he said.

"That is me, Phil. It's ugly, and it's me." She blew her nose again, leaned against the seat and waited for him to drive her back…

"So you want to live as a bigot?" If he slapped her in the face, he couldn't have hurt her more.

"No!" she said, glaring at him. "I don't want to!"

"Then face it down." His tone remained reasonable, but she saw in his eyes how difficult it was for him to say those words.

Face it down. How? How do I face it down? She nodded anyway.

As they continued along the Belt Parkway toward her aunts' place, Danielle's racing thoughts found words. "I'm not revolted by my students, Nicole, or the black men I dated. One was my lover, for God's sake! What is it then? The lascivious leers from the men who looked at me when I dated or talked to a black man?" Then more of the answer struck. "Dad's face when I told him I was dating a Negro student. We were standing around the barbeque in the back yard… I thought he was going to throw up.

They wanted me to stop dating him, but I refused. It seemed wrong. A few days later, Mom scared me with a made up story that Dad had a heart condition. He'd been in bed for three days, and that's when I got scared he'd die, especially when she told me he was really twelve years older than she was. Not two. He'd always looked and acted very young. He had everyone fooled. Anyway, I capitulated… But that's probably when I picked up on that revulsion and internalized it."

"Maybe. Or maybe…" Phil seemed to be thinking something through.

In the silence that followed, a memory of little Thomas Walker, from thirty-two years before, arose. "Phil?" she said, interrupting his thoughts. He gave her his full attention. "When I was in third grade, there was a Negro boy in the second grade."

"In Bayfield? I don't remember any Negroes in our neighborhood."

"You were just three. Anyway, there was one and he was only there a few months. I was walking to school by myself, reading aloud from my Dick and Jane reader, when I saw Thomas walking directly toward me with a big smile. I tried to avoid him because I knew he smelled. It was common knowledge."

"I remember that crap. We didn't get that from home though."

"No, but we got it from somewhere and the idea of being near enough to smell him revolted me. To make matters worse, he was wearing a gray wool suit over a white sweater on a warm fall day. I had on a red plaid cotton dress with an open cardigan. He caught up to me, opened his second grade Dick and Jane reader and looked up at me with real friendly eyes like I was his big sister or something. I was already holding my breath and feeling sorry that someone so nice could smell so bad. I walked faster, but he kept up with me..."

"What happened?"

"I exhaled. And inhaled...No smell. So I walked a little closer to him. Still nothing. I leaned in to him, pretending to read his book, breathed in deeply and inhaled the autumn leaves... And I remember thinking, *Somebody's lied to us.* I was smarter *then* than I am now."

"Some kids thought Negroes smelled, even when I was in high school," said Phil.

"Ten years ago on that acting trip down south, a wealthy theatre patron invited our cast to his huge plantation-like place for lunch. He said the same thing. And his black maid was preparing our lunch. It didn't bother him that she was handling his food."

"It's a disconnect," said Phil.

"It is! – You're dirty and you smell. Here, nurse my baby." She enjoyed a moment of being above it all, then remembered she was a bigot too, and her smile faded.

"When did you disconnect?" Phil asked her.

"Who knows when you absorb this stuff? Maybe it was lying latent within me for years until I found out I'm black." *I said it. I'm black. Not half black. Black.* Something within her relaxed. "Maybe it started when I felt Dad's revulsion in the early sixties."

"Maybe…" Phil seemed to pick up the thought he'd let drop a few minutes before.

"Maybe Dad wasn't feeling revulsion… Maybe it was fear. For you."

"For me?"

"He knew more than we realized about what could happen to you dating that Negro student. Dad and Mom didn't tell us about Emmett Till. But they knew," said Phil. "You were his age."

Inwardly, Danielle cowered from the memory of the newspaper picture of the disfigured face and swollen body in an open coffin, as she considered what her brother said. "Emmett Till was only fourteen years old. I was fourteen in nineteen fifty-five, too. The next year I was taking on my church fellowship for their bigotry." She looked at her brother. "Six years later, I was dating a black student at college… Maybe Dad was afraid for me. Maybe that's why he looked like he was going to vomit when I told him." The memory of a lewd, cold stare she'd gotten from a well-dressed man at a theatre event she'd attended with the black student rose up and frightened her. Neither spoke for a few miles. Then,

"What happened to the little boy…Thomas Walker?" asked Phil.

"Somebody spread a story that he was a homosexual, and his family moved away. Mom told me." Suddenly, Thomas' trusting eyes looked up at her through thirty-two years, and another epiphany struck. "I bet he walked with me that day on the way to school because he saw I was a Negro too and thought he had a friend." Her voice broke on 'friend,' and fresh tears ran down her face.

"Flatbush Avenue," Phil said quietly, turning into the exit.

"Let's stop for flowers," said Danielle.

Chapter Fifteen

"Red roses!" Charlotte graciously accepted them from Phil, and Tessie arranged them in an elegant dark green vase. *They may be old maids but not the distorted ones of my nightmare. In spite of himself, Dad had bragged about them.* Charlotte looked quite modern in a maroon sweater and pants. With her dark brown hair short and curled, she looked nearer fifty-five than sixty-five. She was, after all, a newly retired executive secretary from a Wall Street firm. And Tessie, in her gray mid-calf skirt and white sweater set, looked lovely. Her silvery hair, loosely tied with a gray velvet ribbon, fell below her shoulders, giving her a casually elegant look. Twenty years earlier, she'd completed a career as an assistant in a successful CPA firm. She studied investing at New York University in the evenings and had invested the family's nest egg wisely.

"Where's Danielle's room?" Phil asked, lifting two of the suitcases.

"Follow me," said Charlotte, leading them upstairs to the second floor.

"Glad to be rid of me, Phil?" asked Danielle, picking up the third suitcase.

"Just a little," he teased.

He must be relieved. "I could use a bathroom," she said, hoping red eyes weren't giving her away.

"I'll take you," said Tessie. So they all went upstairs. Danielle splashed cold water on her face and joined them all in her room. A golden glow from the late afternoon sun slanted through the window onto a mahogany rocking chair, drawing her to it. "Did New York Na- Grandma Ruth read here?" she asked settling onto its soft rose cushion.

Charlotte smiled. "She was a great reader. She taught the three R's down South, remember. You would have had a lot in common with her."

Regret touched Danielle's heart. Her eyes followed the vertical lavender lines on old white wallpaper that rose up to the lightly cracked molding at the ceiling. A zipping sound drew Danielle from her thoughts, and she turned around to see Phil take clothes from her wardrobe and hang them in the closet. Charlotte opened the top drawers of an old mahogany bureau with a large framed mirror. "Why don't you and Tessie finish unpacking, while Phil gets the fire started, and I finish dinner. We're having roast loin of pork, collards and mashed sweet potatoes." The menu inspired everyone to action.

Danielle and Tessie made short work of unpacking clothes and putting them into the bureau drawers. A kneehole desk, polished and empty, waited across the room for Danielle to move in. She placed her dream journal and a pencil on the bedside table.

"What's that for? Tessie asked.

"A record of my dreams," said Danielle, taking the fragrant sachets she'd bought in Vermont from her suitcase and putting them on the bureau in front of the mirror.

"I'll help with that," said Tessie, picking up a sachet and sniffing it. "Mmm... pine."

"Take some. I have plenty." Danielle and her elderly aunt smiled at one another in the mirror.

Tessie gestured to a place behind her. "I used to record *my* dreams and interpret them in the morning, sitting on that porch."

"Porch?" She turned. She hadn't even seen the door, but there it was, its windows covered by a sheer white curtain. She opened it and stepped out into the cold dusk and inhaled. It overlooked a narrow back yard one floor below. Ice glistened on the remains of a garden. *I can survive here awhile.* She called out to her aunt who was watching her from the bedroom. "We can sit out here and discuss our dreams."

She heard a chuckle. "We might do well to start that inside. Come back in."

Before they went down to dinner, Danielle pointed to a room down the hall overlooking the street and told her about the dream in which she'd entered that room and found precious jewels, sparkling on black velvet.

"Perhaps the jewels are symbolic of the precious colors combined within you," Tessie said.

Stunned by her aunt's interpretation, she said, "I think you're right! In the dream, I couldn't tell if they were gems or glass, but I knew they were precious."

"Delicious." said Phil, as he scooped an extra helping of mashed sweet potatoes and collards onto his plate. He looked comfortable, sitting at the elegant dining room table in his jeans and beige sweater.

"Mama ordered the meal," Tessie said matter-of-factly. Charlotte rolled her eyes in exasperation at Tessie, and Danielle began to laugh and almost forgot her troubles. They learned Tessie had been divorced after a year of marriage. "He was white and couldn't handle the racial … aspect. And, to be honest, I was tiring of him."

There had to have been pain too, thought Danielle.

"The love of my life was a white man," said Charlotte. "I didn't have the self-esteem or the courage to marry him. Legal or no, it was not accepted. He passed on three years ago." Her voice broke.

"It's all so unfair," said Danielle. "Still, you both took a chance on life and love." *So much for Dad's old maid stories.* She thought about herself and Josh. *Will I end up like them? Independent and unmarried?*

After dinner, Danielle put a plate of ginger snaps and the box of Barricini chocolates from their first visit onto the coffee table. Charlotte and Tessie brought in coffee, cream and sugar, and they settled around a lively fire. Phil sat back and said, "You promised us some more family history."

Danielle's memory of her students' disillusionment rose up within her. "Can we postpone it for tonight? I'm on overwhelm with this black thing."

"Negro situation," said Charlotte. "The word Negro is perfectly fine. It means black."

"The denotation is fine, but the connotations are negative," said Danielle.

"Your father's name, Mac, has some negative connotations, too," Charlotte shot back. Let's get the worst over with. I'll go first." She looked into Danielle's eyes. "Unless you really can't."

"No, let's do it." *Get it over with!* Her eyes darted to the mantle where she'd seen the ghost of her uncle, and she saw the bouquet of red roses in a dark green vase there.

"We visited you in New Crossing once," Charlotte said in an accusing voice.

Tessie's light voice rose to overpower Charlotte's low, well-modulated one. "Not yet, Charlotte. Danielle's 'on overwhelm.' Let's begin at the beginning and give our niece and nephew a picture of their father's life as a boy in South Carolina."

Charlotte frowned. "Did you know your father rode a wild red stallion?" asked Tessie, smiling.

"Yes! His name was Red," Danielle said with relief.

"And no one could ride that horse but him," said Phil.

"Oh no," said Charlotte. "Robert rode him too, but your father always competed with his older brother. Apparently, he chose to alter the truth."

"Older? I thought Dad was older," said Phil.

Charlotte's eyes flashed. "That's because…

"Later, Charlotte," Tessie said sharply. She passed the box of Barricini chocolates and looked into the distant past… "1915 in South Carolina, for a while, was a joyful time for our brother." She smiled at Danielle and Phil. "Your father." Charlotte exhaled impatiently and bit into a ginger snap. Tessie ignored her. "He was eleven years old and already in business shining shoes with his best friend, Shamus, the son of a share cropper. Many a day, they'd ride Red through the meadows to town, Shamus sitting behind him, one arm around Phillip's waist and the other around a wooden box of shoe shine gear."

"Was Grandpa still living on the McKinnon plantation with Jerusha?" Danielle asked.

"No. Papa and Mama lived in a Negro neighborhood, out in the country. We were raised there, but we visited Grandmother Jerusha often." Charlotte sighed. Tessie flashed her sister a stern look and said, "Charlotte hadn't been born yet, so she has no experience of this time."

She talks a story like she's writing it. So does Charlotte. And Dad. Must be all that literature they consumed trying to wipe out their Southern accents with Standard American English.

"As soon as your father and Shamus arrived in town, they would tie Red to a tree and set up for business on a curb in front of the shops to earn money shining the boots of white businessmen. One morning, Papa and I rode to town in his wagon. I bought some necessities Mama wanted from the General Store. Papa still had business, so I bought myself a bag of penny candy and strolled over to see how Philip's business was going. Well, not only had they not made a sale, but Red had dropped a horse biscuit and the smell lay thickly in the warm air. That was why the banker, Mr. Lawson, walked by so quickly with a 'Not today, boy,' when Shamus asked, 'Shine, sir?'

Then your father got a foolish idea. When the lawyer, Mr. Keller, walked their way, your father grabbed a used cloth from the wooden box, ran to where Red was tied and wiped some of the stallion's, ah contribution, onto the cloth. Then, just as Mr. Keller walked by, Phillip dove, as if onto first base, to the back of the man's boot and smeared it with the horse biscuit, as he pretended to wipe it off. 'Can't let you go off to work with this on your boot, sir.' Shamus' eyes burst wide open, and I nearly choked on my penny candy.

'What?' said Mr. Keller. Then he saw his boot. 'Oh. Clean that up, boy!' Shamus pulled out a clean cloth, while Phil removed Mr. Keller's boot, saying, 'We'll have these boots shinin' in no time, Mr. Keller, sir.' I took a walk because I had some nervous laughing to do."

"He could sell you your own shoes," Charlotte said with a wry smile at Danielle's and Phil's laughter. Then, she added with surprising seriousness, "It was a damn fool thing to do! He could have been killed."

"For a prank?" asked Danielle. Tessie nodded in agreement. "Severely whipped at the least, if he were caught."

Danielle exchanged a nervous look with her brother. This was a difficult story to understand.

"He sold us a couple of horse biscuits, too," Phil said.

"Maybe he had to," said Danielle, surprising herself by coming to his rescue for the first time since he threw her out of the house.

"Maybe, because something happened, a couple of years later," said Tessie, who was including the curtains above the window seat in the conversation. "Something happened."

"Well, what?" said Charlotte, raising her voice.

Tessie nodded in the direction of the curtains. "Show your mother respect!"

Charlotte rolled her eyes at Tessie's belief in their long deceased mother's presence among the curtains. Danielle looked to where Tessie had nodded and saw a slight movement of the curtains. Her elderly aunt continued. "Something happened between Phillip and Pa, just before we moved north."

"It's eight-forty five, and I'm not about to lose a good night's sleep over what happened in 1917," Charlotte said. "Danielle and I are retiring."

But Danielle was wide-awake now. "What happened?"

"I don't know," said Tessie, "but overnight, Phillip became a withdrawn and moody boy. Even Grandmother Jerusha couldn't reach him. Soon after, we left Edmundtown and moved north-"

"What did Jerusha look like?" asked Danielle. Tessie paused. "Sorry to interrupt, but I've been wondering… a lot… about her," she said to her aunts.

Tessie smiled. "She looked a lot like you in height and build with high cheekbones. Her skin was a dark coffee. Perhaps Master McKinnon took to her for her beauty."

Danielle's heart trembled open again, as the dream replayed in her mind of a woman in a long dress, standing alone on a railroad platform, getting smaller and smaller watching a train disappear into the distance. She hadn't seen the woman's face, but she'd felt her grief. "Was she sorry to see you go?"

"Oh my yes, but she agreed we should. She was relatively safe, living on the plantation with Master McKinnon, don't forget. And Papa stayed with her when he was working his tailoring business, which was most of the time."

"Master McKinnon… Boy does that sound weird," said Phil. "Was he a decent sort of man… for those times?"

"He was," said Tessie, "but Papa didn't figure his children would be as fortunate as he was. Jerusha's influence went just so far and could quickly end if Master McKinnon had a change of heart, or if he died. So, Papa sent us all up North with Mama. Robert was fifteen, I was twelve…

"Dad was thirteen," said Danielle doing the math.

"And you?" Phil asked Charlotte.

"I was two."

Danielle could see the pieces of a story coming together, and got excited, in spite of herself. "How did you lose your southern accents?"

"You can thank William Shakespeare for that!" said Charlotte, coming to life. "We memorized and read passages an hour before dinner every day in this very house with Mama shouting from the kitchen, "Pronounce the ends of words!"

The two sisters looked at each other and laughed. Tessie said, "On the day Phillip's mood began to lift, he and Robert were practicing a passage from Macbeth. He was fourteen, in high school and just beginning to believe we could actually pass without the sky falling in. The doorbell rang, but the boys didn't answer it. Charlotte and I were helping Mama in the kitchen. The bell kept ringing, so Mama, with us in tow, rushed into the dining room to find Phillip and Robert, each pushing the other toward the door.

'Phillip!' Mama said, 'If this is your teacher again, I'm writing to your father! Open the door, Tessie.'

Well, I was frozen to the spot. 'Is the teacher white?' I asked. I was trembling."

'You are white, now,' said Mama." Danielle exchanged a quick look with her brother. "I still couldn't move, so Phillip opened the door. A workman stood in work clothes, with gardening tools at his side. He wore a straw hat with a brim, which he removed, as he bowed from the waist and said in the broken English of an Italian immigrant, 'Scooza. My name she's-a Domineec, and I come-a to cutta the boosh.'

We breathed a sigh of relief, and Mama informed the man that her sons do the gardening, but to try the elderly couple next door. Then, she closed the door and was telling us to have the passage memorized by dinnertime, when she saw that Phillip was missing.

The doorbell rang again, I froze again, and Mama opened the door. There stood Phillip. Sweeping off an imaginary hat, he bowed from the waist and said, 'Scooza,' and proceeded to imitate the gentleman to a tee, until Mama grabbed him by the collar and pulled him into the house."

Danielle and Phil smiled broadly. They'd seen their father do many imitations.

Charlotte chuckled. "He was the first to get Standard American English down pat too. It was just another accent to him. And he could do a perfect Walter Winchell imitation!" Danielle and Phil exchanged a surprised look at her changed attitude toward him. "He was my hero back then," she grumbled.

"Do you remember why his mood improved?" Danielle asked to draw her out.

"Yes. He was a selfish…"

"Charlotte was too young to understand," said Tessie. Danielle glanced quickly at Phil, as Tessie said carefully, "Your father began to experiment with his talents and newfound freedoms. First of all, he was free of Papa who was down South working for long spells. So he stopped studying. Secondly, he was up North now. Down home, we were Negroes and had only Negro friends… All that changed overnight. Now we were white and made only white friends. The races weren't mixing up here very much either. The terror of being found out was constantly with us at first. Most Negroes could see we were passing. Most whites couldn't. However, we knew the Ku Klux Klan and their sympathizers were lurking somewhere in the close background. Operating on the wrong side of the law, but still operating. Thirdly, Phillip didn't want the college education Papa was offering us. He wanted to go

Chapter Fifteen 177

into business. So, with his charm and a talent for accents, he embraced passing and freedom with his old childhood verve. He quit school and went into sales."

"He told us how he used an Irish accent to make sales in the Irish section and a Jewish one to do the same in the Jewish community," said Phil.

"He did!" said Charlotte, smiling in spite of herself. "He bought a Model T Ford and fine clothes. He looked very dapper in his suits and fedoras."

"He told us how he used Shakespeare to sell the Encyclopedia Americana," said Danielle. "If there was a girl in the family, he'd say to her parents, 'When you educate a boy, you educate one individual. But when you educate a girl, you educate a family.' Then he'd open up the encyclopedia to the passage from Julius Caesar which begins, "There is a tide in the affairs of men / Which taken- which taken…" She snapped her fingers to jog her memory.

"Which taken at the flood leads on to fortune," said Tessie, and Charlotte joined her, "Omitted, all the voyage of their life/ Is bound in shallows and in miseries."

Niece and nephew applauded, and Danielle said carefully, "So, you joined your affairs with those who took the tide at the flood to pass for white, and it led on to fortune?"

"Opportunity and safety," Charlotte said sharply. "Your father, on the other hand, passed for whomever he wanted, wherever and whenever he could." She said that with perfect pronunciation, sounding the h's before the w's in "whom," "where," and "when."

"That's right," said Tessie in kinder tones. "Phillip introduced himself as Mac, an anonymous sort of name, and he passed in white and Negro neighborhoods."

"In Harlem, too?" Danielle looked at Phil. They'd never heard those stories.

"He passed to suit himself. The world was his oyster."

"Until he met Alyerine and got her pregnant," said Charlotte. Tessie glared at her.

"Alyerine?" echoed Danielle, and her stomach tightened, as she looked from Charlotte to Tessie who'd zeroed in on each other. She glanced at Phil and saw that, he too, was riveted. A childish jealousy, for her mother's sake, possessed her. It didn't matter that her folks hadn't met at the time.

Charlotte smiled like the Cheshire Cat. "They were an item for about a year, until Alyerine wanted to get married. But your father wasn't about to limit his freedom by marrying a Negro. None of us were." *How awful... Would I have been any better?*

Tessie picked up the story. "He offered to pay for a safe, for those times, abortion. When Alyerine's brother found out that Phillip wouldn't marry her, he beat your father mercilessly, until Alyerine threw herself between them. Philip escaped into the subway.

"Bleeding and with tears in his eyes, he stumbled in here," said Tessie, turning her fragile figure toward the front door, "on that wintery night in 1933, cradling his left hand in his right. His ring finger was broken."

Their voices dimmed as a memory moved in on Danielle.

"Daddy, what happened to your finger?" asked five-year old Danielle, looking at her father's stiffened left ring finger.

Mac smiled. "Two Mafia thugs pushed me off a moving bus into the street."

"Why?"

"I wouldn't give them my seat. In the fall, my finger was broken." Danielle stared at the stiffened finger on her father's slim, tan-colored hand.

Tessie's gentle voice drifted into Danielle's reverie. "He had to make a choice, and he chose to put the Negro part of his life behind him."

"Mama insisted," said Charlotte. "For too many years, Phillip had been coming home in the early hours, with the smell of liquor on him. Sleeping into the early afternoon, he'd get up to sell encyclopedias then party all night in what he called his 'freedom to choose.'"

"Don't forget he brought in a good share of the income, took the family for a ride into the country every Sunday, and you, Charlotte, you idolized him!" Tessie said.

"He had a good heart back then!"

"He still does!" Tessie turned from her sister and spoke directly to Danielle and Phil. "It was in early spring when his bruises healed, but the bones in his finger had been set improperly, and they fused together, so he'd never be able to make a fist again."

She paused for breath, and Charlotte said, "He was still drinking! One morning, I came downstairs, dressed for school, and saw him asleep at the kitchen table, with a glass of whiskey clasped in his good right hand, and Mama sitting opposite him with a steaming pot of coffee and two cups. Her eyes were red from crying, but determined. By the time I came home from school…"

"And I from work," said Tessie,

"Phillip was in his room and Mama wasn't talking. The next morning, Phillip left the house before we did, drove to Connecticut and began to sell the Encyclopedia Americana… as a white man."

"That's how it happened?" Danielle looked at her brother. Charlotte passed the Barricini chocolates around.

"Day after day, Phillip would come home without making a sale. We thought his spirit was broken," said Tessie.

"He was also mourning a lost love," said Charlotte.

"It wasn't that!" snapped Danielle. "He had trouble selling to New Englanders! Remember, Phil?"

"Yep. He told us he'd speed into Connecticut, talk fast, make glib remarks and get doors slammed in his face. Then a seasoned salesman told him how to talk to a Yankee. So, he slowed down his speech, until it was as slow as maple syrup dripping from a maple tree in early spring, and he knocked on the door of a farmer named Mr. Morrill. Dad introduced himself and the man said, 'I told them not to send a salesman!'

Very slowly, Dad said, 'I know, Mr. Morrill. I know. The sales manager read your letter at our sales meeting this morning and said,

Mr. Morrill does not want us to send a salesman.' Then he looked at me and said, 'Mac, since you are the closest thing to no salesman we have, I'm sending you.'

Danielle felt relief to see Charlotte begrudgingly smile, as Phil continued. "Mr. Morrill invited him to sit on the porch. A cow mooed and Dad said, 'Nice cow you have they-uh.' Mr. Morrill corrected Dad's New England accent and, when he got it right, the old Yankee said, 'Ay-uh,' as only they can, with just the hint of a smile. And, very slowly, Dad opened his briefcase." Danielle looked cautiously at her aunts.

"Then he met Lynn," said Charlotte, with a dryness that puzzled her. "They moved to the Bronx to get married and lived near us for a short time before moving to New England. We remember," she added, with a meaningful look at Tessie. *Is she blaming Mom for the move? Just Mom and not Dad?*

Tessie suggested a glass of Scuppernong, and they all accepted.

"What happened to Alyerine?" asked Danielle.

"She got over him and married someone else," said Charlotte.

She made it sound easy, but Danielle remembered her mother telling her how the beginning of her parents' courtship was rocky. "For a couple of years, your father made trips into New York to visit a girl he'd been involved with. Then one day, he told me he was over her. Danielle had always envisioned the woman as a blond.

It was getting late, but everyone sat back in careful companionship. The roses on the mantle glowed under the soft ceiling light. "Where was Robert during this time?" Phil asked.

Danielle saw Charlotte's eyes darken. "He was out of town working for the railroad as a porter, because he couldn't pass. Just as your father decided to be white, Robert decided to be Negro."

"I bet he did well," said Danielle, picturing her kind uncle helping passengers.

"For the times," said Charlotte. "But the South could be dangerous. Even in the North, he received subtle abuses… all through the fifties and into the sixties, when he retired."

"Where in the North?" asked Danielle.

"His train ran from Manhattan to points south," said Charlotte.

"No abuse in Manhattan, though," said Phil smiling.

"Phil," said Charlotte, "Imagine working long hard hours as a porter. You finally arrive in Manhattan. You're in Penn Station and decide to have a drink with a fellow porter in a bar before going home. It's the North and they serve you. But as soon as you finish your drink, the waiter, if he's that kind, snaps up your glass. You hear the sound of breaking glass and realize it was the one you just drank from. The same thing happens to your co-worker."

Danielle was speechless. In the silence, Phil asked, "What did he do?"

"He chose to socialize in Harlem."

"I can't believe all places in Manhattan were like that," said Danielle.

"They weren't," said Tessie, but you had to know where the friendly places were. The others might not be safe…"

"I was too young to remember him," said Phil, and Danielle heard his regret. He turned to Charlotte. "Earlier, you were going to explain about Uncle Robert's and Dad's ages."

Danielle saw Tessie suddenly sit up, as if on alert, while Charlotte struggled to maintain a neutral tone. "Robert was really the eldest son and had been named Phillip after Papa." Danielle felt her jaw tighten. She looked up at the mantel. "When he was thirteen, Pa had your father's name legally changed to Phillip and Phillip's name to Robert. Mama wouldn't speak to Papa for months." Danielle could barely speak.

"Grandpa switched their names because Robert looked Negro?"

"Yes," said Charlotte. "That's what I believe. He was also a homosexual, and Papa used that as a reason too."

"It must have cut right through him."

"It did…" Her voice broke into a sob, as she rushed from her chair and ran up the staircase. They watched her disappear into the darkness.

"He was a good man," Tessie said softly. "Mama was heart-broken when Papa took his name away from him."

The curtains over the window seat were still. The word, "heart-broken," jogged Danielle's memory, and she leaned forward. "Dad said that once, when he was a boy, Grandma asked him to wait at some bridge to watch for Grandpa – to see if he drove by... with a woman."

"A woman who was white or could pass for white. Mama couldn't pass either," said Tessie. The pain of all those family members who were discarded because of their color seared through Danielle's whole being. From the darkness at the top staircase, Charlotte's voice cut through the room.

"All Mama had was her children. She never had her grandchildren." They turned and looked up. Charlotte's eyes were black with anger.

The evening was definitely over. Danielle and Tessie took the dessert dishes to the kitchen. Phil walked in, zipping up his winter jacket. "Danielle... I just called Josh. He's going to drive you to school tomorrow."

"But I..."

"I really need to borrow your car."

"Are you all right?" He nodded. She didn't believe him.

"I'll leave a note at the apartment to let you know where I parked."

"Okay... Phil? Thanks for getting me here."

Absent-mindedly, he smiled. And was gone.

That night, Danielle lay in her grandmother's bed, desperately tired and unable to sleep. *How could Grandma send Dad to spy on his father? How could Grandpa push Grandma and Uncle Robert to the edges of his life just because they were a shade or two darker? .... I pushed my students to the edge of my life. How could I have done that?* The thought that they were not her family, her blood family, didn't ease her guilt one bit. She remembered Kamara singing, "We be fam-i-ly," just before she shut him down. She turned her face into the pillow to block those images out. An old memory cropped up.

She was eight, barefoot in pink pedal pushers and a cotton shirt, sitting on the warm, back yard lawn in Bayfield, and holding the puppy, Blacky, with a firm grip. Her mother, in mint green shorts and shirt, combed knots from the dog's curly black hair. Little Phil, in a dirty blue shirt and shorts, sat on the grass, digging a hole to China.

Chapter Fifteen

Mac was cooking hamburgers on the outdoor grill, when suddenly he announced, "I want to share some family history with you." Something in his voice had deepened, and they all stopped what they were doing to listen. "We are the McKinnon family. Our family starts with your grandfather. He is Phillip David McKinnon Esquire, the first generation of the McKinnons. I am Phillip David McKinnon, Senior. The second generation. Blond, blue-eyed Phil, holding a little red shovel in his hand, looked on expectantly. The long spatula in his father's hand could have been a sword he was brandishing to announce that the battle was finally won. "Phil, you are Phillip David McKinnon, Junior. You and Danielle are the third generation of the McKinnon family." Danielle looked at them all, petted Blacky, and her heart filled with happiness and pride in the generations of her family.

In her grandmother's bed that night, Danielle turned onto her back, stared up into the darkness and whispered, "What about Jerusha, Dad?" In her mind's eye, the woman was still standing on the wooden railroad platform, watching a train take the McKinnon family north, far away from her. Suddenly, she sat up in bed and cried, "What about my great grandmother, Jerusha?"

Wretched tears slid down her cheeks, and she sat there, waiting, until exhaustion released her back down into a troubled sleep.

Chapter Sixteen

A pair of disembodied eyes, dark and cynical, stared down at her. She tried to move away, but couldn't. A pair of brown eyes changed from confusion to clarity. A multitude of eyes, in various stages of dawning disappointment, looked down. Her heart understood them and grieved. The alarm clock rang, and she awoke.

I've got to face them. Grandmother Ruth's crocheted blanket fell away, as she sat up into the cold air. Her reflection in the mirror of the mahogany bureau mocked her. The red flannel nightgown would no longer offer her a cozy invitation to curl up and enjoy being with herself, ever again. Until she faced them.

Josh is picking me up! She hurried into the shower, thankful no morning sickness churned in her stomach. She dressed in a quiet gray corduroy jumper so she'd fade into the background of her classroom, grabbed her book bag and flew down the stairs so rapidly that she felt like Alice falling into the hole... again.

She tried to breathe normally as she tugged on her boots. Leaning over the window seat, she peeked through the lace curtains. In the cold, white light of morning, fog puffed from the tail pipe of his Josh's yellow sedan. Behind the wet window of the driver's seat, he waved, and her heart fluttered. She'd always wondered what that phrase, "heart fluttered," meant. Now she knew. It was trying to fly, but couldn't.

Slipping into her winter jacket, she threw her book bag over her shoulder and rushed into the cold morning air and down the brick steps. She flew into the open arms of a distinguished looking man in an open wool coat over a business suit and kissed a tender lover. His warm mouth closed over hers, and her mind clouded up, as she tried to remember why they separated. Once in the car, Josh said, "Sharon's in therapy with her mother." His voice was warm and deep.

A flood of hope washed through her, rendering her almost speechless. "And?"

"They met once with Alison, but they haven't made a second appointment yet."

"Do you think they'll stick?" She wanted to say, "stick it out," but "stick" was all she could manage.

"I don't know. Kathy loves Sharon, even though she doesn't always show it. They're a lot alike." Josh smiled. "We're not out of the woods, yet."

"I know."

"Sharon accepted your earrings, called them 'pretty' and put them into her jewelry box, but she hasn't worn them, yet."

"At least she didn't do a war dance on them." The wise crack forced her to look into that mirror herself. "Josh, last night, I learned my father had fallen in love with a woman. It was a couple of years before he met Mom. Even so, I felt hurt and jealous for her."

Josh glanced at her quickly. "Like Sharon does for Kathy?"

"Yes." She studied the curve of his aquiline profile, his thin lips and bearded chin, and she wanted to slide her fingers over them. But he was driving, and they'd had close calls before.

"I hired Andrew Davis," he said, "and gave him free rein to use his discretion in sending black people out to all the client companies."

"Really? Weren't you worried about your business?"

"Yes, and I told him. He's such a nice guy. No chip on his shoulder. Most of the clients like him."

"And the others?"

"The hell with them."

Danielle's voice shook. "You've been rebuilding your life, while I've been destroying mine." She told him what she said to her students.

"You can handle this, Danielle. I know you can. Follow your heart." The car slowed to a stop. "Call me tonight," he said, and kissed her.

Chapter Seventeen

Five minutes before her Literary Arts class was due to begin, Danielle's reservoir of inspiration, like her first container of coffee, was on empty. *What do I do now? What do I say?... Be honest.* She gripped her pen and wrote an honest note about herself on a piece of composition paper, cringed, crumpled it up and shoved it into her pocket. *I don't have to tell them that! I just have to apologize.*

She took a piece of chalk from the blackboard tray and wrote Bigot's 'R Us, with the R reversed across the top of the blackboard. It was a take-off on the popular toy store chain, Toys 'R Us. Then she paced the perimeter of the room looking for inspiration from pictures of Ralph Waldo Emerson, Frederick Douglas, Henry David Thoreau and Bronson Alcott. *I've violated that heritage.* She returned to Bigots 'R Us.

The bell rang, and like Pavlov's dog, she checked her Aim and Do Now. They weren't there! *I'm not ready!* She grabbed a piece of chalk and wrote:

Aim: To examine prejudice.
Do Now:

She drew a blank. The door opened, and she stood there, with her back to the students of her favorite class and listened to their footsteps enter the quiet room. *What do I do? What do I want them to do?* She listened to chairs scrape the floor, and book bags zip and unzip in the silent room where Kamara's song had set such a happy tone just two mornings before.

"Bigots 'R Us... That your idea of Standard American English, Ms. McKinnon?" The voice was guarded and bordering on unfriendly. Kamara was looking in from just outside the door.

Danielle turned to face the dark, cynical eyes from her dream. "No, but life seems backward and upside down now." He didn't smile. She

Chapter Seventeen

looked at the class. No one was smiling. Kamara was still standing by the threshold. *Please stay!* Tamika was looking at her in the same way she had looked at Dr. James on the morning before Christmas break, when he'd written up Danielle for giving the class a holiday breakfast of juice and doughnuts. She knew the look of a class who didn't trust a teacher or an assistant principal. This look was trained on her now. "I apologize to all of you," she said.

"What's your Do Now?" Louis said coldly.

"I thought we could — try a transcendental writing exercise as we read Self Reliance." No response. "I'll join you." She fumbled for the crumbled note in her pocket and held it up. "I have mine." *What am I doing?*

The students looked at the Aim, to examine prejudice, and looked at her. "I would like — to invite you to write down something bigoted about a fictional character or someone you know or- or yourself, if you like," – *They're still listening.* – "or just something you don't like about yourself that you want changed."

"Like a confession?" Marisa asked quietly.

"Yes, but with a need to change it, to transcend it, because it hurts so much." She almost sobbed on the last words. She looked down and breathed deeply to regain self-control. She couldn't say more without crying, and she mustn't cry.

"Let's do it," said Tamika. Danielle looked up to see her student stand and turn to her classmates who nodded in silent agreement. Tamika looked professional, as she walked to a shelf and took a handful of composition paper from a stack beside the Remus hat. In a Hail Mary attempt at self-control, Danielle quickly turned back to the blackboard and wrote:

Do Now: Describe the bigoted actions of a real person or a fictional character. Include your reactions.

Out of the corner of her eye, she saw Chang, in a crisp white shirt and jeans, accept a sheet of paper from Tamika. She heard pens click open and the whispering sound of pencils on paper. She sat at her desk, smoothed out her own crumpled note and wrote more. She thought of

Kamara, quickly looked up and breathed more easily to see him seated and writing. She cleared her throat. "When we finish, we'll …we'll…"

"Put them into the Remus hat, jumble them up and read each one aloud?" suggested Tamika.

"No!" She looked at the class! They looked at her. "Unless you want to."

"Let's do it," said Kamara.

"Don't sign it!" said Louis.

"If we're not going to sign it, let's write about ourselves," said Marisa.

Before Danielle's incredulous eyes, they started crossing out and re-writing. She saw fear flash in Erica's eyes and identified with her. Her own body trembled, as she folded her paper, walked across the room, took the Remus hat from the shelf, placed it on her desk and dropped her note into it. Each student followed suit. Tamika picked up the hat and shook it until the notes were thoroughly jumbled.

Danielle stifled the impulse to say, "Respect everyone's privacy, as the notes are being read." *I have no right to tell them anything. I'm no longer their teacher.* She took a seat in the last row of the small class.

"Who'll go first?" asked Tamika.

Danielle thought she'd really fallen down the rabbit hole, when Erika walked to the front of the class, took a note from the hat, unfolded it and read, "I have this fear I'm not as smart as the Jews and that makes me want to hate them." The girl looked like she might be ill. "That's not mine. Somebody else wrote it." Silence. She threw the note into the wastebasket and sat down, thereby establishing a precedent for disposing of the notes. Danielle didn't look for the writer.

Marisa stood and looked away from the hat, as she pulled out a note: "When I was little my mother always said, 'Don't trust the Slant Eyes.' Even though I know it's not true, it got into me, and it makes me sick of myself." Marisa crumpled the paper and threw it into the wastebasket, real hard, thereby setting a precedent for vehemence in disposing of the notes. No one turned to look at Chang. Danielle loved the class even more for that.

Louis went next. "My father treats my mother like an inferior. I look just like her, and I feel inferior too." Louis trashed the paper. *Was that Erica's?*

Danielle took her turn. "I was just beginning to trust white people, when the person I trusted most turned on us. I don't trust any of them now." She simply dropped the note into the wastebasket and sat down. *Whoever it was pegged me.*

Jamal, the sketcher, picked a note and read, "I overheard someone say that light skin Spanish girls are well-adjusted but dark skin ones are moody. Well, why do you think we're moody! People ignore me and leave me out of too many things. Social things." As Jamal trashed the note, a muffled, high sound of crying pierced the room. No one looked around, but, from her seat in the second row, Danielle saw Tamika place a gentle hand upon the bent back of a dark Spanish girl.

As Chang read, Danielle looked down, and her face burned. "I pushed you to the edges of my life, by not telling you I'm black and that I'm not sure I want a black child. And I lost you. Once my family had compelling reasons to hide, but I followed fearfully in their tradition, proving Emerson right. 'A foolish consistency is the hobgoblin of little minds.'" Chang trashed it with energy.

The next fifteen pulls from the Remus hat filled most of the period. After the last note was torpedoed into the waste-basket, after a silence punctuated by the blowing of noses, quiet crying and mumbled words like prayers, Louis looked around and asked, "How do we transcend this?"

"We could write about it," offered Danielle.

"We just did," said Erica.

"Let's forgive ourselves," said Tamika.

"And each other," said Chang.

"Kamara stood. "Burn them! Forgive, forgive and write later."

Danielle stood, mentally choosing her words with care. *There's a fire law. We can't do that. I'm sorry.* She looked into Kamara's eyes. "Burn them!" she said.

Kamara and Chang had matches lit before she could retract her statement, so she assigned herself to damage control. But the hiss of ignited paper and the sight of flames filling the wastebasket drew them all around the pile of vile burning notes, and they stood together to begin their transcendence.

As the flames died, smoke drifted upwards and two students coughed. An almost imperceptible tap on the door made Danielle whirl around! Mr. Spatz was staring at them through the window and mouthing, "Dr. James," as he pointed down the hall.

"Block the view," said Kamara, placing his six foot two height in front of the wastebasket. Smoke rose around him. Louis opened the window. Chang waved the Remus hat and tried futilely to disperse the smoke.

Dr. James appeared outside the window of the door. Sniffing. The fumes were in the hall! In a flash, Mr. Spatz's arm wrapped around Dr. James' shoulder, turned him away from the classroom window, while his other arm pointed in a "They went that-away!" gesture, and propelled the assistant principal down the hall.

Danielle dashed to her desk drawer, pulled out her second container of coffee, uncapped it, dashed back through the students and poured the black liquid into the smoking wastebasket. When she finished, she looked up to see the class was standing around her, waiting, giving her a chance to be their teacher again. "Most everyone's got something to transcend," she said and didn't care that tears were running down her cheeks. "But not everyone does something about it. We did." She looked at each of them. "Keep a private notebook of your reactions. You will get credit for keeping the notebook. I won't read it. I'll just check for written pages."

"Are you going to keep a private notebook?" asked Kamara.

"Yes." The bell rang and class doors opened. Dr. James dashed by, still looking for the arsonist. Danielle looked for the wastebasket. It was gone!

Mr. Spatz walked in. His face was one big question mark. On his way out, Louis gently patted his shoulder. Another student patted his arm. Tamika and Marisa smiled gently at him. Erika said, "See you for our next discussion, Mr. Spatz." Danielle was surprised to see she seemed to be looking forward to it. Kamara raised an arm with an open palm, and they high fived each other, as he strolled out with the wastebasket under his other arm.

When the last student left, Danielle approached her colleague.

"What did you do?" he asked.

"Became a teacher."

At lunch, Danielle asked Nicole to join her at a small corner table, blurted out the story of what just happened and added, "I know you knew I was lying before. I feel terrible…"

"Hey! You found your way out of it, and, teacher that you are, you opened that route for your students."

"Tamika really did that. Kamara. And Marisa, Chang and…"

"You played a part in this transcendence, too. I'm going to do the Remus exercise, as soon as I get home."

"Really?" *She just named it!*

"Really. But I'll light a small fire in a deep sink."

Danielle moved, stunned but hopeful, through the day. She'd heard Nicole's gentle rebuke. The fire could have had tragic consequences, and all because she wanted to dispel her guilt. She vowed never to be so careless again. After the last class, she corrected papers, prepared for the next day and jotted down some ideas for the creative writing contest.

It was five o'clock, when she called Josh at his office. "Hi," was all she said, or thought she said.

"It went well, didn't it?"

"Oh yes. From the moment you picked me up, it's been a charmed day."

"Have Chinese take-out with Sharon and me tonight. Maybe the charm will still be in effect."

Who's going to cast the spell like those here did? "I'll pick up my car and be on my way."

Before leaving, she called her aunts. Charlotte picked up the phone. "Oh, Danielle, I hope I didn't upset you too much with my outburst last night. What happened to Robert still hurts me."

"Listen, if we're going to catch up on thirty lost years, we've got to be prepared for outbreaks. I got to know you better for it, and I'm glad it happened. Now."

They laughed. "I probably ruined your sleep," Charlotte said.

"You didn't. I called to let you know I'll be having dinner with Josh and Sharon."

"Have a good time." Danielle warmed to the smile in her aunt's voice.

Chapter Eighteen

Dusk was darkening into night, as Danielle drew her scarf to her neck and buzzed Josh's penthouse. Her key lay on the bottom of her book bag. *Is it only two weeks, since I walked out of this place that was to be home with a husband and two daughters?*

"Who is it?" Josh's deep voice stirred her.

"Danielle." Her heart was fluttering again.

"Of the charmed day?"

"Yes," she laughed.

The buzzer buzzed, she walked in and took the elevator to the top floor. Josh met her by the door. "Throw out your key?" he asked, helping her out of her coat?

"No, but it didn't seem right just to walk in." She turned around and got lost in his kiss. Just for a moment. "Where's Sharon?"

"Out, but she'll be back soon."

"That sounds like an improvement."

"It is…" He paused, and she thought he was going to say more, but he smiled and took her hand. "So, tell me what happened?" They walked into the living room, settled onto the couch, and she told him about her charmed day.

He was laughing as she finished. "Incredible. I knew you could do it."

"Tamika did it, Kamara and the others. Not to mention Richard Spatz!"

"I wish I could have been there." He leaned back onto the couch, and she watched his thoughts travel. "How do you feel now?" he asked.

She looked into a painting of the Venice Canal on the opposite wall, as she described her inner journey. "I feel… lighter, freer of bigotry. And grateful. So grateful.

I'm a teacher again. I hope. Other than that, it's like I'm floating on a cloud, changing."

He looked distressed. "I'm sorry. I meant to say, how do you feel about having the baby?"

Her cloud jolted to a stop. "I haven't gotten that far yet."

He caressed the edges of her fingers. "How do we solve this?"

She swallowed. "I'm not an oracle, but I'd say we need to give ourselves more time, you, Sharon and I."

"How long?" They savored a kiss because she didn't have an answer and he knew it. "I'll call the restaurant. What'll you have?"

"A small hot and sour soup and moo-shoo vegetables with shrimp on brown rice." She watched him punch in the phone number. "Does Sharon know I'm here?"

"No. I haven't seen her since she left for school."

Danielle breathed in deeply and exhaled. Josh's voice, ordering the food, faded into the background, as, buoyed by the remnants of her charmed day, she decided what she'd say to Sharon.

Twenty minutes later, after talking companionably about Josh's plans to wrap up his search firm business, Danielle was brewing a smoky-scented tea. Josh was setting three soup bowls on the table, when Sharon burst into the kitchen.

"Dad! Guess what happened?"

Danielle smiled at her. "Hi." She saw the girl's smooth switch to indifference.

"Uh – hi," she said, and busied herself with taking off her black leather jacket.

"What happened?" asked her father.

"I'll talk to you later." Slim and graceful, she walked back through the swinging door. Danielle noticed the slightly snug fit of her black denim pants balanced by the engaging curves of her aquamarine sweater, and matching scrunchie that complimented her dark brown ponytail.

"Pretty outfit!" she called out to Sharon.

"Thanks." She was already down the hallway.

"Chinese tonight," called out Josh, holding open the swinging door.

"I ordered us Won Ton soup and General Tso's Chicken!" Danielle smiled. It was Sharon's favorite. When there was no response, Josh called again, "It'll be here soon."

"Call me when it comes," Sharon yelled, and they heard her bedroom door close.

Ten minutes later, sitting around the kitchen table, Sharon laconically pushed the wontons through the broth with her soupspoon, while Josh devoured his. Danielle sipped her hot and sour soup and stifled the impulse to beam and chatter into the silence, in an effort to break through the tension. *When has that ever worked?*

"How's school?" Josh asked Sharon.

"Okay."

"Tell her about your day!" he said to Danielle.

Her first impulse was to refuse, but when she saw the plea in his eyes, she braced herself with another spoonful of soup and went for the short version. "Two days ago, I offended my students. They found out I'm black and hadn't told them. I tried to explain why I wanted to pass for white, and someone asked what I'd do if the baby is black."

"Like – would the kid blow your cover?"

"Yesss," Danielle inadvertently hissed at being nailed by Sharon, of all people. She paused to regain her composure. *At least she's not a racist.* "Today, I apologized. We started talking about prejudice and one thing led to another, and they pretty much invented an exercise in which we'd each write a couple of lines, describing a personal prejudice, then put the notes, unsigned, in a hat and take turns reading them to tell the truth and shame the devil, so to speak, and hopefully transcend the prejudice."

"You wrote one, too?"

Danielle nodded. Sharon snorted and began to eat, and Danielle went on alert. *Don't tell her about the fire!* "It was a challenging exercise," she said instead.

Josh, having missed the last interchange as he set out dinner plates and put serving spoons in the opened cardboard containers, said, "But the most exciting part happened when..." Danielle interrupted him.

"This isn't what I really wanted to talk about."

Sharon took in the two of them and spooned a generous portion of General Tso's Chicken over her fried rice. "What's the most exciting part," she asked her father.

"Let Danielle continue," said Josh.

"It's better I don't say anymore for now," Danielle said. Sharon turned her attention to her dinner.

Danielle took the plunge. "There's something else I really want to tell you. It shook me up last night and made me think about our relationship in a new way." She watched Sharon maintain her indifference, take a mouthful of food and calmly chew. *Be careful!* "I found out from my aunts - Oh, did you know I moved in with my aunts?" – Sharon glanced at her and kept eating. "Well, they, my aunts, told me that my father had once fallen in love with a girl from Harlem."

"When?" Sharon looked up with interest, reminding Danielle how much Sharon had liked Mac during the Christmas visit.

"Oh, years ago – in the late thirties, when he was young – before he met my mother. But he didn't want to get married and be known as a Negro. That's what they were called back then. Negroes."

Sharon stared at her. "I know. What happened?"

"Their relationship ended. Anyway, last night, when I heard my father had loved another woman, I got jealous. I immediately thought of this woman as an intruder and wanted to protect my mother. And all this happened before my parents even met!" Danielle and Sharon were finally looking at each other, and for a moment neither moved. Danielle saw vulnerability flicker in the girl's eyes, and she said, "So I think I understand what you're going through with your father and me."

Sharon set down her fork, stood, and in a hard voice breaking, said, "I don't think you understand me." She turned and quickly walked from the kitchen.

Danielle got up and ran after her. "Sharon." The bedroom door slammed. She knocked softly. "Sharon, I'm saying this wrong. Of course, I can't know what you're going through, nobody can, but I had a similar experience, and I'm sensitive to your feelings." She heard a muffled sob. "Sharon? I'm sorry. I didn't mean to hurt you." She turned, saw Josh's distress and covered her face with her hands. Tears seeped through her fingers. It was a while before she realized he was holding her and she was sobbing. She felt gentle lips on her forehead. "I made a real mess."

"No, you didn't. It's just going to take time. Like you said."

"I'd better go."

He held her. "You haven't eaten."

"I can't."

"Take the moo-shoo." He recapped the container, put it in the container and gently pushed it into her hands.

Wrapped in their jackets and scarves, Danielle and Josh walked hand-in-hand through the crunching snow to her car.

"Don't mention the fire."

"I got that. Don't worry." They held each other in the cold night. As she got into the driver's seat, he said, "Save the week-end for me. Okay? I'll ask my parents to stay with her."

"Okay." She started the ignition and drove off, lonely but free, ten blocks away to her aunts' home.

Chapter Nineteen

She stood in the shadows of the foyer and listened to her aunts' muted voices off in the kitchen. She wanted to nurse her wounds in solitude, but if she snuck upstairs without even saying goodnight, she might offend them. *I've offended enough people for a lifetime.* Besides, an aromatic blend of onions and peppers filled the air.

She found Tessie and Charlotte, sitting opposite each other at a rectangular wooden table. Six people once sat there… Grandpa and Grandma McKinnon, Robert, Dad, Tessie and Charlotte. She remembered them young and vibrant. Her aunts stopped eating and looked up at her from large green bowls of chicken vegetable soup. A circular, red plastic clock above the table said eight-fifteen. Opaque beige curtains with red, green and brown Amish symbols, partially opened to the black night, pulled the color scheme together in a homey way. The large kitchen's architecture, with its simple lines and gentle arches from a more elegant time, stood quietly aloof.

"Back so soon?" asked Tessie.

Danielle forced a smile and put her cardboard container onto the table. "Anyone for Moo-shoo with shrimp?"

"Not I, but there's plenty of soup for you."

Danielle peered into the pot and inhaled deeply. Parsley, basil and rosemary floated in a broth with chicken, onions, garlic and peppers. "You made it from scratch."

"Of course we did," said Tessie. Danielle took a soup bowl and dinner plate from the wooden corner cabinet.

"Bring me a plate. I'll have some Moo-shoo too," said Charlotte.

Danielle turned to serve Charlotte and caught them looking at her. "Sharon's not feeling well, so I… left early." Her aunts accepted her excuse in silence and continued to eat. She knew they didn't buy it. *My eyes are probably red.* "I told her I understood how she felt about my being with Josh because, last night, when I heard about my father falling in love with another woman, I felt jealous."

"Good grief," said Charlotte. And Tessie added, "You tell Sharon too much."

Danielle sat down, swallowed a mouthful of soup, and they ate in silence for a minute or so.

"I was livid, when I discovered Papa was cheating on Mama!" said Charlotte.

"I was heart-broken," said Tessie. She tapped her soup spoon on the table near Danielle. "You and Josh aren't cheating on that child's mother, and she knows it. But I'll bet she's hoping her parents will get back together. Somehow," she said, with a faraway look in her eyes.

"If she can just get rid of you," said Charlotte.

They understand her. Danielle's hunger struck, and she began to eat. "I'm glad I'm living here." Charlotte smiled, Tessie patted her hand, and Danielle told them what happened at school. "It may be a little early to know for certain, but I think the aversion I sometimes feel at being black is melting away."

"Good. Because you are part Negro," said Charlotte. "However!" She spoke with authority. "You can pass for white without being prejudiced or filled with self-hatred."

Tessie nodded. "I think what was happening to you and what is obviously happening to your father is that neither one of you has had an opportunity to talk those feelings out, as you did in class today."

"But!" said Charlotte, "passing for white is one decision and having an abortion is an entirely different one. Take time to decide what you want to do. I think Sharon will make that time available."

"Perhaps I should thank her," said Danielle.

"I wouldn't go that far."

Chapter Twenty

Maybe they're right. The dishes were done, and Danielle was exhausted. She bade her aunts a good night, hurried upstairs, showered, slipped into her red flannel nightgown and robe, padded quickly back to her bedroom and closed the door.

She was untying her robe, when an almost palpable presence stopped her, and it seemed to come from the porch. Reluctantly, she opened the door and, leaving it ajar, pulled the robe around herself, and walked in slippers across the cold cement. Shivering, she looked from the railing down onto the little garden of unpicked vegetables. *Squash? Cabbage?* They were iced over now and glistening in the black air. "Who is it?" she asked. And waited. A cold breeze penetrated her flannel robe, moving her back toward the bedroom. At the threshold, she looked back, whispered, "Grandmother Ruth?" and stood there a while longer. Then she stepped into the warm bedroom and guiltily shut the door.

She almost called her again, when with a start, she remembered she'd already seen one ghost in the living room and wasn't sure she wanted to experience another. *But she's my grandmother, and this is her room.* Settling cautiously onto the cushioned rocking chair, she rocked and rocked, until she warmed up and calmed down. "I'm glad you're here, if you are… here, Grandma Ruth," she said bravely, settled back into the cushions and rocked some more.

Charlotte's words replayed in her mind: *Passing for white is one decision, and having an abortion is an entirely different one. Take time to decide what you want to do.*

The possible presence of her grandmother receded, as she caressed her belly and said quietly, "What are we going to do, Little One? We're back to square one. I'm a single mother and may continue to be single. I have to work and you won't have me around during the day like I did with *my* mother…We could live in Greenwich Village where you could attend The Little Red Schoolhouse! You'd get a wonderful education there, and maybe no one would even care that you're English, Jewish, African and Native American, Irish, Scotch and Welsh."

She remembered a dream she had had only a month before, of walking into a room down the hall and discovering colorful jewels on black velvet. "Your Great Aunt Tessie thinks those jewels represent us. I didn't even know I was black when I had that dream." She smiled. "That was the morning I thought you choked me for laughing at that stupid rhyme. *Don't need a disclaimer – Abortion's a no-brainer!* Did you?"

She looked toward the porch and imagined herself sitting out there on a summer's day, holding her baby in a soft, white blanket. "You'd be born in August." She was contentedly rocking, when she felt the trap snap into place. Suddenly, she was on her feet, the chair rocking wildly into the backs of her calves. "I forgot about becoming an assistant principal! What am I going to do about that?" She paced the room like a caged animal, talking loudly now. "If you are here, Little One, maybe you need to be a part of this decision. Is this really the right time for you to come in?"

The curtains inside the porch door moved slightly. "Grandmother Ruth, the baby and I can't hide from the world with your daughters! Where in the world can I go to bring this girl up whole? Where?" A knock on the door startled her.

"Are you all right, Danielle?" It was Charlotte's voice.

"Yes! Yes." She opened the door and saw her aunts' concerned faces. "Sorry. I talk to myself sometimes."

"It sounded like an out and out battle to me," said Charlotte. They waited.

"I got carried away." She forced a laugh.

"I've done that," said Tessie. "Nighty-night." She pulled a worried-looking Charlotte down the hall. Danielle gently closed the door.

Slipping between the sheets and pulling the crocheted blanket over herself, she shut off the bedside light, lay on her back and listened to her grandmother's chair rock slowly to a stop.

She placed what she hoped was a calming hand over The Little One. Then she looked up into the darkness with tear-filled eyes, hating the injustices of racism, of anti-Semitism and mostly of how the shade of a little girl's skin could warp her life. *How do I guide such a child? Alone.* She fell asleep wondering if Josh had talked with Sharon.

Chapter Twenty-One

At five o'clock the following morning, Danielle awoke to a mild case of morning sickness. By six, she was on the road to work, and by seven, she entered school with two coffees, a warm buttered bagel and an hour and a half to spare before class began. Snuggling into an enclosed telephone booth, she sat down, and with her book bag between her feet, a steaming container of coffee and a small pile of dimes and nickels on the counter, she called Phil at her apartment. They hadn't spoken since he took off with her car. "How are you?"

"Fine, now." There was a smile in his voice. "After lecturing you on your racial challenges and then listening to our aunts' stories about the rest of our family, I decided to put my own life in order."

He hasn't sounded this happy since-

"I called Alma,"

I knew it!

And we met at a coffee shop on 125th Street!"

"And?"

"We talked. We're... getting to know each other again."

"Wonderful." She felt outrageously happy for him and exquisitely sad for herself.

"Can you and Josh join us at the club Saturday night? My melody's debuting."

"You finished it?"

"Yes, and I'm calling it Jerusha."

Her breath caught. "I'm coming! I'll ask Josh, but I'll definitely be there... Jerusha?"

"Yes. Dinner is at six. I start work at eight. See you then."

Immediately, she dialed Josh, and while waiting for him to answer, she remembered when her brother last sounded so happy. He was dating Alma and studying for a degree in Music History in college.

Ambivalent feelings squeezed at her heart until Josh's deep voice touched it through the phone lines. "Hi! The weekend is free, and Sharon is staying with my parents. What do you want to do?"

The aroma of fried chicken and curried shrimp blended in the air. A blue-white spotlight shone down on the band and the first row of round tables at which Danielle, Josh and Alma sat, their coffees abandoned. To listen. A Celtic-sounding melody, mingling with African rhythms, haunted the hushed room. Josh's fingers tapped to its rhythm and Danielle's heart opened to it.

Across from her sat Alma Walker. Her slim, sensuous body moved ever so subtly to the music. Her dark eyes were watching Phil's hands move deftly from drumsticks to brushes. She was no longer the prim college girl in denims and sneakers with straightened hair. Her Afro framed a pretty face that made Danielle think of Angela Davis. A long, blue-green sheath highlighted her chocolate complexion.

When the piece ended, Phil sat behind his drums and just looked at Alma. Danielle doubted he heard the swelling applause. Alma motioned for him to stand. He stood and accepted the applause with a nod and a smile. His fellow musicians, black and white, stood and applauded too. Their little table joined in and, when they all sat down, the band slipped into a Duke Ellington medley.

Danielle lifted her coffee cup to toast her brother and felt tears prick her eyes. *He got it! He found his melody.*

"Who's Jerusha," asked Josh.

"Our great grandmother," Danielle said, and unexpected pride straightened her back.

"Did you know her?" asked Alma.

"Yes." Josh looked surprised, Alma looked impressed and Danielle looked into her empty coffee cup and remembered a dream in which a woman in a long, old fashioned dress watched a locomotive pull away from a wooden station platform and leave her standing there.

The waiter refilled their cups, and the two women moved easily into shoptalk. "How are your students' reading levels?" Danielle asked.

"For most, not nearly good enough. I stopped teaching third grade and took an administrative position last year to make some major changes – cut class size, hold back students who fail, fire ineffective teachers and get parents more involved."

"Sounds familiar." Jealousy tightened Danielle's voice. *I have to give up my administrative position before it even begins.*

"It's an uphill battle," said Alma.

"I'm glad you're in there pitching. The system needs you!" Danielle smiled, looked at life from the sidelines, and wanted to cry.

"It Don't Mean a Thing" ended the set, and their little party joined the applause. Phil joined them. A waiter placed a bottle of champagne and four champagne flutes on their table. "From the management," he said and high-fived Phil. Congratulations, man." He popped the cork and poured.

Alma lifted her champagne flute. "To a gifted musician."

Danielle and Josh clinked glasses and watched Phil and Alma get lost in each other's eyes. When Phil remembered where he was, Josh asked him, "What inspired you to write a melody to your great grandmother?"

"She's a mystery. All we know is that she was a quadroon, a former slave and kept mistress of McKinnon, the plantation owner, who was our great grandfather."

As he talked, Danielle felt her great grandmother's searing loneliness as the train transported her family North in quest of the American dream. She barely felt Josh wipe a tear from her cheek.

Phil turned to Alma. "There's someone I want you to meet," he said, standing up and taking her hand. They picked up their champagne glasses. Danielle and Josh watched them disappear into the crowd.

"You may have a black sister-in-law," Josh said. "How will you pass then?"

"Family can know. School can know." She looked away. "I don't know."

"Life's not that hopeless."

She turned on him. "Where's the hope in our relationship?"

"I don't know, but you're changing the subject."

She needed to escape. "I have to use the bathroom." She stood and walked away, but not before she saw the hurt in his eyes. Guilt seared through her.

The women's room was just past the bar. Two chairs faced each other just where she and Josh had sat and committed to having the baby. She froze.

A hand waved into her peripheral vision, and she looked into the smiling, thick-lashed eyes of the well-worn woman. She was still cradling an oversized martini glass in fingers with silver and maroon claw-like nails, and her red-gray hair was still pulled back into a ponytail. But her eye make-up and lipstick were peach now. Her earrings were gold with a half moon dangling from one ear and a star from the other, reminding Danielle of her dream.

"How's the baby, Ms. Bronte?" she asked in a gravelly voice.

Danielle had no reason to equivocate with this woman. No reason at all. "Messing up my career. I don't know if I want it." She motioned to where Josh waited out of sight across the room. "Our relationship is… very fragile. He has to choose between his daughter from his first marriage and me, and he's choosing his daughter. Well, he has to." She intended to laugh it off, but cried instead.

At some point, after she was gently pushed into a chair and tissue was stuffed into her hand, she blew her nose, wiped away her tears and looked into the woman's attentive eyes. "What am I doing?" she asked apologetically.

The hand with the long peach-colored claws gently squeezed Danielle's arm. "You're saying something – talking it out – so you can hear it." Danielle talked out her conflicting and confused feelings, and the woman listened quietly. Then she said, "Whatever you do, make sure it's your decision and your decision only. And don't be afraid to change your mind. The situation is very complicated, and you have to live with yourself."

Fifteen minutes later, Danielle returned to a lost and worried looking Josh. He rose quickly to his feet and embraced her. "I was about to look for you. Are you all right?"

They sat down and looked at one another. "I may go to Connecticut on the winter break. I may have it done there, near my mother," she said.

"The abortion?"

Thinking she might have heard hope in his voice, she said firmly, "Not for you or Sharon! – For my freedom. I have to support myself."

Danielle stood her ground shakily in this new space, relieved that racial prejudice no longer manipulated her, but unnerved by her freedom to choose.

A long moment later, Josh said, "If you want me, I'll be there."

"I do," she said.

Chapter Twenty-Two

The Sweet

The days between mid-January and February 14th were bittersweet.

Danielle's Literary Arts class began outlining and writing their short stories. Enthusiasm was high. "I want to write about Uncle Remus and why he wrote his stories," Tamika said.

"He didn't write them. Joel Chandler Harris, a white man on the plantation, did," said Danielle.

Kamara was on his feet. "What kinda shi…" He stopped in mid-curse, and Danielle busied herself, keeping a straight face. "No honky could…" He stopped again. Determined not to smile, she looked at him and waited. In very measured words, he began again. "Excuuse me, but no white man could just make up those stories. He wouldn't even think of them. He had no reason to!" The class was on alert.

"Maybe Uncle Remus wrote a few, and Mr. Harris wrote a few more," said Chang.

"Maybe Uncle Remus didn't know how to write. He was a slave," said Marisa.

"Damn," said Kamara. "I'll bet Joel Chandler – what's his name? – Harris wrote down all the stories and got credit for it!"

"Maybe. There were rabbit tales from Africa the slaves knew," said Danielle. She saw Tamika's eyes shining, and said to her, "I think you're stirring up a hornet's nest. Go for it! Do some research and see what you can find out. Then bring your own imagination into the story and have fun."

"Whitey!" muttered Kamara. "There he goes again." His hand gravitated to his heart.

"That's our culture. Uncle Remus was a..a.."

"A bard?" suggested Danielle, "who told true stories in code, using animals instead of people?"

"What's a bard?" asked Louis.

Jamal spoke quietly as he sketched. "A story-teller, usually a poet, who celebrated the accomplishments of heroes."

"That fits," said Kamara.

"Uncle Remus was a hero? Like Odysseus?" Louis asked. They had all read the *Odyssey* in ninth grade.

"Maybe not just like him, but he had his odyssey," said Chang.

"Because he represents the slaves, he represents our ancestors-who-were-heroes!" said Kamara, strutting to the rhythm of his words and high fiving Jamal.

"Let me at this story," said Tamika.

"You better do it right!" said Kamara.

"Write your own!" Tamika shot back. "Probably no one knows the truth anymore."

"I'm going to write about the Remus Exercise," said Marisa.

Danielle's hands flew to her head. "You'll blow our cover!" she said, laughing, then stopped short. *Nicole coined the term Remus Exercise.* "Where did you hear that?"

"Ms. Johnson's students are doing it in class, except they're using a shredder instead of a...fire."

Danielle remembered Nicole Johnson's gentle criticism. Her face reddened. "I was out of line allowing a fire. It was dangerous." She felt as though they were all walking through a land mine. "The challenge is to find a way to tell the truth responsibly. The important thing's to tell what's happened to us on the inside," Tamika said. "For me, I didn't actually mind being black before the exercise, but I'm proud of it now. I don't want to be anyone else but me!" Danielle was stunned by Tamika's admission. *So that was why she was always role-modeling me so closely? Because she wished she was white?* She regretted every moment she'd deceived the girl.

"My racial prejudices are melting away, too," said Danielle.

"Mine too. I feel differently about Jews now," Louis said.

"Me too," said Erica. All eyes flew to her neck. The swastika was gone. "I buried it in the garbage at home, and my father threw it down the incinerator." She giggled nervously. "He didn't know it was in there. It's gone," she said bravely looking around at her fellow students and receiving their gentle smiles.

"Who's going to see this stuff," said Kamara.

"Why? Are you going to write a Whitey story?" Louis asked.

"It's not the white man. Just some of them," said Kamara.

"That's okay if you make that clear," said Tamika. Then she added, "These stories are going to be good. I just feel it."

"We should make a book of them and print copies for each of us," said Luis. They all looked at Danielle.

"Can we?" asked Marisa.

"Yes," Danielle said and looked at Kamara. But don't let that inhibit what you write. If you're uncomfortable about being published, I'll leave your story out."

"Uncomfortable?" said the young man. "I'll be available for autographs."

"Me too!" said Louis, holding up his pen, as if to write. Marisa laughed, and Erica smiled a beautiful smile.

High on her students, Danielle floated into the English office and sat beside Nicole. Dr. Norton faced them from behind his desk and handed each woman a set of papers. "Here's the schedule for the English Regents," he said and smiled at her. Danielle took her set, aware that he was addressing just her again. "You need to tally the numbers of students taking the tests and assign them to the right sized rooms. Also, assign room proctors and relief proctors…" His instructions became a drone in the background of Danielle's mind where Kamara's strutting and Tamika's shining eyes were being replayed. "When can you have it ready, Ms. McKinnon?"

She came to and smiled at him. "I'm sorry. I was just thinking about my class." Silence. "They were debating whether or not Joel Chandler Harris or Uncle Remus himself had created the stories Chandler Harris gets all the credit for." Dr. Norton stared at her. She looked at Nicole, who was smiling into her notebook, and she leaned in to read her notes. "So, we're assigning rooms and proctors?"

"And correcting rooms," her colleague said.

The very thought of all that testing, marking, tallying and proctoring drained her, and she drew a blank. She looked at Nicole. "Any suggestions?"

"I could do the tallying and assign the rooms, while you select the readers for the listening part of the test and see if we can get into the library to correct papers as a department. Then we can meet and select proctors together from the list of English teachers."

"You gave me the easy part," Danielle said, "but I'll take it." She turned to Dr. Norton.

"What do you think?"

"You're teaching Uncle Remus?"

"One of the students is researching Joel Chandler Harris for a writing project."

"Don't mention that when you go before the board for your oral exam." He shook his head. "Now then, you have one huge organizational task to give the regents, correct them and send them out, a second to bring the school year to a close for all English classes and a third to begin planning for the fall term."

"That's a lot of organizational work," she said, scanning the previous year's outlines, as he handed them out.

"No time for a Literary Arts class, I'm afraid." He smiled. "Probably for the best. Program yourself a small, quiet senior class or a reading class with a paraprofessional." She looked at him in horror. "You'll need to devote your energy to your new job," he said, smiling paternally at her, and he kept talking. He was still interacting only with her, Danielle noticed, while both women took notes.

His instructions droned on, while her thoughts screamed, *I'm trading in a profession for one I'm not good at, that I don't even like!* She looked at Nicole taking notes. *She's having a good time! What's she thinking about?* Danielle knew her brilliant colleague could inspire both faculty and students. She looked down at her notes. *Why did I want this job in the first place? For prestige? No. To please Dad!* She put down her pencil, a simple enough act but as powerful as if she'd cleaved heavy chains with which she'd enslaved herself. "I'm not good at this," she said aloud.

"At what dear?" asked Dr. Norton.

"At doing the work of a Department Head. I'm not good at it."

"Of course you are." He inclined his head toward Nicole, without looking at her. "Delegate. It's all in the delegation."

"I can delegate because Nicole is so good at this. She should head the department. Thank God you chose her as the back-up!" She turned to her colleague who, with mouth open, held a pencil somewhere in space over her notebook. "I'll assist you."

"Danielle, Danielle." Dr. Norton's voice massaged the air around her. "Think it over. Try it for a term, a year before deciding. You're turning your back on a brilliant career."

"For which I have no interest or talent, Dr. Norton. I want my classes."

"Then keep your Literary Arts class if that will work for you."

"No, you're right. I'd have no time to teach it, to direct a play, run a writing contest or coach students for the city Shakespeare Contest." She was talking to his back. He was pulling a document from his file.

"At least sleep on it," he said, handing her the document. "This is the contract you will sign. That will be your starting salary." He pointed as if he were clinching a business deal. She knew what the salary was, but she looked anyway.

Unmoved, she looked up at him, her eyes never leaving his face. "Nicole Johnson is better qualified. She's a fine teacher, and she has the organizational skills for the job. She has the balance." Danielle felt her dignity in that moment, but just for a moment, before she added, "I don't. I'm unbalanced." She heard how it sounded and giggled.

"I wish you would reconsider." A hardening in his voice caused her to sober up.

"I'll sleep on it," she said carefully, "but if I decide to remain a

Chapter Twenty-Two

teacher, I'll assist Ms. Johnson over the summer." He didn't reply. "She and I will just exchange roles."

"Don't do anything rash," he said.

"No, of course not."

"We should get this settled soon, before we proceed."

"Yes, yes, of course." *What is he saying?*

"I'll give you until after the Passover-Easter Break to think about it." *Oh no…*

Outside in the hallway, Nicole asked, "Are you sure you want to do this?"

"Absolutely. You're perfect for the job. And you know it. You've been guiding me all spring."

"Just be certain. Okay?"

"Okay."

It wasn't until they parted that Danielle could deal with Dr. Norton's threat. She unlocked the door to the dark book room, shut it behind her and switched on the overhead light. The sparkling brass chandelier lit clean, organized shelves. Nicole had led her in organizing this once dirty, disorganized room during Christmas vacation. Danielle, the new department head in training, had only helped, but she'd gotten the credit. "Delegation," she sneered aloud, as she sat on a polished wooden bench in the far corner, where she could examine her feelings. *I should have seen it before, but I wanted to please Dad, to make him proud… with my appointment.* An anguished, "Oh!" popped out of her, filling the quiet room, and she said, "Dr. Norton didn't come right out and say it, but he doesn't want Nicole in that position."

Her eyes roamed the bookshelves. She was talking softly now. "He gave me until the end of the Passover-Easter Break to *think* about it. That's in the Spring. I've got some time." She spotted Emerson's "Self-Reliance," paused and took a volume from the shelf. "They know this," she murmured, as she flipped through the pages. Then she shut off the lights, left the book room and roamed along the empty corridor, as the seed of an idea took root.

PART THREE

Chapter Twenty-Three

...and The BITTER

What to do about the Little One...It was late January, as Danielle looked up from correcting papers at her bedroom desk in Brooklyn. The first trimester would be over in mid-February. Just thinking about it exhausted her. *I'll be too isolated caring for a baby in my Gramercy apartment. How can I do this alone? I can't live with Charlotte and Tessie, if they're going to influence her to join their outdated lifestyle, passing for white and hiding out in this house... Would Phil and Alma raise her?* Embarrassed, she covered her face with her hands. Then she indulged in a momentary but unrealistic vision of her mother and father beaming down upon their granddaughter the way they used to beam down upon her, and she dissolved into tears.

She steeled herself to imagine entering the abortion clinic in Connecticut, but her vision blurred at the door. She sat back in her chair and remembered how she'd rejoiced when Roe vs. Wade became law. *Thank God! Now women won't have to die in unsafe abortions while the rich fly to another country for safe ones.* Then the mixed blessing hit her smack in the face. *Now we have the freedom to kill.* That thought kicked off an old inner conflict.

It's legal.
That doesn't make it any easier.
Live in Manhattan. It makes room for everyone.
With or without a child.
Without a child. The momentary relief she felt was undeniable.

After dinner, one night in early February, Charlotte sat down at the baby grand and began to play the opening bars of *Afternoon of a Faun*. Danielle, with a class set of composition papers, slipped out of her shoes and relaxed on the window seat with her back against the mahogany partition and her legs stretched out on the blue-green velvet cushion. But instead of marking papers, she gazed through the sheer curtains. Outside, snow piles were disappearing into the darkness and just enough cold air seeped through the window to make the large living room feel cozy.

Tessie settled into a cornflower blue rocking chair to crochet something pink. Danielle's eyes narrowed and her stomach tightened. *It's for the baby.* In the soft yellow lamplight, the old woman's face had a youthful glow and her long sliver hair shimmered like floss, reminding Danielle of the angel on top of the Christmas tree at her parents' home in Connecticut. Tessie glanced up from her knitting and smiled. "Do you miss Josh?"

Danielle nodded and her anger surfaced.

"Invite him over," said Charlotte.

"He'd have to get Sharon to come with him. That'd be a cold day in hell!"

Tessie's crochet needles poised in mid-stitch. "He needs help with that child!"

"I'm busy with mine!" she snapped before she could catch herself. The window seat no longer felt cozy. She rose. "Sorry. That was unnecessary. Maybe I'll feel more like coping after a night's sleep." But the genuine concern in Tessie's eyes held her there. So, when the phone rang, she dashed for it to break away from her aunt's perceptive gaze.

"Hello?" She waited impatiently through a long pause. "Hello!"

"Charlotte?" said her father, and her breath caught.

"Dad?" She'd forgotten that he periodically checked in on his family. Charlotte stopped playing, Tessie stopped crocheting and Danielle stared at her reflection standing in the long, dark, curtained window across the room. A second phone clicked on. "Hi, honey!"

"Hi, Mom." She felt like a little girl.

Chapter Twenty-Three

"What are you doing there?" her father asked. "We didn't know you were… in contact with your aunts."

"I live here." She saw her reflection enjoy a measure of vengeance. "Phil has my apartment for the time being."

"I see."

"When are we going to see you?" asked her mother.

She wanted to scream, "Valentine's Day! Abortion Day!" Instead, she said, "February fourteenth. Winter break."

"Can you come home earlier? So we can talk?" asked Mac.

Now he wants to talk! What's he up to? "I have school on the thirteenth. I'll pack a bag and take Amtrak after my last class." *I'm not going to be there any longer than I have to be.*

"The train's a good idea," said her mother. "I'll meet you."

"I've done a lot of thinking since the last time you were here," said her father.

"So have I." *He's not selling me another pile of horseshit!*

"The abortion's your decision. I was out of line pushing my--"

"I haven't made up my mind yet," she said in a breaking voice. "I have to go."

She heard her mother call her name, as she whirled around in the direction of the piano and held out the phone to Charlotte, who quickly slid off the bench and took it.

As she ran up the stairs, she heard Charlotte say, "Mac?" More words were spoken, too softly for her to hear. At the top of the stairs, she stood in the shadows and listened. "It's an emotional time for a woman. She'll be fine," said Charlotte.

For someone who's so angry with him, she's awfully nice! An overhead light glowed on silvery floss at the foot of the stairs, and she looked down into the compassionate eyes of her Christmas angel, whose shadowed features looked like a woodcarving. Danielle half-waved and rushed into her room.

When her alarm clock rang the next morning, Danielle awoke to a revolving dream image of a cloud-like carousel in pastels with girls and boys, no older than three, riding pink and blue horses. She heard carnival music and children chanting: *He needs help with that child! I'm busy with mine!* He needs help with that child! I'm busy with mine, over and over, as the carousel turned and turned.

Exhausted, she shut off the clock, picked up her dream journal, jotted down "carousel" and slogged into the bathroom accompanied by the chant. "Stop!" she said.

But the dream was on automatic replay that morning and all that afternoon. It was wearing her down, and the appointment for the abortion was days away. She had to decide soon. At the end of the school day, feeling even more exhausted, she drove directly to her aunts' house. Charlotte's car was not in the driveway. She walked into the house and called out their names, just to be sure. *They're probably grocery shopping.* In the kitchen, she made herself a cup of chamomile tea, then returned to the living room and sat with her legs stretched out along the window seat.

The carousel and the chant played on. She had to silence it. I have to decide now! She scanned the room, knowing she was not alone, and pulled the sheer curtain aside to look out the window, away from them… the listeners. The last of the sun's rays fell upon her parked car and the snow piles. Charlotte and Tessie would return soon. She knew her decision, and she had to face it now, even if the family ghosts were there. Let them listen.

She sat up, took a deep breath and said over the carousel, "I don't know how I'll raise you… but I'll do it, Little One. I'll take a sabbatical for six months or, maybe a year. We'll live here for a while. Then we'll move to Gramercy Park."

She remembered when she first suggested to the fetus that they try a life together… her enthusiasm and hope, her frequent chats with the unborn child and her certainty that it was a girl. "I must have been living in a bubble!" she burst out. "But I'll have you anyway… I know you too well." Exhausted, she leaned back against the mahogany partition of the window seat and closed her eyes….The carousel was finally stopping, and she just wanted to sleep…

And I know you too well. Danielle's eyes slitted open. There was nothing to see but fading light on the curtain and the mahogany partition opposite her. The voice had come from within. She closed her eyes again and was drifting into sleep, when she felt wetness between her legs. Carefully, afraid to move, she pulled up her skirt, pulled open her underpants and saw blood, dark red and spreading.

"Nooo," she whispered. In that instant, everything began to change. "No, no please, Little One. Don't go. Please!" She carefully replaced her clothes and, gently, very gently, lay flat upon the window seat, with the palms of her hands over her womb, and she prayed until her terror was reduced to fear. She felt no more blood flowing, but she dared not move. The last rays of the sun were slipping into dusk. She closed her eyes and was trying to breathe calmness into her body, when exhaustion finally took her. "I love you," she said, just before falling into a deep sleep.

A golden glow pervaded a dream she was forgetting and warmth flooded her midsection, as she opened her eyes. Silvery-haired Tessie was sitting beside her on the window seat. The old woman's cool, papery hands lay gently over her own, which still covered her womb.

"How do you feel?" her aunt asked.

"My stomach feels warm, but your hands are cool."

"That was Mama."

"Oh, for God's sake, Tessie!" Charlotte, in a full-length apron over her slacks and sweater, stood behind her sister, and looked down at Danielle. "You were fast asleep, when we came in. Are you all right?"

"Just groggy," Danielle lied.

"We have vegetable soup, broiled halibut, carrots and mashed potatoes." Her stomach revolted, but she raised herself carefully onto her elbows.

"Sounds good. I have to use the bathroom first."

"No hurry. Dinner isn't for half an hour yet. I need your help, Tessie." Tessie patted Danielle's hand and followed Charlotte into the kitchen.

The velvet window seat, where she'd lain, was dry and so was the back of her skirt. Like an old lady, she carefully climbed the stairs to the upstairs bathroom… No new blood. "Give me another chance."

Chapter Twenty-Four

Danielle's doctor prescribed a few days of bed rest. Charlotte and Tessie fed her nourishing soups, steaks, collards and beets to build her up. She called the school to say she'd be out sick for the rest of the week. Then she left a message for Dr. Norton to tell the substitute to let her Literary Arts class work on their short stories, instead of using her substitute lesson plans. She spent the time lounging on the window seat, correcting compositions, reading, talking to the Little One and sleeping.

By the weekend, her energy along with her mood, bounced back. A partial reprise of the carousel chant from her dream, "He needs help with that child, He needs help with that child," revved up, and she called Josh.

The following evening, she joined him and Sharon for Chinese take-out at his place. She chose egg drop soup and vegetable chow mein because they were mild. After dinner, she said, "Let's hang out in the living room for a while.

"Why?" Sharon asked.

"To talk… about us." The girl made her usual deprecating noise.

"Come on," said Josh. Sharon slumped into the wing chair and stared at the grandfather clock. Danielle and Josh sat on opposite ends of the couch.

She smiled at Sharon. "Remember when you said I didn't want a baby because it might blow my cover?" Like a cat, ready to fend off an attack, Sharon slowly straightened up in her chair. "You were right," Danielle said quickly, "but there was more. Even when I no longer cared about the race thing, I still didn't want a baby."

"You didn't want me either. You want him."

"Sharon," said Josh in his reasonable tone.

Chapter Twenty-Four

"You don't want me either," she said to her father. "I'm a responsibility, and you're the suffering hero!"

"That's not fair!" Josh's rational tone disappeared.

Sharon faced her father. "My mother said you wanted her to have an abortion when she was pregnant with me!" Silence. Danielle looked at Josh, saw it was true and remembered how abandoned she'd felt when he'd suggested she get an abortion. "You didn't want me then, and you still don't want me, now!" Sharon got up and headed for the coat closet. "That's okay. I have friends."

I left him too, thought Danielle.

Josh was on his feet to block her way to the door, yelling, "You're making a mountain out of a mole hill! Sit down!"

Coat over her arm, Sharon picked up speed to reach the door first. Josh broke into a run and got there ahead of her.

"Let me out," she said, leveling her eyes at his. Neither moved.

"Maybe Sharon's right," said Danielle, matching their decibel. She heard her own anger too. They turned and stared at her. Josh looked betrayed, and Sharon looked suspicious. "Maybe you're conflicted, Josh," she said, and her voice softened.

Sharon refocused on her father. "You don't want me, do you? Admit it." Her pain and anger silenced him.

Danielle spoke quickly. "I know you love Sharon more than anything, more than she knows. But remember when we started dating and you told me you weren't cut out to be a… father? That Sharon would be better off with her mother? You didn't want the responsibility?" Josh turned to her, and she felt the sting of his anger before he turned back to his daughter.

"I was reeling from the divorce back then and couldn't imagine raising a child alone. It terrified me. And everyone said a girl should be raised by her mother," said Josh.

"So you were off the hook!" said Sharon.

"I'm past that, now. I want you to live here with me." His voice broke with the truth of it. Neither spoke, as they stood by the door.

Danielle talked to keep Sharon from leaving. "I wasn't happy about having my child either. The responsibility. I told the same thing to her, three nights ago, and she started to leave me. I began to bleed." Danielle's voice trembled to a stop. Josh and Sharon were still staring at each other. *Didn't they hear a word I said?*

She slipped behind them and took her coat from the closet. They turned as one to look at her. Danielle and Sharon locked eyes. "I want two daughters, if that's possible," she said and tears pricked her eyes. It only took a moment to wipe them, but, when she looked up, Sharon and Josh were hugging each other. Sharon was crying. Josh was too, only he made the squeaking sound of a man trying not to. Danielle stood right next to them, but they seemed to be in their own world. Father and daughter. She sensed the child within her, smiled and slipped into her coat.

Josh looked at her. "Where are you going?"

"You two really have a lot to talk about… this time," she said, remembering all the other times they shut her out to talk, and she smiled a partly encouraging, partly gotcha smile and opened the door.

"Thanks," said Josh.

She looked back at them. "I hope you'll include me… soon."

She found Charlotte and Tessie having tea by the fire. They looked up expectantly, but with good manners, asked no questions.

"May I join you?"

"Of course," said Tessie.

Danielle took a cup and saucer from the china cabinet. After a peaceful sip of tea, she gazed into the crackling fire and said, "I took your advice, Tessie. I visited Josh and Sharon and gave him help with that child. I hope."

"That's nice," said Tessie. Charlotte pushed a dish of homemade peanut butter cookies toward her. Danielle took a bite and told them what happened.

Chapter Twenty-Four

Her aunts didn't speak when she finished, and Danielle wondered if she'd said too much. Then Charlotte said, "I hope this works out for you."

"You'll always have a home here," said Tessie.

They avoided further discussion of her strange story, and she loved them for that.

The three lingered over a second cup of tea and talked until Danielle excused herself to go to sleep and to allow her child to get strong.

Chapter Twenty-Five

The woods are lovely, dark and deep,
But I have promises to keep,
And miles to go before I sleep,
And miles to go before I sleep.

— *Robert Frost*

Daylight was leaving the wood, as the train sped through the winter countryside past black-branched trees in crusted snow. Robert Frost country… My Literary Arts class would enjoy reading his poems aloud. She jotted down a few titles, snuggled cozily into her seat, and gazed out the window. She remembered the tomboy she was, racing through those Connecticut woods with her shaggy, black mongrel running ahead of her, circling back and running ahead again. Her heart yearned to hold Jerusha's little hand and to introduce her to those mystical New England grounds, just by walking on them. As her mother had done with her. In this reverie, Jerusha's complexion was dark olive, just like Danielle's. Just like her father's.

A memory suddenly arose of how her father had once discouraged her from traveling too far outside of New England. "You can learn all you'll ever need to know in your own back yard," he'd said, and quoted a line of poetry about the universe in a leaf of grass. He'd stumbled onto great literature, while erasing all vestiges of a southern accent from his speech. Danielle enjoyed the poetry, but somehow she'd also received the message that she'd be in danger if she strayed too far from that yard. How he had panicked when she'd gotten an acting job with a dinner theatre chain down south. It was nineteen sixty-nine, and she was twenty-eight years old. "You know how dark you get with a tan! And those stages in the round. You'd be a perfect target for someone who

Chapter Twenty-Four

mistook you for a Negro."

Danielle, badly bitten by the acting bug, didn't listen until her mother said, "Get your hair straightened, just in case he's right." She did, and he was.

First, there was the incident in Nashville, Tennessee. She'd lost her way on an empty back street and asked the only person around, an old black man, swaying with drink, for directions to the Grand Ole Opry, where she was to meet up with her fellow actors for dinner and a show. Suddenly, a car screeched to the curb beside them. A white man her age rolled down his window, and with a lewd smile, beckoned her into his car. She quickly thanked the old black man and ran. A block away, she was among people again and in sight of the opera house.

Then the acting troupe went to Jackson, Mississippi. They were performing in a Broadway comedy that had recently closed. The audiences seemed friendly. One night the show was stopped so actors and audience, northerners and southerners, could gather together around a television set in the lobby to watch Neil Armstrong, Edwin Aldrin and Michael Collins descend from Apollo Eleven and walk on the moon. They all shared an American moment together. She'd had two dates while she was there, a dinner date with a young white man who attended the show… and a party with food and dancing with a young black man who worked in the kitchen at the dinner theatre. Her experience in Tennessee should have made her cautious. But the dates were platonic, she didn't challenge anyone's views, and she remained safe.

Then one night, a rich theatre patron invited the cast to dinner at a restaurant in a nearby city, where tension among people, now calling themselves Black, had been thick with barely concealed anger. He talked of very little but the inferiority of Negroes. He even insisted they smelled…

Danielle stared in horror at these memories. How naïve she'd been. And though she feared airplanes, she'd run up the steps of that plane in Jackson to go home.

She relaxed into the train's soft seat and closed her eyes. Jackson, Mississippi…Like a snake, a newspaper article and two pictures of Emmett Till slithered into her mind, and she remembered they were both fourteen in 1955. She was fifteen when she'd challenged her youth fellowship at church in Connecticut for saying Negroes were slow, lazy and smelled, and they wouldn't marry one. "I'd marry one!" she'd said, kicking off an explosive reaction from her fellowship. She hadn't known about Emmett Till, hadn't read the news article or seen the photos for many, many years. Now she recalled the picture of him, not long before he was murdered. He was standing beside his young mother. Both had healthy complexions and abundant hair. Both were smiling. She also saw the picture of the open casket his mother had insisted upon. His corpse looked old, very old. His face and neck were swollen in his black suit, and his hair was sparse. One eye was gouged out; the other was slightly open and, to Danielle, looked inexpressibly sad. The sides of his mouth were pulled down in what must have been an undertaker's attempt to tie it shut. He looked helpless.

My parents must have known about Emmett Till when I traveled to Tennessee and Mississippi to act in dinner theatres! He too would have been twenty-eight if he'd lived. Mom and Dad never told me about him. Never told me about my race. If they did, I would have been terrified. I might have passed for white like the rest of the family. Dad…

She remembered her father often quoting the lines,

>"Oh, what a tangled web we weave,
>When first we practice to deceive."

Dad quoted that couplet so many times over the years to teach us honesty. It never even occurred to me he was speaking from experience. He passed for white in exchange for a safer life, access to liberty and the pursuit of happiness. He couldn't have foreseen all the lies he and Mom would tell… or the separation from his family. What a heavy weight. And they lifted it off our shoulders by deceiving us, too… Oh Dad…

The trees blurred, as she imagined herself saying, "I accept what you've chosen for yourself, Dad, and I won't say anything, when I'm in

Chapter Twenty-Five

New Crossing. But, would you pass for the mixture you really are when you and Mom visit my daughter and me where we live?" In this reverie, five-year old Jerusha was smiling up at Mac, and her complexion was the color of coffee mixed with milk. *I want the Little One to have you for a grandfather. Tears rolled down her face. I want Jerusha to walk the New England woods with Mom and me, three generations of McKinnon women with our current dog, continuing our tradition.* She imagined her daughter at twelve, dashing through the woods with her shaggy black mongrel running ahead of her, circling back and running ahead again. Her complexion was black.

From the window, she spotted her mother waiting for her at the railroad tracks, holding her beige cashmere coat closed at her throat against the chilly whoosh of the train, and she remembered meeting her there, a mere thirteen years before in 1969, when she flew back in from Mississippi. The train stopped and, as she climbed down, she thought, *If something bad, really bad, had happened to me in Mississippi, would Mom have insisted upon an open coffin?* Fear, like a snake, coiled itself within the pit of her stomach. She rushed into her mother's open arms.

At sixty, Lynn looked fifty and fit. *Nerves are probably wracking her body. That's my fault.* A minimum of powder and lipstick comprised her make-up. Her well-defined eyebrows framed beautiful but unhappy eyes. *My fault, too.*

"I like your new coat. It's you," said her Mom. She was referring to the casual long-waisted drape and velvet collar. She touched it and gave her daughter an affectionate smile.

"Josh and I picked it out at Bloomingdales. It's my Christmas present!" Both women's faces fell, as the word, Christmas, brought back that awful night.

Wind whipped along the station's platform. "Let's go home," her mother said. As Danielle walked beside her, the memory of her narrow escape in Jackson, Mississippi returned. *He didn't follow me. I would have heard his car or his footsteps... Why? What happened to the drunken old man?* It hadn't even occurred to her to wonder. Now she prayed for him.

Chapter Twenty-Six

Darkness moved in on New Crossing, as Danielle walked quickly after her mother, whose flowing cashmere coat blew open in the cold night air. "Slow down for a pregnant woman," she wanted to joke, but thought better of it. She was breathless when she finally caught up with her in the crowded town hall parking lot. "The devil chasing you?" she asked. No answer. She glanced up quickly to see a yellow glow from lights within the stately building. "What's going on in there?"

Still not answering, her mother stepped quickly into her Chevy Malibu and started the ignition. "Nice car," said Danielle, promptly shutting the door. "Right out of Dad's showroom? It smells new… Or is it that spray stuff?" The car swerved onto Oak Street throwing her against the door. "Careful!"

"Sorry, honey. Dinner's ready. Hungry?"

"I'm getting there," Danielle lied. The thought of trying out her imaginary conversation on her father had ruined her appetite. "How's Dad?"

"Looking forward to seeing you." They turned onto the country road. In only eight minutes they'd arrive at what used to be home, and the pain of its loss gripped Danielle again. "I understand him better than I did at Christmas. I really want to talk to you both."

"He may be a while."

"Oh." She thought all decks would be cleared for her visit. "Still at work?"

Her mother's tense long-lashed hazel eyes were her prettiest feature. "He's at the Town Hall."

"We just passed it!" *Ran past it!* "Why didn't you tell me?" Her mother focused on the road she knew like the back of her hand. "Mom?"

Chapter Twenty-Six

"The Haley family is contesting the sale of the Richardson house." Danielle's stomach turned over, as the Christmas Eve nightmare, less than two months before, moved in on her.

"I don't want that house. Why is he so stubborn? To keep the Haley family out?" The car sped through the darkness.

"This whole thing's been in limbo since Christmas," said her mother in a tight voice.

Your father's been depressed and impossible to talk to. He's barely gotten through his work hours at the showroom. Then three nights ago, Roger Preston called."

"The banker?" Her mother nodded. "Why didn't you say anything?"

"We didn't want you upset, in your condition."

"I'm not going to have the abortion so don't worry."

Her mother hit the brakes, pulled off the road, stopped and looked at her. "Why?"

"I want… her." Her voice broke. "I came home to tell you and Dad in person… So, Roger Preston called and…"

Carefully her mother said, "Do you remember Reverend Johnson, the black preacher from Milltown?"

"Sort of. I remember snooping around Dad's desk one Christmas, when I was about thirteen, and finding a check for a hundred dollars written out to him. Dad told me he'd had a good year and wanted to share with those who were less fortunate than we were. Then he said, 'Who knows, though? He may spend it all on liquor.' And he laughed."

Suddenly, Danielle had an epiphany. "Mom, that was before you and Dad started your nightly cocktails… That was in the sixties, right after I graduated college and moved out into the world. Did you two start drinking because you were both nervous people would see I'm black?"

Her Mom looked at her. "Nervous? Terrified. No one was black then. They were Negro, and Negroes were in much more danger than blacks are today… Yes, drinking reduced our constant tension." She took her daughter's hand in hers and said, "Anyway, Reverend Johnson's also a lawyer, and he's representing the Haley family."

"Against Dad?"

"Not exactly. Tom started to show the house again, so the Haleys contested it. Tom and Roger asked your father to stop by to give them moral support."

"Moral? More like credence." Her mother was quiet. "How can they block it?"

"The covenants… racial housing laws."

"Oh, come on! In 1982?"

"We still have them. You know that!" her mother snapped, but her voice broke, and Danielle saw tears run down her cheeks. She rummaged through her pocketbook and pulled out a hankie. "Jim Crow Laws prevented your father and me from marrying here back in the forties. That's why we got married in New York." She sounded very weary, and, for the first time in her life, Danielle feared for her mother's health. "Connecticut still has Blue Laws in New Crossing too. You know that."

"No one's contesting Josh's moving into New Crossing," Danielle said quietly.

"They decided to let him slip by because the Jews would put up such a fight and because they could use him as a hedge against a charge of racism if the Haley family tried to move in again."

Josh is the cork. Just like in school. They sat in silence. As her mother was wiping her eyes, a sick sensation jogged Danielle's memory. *Hey Mac! Want to go down South and shoot niggers?"* She looked at her mother. "Dad told me, once, that someone in town invited him to go down South and shoot Negroes."

"When?" her mother asked sharply.

"When I was fourteen."

"You remembered that?"

"It's not something you forget." The memories kept coming. "I asked him why he never joined clubs with the other businessmen. He said he didn't want to be a member of a club where some people were left out, that clubs did background checks and, then he told me about this guy, who wanted them to kill Negroes."

"Tom Page," her mother said.

Danielle's eyes widened. "The real estate agent? Didn't he sell Dad the house?"

"Yes."

"My God! How could you live in a neighborhood like that?"

"The neighborhood wasn't like that! Tom Page was. And a Tom Page could have lived anywhere back then. Emmett Till…"

As Danielle watched her pause and regain self-control, she thought of all the years this woman who'd given her birth, who'd once wanted to abort her, had turned a corner to protect her from this dark and dangerous… society. She placed a hand on her arm and humbly asked, "Do you want to go back to the Town Hall?"

Her mother nodded and made a U-turn on the lonely country road. On the way, Danielle said, "You knew about Emmett Till."

"Of course." Nothing more was said.

It was pitch black, as they climbed the steps of the two hundred year old, brownstone edifice. Cold air blew into their faces, freezing their ears and noses. The meeting sign that swung on chains from a low wooden frame was barely discernible, announcing,

Meeting: 7 P.M. The topic wasn't posted.

Macabre was never a word Danielle had associated with this building before that night. Justice was. As a high school student in Social Studies class, she'd sat in on Town Hall meetings. The class of fifty-nine, her class, graduated in the auditorium.

The interior of the building was simple with dark wood, solid beige walls, tall windows and a large bronze chandelier, glowing with electric candles. Middle and side aisles flanked twenty rows of seats on the first floor. A second floor balcony, seven rows deep, was a horseshoe overlooking two speaker's stands on the stage below.

At the auditorium's entrance, Danielle and her mother looked for Mac. They saw Reverend/Attorney Johnson, dark and dignified in a navy suit, standing behind the podium to the audience's left and listening attentively to real estate agent, Tom Page, who casually slouched onto his podium at the opposite side of the stage. His blue eyes matched his blue suit, and they lit up when he saw Danielle. "Here comes the proper owner of that house right now," he said with a slur, listing to his right as he waved.

"Welcome home, Danielle!"

She stared at him. *He wanted to drive down south to shoot Negroes. Did he go?* There was a slight stir as the townsfolk looked back at her, rippling a tension in the air Danielle had thought was just within herself.

"Over there!" whispered Lynn, pointing to Mac, who stood up at his seat a few rows in front of Tom. Her father smiled, pointed to empty seats in the last row and walked back to join them. He looked older and sadder in the short time since Danielle saw him. Still she thought, *If Dad supports that man, he's no better than Tom Page is.* Afraid of what she would discover about him, she pushed past her mother to the third seat from the aisle, forcing her Mom to sit between her father and herself. She concentrated on the speakers. Tom Page was speaking.

"The laws of this town are very clear on the issue of residency, Reverend Johnson," he said, as if to an unschooled boy.

"Those laws ignore the 1968 Fair Housing Act." A murmuring arose and drew Danielle's attention to the Haley family two rows in front of Attorney Johnson. Leo Haley sat still as a statue in his dark brown suit and tie. Danielle wondered if his powerful hands were opening and closing into fists, as they did on the night of the Wassail party. Viola Haley looked lovely in a gray suit with a silk rose scarf at her neck. Their two pre-teen boys, one in a blue and the other in a green crew neck sweater over white shirts and dark slacks, sat straight-backed and attentive.

Attorney Johnson raised his voice. "The laws of this town are blue, Mr. Page! It is 1982 and they..."

"Prohibit residence by blacks!" interrupted Tom, as if quoting well-known wisdom. Danielle was unaware her own hands were opening and closing into fists, until her mother tapped the closest one.

Chapter Twenty-Six

"They also prohibit the residency of Jews, Mr. Preston. Why are you not trying to block the residency of Joshua Freedman?"

Danielle leaned forward. Apparently, Tom had no answer because he looked at his notes, swayed slightly and said, as if to a recalcitrant child, "Reverend Johnson, Reverend Johnson," and he cleared his throat.

Danielle felt a man's moist hands settle onto the shoulders of her blouse and massage them. She looked around into the handsome face of the aging banker, Roger Preston, still slim in his Brooks Brothers suit. He trained his charismatic smile on her. *Did he murder Negroes with Tom?* She pulled away, and he leaned past her to whisper, "Hi, Lynn, glad you're here. Mac, Tom's had a few. We need your verbal ability."

"Let him handle it," said Mac.

Tom got his voice back and shouted, "The laws of this town…"

"The laws of this town are giving us the blues, Mr. Page!" interrupted Attorney Johnson, sounding like the reverend he was, elongating the uuu in blues. Laughter erupted, then quickly stopped, as if the town had surprised itself. Danielle and her mother exchanged a careful look. Leo Haley relaxed his rigid posture and looked around at Mac. Danielle looked at her father. His eyes, riveted upon the Reverend, were unreadable. "And the laws of this country override the laws of this town." Perhaps it was Attorney Johnson's rising intonation and extended "i" in override that caused sporadic applause.

A boy with curly red hair and a freckled face turned in his seat and looked around at his neighbors. *Jamie Townsend! He must be in Junior High School by now.* Danielle remembered him, only a year before, as the shy newsboy, who delivered their Sunday paper. He'd undergone a growth spurt since then. He saw Danielle and waved. She waved back.

Attorney Johnson continued. Jamie turned back around, and the audience quieted.

"On December twenty-second of 1981, Mr. Haley exchanged a gentleman's agreement with Mr. Patrick Richardson to purchase his house on twenty-two Liberty Circle. The legalities were postponed until after Christmas." He paused and looked at Mac, as if waiting for him to respond. All of New Crossing waited.

Tom burst out, "Mr. McKinnon put a binder on that house and, uh… Tell 'im Mac! Come up here and set these people straight."

The Haley family turned as one, to look at Danielle's father. Everyone in the room strained to see him. Danielle looked and saw a grim, aging man, her father, looking back at her, and she felt a deep sorrow.

"Mac!" yelled Tom from the podium.

"Mac," said Roger gently, as if to massage him with his oily voice. Danielle's skin crawled. He was still behind her.

She leaned across her mother and whispered, "Dad, it's your choice. You don't have to do it." Lynn reached out to him, but dropped her hand as Mac rose, and Danielle watched him walk to the stage to live out yet another condition of the fine print in his contract to pass for white, the public sacrifice of his honor. She doubted, however, that a public, who so liked him, would see past his salesman's skills. Her stomach tightened as he mounted the steps to the podium. Tom stepped down, slapped a fraternal hand on his shoulder, lost his balance, grabbed Mac's jacket and clutched the railing and stumbled down the aisle toward the back of the auditorium.

Reverend/Attorney Johnson looked with interest at Mac, confusing Danielle, who cringed with embarrassment at the memory of her father's words: "Who knows? He may spend it all on liquor." She couldn't see her father's expression, as he faced the reverend during that long moment. Then, he turned to the audience, his audience of neighbors, friends and business associates, and smiled.

"Good evening." Smiles and murmurs of greeting welcomed him, and Danielle wondered if he felt any of the shame she felt for him. "I caused this confusion when I neglected to close on Pat Richardson's house. Danielle's and her fiance's plans to move to Connecticut were up in the air, at that time, and perhaps still are." He looked at her and bile rose up in her throat. She forced it back down. *Does he think he can manipulate me too?* She sat back and crossed her arms.

"Do you have a binder on the house, Mr. McKinnon?" Attorney Johnson asked.

Mac turned to him. "I have withdrawn it."

"Irreverent!" slurred the inebriated Tom, walking unsteadily to the back of the room. "Whether Mac has a binder or not, this house will not go to a nig… The precedent is set!" He plopped down onto Mac's empty aisle seat, and Lynn moved close to Danielle.

"That precedent will not stand up in a Court of Appeal! The Fair Housing Act became the law of the land during Lyndon Johnson's administration," said the attorney.

Jamie stood up and raised his hand. "Mr. McKinnon? Reverend Johnson?" The two men looked at the red-haired boy.

"Yes, young man?" said Reverend Johnson.

"Can we… Can we set a new precedent?"

"A new precedent?" repeated Mac, an ironic smile curving his thin lips.

"A new precedent?" echoed Reverend Johnson, as one would in his church. He was looking at Mac when he said it, and Mac turned to look at him.

Beside Lynn, at the back of the room, Tom Page scrambled to stand, and he leaned on the chair in front of him. "Jamie, this is a restricted community. A person of color has never lived in New Crossing, son." The smell of whiskey spiked the air around him. "There is shimply no president!"

A man's strong voice overrode Tom's. "A new precedent was set, Jamie." Even though Danielle was looking straight at her father, it took her a full moment to realize that he was the one who'd spoken. She felt her mother stand and saw her hold her husband's gaze, until he refocused on the people of New Crossing. "A new precedent was set the day I moved into this community."

In the quiet, Tom called out, "Mac, wha the hell?"

"I owe all of you an explanation. And I owe my daughter an apology." Danielle couldn't move. "Over Christmas, my daughter, with her fiancé, Joshua Freedman, told us she was pregnant. I encouraged her to get an abortion. Then she found out the child might be born black. You see, I'd kept her heritage from her, but her mother had the good sense to tell her the truth that night. Danielle guessed my motives and accused me of genocide for suggesting an abortion, and I… threw her out of the house." A look of self-disgust appeared on his face, as ironically he seemed to gain in stature.

Danielle rose to her feet and stood for her father. Mac continued. "But that word, genocide, and a forgotten childhood memory that has returned so clearly with it, pursued me constantly."

The quiet room went silent.

"I was five or six, in the woods of South Carolina at the edge of the Negro quarters, where my older sister was shaking tree branches with a stick to loosen the ripe pecans. I was crawling on the ground to pick them up and put them into a basket. We were so involved in our harvest that we didn't see the charred remains of a man hanging from a tree next to us until…" His composed voice began to break. "I looked up and saw my Uncle Luke before I saw his corpse, and I… reached out to him…" Mac was crying openly now, his head down, his hand covering his eyes. When his shoulders stopped heaving, he pulled a handkerchief from his jacket pocket, blew his nose and looked back at the townsfolk. "His charred flesh stuck to my hand. My sister Tessie later told me I tried to shake it off and, when I couldn't, I started to scream. She grabbed my other hand, and we ran deep into the Negro area, where the white man couldn't hear me." Mac held out his right hand. "To this day, this hand shakes, whenever I'm afraid of being exposed." Danielle saw that his hand was still. Hot tears washed down her face. "I was twelve when we moved up North, and though I'd blocked out that particular incident, I've been running from fear all my life.

"I passed for white to provide for myself and for my family. But, in my need to protect my American dream…" Mac looked at Leo Haley, and the town heard his shame as he said, "I did to Mr. Haley what I, by the mere shade of my skin, could avoid having done to me."

In the silent room, people looked toward the Haley family and back to Mac. Danielle's eyes remained riveted on her father. Mac McKinnon faced his neighbors, friends and business associates. "A black man lives in New Crossing, Connecticut. That precedent was set over twenty-five years ago."

Chapter Twenty-Six

Danielle watched her father step down from the podium into the stunned auditorium. A remembered feeling of family pride returned. Reverend Johnson stood and followed him.

Next to Lynn, Tom Page uttered an obscenity. A number of citizens began to walk toward Mac. "I'll get security," her mother whispered, and dashed off. Danielle ran up the aisle between them and her father, hoping the presence of a pregnant woman would deter any violence. As she ran, she saw some people with angry stares frozen on their faces, and some turn away. But she also saw people wipe tears from their eyes, reach out to pat his shoulder or to shake his hand.

"Good going, Mac."

"Wow!"

"That took courage!"

She heard all this and saw Mac's next-door neighbor, Pat Richardson, wrap him in a bear hug. "I deceived you," said Mac.

"I guessed a long time ago, so I really didn't think you'd mind my selling the house to the Haley family."

Lynn was panting when she caught up with Danielle. They held hands and looked around. They saw Tom Page weave toward Roger Preston, who stiffened, turned away and walked from the room, deserting him. They saw Tom swerve around, see Mac, smile terribly, mutter, "Damn you!" raise a fist and go after him.

The people of New Crossing also saw Leo Haley step into Tom's path, and they watched Tom turn and look to them for help. They witnessed his disbelief, as they stood there, and his ignorant surprise as the security guards secured his arms and walked him from the building.

Chapter Twenty-Seven

*"Great Spirit, Help me never to judge another,
Until I have walked a mile in his moccasins."*
—*Native American Proverb*

That night, Danielle and her parents coined a new phrase. It all started in the cocktail hour before dinner when they were sitting in the family room before the fireplace and the framed drawing of the Native American riding bareback, guiding his pony away from the viewer. Her folks sat on the couch and she on an overstuffed chair to their right. Mac stood and raised his crystal tumbler of scotch. Her mother raised her scotch, Danielle her Perrier, and they waited. And waited. "I'm stumped," he finally said. "I can't find words that include every member of our dispersed family."

A hard laugh escaped Danielle and, with it, something else she didn't know was within her. "Our family relationships are like broken pieces of a puzzle," she said. "Let's see… what can we call them? Broken puzzle? Not really a family?" They all tried for a name, but were stumped.

During her mother's tasty dinner of broiled steaks, corn soufflé, salad and Merlot, a glass of which Danielle allowed herself to celebrate her father's triumphant turn around at the Town Hall, she was still at it. It seemed a safe and silly conversation, but it fueled something deep within her, even as she saw that her parents had stopped participating.

It became a rant. "Josh's parents would just say, 'Family.' They even call *me* family. We need a word or phrase to identify you Dad, Mom, Phil, Alma, Tessie and Charlotte, most of whom have separated from one another." She sipped her wine and chattered on – "Josh… Sharon who wants nothing to do with me, and Josh's parents whom you two have never even met!" She saw her father looking down at his hands, and her mother's brow tensing, as she stared at her wine goblet. They'd stopped eating. *Why am I doing this? Haven't they had enough?* She rejected the caution, even as it entered her mind. "And what about all those secret ancestors? How do I explain to the Little One why I'm calling her Jerusha? Tell her I read the name in a book?"

"Enough," her mother shouted. "That's the final straw. We'll become a family. Probably."

Danielle was taken aback. "*Final straw?* What happened to the last straw?"

"You passed that a long time ago," Lynn said with a leveling look.

Mac looked up and slowly raised his wine glass. "To the Family… Probable."

"The Family Probable," Danielle said, considering the name as she gazed at the drawing of the Native American. She almost apologized then, but the best she could do was raise her glass and say, "You've always had a way with words, Dad." Her mother joined the toast, and they laughed weakly, but laughed together for the first time in nearly two months. All of a sudden, one piece of the puzzle fell into place. She knew they felt it too, as they looked at each other. "I think the three of us are a family again," she said. They laughed a little and cried a little too.

To avoid more pain or becoming maudlin… or just to shut me up, Danielle thought in retrospect, her frazzled Mom started barking orders! "Danielle, get yourself on the phone and invite the family probable over for the weekend after next. Saturday and Sunday. Mac, clear the table and set it for dessert. The pecan pie is ready. I'll make the coffee."

Danielle practically jumped onto the couch for the phone by the fireplace in her rush to obey her mother's orders and to avoid saying something she vaguely felt she might regret for the rest of her life.

She saved Josh for the last and told him the whole story, including the conversation that prompted the call. "Then Dad told Reverend Johnson why Tom and Roger were letting you move into the neighborhood."

"Why?"

"Letting in a Jew would be their hedge against a charge of racism!"

"He said that?"

"Yes. Then, Reverend Johnson introduced Dad to a college senior from his church and told us that Dad was responsible for his Howard University education."

"He paid for his education?"

"Why not, he owed them!"

"Is it fair to judge him?"

"I guess not. Dad has been giving money to the Baptist Church for years. I wish you could have been there. Can you come for the weekend? Phil and Alma are coming on Saturday, and Charlotte and Tessie are deciding."

"I'll be there. I'll offer Charlotte and Tessie a ride so they won't have to drive, if you tell them I'll be calling. I haven't met them yet."

"So what's new?" When he didn't respond again, she said, "Am I judging again?"

"Maybe," he said gently. "You've been through a lot."

"I'll call them," she said, and changed the subject. "Guess what?"

"What?"

"My parents seem really happy about the baby."

"So am I." She heard the truth of it in his voice, and took a chance on happiness.

"Your folks are still in Florida. We'll get them next time. But bring Sharon. She's a Probable, too."

"I will. If I have to drag her by the hair."

Danielle laughed, and they said goodnight. When she hung up the phone, she considered the American Indian proverb on the wall in front of her and recognized the wisdom in it, even as it slipped away.

PART FOUR

A Few Celebrations

Chapter Twenty-Eight

Whenever Danielle recalled that first meeting of the Family Probable at Mac and Lynn's home in Connecticut, it seemed to be backlit by a golden glow, and she was certain the fireplace was not responsible. At first however, they were all on their best behavior and all a bit stiff as they sat down to dinner. Then Phil's fiancé Alma, striking in a full Afro and purple jumpsuit, said, "How do you season the roast beef, Lynn? It's delicious."

"I just stuff it with slices of onions, then salt and pepper it. We can do it together next time."

"That's how Mama did it," said Tessie. In a navy dress with a matching velvet ribbon tying back her silvery hair, the girl she once was smiled out at them.

"I learned by watching your mother," said Lynn, "but my cooking never tasted as good as Ruth's, and Mac was never quite satisfied." She flashed him a hazel-eyed tease.

"You're exaggerating," Mac said, smiling.

"You're a fine cook," said Charlotte, looking professional in her brown merino jacket and skirt. "Even Tessie and I never mastered all the southern cooking secrets Mama tried to pass on to us. We were too absorbed in our careers and Manhattan restaurants."

Excruciating boredom announced itself in Sharon's sigh, as she gave her father a look that clearly said, "When are we going home?"

To interest her, Danielle asked Alma, "What do you think of the New York City school system?" Everyone spoke up.

"Your salaries are too low," Josh said.

"But we've got a pension and a tax deferred annuity," said Alma.

"And you have health benefits," Phil said.

Alma looked pointedly at Danielle. "Every last one of us is well taken care of, no matter what."

"Even the dysfunctional teachers," said Danielle, reading her. "There's so much red tape and paperwork involved in firing them that they slip by."

"That's messed up," said Sharon, and Danielle relaxed.

"It certainly is," said Tessie, once an accountant's assistant in an orderly office.

"It's a huge unwieldy organization," said Alma, "and the students' needs often slip between the cracks."

"I don't know how you put up with some of those students," said Charlotte, who'd been an executive secretary with very little back talk in her domain.

"I think she enjoys them," said Lynn.

"They're not getting a fair shake in the system, and they know it," said Danielle.

Charlotte poured gravy onto her roast beef and potatoes. "We didn't either, but we made the best of it."

"By hiding your heritage to succeed in this… free country," said Danielle. "It's time now to walk the walk. Martin Luther King changed the playing field. He inspired a nation… and gave his life." She looked at her father who seemed lost in his thoughts.

After dinner, they gathered around the fire in the family room. Josh sat between Danielle and Sharon on a couch facing the fireplace. Tessie and Mac shared a love seat to their right, and Phil and Alma shared one to their left. Lynn and Charlotte sat in chairs near the kitchen to serve everyone. When Danielle tried to help, they insisted she relax and get strong.

Chapter Twenty-Eight

Lynn handed Mac a bottle and a bottle opener. "From Charlotte and Tessie."

"Scuppernong. I haven't had this in years! It was Mama's favorite," said Mac.

"My grandmother's, too!" Alma said."

"Where are your folks from?" asked Tessie.

"South Carolina."

"Our family is too!"

"Let's drink to that, seeing you're all going to stay the night," said Mac, pulling the cork from the bottle of dessert wine.

As he poured, Tessie told Alma, "This is a special day for us. Over the years, we saw our brother for an occasional visit, and we talked to everyone else by telephone on the holidays, but… I imagine Phil told you the story of what happened."

"Yes, he did." Alma smiled politely and looked down.

"Make the toast, Mac," Charlotte said softly.

They all held their glasses and turned to him. He'd dressed casually in a maroon Perry Como vest, shirt and brown slacks. Danielle, who knew how easily her father could turn a phrase and make a toast to charm his company, was confused to see him lift his glass, as if it were the heaviest weight in the world. The golden liquid glowed before the fire, as he searched for words. "To our South Carolinian roots and to our family being together… again." He paused to look at Danielle. "And, though it's a little late… to my grand-daughter who'll be born in August." Danielle raised her glass of Pellegrino to her father before joining in the group toast.

She felt Josh's arm around her waist and looked around. Sharon, sitting on his other side, avoided her eyes as she clinked her glass of coke with everyone. *Give her time.*

Her mother served coffee and tea. When Charlotte put a plate of molasses cookies she'd baked onto the coffee table, Danielle said, "We had these with Grandma Ruth's sandwiches on that last drive home from Brooklyn, in nineteen forty-something." She looked at her father, who still seemed lost in thought. But when she said, "Remember how good those sandwiches tasted, Dad?" he smiled and nodded. She saw Sharon give Josh a mischievous grin and recalled how the girl had ridiculed her on the drive to Connecticut for Christmas, when Danielle said those sandwiches were better than any food she'd ever tasted.

"But was it the best food you've ever tasted?" Sharon asked Mac.

"The best food? Well, I wouldn't go that far, but they sure were good," he said. Sharon gave Danielle a playful gotcha look.

"They were the best sandwiches I've ever tasted," Danielle said smiling, just before inhaling sharply with a sudden epiphany. "They were made with Grandmother Ruth's love. She made them on the last day Phil and I saw her."

"I believe that can happen," said Alma.

"Wow," said Sharon.

"That's Mama, all right," said Tessie. Then she patted Mac's hand and looked up at him with a sweet smile and said, "Have you heard *Jerusha?*"

Mac's expression saddened, and Danielle knew he thought Tessie had slipped into the past and had heard her long-deceased grandmother. Gently, he put his arm around Tessie's fragile frame. "You've heard her?"

"No, not yet."

Danielle, Josh, Phil and Alma laughed. "She's referring to a tune I wrote," Phil explained.

"You wrote a melody to Jerusha?" asked Mac, looking at his son, as if for the first time.

"It's a blend of African and Celtic rhythms, and it's beautiful," said Danielle.

"As was she," Mac said softly to Phil.

For the first time in years, Danielle witnessed a vulnerable exchange between her father and her brother. She and her mother acknowledged it in a glance. "I'm naming the Little One after her," said Danielle.

"Jeruusha," said Sharon, elongating her name with a groan. "Are you really calling her that?"

Chapter Twenty-Eight

Danielle felt her back straighten. "Yes. It was her great, great grandmother's name."

"That's quite an old-fashioned name for a twentieth century little girl," said Mac.

"Sounds biblical," said Charlotte.

Sharon joined forces with them, took center stage and drove the point home. "Jeruuu-sha! Abidiii-ah! Come to the dinner table!" she said, imitating her grandmother Bess' Brooklyn accent. Everyone laughed. Danielle smiled absently, as the memory of a recurrent dream moved in on her: A locomotive pulling away from the station, leaving behind a Negro woman in a long dark dress.

"Call her Jerri-Anne," said Sharon over the noise of the train.

"What?"

"Call her Jerri-Anne… at least for school."

"I like Jerri-Anne," said Tessie.

Everyone tested the name aloud, as if tasting a nice new wine.

"It would just be a nickname," said Charlotte, lightly tapping Danielle's hand.

Common sense won out. Danielle picked up Josh's unfinished glass of Scuppernong, faced Sharon and said, "To Jerri-Anne," and knocked it back.

Mac raised his glass. "And to my Grandmother Jerusha." He drank, set down the glass and turned to Tessie. "It's high time I claimed her."

"We're finally coming full circle since that day," Tessie said.

"What day?" Danielle asked.

"Might as well tell it," Mac said.

Tessie placed her fragile hand over her brother's strong one. "That day on the McKinnon plantation, when your grandfather lost his temper and shoved your father across Grandmother Jerusha's kitchen."

"What's all this about?" Charlotte asked sharply. Danielle stared at her aunt. *She doesn't know?*

They all waited as Tessie looked sternly into the eyes of those gathered there. "Pa was under a lot of pressure back then, working his tailoring business down South, while buying us a house up North… and white birth certificates."

Danielle's mouth dropped open. "Isn't that kind of like being an illegal immigrant?"

"Under the Jim Crow Laws, yes," said Mac.

Tessie turned to her brother. "Maybe I should have talked to you, helped you to understand why Papa acted as he did, when you refused to break off your friendship with Shamus and start acting like a white boy."

"It wouldn't have mattered," Mac said quietly. "I would have refused anyway."

Phil leaned toward his father. "Tessie and Charlotte told us about your shoeshine business with Shamus."

"Shamus," said Mac, "Shamus. The best friend I ever had."

"What happened?" whispered Danielle.

Mac looked into the fireplace, as if into a long dark tunnel. "One day, in the summer of …1914, Shamus and I were sitting on the curb outside of Mr. Potter's bakery on Main Street, in South Carolina, shining shoes. It was a good day, and we'd dropped many coins into the shoe supply box to share later, when a rough hand grabbed me by the collar of my shirt and pulled me to my feet. I looked up and saw my father's eyes boring into mine. Before I could tell him how much money we'd made, he said, 'You are not to shine shoes or to associate with nigras, anymore!'"

"Nigras?" said Sharon. She'd moved away from her father and was sitting cross-legged in jeans and a sweater on the rug beside Mac.

He nodded and looked back into the flames. "Pa dragged me, arguing and pulling away from him, tied my horse to his carriage, and we drove off, leaving Shamus at the curb with the wooden shoe supply box at his feet. All the while, I kept saying, 'We're nigras, Pa. Shamus is my best friend.' My life had just turned upside down."

"That's messed up," said Sharon. "How old were you?"

"Nine."

Chapter Twenty-Eight

"That's really messed up."

"All I knew was that I wasn't going to lose my friend, and I was still trying to convince Papa of that, when he pushed open the door of my grandmother's kitchen. She was kneading dough at a long wooden table. He shoved me across the kitchen floor, where I collided with a flour sack on the table, fell and hit my head. The next thing I remember was Grandmother Jerusha sitting on the wooden floor, cradling me in her arms. Blood was on a damp cloth with which she was dabbing my forehead."

"Papa dragged me to my feet and stood me beside him in front of a mirror on the wall. I saw my face covered in flour and blood, felt his tight grip on my arm and heard hardness in his voice. 'Look at yourself, Phillip. Look! What color do you see?' I saw my grandmother's reflection as she appeared at my other side. She was black. My father and I had dark olive complexions." Danielle got chills; she'd lived a similar scene with her father just that past Christmas.

"A light skin nigra," I said.

"What color!" he yelled.

"The boy needs time," said my grandmother.

"You see a white boy!" When I didn't answer, he yelled louder, "A white boy!"

"I kept looking at their reflections and at my own. Even now, I can see how much this moment cost each of them. It cost me, too, but I didn't see it then."

"You were so young," said Danielle. She wanted to reach out to him, to make the pain go away. She saw tears in Phil's eyes and felt the rapt attention of the rest.

"He kept peppering me with questions… 'Do you want equality, Phillip?'

"Yes, Pa, but so does Shamus."

'Do you want opportunity?'

"Yes Pa. Shamus wants it too."

'The respect of your neighbors and friends?'

"I have that, Pa!"

Then, he asked, 'Do you want a business of your own?'

"Oh, how I wanted a business of my own, just like Pa! I began to let go of my loyalty to Shamus... I can still feel it, the moment I began to sell out." Mac bent over, covering his face with his hands.

"You were just a child," said Danielle, reaching out to him.

With brutal self-control, he looked up and chilled them with an ironic laugh. "Two years later, I had a business. A watermelon business. I was eleven and in charge of a group of Negroes, who were my friends before I... placed myself above them." He looked back into the fire. "I stood on the open back of a truck, a pad and pencil in my hand, ordering them to hurry up and load the watermelons onto it. The more I yelled, the more slowly they moved. Shamus, with sweat rolling down his face and neck, held a huge watermelon in his arms. When he looked in my eyes and slowed his pace, I yelled, "Move you lazy nigger!"

"What did you say?" He sounded like he'd been kicked in the stomach."

"Time is money! Earn your pay," I yelled to soften it. He didn't move. I couldn't look at him, so I turned away and pretended to write on my pad."

"I heard the watermelon thud onto the hard dry ground, just before he was up on the truck, grabbing my arm and pulling me around, saying, "Who do you think you are?"

"Suddenly, we were fighting. He was my age, but smaller than I was. We fell off the truck, struggling to beat each other up. Shamus won. I lay on the ground, too winded to move. He stood over me. The rest of the boys just stood there, watching. I climbed back onto the truck and picked up my pad and pencil. Shamus could have pulled me back down. When I turned around, I saw him walking down the road, away from his job... and away from me. I looked down to avoid the other boys' eyes, saw the raw, red meat of the crushed watermelon in the dirt... and I vomited."

Mac continued to stare into the fire. "You were so young," said Charlotte, offering her words like a balm to soothe his anguished spirit.

Danielle looked at her father's back. Just beyond his left shoulder, to the side of the fireplace, hung a small, framed ink drawing of a Native American on horseback, moving along a path away from the viewer. Underneath the drawing were the words she knew so well. "Great Spirit, help me never to judge another, until I have walked a mile in his mocassins." It opened up Danielle's memory, back in time to nineteen sixty-three, and though she felt the others around them, it was as though she and her father were alone by that fire. "Dad?" she said, in a small voice, to her father's back.

Mac turned and looked at her with the lonely eyes of the self-condemned and, with a breaking heart, she called him back. "Remember when I was in high school, and we were talking about that drawing behind you of the Native American, and I said that I loved to write, and you said that maybe one day I might write a story about a fellow, who meant no one harm, but who was beset by others?" He nodded. "You didn't say you were a little fellow when they got to you."

"Don't let me off the hook Danielle, when you tell your story."

"They got to you… your father, the Klan, society."

"Tell the truth."

"The truth is an indictment of the times."

"And of one who turned his back on his family and friends."

"Who lost his way…"

"Don't do this for me."

"May I do it for your grand-daughter?"

Mac looked at her with a crooked smile. "Just now, you reminded me of your great grandmother, Jerusha."

"Jerusha?"

"She loved so hard, you had to love back."

Chapter Twenty-Nine

The oral interpretations of the short stories were due, and Danielle knew her Literary Arts class would be in a stir, calming their nerves. She wanted to be in her classroom early to help the young performers. But she found herself sitting in the English office, still trying to decide what to do about Dr. Norton's aversion to recommending Nicole Johnson to replace him as head of the English Department.

The bell rang, propelling her to her feet. She scooped up an armful of their short story booklets she'd Xeroxed and stapled. Jamal, to his classmates' delight, created the cover, a cartoon collage depicting his fellow students in various stages of angst, under the title, In Search of That Iron String.

She rounded the corner a minute late, just as Kamara was ushering Mr. Spatz into her classroom, and she wondered if her colleague had the time, with his history mid-terms, to listen to their stories. Kamara seemed to think he did.

Pre-performance nerves vibrated throughout the room. Some students were pacing and muttering their lines. Others were panting, shaking out their hands or running in place to release their tension. Still others just sat and read over their work. Kamara chose to release his tension by picking on Danielle. "You're late!"

"So are you." She was nervous, too. *Is this plan going to work?* She waved to Mr. Spatz and addressed the class. "Okay, take your seats. I have an announcement, and I want you to be the first to know."

"You're getting married?" asked Kamara. "It's about time." He looked very pleased with himself.

Wide-eyed with shock, the class looked up to see if she was offended. Mr. Spatz raised an avuncular eyebrow, leaned into Kamara and said quietly, "You're way out of line."

Tamika swatted him with her notebook. "That's her business!"

"Sorry," Kamara said, trying to look sorry.

Danielle gave him a quick nod and made her announcement. "Ms. Johnson will be the new head of the English Department this fall." Everyone cheered. As they began to quiet down, she raised her voice. "Before we start our oral interpretations, I have an oral pop quiz for you, good for extra credit, based on the transcendentalists and their influence on our history."

The class groaned. "That was the first marking period! Give us a break! We've got enough work with these oral interpretations!"

"Are you punishing us because of what I just said?" asked Kamara.

"No. Now, this is just a hypothetical situation, and I don't expect it to happen, but, if someone tried to block Ms. Johnson's appointment unjustly" – The complaining ceased! "and if you had evidence…"

"If?" Kamara asked into the quiet.

"If. What could you do to bring about justice?"

At first, no one spoke, while the students absorbed what was both said and unsaid. Then, Marisa raised her hand. "Write petitions!" she said, and the quiz was on!

"Signed by students and teachers," said Chang.

"Organize a non-violent protest," said Kamara, banging his fist on the desk.

"Make signs!" said Jamal, picking up his pencil and sketching in his notebook.

"Put out an extra edition of the school newspaper," said Erica.

"Get a reporter from the New York Times to cover it!" Tamika said, jumping up.

"You don't know anyone from the New York Times," Louis said.

Crestfallen, Tamika sat down. Silence.

"I do," said Mr. Spatz.

Danielle smiled. "Good. You all get extra credit. Time for the oral interpretations," she said, before any more questions were asked. Tamika stood, exhaled and took center stage under the poster of Frederick Douglass.

After the last story was told on Friday of that week, Danielle presented them each with a volume of "In Search of That Iron String," and reviewed the vacation homework.

H.W. 1. Take notes from an encyclopedia on the life of Frederick Douglass.

2. Bring the notes to class for a discussion.

That week before the Passover-Easter break, when Jews and Christians the world over would retell ancient stories of courage and transcendence, also became a time of new storytelling in the same spirit. It was one in which the news of Danielle's pop quiz, as did the plagues of old, reached the appropriate ears and, by the end of the week, Dr. Norton officially announced the appointment of Ms. Nicole Johnson to succeed him as the head of the English Department.

Chapter Thirty

The Holidays — Easter

*"He walks in the garden with me,
While the dew is still on the roses…"*

"That's too much work for you, Charlotte," said Mac, solicitously taking charge from his phone in New Crossing, Connecticut. In Brooklyn, Charlotte's smile faded.

"It's not too much work. I just retired from running an entire office, for Pete's sake," said his sixty-six year old "little sister" from her phone in Brooklyn. Sitting straight backed in her Queen Anne chair in a crisp, white shirt and brown slacks with a telephone on her lap and a pad and pencil on the chair's cushioned arm, she looked like an office executive to Danielle, who was lounging in her bathrobe on the window seat across the living room, listening in on the extension line and sipping her morning coffee.

It was a month before Easter, and Charlotte had called to invite "The Family Probable" to dinner on Easter Sunday. Everyone had accepted with thanks, except for Mac, who, feeling his old self, had slipped into his salesman's persona.

Danielle watched her aunt's mouth move into a thin straight line. *Dad's met his match!* She struggled to keep a straight face, as her father continued. "Tessie's fragile and Danielle's pregnant. All the work will fall onto your shoulders." When he didn't hear an objection, he zeroed in to close the deal. "Lynn and I will pick up you, Tessie and Danielle, if she's going to church –

"I'm going," said Danielle. *I'm not going to miss this. I'll see Josh and Sharon later.*

"Fine," said the master salesman. "After church, we'll meet everyone else at a nearby restaurant for dinner. Choose one and make the reservations, Charlotte, and we'll go back to the house later."

But he hadn't seen Charlotte's eyes narrowing, and like a cat with her ears back, getting ready to attack. "We're not helpless here, and it's high time you came home for Easter, you damned prodigal!" said his little sister.

Danielle's laughter rang out over the phone lines. "See you at the house for dinner, Dad."

So, on Easter Sunday, the second meeting of the Family Probable arrived in Charlotte's and Tessie's back yard for cocktails. Except for an occasional perennial flower in the grass, there was no garden in bloom on that day. However, an Easter Lily, brought by Lynn, reached out from amidst crystal glasses and hors d'oeuvres on a wrought iron table, and scented the warm April air.

Charlotte looked smart in her navy pants suit. Mac draped his suit jacket over the back of a lawn chair, loosened his necktie and unbuttoned his starched shirt at the neck. Josh and Phil gratefully followed his lead. Danielle and Sharon served drinks and chilled shrimp with a dipping sauce.

A perfect afternoon, and yet a feeling that something was missing haunted Danielle. She looked around, but only saw her mother smiling at Sharon. "Pink ballerina shoes! How lovely. Did you choose that outfit yourself?"

"Grandma did. She said I had to wear them today," the pretty teenager said. Then imitating her Grandmother Bess, she shook her forefinger and said in a Jewish-New York accent, "Be nice! Make your father proud!" Everyone laughed and Sharon was delighted with center stage.

"You have a million dollar smile, young lady," said Mac, raising his glass to her.

"I hope your parents will be able to join us next year," Lynn said to Josh.

"So do I," said Charlotte, and Tessie nodded.

"And I'd be proud to have a second daughter in the family," said Mac

Chapter Thirty

and shot Josh a sharp look. That was as close as Danielle's family came to asking, "When are you two getting married?"

Mac's remark about a second daughter caused unexpected jealousy to zing through Danielle. She thought she quelled it quickly enough, but Sharon leaned into her, looked directly into her eyes and said quietly, "You were jealous just now, weren't you?"

"No, of course not. You would be an… addition. A good one."

"You were jealous. Of me. I saw it."

"You did?"

"That jealousy straight talk hurts, doesn't it?"

Danielle glanced around. No one was close enough to hear. "Yes, it does." Sharon laughed, not unkindly. Danielle laughed too and felt an impulse to hug her, but she held back.

Sharon grinned. "We're just a couple of jealous bitches."

"We are," said Danielle, and, shocked that she agreed, was about to clean up the language, but stopped short. *We've made a connection!*

"What are you two laughing about," asked Mac from across the yard.

"Oh, nothing," giggled Sharon.

"Just girl talk," laughed Danielle, and the two bitches took a walk around the block to get control of themselves.

So when they returned, and Phil, his suit jacket back on, took Alma's hand and said, "We have an announcement," Danielle was unprepared, as his words, "We're getting married," rolled over her. Her world shifted into slow motion, and she looked around for Josh. His hand found hers, she searched his eyes, he smiled uncomfortably, and she looked back at the radiant couple.

Silver-haired Tessie, like an ancient garden sprite, floated in her lavender silk dress to embrace her handsome nephew. "You remind me of your father the day he announced his engagement to Lynn." She smiled into Alma's eyes as she framed the black woman's face with her light brown hands and hugged her. Her long hair like silver netting blew over Alma's afro, and her lavender dress blended into the young woman's vibrant rose one. "God bless you both."

"You'll need it," said Charlotte, approaching them with open arms.

Danielle watched her father shake his head, as if a good-natured joke had been played on him, and she heard him say to Lynn, "The best laid plans…" They rose and embraced the couple.

Danielle and Josh waited in line. Because she dared not look at him, she felt his masculinity all the more strongly, so sensuous in his navy slacks, shirt open at the neck, loosened tie. She saw Sharon standing on Josh's other side and leaned in to smile, but the girl was looking the other way. *I forgot about her when Phil announced their marriage. Are the battle lines being redrawn?* Danielle felt her heart breaking, as she embraced Phil and Alma and pretended all her tears were happy ones. Mercifully, Charlotte announced dinner, and they left the garden.

In the living room, Danielle looked at Sharon, but the girl still wasn't meeting her eyes. *How long?*

Charlotte's loud, "No, Mac!" snapped her back into the moment, and she saw her father freeze at the forbidden coat closet door, his suit jacket in one hand and a coat hanger in the other, staring at his sister. "I didn't mean to startle you, but Mama's and Robert's ashes are still in there. Use the hooks outside." All eyes looked down upon two boxes on a table in the closet.

"We need to get them home to South Carolina," Mac said in a hoarse voice.

At the dining room table, Tessie asked Mac to say grace, and as he gave thanks for the family being together again, his voice deepened in that strange way that always mystified Danielle and Phil. They glanced up at each other from the prayer and saw Tessie and Charlotte looking at one another too. Later, Danielle said to her brother, "I guess there are secrets we'll never know."

"And perhaps shouldn't," he said, putting an arm around her shoulders.

Dinner was a traditional meal of roast lamb, new potatoes and a sautéed medley of broccoli, carrots and peas.

In the break between dinner and dessert, Danielle whispered to her mother, "I have the best room in the house. Want to see it?" The two women were disappearing up the stairs in a flurry of magenta and green when, "Where are you going?" – stopped them. They turned to Sharon.

"Come on," said Danielle. Her mother held out her hand and they waited for her.

Upstairs in Grandma Ruth's bedroom, she watched her mother and Sharon look around at the yellowed wallpaper decorated with roses and vines and the mahogany furniture so comfortably lived in. "I haven't been in this house since Phil was two, and you were six," said her mother. Danielle remembered her as a thin, nervous young woman with long light brown hair. Since then she'd gained about twelve pounds and was still trim. The gray in her hair was barely discernible. Since the truth had come out about Mac's passing for white, she'd begun to relax.

Danielle watched her mother's reflection in the mahogany dresser mirror pick up a bound copy of *In Search of That Iron String*, laugh at the cartooned cover and look up to see a smile of self-worth on her daughter's face. "Your Literary Arts class. How are Kamara and the others?"

"Wonderful!"

"You know about them?" Sharon asked, her eyes wide-open in amazement. *Is she play-acting?*

Her mother laughed. "Before Danielle got herself thrown out of the house, she told us all about her – adventures in the high school."

Sharon smiled. *She looks like she wants to belong.* Mom's magical touch.

"Would you like that copy, Mom?"

"I was just about to ask you for it," she said, settling into the rocking chair.

"Can I have one too?" asked Sharon.

"Sure. I have extras." She took one from her desk and handing it to her said, "Let's get comfortable on the bed. Pull your chair along side us, Mom." She did and that put Sharon between them. Danielle slipped a pillow between Sharon's back and the headboard. Then, she lay back with the other pillow under her head and relaxed as her mother and Sharon opened their booklets and read.

"I didn't think your students could write this well," Sharon said.

"They're an extraordinary class, and they work hard to make the grade, and then more."

"What year are you in, Sharon?" asked Danielle's Mom. It was a simple enough question, but it opened the floodgates and Sharon, happy being the center of attention, told them how she'd dropped her grade point average in the past year, but that she wanted to bring it up again and go to college.

"I'm here to help with English anytime," said Danielle. "You just have to ask."

Sharon hesitated, and Danielle's magical mother smoothed the way. "What would you like to be?"

"A model! Or maybe a psychologist like my father. Or a chef like my mother."

"You'll do well in whatever you choose," she said, and they chatted about Sharon's future until Charlotte called to tell them that dessert was ready.

Sharon was still chatting as they descended the staircase. *It feels like we're a family. Is it possible? Or is it just Mom?*

PASSOVER

The Lord, he freed the slaves from Egypt,

Out of the hands of their oppressors.

If that was all He did for us, then Dayenu.

Day-day-yenu, day-day-yenu, day day-yenu,

It's good enough for me! Dayenu, etc.

"Dayenu," with its many verses and refrains, telling how God helped the Hebrews in their escape from the Pharaoh and on to freedom, was a Passover favorite around the dining room table in the Brooklyn apartment of Grandma Bess and Grandpa Jake. Danielle joined the rest in

Chapter Thirty

the pure joy that escalated, as they sang and celebrated the courage to be grateful for whatever the Lord decides to give you.

The motley crew of cousins, nieces, nephews, sons, daughters, husbands and wives, representing self-made businessmen, teachers, secretaries, office managers, accountants, a banker and a performer, sliced right through the trivia of their job descriptions and reverted to the playful teasing that, Josh warned Danielle, had been leveling their playing field since childhood. At the table, it started with the maneuvering to beat the other guy to the dark turkey meat before it was gone.

Danielle enjoyed their antics. In her fifth month of pregnancy, she was just showing under her purple silk shirtdress and jacket, and, remarkably, no one had said anything. Until Josh's Aunt Harriet, in stylish high heel shoes, clicked across the parquet floor to Josh, pecked on his chest with an exquisite, long fingernail and asked, "So? When are you getting married?"

"We haven't decided yet," said Josh, without missing a beat.

Aunt Harriet arched an eyebrow over her perceptive, mascaraed eyes and, with a look, invited Danielle to join her in pressuring Josh.

Danielle glanced around. Only Sharon and her grandparents seemed to have heard. Quietly, she said, "We're taking it step by step."

Aunt Harriet said, also quietly, "Step by step?" and she eyed Danielle's belly. "You don't have much time to step!"

When she moved on, Danielle said, "I looked like the weak and foolish little woman. I should have helped her take you on!"

"Thank you for understanding," he said, just before his daughter of all people, with Grandma Bess and Grandpa Jake in tow, did. She walked up to them and tapped on her father's chest. "So? When are you getting married?" she demanded in perfect imitation of Aunt Harriet. But loudly. The room fell silent; everyone listened.

Josh and Danielle looked at each other. Danielle's mind raced. *Why? Is she just seduced by the chance to take center stage? Does she mean it only as a joke?*

"So when are you?" asked Grandma Bess, eyeing her son.

"Set a date while your daughter's in a good mood," said Grandpa

Jake, putting an arm around Sharon's shoulders. "She's still smiling. And I want to be around to dance at your wedding."

Danielle looked at her. Sharon was smiling, but her eyes were non-committal.

Josh's strong gentle hand covered Danielle's. "July 4th. The anniversary of the weekend we met." Danielle glowed as if in the light of exploding firecrackers. He reached out to Sharon with his other hand and she reached back.

The whole room exploded with congratulations, laughter and hugs. Danielle's mind kept racing. *Mom and Dad and my aunts have to meet Bess and Jake! And Aunt Harriet and…* She looked around at the small crowd just in the room… *Perhaps a low-keyed celebration in a place large enough for family and friends? Large! Large!!*

She looked around for Sharon and saw her among aunts, uncles and cousins getting hugs and sharing laughter. *Will this work? Or will I have to move in with my aunts again?* She saw Sharon's laser-like attention focus onto her grandfather as his authoritative voice began to rumble throughout the gathering and watched her move closer to catch his words.

"It won't be easy to get a hall on such short notice," Grandpa Jake was saying, "but I'll make a call." He started to dash off, but Grandma Bess grabbed his hand, stopping him. He looked at her. "What?"

"She has a father, Jacob!" He looked abashed, and Bess turned to Danielle. "Do you feel well enough to have such a large celebration in just three months, bubala?"

"Yes," she lied. *As soon as possible.*

"No, you don't." She felt Josh's arm around her waist. "We'll have a small, family wedding on July fourth and the large celebration in late autumn. Right now, we'll plan this July one with just the two of you and Danielle's parents."

"And Sharon, of course," said Danielle.

"You'll like Mac, Grandpa," she said. "He's cool."

"He is?" Jake said, and smiled foolishly at Danielle. "I forgot all about him." Then his face became serious, and he gestured helplessly. On such short notice, it's going to be a modest affair. Will that be good enough for you?"

She saw he wanted to give them the world. "Dayenu," she said and broke into a smile. "It's more than good enough for me."

In the happy melee that followed, Josh embraced Danielle and whispered into her ear, "I don't know why she changed her mind, but something tells me not to ask."

"I agree," she said, but privately wondered if the time she and Sharon spent with her magical mom inspired the change.

Chapter Thirty-One

"Love in the open hand,
No thing but that."
Edna St. Vincent Millay

JERUSHA

1916 – South Carolina

The Negro woman didn't care that she was dressed too elegantly for her race. She stood alone on the wooden train platform and blew a kiss to her family who waved from the windows. But she didn't wave back. That would be too final. Only moments ago, they were all on the platform, embracing. She could still feel where their hands touched and their lips kissed.

Her dark blue dress with a high neck draped down over her full figure and ended smartly above new shoes. She watched her family of southern country Negroes beginning to adjust to their stylish northern city attire. They were dressed so well because her son, Phillip, was a tailor... because the white man who kept her and sired Phillip, sent him to tailoring school and provided him with clients from among his own friends and associates. Now, to insure opportunity for *his* family, Phillip gave himself the title of Esquire, the first in the family line, and he was moving them North. He'd divide his time between his lucrative tailoring business in South Carolina and his family in Brooklyn, New York.

Minutes before, Jerusha had taken her daughter's arm and said, "Family, Thelma May. Stay by your family." Thelma Mae, eighteen and stunning in a long green dress, her light brown hair in an upsweep, appeared as white as her white father. "Family, you hear?" she said, gently shaking her. Jerusha looked like her daughter's Negro servant.

Chapter Thirty-One

She kissed her son's wife Ruth, plain and dark in a long navy dress, and stroked the tender, dark olive cheek of little Charlotte, not quite two, appearing to lecture in baby-talk from her mother's arms. "Maybe she'll become a school marm like you," she told her daughter-in-law and laughed shakily. She felt fourteen-year old Tessie's arms wrap around her, smelled the newness of her granddaughter's cotton calico dress and the sweetness of the girl. "Tell your Mama to send pictures." Tessie nodded vigorously, bouncing a calico ribbon about her long curly brown hair.

"I will, but I'm coming back to visit you."

"I'd love that," she said, and smiled radiantly because she couldn't say more without crying.

Her two grandsons waited their turn behind Tessie. They looked so grown up in their dark brown knickers and white long-sleeved shirts. They were twelve year old Robert, a dark, delicate boy, so recently wounded, when his father had taken the family name from him and given it to his younger brother, eleven year old Phillip, who, like his father, was Mediterranean-looking, masculine and entrepreneurial. She took one boy in each arm and kissed them. "Take care of each other and your sister, you hear?"

Her heart expanded with love for her son, who had the wrenching task of moving the family North. He stood tall and handsome in a three-piece suit, as he checked the time on a gold watch, attached by a gold chain to his vest pocket. The watch was a gift from his white father. He looked up. "Time to board." He kissed his mother's forehead and said, "See you soon, Mama." She touched his cheek. He'd be back often. His business was in town.

She stood alone now on the wooden platform. The train whistled. The slow chug of the engine sounded like a funeral march to her as the train left the station. Still, she smiled. It picked up speed, and her heart quickened. *Two won't pass.* She saw Thelma Mae, gathering her green shawl around her shoulders, already separating herself from the rest. "Family, Thelma Mae!" she cried out. Breaking her resolve, she waved, and tears streamed down her face.

She didn't feel the wind of the departing train rippling her beautiful long dress or smell its smoky residue, as it settled onto her black face and hair. Nor did she realize the hand she just waved was reaching out to them. She only saw the train become smaller and smaller until it disappeared among the trees.

Danielle's Dream

1982 – Brooklyn, New York

At the doorway to her recurrent dream, Danielle watched the Negro woman standing alone on the wooden platform. She, too, watched the train get smaller and smaller until it disappeared among the trees. But this time, she crossed the threshold. Her multi-colored twentieth century sundress billowed in the warm nineteenth century air as she walked toward the bereft woman, whose black features were so much like her dark olive ones. Great granddaughter and great grandmother from different American centuries recognized each other, and their surprised reunion banished grief. They talked and laughed easily together and said many things. Then Danielle reached out to her and was startled awake by the gentle strength of the hand that pulled her up!

"Jerusha!" she cried out, sitting bolt upright in bed. The arm of her white cotton nightgown was extended; her hand was pulsing from her great grandmother Jerusha's firm grasp. A warm June breeze drifted through the screened window in the pre-dawn light of her grandmother Ruth's bedroom. She drew in her arm, looked with wonder at her pulsing palm, then laid it over her womb and sat between the two worlds until the pulsing receded. Only then did she record the incident in her dream book. Their words were beyond recall by then, but she remembered their radiant faces, wrote, "Love..." and got ready for school.

Slipping a light blue cotton dress over her rounded belly, Danielle looked in the mirror of the mahogany dresser and saw the proverbial glow of an expectant mother. Still entranced by her strange dream, she stepped from her bedroom onto the veranda and gazed out over the garden on that still June morning. *August will be lovely, Jerusha, warm and lovely.* The nickname, Jerri-Anne, didn't come easily to her. Others could use it.

She remembered a cold winter's night, just a few months before, when ice and snow covered the garden. "The garden!" she said aloud. "That's what was missing on Easter Sunday!" She looked down upon the narrow yard, green with grass, and a few rogue red tulips. *Did I imagine those frozen vegetables? A garden never picked?* "Grandmother Ruth?" she whispered. As if in answer, gentle breezes rippled her dress just above her belly, and she lingered there until she remembered it was the last day of school. The air became still again, she noticed, as she left the veranda.

Along the hallway, she met Tessie, in a blue nightgown, sleepily wending her way to the bathroom. "Tessie?" The old woman stopped, placed her hand against the wall, and looked up at her. "When did Grandma pass on?"

"June, nineteen sixty-three," she answered without hesitation. "Shortly after your graduation. Tessie seemed to look back in time. "She was so proud of you. Why do you ask?"

"I was wondering if she'd done any gardening that spring… I guess she didn't."

"She did." A chill played along Danielle's arms. "Charlotte and I did most of it, of course, and Mama did a little weeding… After a while, she sat on a lounge chair out of the sun, and watched us. One night, she passed on, and we let the garden go."

They continued to look at each other. *Did Tessie see the frozen garden, too?*

"Would you like to come over and help us in the garden this summer, if you can find time with all you have to do?"

"Yes!" Ten blocks from their apartment would be such an easy walk.

Chapter Thirty-Two

You have seen how a man was made a slave;
you shall see how a slave was made a man.
— Frederick Douglass

Last day of school. Time for a party. The genealogies had arrived from the Schomburg Library two weeks before. She'd waited for her Literary Arts class to finish their work and secure their marks and graduation, before telling them. They decided to save the letters for this final celebration.

She wheeled her aunts' grocery cart out of the Tudor house, packed it and a bag containing yellow paper plates, cups, napkins and tablecloth into the trunk of her car and drove to school. At the deli, she ordered just one black coffee to go, a variety of pastries for five classes and punch. Then she parked her car, packed the paper products into the grocery cart, slung a considerably lightened book bag over her shoulder and rolled the cart up the teachers' ramp. Her light blue dress blew gracefully over little Jerusha's abode. She couldn't stop smiling.

"Hold on! I'll get it." Felix Mendez, the security guard, ran down the ramp and took the cart from her. "No parties," he said, trying unsuccessfully to look official. Just for a moment. "What have you got this time?" He selected an almond croissant.

After checking in and collecting her mail, she took the elevator to the fourth floor and left everything but the coffee in her room. Her Literary Arts students had volunteered to arrive early and set up the party. With a notebook and a small purse, she blew into the English department, lighter than a summer breeze, to check in with Dr. Norton and Nicole. She'd assist her colleague for the rest of June.

Chapter Thirty-Two

The door to Dr. Norton's office was ajar. Odd. He usually locked it. She knocked and peeked inside. Nicole looked up from his desk and smiled. Her pinkish gold wire glasses matched her trim mauve blazer. "Morning! Dr. Norton was called down to the Board again. I think it's going to be just the two of us for the rest of the month."

"We can do it," said Danielle, walking in and sitting down. "We've done it before."

"I'll miss you," said Nicole, "but I'll be at your wedding celebration in October. The invitation arrived yesterday." Danielle heard a personal as well as a professional tone in her voice. They didn't have a friendship outside of school, but...

"I'll miss you, too. How about visiting, when the baby's born?"

"I thought you'd never ask."

On her way back to class, Danielle marveled at the veils that were still falling away in her expanding world, and she felt embarrassed at the limits of her old life, as it was, just a year before.

They didn't see her, at first, as she stood quietly in the doorway taking mental snap-shots of them. Marisa's wavy, black hair fell to the shoulders of her pink tee shirt over jeans, displaying her astrological sign, Libra, in silver sequins. She'd covered the long table with the yellow tablecloth and set out the matching paper plates, napkins and cups. Luis, in a black and red shirt over black jeans, and Chang, in a blue denim suit, shook large containers of punch, opened them and filled the glasses.

Luis spilled juice on the tablecloth. "Damn!" He looked up and saw her. "Sorry."

"I dropped half a container on the floor once," she said, crossing the fingers of one hand behind her back, as she walked over and dabbed it up with a yellow napkin.

Tamika carried her carefully arranged tray of almond croissants, cinnamon sticks, chocolate brioche and biscotti to the table. Her hair was in blue-ribboned corn rows.

The front of her bright blue tee shirt over her jeans announced she was an Aquarius. The tail of the fish wrapped around her back.

Jamal, the sketcher, in a brown suit and tie that Danielle guessed was his Sunday best, and Erica, in a pink shirtdress and little pink earrings, eradicating her former severe look, arranged the desk-chairs into concentric circles.

Kamara, in a new black tee shirt over new jeans, had his back to her as he wrote the Aim on the blackboard. Danielle smiled. Over six feet, he moved with grace and confidence. *When did that happen?* She watched him write:

Aim: To prepare for our future as we

Do Now: learn about our past!!!

Danielle applauded. "Beautiful."

He turned around and smiled. "Thank you."

She wanted to cry, he was so polite, even as he usurped her job. They all seemed so mature this morning, straight-backed, well dressed and quiet. Too quiet! *We're all thinking the same thing*, she thought and wished she'd remembered the camera. *I'll bring it for graduation.*

"I have your genealogies." She put them into the Remus hat and placed it on her desk. "I need two volunteers to hand them out." Erica and Luis were the first to volunteer. The silence was broken, as they called out names and the others called out,

"Right here!"

"I can't wait!"

"Where's mine?"

Suddenly, it was quiet again, except for the tearing of paper envelopes and the unfolding of documents. They turned or moved away from one another for privacy.

Danielle held her letter, already opened, and watched them.

"Oh!" Disbelief, like a cry, escaped from Tamika. "My great, great grandmother was Anna May Johnson, the daughter of a plantation owner!"

"Maybe she ran a plantation like you try to run this class," Luis said helpfully, and turned back to his own document, abandoning Tamika to her new white ancestor. Danielle grinned.

Chapter Thirty-Two

Chang looked embarrassed. "My great grandmother was married twice."

"My great, great, great grandfather was Othello, a slave to her!" said Tamika.

"Othello? Damn," muttered Kamara.

"Maybe they loved each other," Marisa said gently. "That did happen."

"I think so too," said Danielle. "My great grandfather's family owned slaves and my great grandmother was one of his slaves. After emancipation, my great grandfather kept her and their two children in a cabin on the plantation, where she worked as a servant."

"Oh my," said Tamika, and exhaled loudly as she absorbed the news. Then, she added, I'm Ashanti and French, mainly."

"I'm Dominican and Spanish. I knew that!" said Luis. "Oh, wait a minute." He kept on reading.

Danielle saw Marisa, sober faced but apparently unsurprised, look up from her document. Instead of sharing her news, she asked Erica, "What's your background?"

"German and Puerto Rican."

"Welcome to the neighborhood," said Marisa.

Erica blushed "And you?"

"I'm Puerto Rican, Danish, Jewish, Greek and….."

"How did that happen?" asked Luis, during Marisa's lengthy pause.

"I'll explain it to you later," said Kamara, and everyone laughed.

"And Mexican," Marisa finished in a trembling voice that caused everyone to look at her. "I'm here illegally." Her fellow students' voices surrounded her like a fence.

"Don't tell anyone else."

"Graduate before you do anything. It's only a week off."

"And go to Fordham anyway. You'll figure out something."

"We've been together since kindergarten. You're an American, and that's that!"

Danielle's thoughts were spinning. "I don't know the legalities of this, but if you need someone to sponsor you, I'd be proud to do it."

"And, if you need someone to marry you, I'll do it!" Everyone looked at Luis. "Until you get your citizenship. We'll just be friends."

Luis' extraordinary generosity moved everyone. Tears welled up in Marisa's eyes, as she said, "Thank you, Luis. And everybody. I have a lot to think about. Let's get back to our party now but… Ms. McKinnon, can we sit down and talk sometime next week?"

"Absolutely." Danielle saw Jamal quietly sketching Marisa, and she asked him,

"What's your ancestry?" Then thinking he might be too shy to say, she said, "If you want to share it, that is."

He smiled. "Ashanti, English and French," and surprised her by asking, "What's yours?"

"Mainly Irish and Yoruba."

"Yoruba and Irish!" said Kamara striding toward her, hand raised. They high-fived.

"Mc Kin!" Danielle said softly, and they high-fived again.

"Might have known," said Luis. Everyone laughed and talked more freely about their backgrounds.

Danielle was oblivious to the noise they were making, until Mr. Spatz looked in and asked, "Is everything all right?" It was his free period, and he'd been invited, as usual. Three students near the door ushered him into the room and to the refreshment table.

Little Jerusha began kicking Danielle. She placed a hand over her womb and felt serenity there.

"Everything okay, Ms. McKinnon?" called out Tamika and was by her side in an instant. As one, the class quietly turned to them.

"She's celebrating, too," said her mother.

Spontaneously, Tamika lifted her hands to feel the baby kick, then stopped.

"Go ahead," she said. The girl laid her hands on Danielle's belly and cooed softly.

Danielle felt the energy and said, "This is your third blessing of the morning, Jerusha."

Chapter Thirty-Two

"Jeruuusha," the class moaned in unison, and Danielle heard the familiar veto.

"Give her a break!" said Kamara, walking over and looking down at the baby's abode like a protective big brother.

"We're nick-naming her Jerri-Anne," she said, looking up at Kamara with resignation. Tamika removed her hands, and Kamara looked down curiously. "Go ahead," Danielle said. Very gently, Kamara placed his large hands over her womb, and, in quiet wonder said, "Oh, man. She's alive and kicking."

In that moment, the assistant principal burst through the door, breaking into this still, sacred moment. "Ms. McKinnon!" he said, as if he'd just caught her in a depraved act. Danielle and Kamara looked at him. The class and Mr. Spatz looked at him.

"Good Morning, Mr. James," said Danielle quietly. Kamara stood beside her.

Speechless, the assistant principal flipped open his note pad, looked around and saw the pastry table. "A party too?" He clicked open his ball point pen and began to write.

For a second, no one moved. Then, with a smile, Mr. Spatz walked over to Mr. James, put an arm around his shoulder and guided him into the midst of Danielle's students. "We have a lot to celebrate here, Mr. James. Our roots! A baby!"

The students followed his lead. "My graduation," said Kamara, walking over and offering Mr. James his raised palm for a high five. The unnerved assistant principal tapped Kamara's palm with his notebook.

"Thanks, man," said Kamara, eyes twinkling with charm. From the buffet table, Danielle watched the scene with growing fascination.

"Punch?" asked Louis, a little too loudly. Mr. James jumped back, before he saw the glass of juice the young man was offering.

He shoved the open pen into his jacket pocket and took the glass. "Uh, thank you."

"Have you seen our project?" Tamika asked, taking his arm with the notebook and leading him to the bulletin board, showcasing their short stories. The title page with the cartoon characters was displayed at the center.

"In Search of That Iron String?" He frowned. "What iron string?"

"The one inside," boomed Kamara. Mr. James looked up and his eyes widened, as Kamara, like a preacher, intoned, "Trust thyself: Every heart vibrates to that iron string!" and added confidentially, "Ralph Waldo Emerson."

At the buffet table, Danielle was fighting off an attack of the giggles.

Respectfully, Jamal said, "That pen you put in your pocket, Sir, is leaking." As Mr. James quickly retrieved it and Marisa handed him napkins, Kamara sent Danielle a victorious look, which she returned.

She ached to join them, but somehow she knew she had to remain where she was as the tour continued. *They can make it in this world. Please God.*

Marisa gestured to the opposite bulletin board, which displayed their persuasive speeches. "We also read selections from *The Life of Frederick Douglass, an American Slave,* and gave speeches on how those slave days still affect our country today. Even affects this school."

She said it innocently enough, but Mr. James looked around like one about to be caught in a cover up. "Good work, good work," he mumbled.

"We have a good teacher," Jamal said quietly. Mr. James mumbled again.

"What did you say?" Chang asked politely, adjusting his glasses and squinting his eyes, as if to hear him more clearly by reading his lips.

Tamika, who'd removed the pastry tray from the buffet table, held the delicacies before Mr. James, who grabbed a chocolate brioche and shoved it into his mouth.

Better that than your foot, thought Danielle, smiling from across the room.

"Welcome to the party, Mr. James," said Tamika, and he nodded, chewed and listened to the savvy but kind seniors from her Literary Arts class.

When Mr. James read a line aloud from Marisa's speech and said, "Nice," Mr. Spatz slipped away from the group and joined Danielle at the buffet table.

He poured them both some punch, and they tapped their paper glasses together in a toast. "You've won this round," he said.

"We've won it. I have to talk to you later about the next one. Marisa's here illegally." He nodded.

At the close of that last school day, Danielle walked into her empty classroom and looked around. The Short Story bulletin board faced the Persuasive Speeches bulletin board. In front of the room, above the blackboard, a poster of Frederick Douglass, flanked by pictures of other great men and women, looked out over the quiet room that had been so vibrantly alive with the studies of the humanities. Her Literary Arts class was becoming history.

She removed the Remus hat from her desk and carefully placed it into her aunts' cart. It had been Grandmother Ruth's gardening hat once, and now she would offer it to Tessie. But a deep love prompted her to pick it up again. "I've got it for today," she told the room, and placing it on her head, rolled the cart through the doorway, paused at the threshold, looked back and gently closed the door.

Chapter Thirty-Three

She knew he'd be there, the man she would marry. They enjoyed a leisurely kiss and embrace in front of the school building before he packed the cart into the trunk. "Do you mind if we leave your car in the garage for now, Farmer Brown?"

"No." She laughed and slipped into the passenger seat of his car before she saw Sharon. In the back seat. Smiling. "Hi!"

"Hi."

Danielle could see the straw hat amused her too, and felt a wisecrack coming. She looked at Josh, but he just smiled and started the car. Knowing how the girl loved center stage, Danielle took a chance and turned around in the front seat to include her in the circle. "Another astrology shirt! I like it." Sharon sported Gemini in gold sequins on a green tee shirt over jeans.

"Thanks. What do you mean, another?"

"Two girls from the Literary Arts class wore astrology shirts today."

"Which ones? I'm reading their stories."

"Really? Tamika is an Aquarius, and Marisa's a Libra."

"They're good writers."

"So are you. How did your English exam go?"

"Aced it!"

"Congratulations!"

"I got some tutoring from Ms. Parker, my English teacher."

Danielle smiled. *So she rejected my offer to tutor her.*

"She's a lot like you." It sounded like a compliment. Danielle risked a smile and glanced at Josh who was turning onto the Long Island Expressway. "Where're we going?"

"I heard about a place to get a good buy on a bassinet and a stroller," he said. "Then, we'll have a seaside dinner."

Chapter Thirty-Three

She looked at Sharon who was studying her. "How does that sound?"

"Okay… When are you moving back?"

"Last day of school."

"I'm taking a week's vacation at the beach with my Mom right after school."

"How wonderful!"

"For you, too. Won't you want a little honeymoon before Jerri-Anne comes?"

"Yes," laughed Danielle. Sharon was still studying her.

"I'm moving back in with my mother."

Oddly enough, Danielle felt no desire to cheer, do cart wheels or praise the gods. "Is that what you want?" The girl nodded. Josh glanced at them both, and back to the road. "Then I'm happy for you. You'll still have a home with us, though."

"I want to keep my room."

"I told her we'd discuss it with you," Josh said to Danielle.

Just a ripple of tension was back. "It's a good idea. We still have a room for the nursery. We're all set." *Maybe one cartwheel.* In the silence that followed, a little foot tapped from within her serene place, reminding Danielle of her students and how much she missed them. "My Literary Arts class disapproved of Jerusha for a name, but they liked Jerri-Anne," she said.

"You told them?"

"Yes," said Danielle. Sharon squealed in delight, and Josh smiled. "I even let them feel the baby kick."

"You did?" said father and daughter in surprise.

"Is that… proper?" asked Josh.

"For us it was." *How can I explain to them… the family love we had?* "The assistant principal almost had a fit though."

"What did he do?" asked Sharon, obviously wanting the gossip. *Why not? It's harmless enough.* "Well, first the history teacher, Mr. Spatz, put an arm around his shoulder and gave him a big smile." Sharon giggled, Josh smiled, and Danielle related the unwitting comedy performed by her students and the assistant principal.

After getting good buys on a good quality bassinet and stroller, they ordered lobster dinners with a seaside view near the restaurant in which, just that January, they'd had such a wretched time. "Why are you wearing that straw hat?" Sharon asked, grinning at her father. *Is she inviting him to gang up on me again? Not this time!*

Danielle took center stage for herself. "I was wondering when you'd ask. We called it the Remus hat." Leaving out details that would violate her students' confidences, she told them that it had once been her grandmother's gardening hat, that it got it's name as the Remus hat when Kamara used it as a costume piece for an oral interpretation of an Uncle Remus story, how it then became the crucible into which Danielle and her students had thrown their written admissions of bigotry after reading them aloud, and finally that it held the genealogies which caused such a stir just that morning.

"It will be a gardening hat again, this time, for Aunt Tessie. I wore it this afternoon because I... couldn't bear to part with it... yet." She looked out onto the tranquil ocean.

Into the long moment that followed, Josh asked, "So, what will Jerri-Anne grow up to be?"

He's trying to cheer me up. She played along. "Maybe she'll become head of the Department of Education and lead them into a New Age where they'll level the playing field for the students." She began to cheer up.

"That would be good," said Josh. "Or maybe she'll become the head of your union and lead them into a New Age where they'll no longer protect the jobs of teachers who aren't working in the students' best interest."

"Forget the small stuff!" said Sharon, leaning in to recapture center stage. "Maybe she'll become the first woman president of the United States and level the playing field for all of us!" The high energy at the table halted in mid-air, and like a Tom and Jerry cartoon, plummeted. Sharon looked quickly from Josh to Danielle and back to Josh. "What did I say?"

Chapter Thirty-Three

"Jerri-Anne will be black," said Josh.

"So?"

Danielle felt the pressure of his hand on hers affirm his love and support. She looked at Sharon. "I'm afraid we won't see a black president in our lifetime."

"Oh. Bummer," said Sharon. Lovingly, Danielle moved her free hand over her belly.

EPILOGUE

"Time and again history has shown us that there is nothing – NOTHING – more powerful than ordinary citizens coming together for a just cause." —Michelle Obama

Twenty-Six Years Later

"The time has come to affirm our enduring spirit; to choose our better history; to carry forward that precious gift, that noble idea, passed on from generation to generation: the God-given promise that all are equal, all are free, and all deserve a chance to pursue their full measure of happiness."

Barack Hussein Obama
January 20, 2009

It didn't happen in Mac or Lynn's lifetime, or in Grandpa Jake's, and certainly not in Tessie's. On the day it did happen, Danielle and Josh hosted a celebration brunch in their Greenwich Village duplex for the six family members who would be there.

As she arranged drinks along a table overlooking West Eleventh Street, she remembered how Sharon had surprised her and Josh that first year by offering to share the upstairs apartment with Marisa. In the second year, Marisa married a young American student she'd met and fallen in love with at Fordham University.

That year marked a turning point for Sharon, who began a friendship with Marisa and graduated from high school. The following year, she went to New York University and majored in Culinary Arts. Upon graduation, she joined her mother and stepfather in building their restaurant businesses in Brooklyn.

Danielle was roused from her reverie, when Josh joined her to pour a cup of tea and a cup of coffee. They gazed together through the tall windows at the old-fashioned tree-lined street of townhouses and low apartment buildings. They loved this home their parents had made affordable with generous wedding gifts of a down payment. *Who would have thought the prices would have risen so drastically since then?*

Everyone dressed for comfort that day. Danielle wore a red velvet pants suit, and Josh wore jeans and a blue pullover sweater. Their curly heads sported strands of gray, but they looked and felt like vibrant fifty year olds.

They joined the rest of the family who were relaxing on sturdy brown cushioned chairs and couches that had weathered years of happy, energetic children. The furniture stood on parquet floors before a wooden coffee table within reach of everyone. Josh set coffee and tea before Charlotte and Bess, sitting companionably in cushioned armchairs. To their right, he and Danielle settled onto the center couch and to their right, Phil and Alma, in jeans and sweaters, snuggled on the love seat. Their children were in college.

A fireplace glowed before them, but they ignored it to concentrate on the television screen. As the camera panned the crowd with close-ups, Danielle leaned forward to peer through the million or so people who packed the National Mall from the Capitol to the Washington Monument and beyond. Gently, Josh massaged the back of her neck. "She'll be home in a couple of days. She gave her word." He was referring to the girl once nick-named Jerrie-Anne, who had reclaimed her great-great grandmother's name in high school. Jerusha Freedman was somewhere in the National Mall with three friends, who'd worked together in New York on the Obama election. They'd be staying on after the swearing in for a few days with friends who lived in Washington to go to the Neighborhood Inaugural Ball and to mingle with the peaceful revelers at the Robert F. Kennedy Stadium. She'd sounded so happy when she called.

Two months before, right after the November election, when Jerusha had announced these plans, Danielle panicked. "Oh no, that could be dangerous!" was on her lips, when the words were suddenly roadblocked by the memory of the peaceful March on Washington she'd missed in 1963 because her parents had been afraid for her. She looked at Josh, and they exchanged a look of shared consent and concern. "It'll be an experience that will inspire you all your life," she said, hugged her daughter and cried.

"Mom, I know the happy ending hasn't arrived, and it may not for a long time," said Jerusha gently. "I hear how angry some people become when they say things like, 'That Kenyan!' and I see their expressions when they talk about our people. But mostly people are positive. Danielle relaxed a bit. Jerusha was perceptive and had good judgment. *More so than I had at her age.*

"Stay together with your friends and check in with us every day on your cell phone," her father had said. He handed her extra cash. "I'm proud of you. And a little jealous."

The phone rang. Josh answered and put it on speakerphone. "It's Sharon! She only has a minute." She and her husband Gary were busy managing a popular tavern they'd bought from her mother and father-in-law.

"Hey!" said Sharon. "Listen, when Jerusha calls, tell her I was the one who said she could become the first woman president and you two blew me off, saying an African American could never be elected President in our lifetime!"

"Touche," said Josh, Danielle laughed and they asked about their grandson Gary Jr. who was adjusting to life as a freshman in Brooklyn College.

"He's great," said Sharon, and they thrilled to hear her joy.

"Come for dinner Saturday. Jerusha will be back and we'll all have lots of news."

"We'll be there!" said Sharon.

Josh clicked off the speakerphone, checked the time and announced, "Forty-five minutes before the inauguration!" They drank tea and coffee and nibbled on mini bagels and croissants from a local bakery. Brunch would be a vegetable omelet and potato pancakes that were warming in the oven. Chilled champagne was at the ready.

"Let's take a stroll into the Village after the ceremony," said Danielle, sipping coffee and still scrutinizing the crowds on television.

"Have you found Jerusha yet?" teased Charlotte. Spry and alert at ninety-three, Danielle's aunt, in a maroon slacks and sweater set, nursed a cup of coffee and mused, "My grand niece. She gets herself a double Master's degree in American History and Government, takes a year of study abroad and then becomes a Community Organizer... whatever that is."

"She's been discovering that for herself the last couple of years," said Josh.

"Brave new world that has such people in it," said Danielle.

"And that had such people in it, too," said Phil.

"Then play a little ancestor music," his sister said playfully standing and raising her mug in a toast. Josh lowered the volume on the TV.

There was some chuckling, as Phil walked over to the piano, sat down and played the familiar strains of "Jerusha." Danielle began. "Here's to Mom and Dad for taking a chance on a mixed marriage in the *forties* and raising us in that world."

Phil kept playing, as he said, "And who had the courage to speak out about passing, however late."

Charlotte raised her mug. "To *my* parents, Ruth and Phillip McKinnon, Esquire, who moved our family up North to pass for white. I know it's frowned upon today, but even that was dangerous. My very white-looking aunt, Thelma-Mae, left home and tried to blend into the white world. One day, her letters stopped coming. Papa left work and looked for her for two weeks. He was told she'd drowned in a boating accident. That's all he could find out. She closed her eyes against other terrifying scenarios.

Beside her, eighty-eight year old Bess Friedman leaned forward in her armchair and looked at each one. Eyes dark with memories, she said, "You would have had to live through those years to understand. It might have been a holocaust for the Black people, too, if they weren't needed as laborers. You did what you had to do to survive. And you weren't always right." A silent toast of raised cups and mugs were raised.

Danielle placed her hand over her mother-in-law's. "To Jacob Freedman, who welcomed a pregnant gentile into his family and loved her like a daughter."

Alma raised her cup of tea. "To both of your families, who spoke and acted on behalf of the rights of others. I believe that's what really moves humanity forward."

Phil continued to play the piano as he said, " To Alma's parents who endured an unspeakable tragedy within their family, not unlike that of Emmett Till, but who still fought in this country's armed forces and raised their children to cautiously show good will to others."

Josh raised his mug. "In that spirit, may we, as a people, now treat our Muslim brothers and sisters with decency. We meet them everyday in this town. They're a peaceful people."

Silent nods and voiced "Amens" answered him.

"And here's to my sister, Tessie," said Charlotte with a smile, who convinced me to tell people I'm Negro, I mean, Black, ah! African American, so Jerusha wouldn't get a complex."

Emotions shook their laughter, and all eyes turned to a framed photograph by the fireplace. Danielle's heart filled with joy whenever she looked at her slim, energetic daughter with a dark coffee brown complexion and warm, intelligent eyes. The picture was taken on the day she graduated from high school. One arm was around her Grandmother Lynn and the other around her Grandfather Mac. Both tearful grandparents looked proud and happy. "She was their darling," said Danielle.

"Grandpa Jake loved her too, and so do I," said Bess with tears in her eyes.

"Jerusha was only seven, when Tessie passed on" said Phil, "but I remember her talking to her great aunt as if she were here…"

"She still dreams of her," said Danielle with a knowing smile. Suddenly the faces of Tamika, Kamara, Marisa, Luis, Chang, Jamal and the rest of her Literary Arts class rose up in her memory. She raised her mug again: "To a class I once had the privilege to teach. I set out to save them… and they saved me." *Where are they now? How are they? Maybe Nicole knows.* They were meeting for lunch the next day to toast Obama.

Phil kept playing as he said, "To Great Grandmother Jerusha, who encouraged her family to move north even though it meant she'd be left behind and lonely."

"And to our Great Grandfather McKinnon," said Danielle, "who once owned Jerusha as a slave and, after Emancipation, retained her as a kept woman, educated their son, our grandfather, to become a tailor, provided him with clients and helped him move his family North to the freedom and opportunity he couldn't or wouldn't provide."

Uncertainty, it seemed, caused their silence. "Yes," she said, " To Great Grandfather McKinnon. He's also a piece of our puzzle." And they toasted him.

The timer on the stove rang! All eyes flew to the television. "Seven minutes," said Phil. He stopped playing and started opening the champagne.

Danielle and Alma collected dirty dishes on their dash from the room. In the kitchen, they overheard bits of conversation…

"Sasha's so cute," said Charlotte with a laugh.

"Did you hear? Malia was born on the fourth of July!" said Phil. The two women smiled at each other and kept listening.

"Michelle will be promoting a healthier lifestyle," said Josh.

Danielle glanced at the Obama family picture she'd put among the gallery of family photos on the refrigerator, as they listened.

They heard Bess say, "Do you think President Obama will get a health care plan passed?"

"No one has so far," said Phil.

"*Obama will!*" Alma called to her husband. She picked up the covered plate of potato pancakes and walked quickly into the living room.

Alone in the kitchen, Danielle closed her eyes and prayed for her daughter's safety. When she opened them, Josh was at her side. "She'll be fine," he said, kissed her and picked up the tray of covered omelets.

"It's starting!" Phil called. They rushed back into the living room. Josh put the tray on the coffee table. Then each person stood, held up a glass of champagne and turned to the television to take part in the next chapter of their country's history, as a stately black man stepped forward, placed his hand on the Lincoln Bible and took the vows of the President of the United States of America.

Chronology of the Historical Novel, *Jerusha*

1861 – Jerusha is born into slavery on the McKinnon plantation in South Carolina.

1863 – Abraham Lincoln delivers the Emancipation Proclamation. Jerusha grows up on the McKinnon plantation. She becomes the kept woman of Master McKinnon and lives in a cabin with their two children, Phillip and Thelma Mae. To please Jerusha, Master McKinnon sends Phillip, to tailoring school and provides him with his rich and influential friends as clients.

1901 – Phillip marries Ruth Williams, daughter of a sharecropper.

1902 – Tessie is born to Phillip and Ruth.

1903 – Phillip Junior is born to Phillip and Ruth.

1905 – Robert is born to Phillip and Ruth.

Note: Because Robert can pass for white and Phillip Junior cannot, Philip Senior legally changes Robert's name to Phillip and Phillip's name to Robert.

1914 – Charlotte is born to Phillip and Ruth.

1915 – Lynn Barnes is born in Massachusetts.

1916 – Phillip Senior moves his wife Ruth and their four children, Tessie, Phillip Jr., Robert and Charlotte, north to New York, and later, to Massachusetts.

1939 – Phillip Jr. (Mac) intermarries with Lynn.

1941 – Danielle McKinnon is born to Mac and Lynn.

1946 – Phil McKinnon the third is born to Mac and Lynn.

Acknowledgments

First of all, I want to acknowledge my country, the United States of America. We are a complex mix of people, who are getting ever closer to realizing our founding fathers' vision of equality and justice for all.

I also want to acknowledge my students for all they taught me.

Specifically, I want to thank Meredith Sue Willis, an accomplished novelist and teacher of novel writing at New York University, who guided me in the technique of the craft, while leaving me free to discover my own story.

I'm also grateful to writers William Pace, Loren-Paul Caplin and Jennifer Bell of the New School University in Manhattan who taught me the craft of screenwriting.

Years before, the fine black actor and teacher, Earle Hyman, set me on the path to searching for the concrete and mystical approach to interpreting a role in a play. And earlier, English teacher, Mr. Ed Smith of Classical High School in Springfield, Massachusetts, taught the art of questioning, listening and thinking independently so we, his students, might speak our truths... even as those truths change.

Somehow all of these teachings came together to guide me in writing this historical novel.

The design of Aline Hoffman's book cover is alive with the love and pain of this story. I am so fortunate to have worked with her on it.

Anstiss Morrill and Phyllis Nahman edited Jerusha with sensitivity and skill. History Department Chairperson, Joye Bowman, made helpful introductions at the University of Massachusetts.

So many people encouraged me along the way.

The owner, manager and all the people who work at a local restaurant, ironically called The Black Sheep, welcome writers to work as they eat. They provided me with a refuge.

Jeffrey Cohen, the love of my life, was once a supportive presence and is now an inspiring spirit.

I so value my brother Bill who always tells me the truth.

I am still in awe of the courage of my white mother and black father who dared to pass for white during the 1940s and on through the 1980s to raise a family side by side with people, some fair and just, some dangerously prejudiced.

My heart reaches out to all of my black ancestors of whom I know so little…

Author Note

Dolores McCullough was inspired to write *Jerusha* when, at age thirty-nine, she found out she was black and her father was passing for white. She embarked on a frustrating attempt to learn about her family history, especially about her great, great grandmother, a slave who, after Emancipation, became the kept woman of her former owner. (She wrote an earlier version of this story in a screenplay, *McKin*.)

In New York City, she studied acting at HB Studio, but earned her living teaching high school English, speech, and acting to mostly African- and Hispanic-American students who travelled from uptown ghettoes to study in mid-town Manhattan. She directed them in plays as diverse as *A Raisin in the Sun* by Lorraine Hansberry, *A Fiddler on the Roof*, the musical on the Jewish pilgrimage from Russia to the U.S., and Anton Chekhov's *The Marriage Proposal*.

After school, she co-produced Theatre 77 Rep Off-Off Broadway in the east 20s. She lived in Greenwich Village.

Earlier, she researched and wrote a one-person play, *A Rainbow in the Night*, on the New England poet, Edna St. Vincent Millay, and performed it at colleges, universities and small theaters along the eastern seaboard.

Recently, in tribute to the Muslim people of this country, she wrote an article, "Of Islam," on a true experience she had with a Muslim cab driver and a Muslim hair stylist,